I0532593

THE
TRANSLATED
MAN

AND OTHER STORIES

BY

CHRIS BRAAK

First published 2007 by Threat Quality Press,
Copyright © 2007 by Chris Braak

"The Hangman's Daughter" first published in Black
Gate Magazine, 2010,
Copyright © 2010 by Chris Braak

"Elijah Beckett's Job" first published on Threat
Quality Press, 2010,
Copyright © 2010 by Chris Braak

All rights reserved. Except as permitted under the
U.S. Copyright Act of 1976, no part of this
publication may be reproduced, distributed, or
transmitted in any form or by any means, or stored
in a database or retrieval system, without the prior
written permission of the publisher.

Threat Quality Press
1299 New Gulph Road
Gulph Mills, PA 19428

The characters and events in this book are fictitious.
Any similarity to real persons, living or dead, is
coincidental and not intended by the author.

ONE: BENEATH THE CITY

In the labyrinth called the Arcadium, the low roads and covered alleys beneath the city's merchant district, Elijah Beckett, Detective-Inspector of the Coroners' Division of the Imperial Guard, thumbed the hammer back on his massive revolver, and crouched beneath one of the broken phlogiston lanterns. It leaked its spent, silvery-gray fuel onto his leather hat, splattering down his heavy wool coat and forming a little puddle by his feet, but at least it didn't light him up. Most of the regularly-spaced lamps had been broken, and probably long ago. The remaining lamps provided only a bare, dull, eerie blue glow, turning the dark spaces into a nest of suggestive shadows. The occasional sunbeam that broke through the city's chilly, cloudy, smoky sky rarely broke through the mountain of architecture, and the last dregs of weak sunlight were eaten up well before they made it down to where Beckett now stood.

The closest working lamp was about twenty feet away, and it pulsed a deep, eldritch blue. Beckett tugged his hat down to blot the glare out of his eyes, and tried to spot the Reanimate, the hideous undead chimera that he knew was shambling in the dark beyond the light. He hefted his revolver and waited. Waiting was the only part of his job that got easier as he got older: as the frigid ache of his sickness vied with the warm lassitude of his last veneine injection, he found that stillness had become his natural state of being.

Something big lurched in the darkness at the end of the alley, just beyond the light, causing a kaleidoscopic swirl of black shapes. The shadows made it impossible to track the thing's movement. Beckett briefly debated finding a new position. If the Reanimate knew where he was, it would try to move around behind him. On the other hand, if it didn't know where he was, moving might alert it to his presence. Beckett squashed the jittery instinct that told him to move. Patience had gotten him this far, patience would get him the rest of the way.

There was a faint rapping on the sooty stone wall by his ear. This was Skinner, Beckett's assigned knocker. She'd been keeping track of the Reanimate and its master, using her uncanny ability to hear sounds from hundreds of yards away, and to project the tapping sound that was a knocker's signature. Skinner's intricate double-rhythmic code jittered on the wall. *Thirty-five feet,* Beckett translated mentally. *It doesn't know I'm here yet. Keep waiting.*

The Reanimate's lurching footsteps grew louder. Beckett strained his eyes against the unyielding dark, and could make out a vague adumbration, a hazy, hideous silhouette slowly shuffling into the lamp light. The shape moved steadily, painfully, its mismatched limbs poorly-knit together, and Beckett could make out more and more as the blue glow from the lamp cast itself on the Reanimate's form. It was a big hulking thing, even hunched over. The Reanimate kept its nose near the ground, because smell and hearing were the only senses that didn't rot away after its undeath, and now the thing snuffled around for Beckett's scent. The Reanimate tilted its head up as it caught an odor, and now the dim phlogiston light fell upon its face.

The creature was horrific. It was a patchwork of dead, leathery human and sharpsie skin, scales and lank tufts of hair. Its eyes had rotted away, because the eyes were always the first things to go; they left two great, black, gaping sores in the creature's face, and slimy black ichor dribbled down its cheeks like tears. The thing's lower jaw had been replaced with an iron facsimile; its master had fixed long iron nails to it in place of teeth. The thing had two arms, made of thick, gnarled muscle; their pebbly skin and stubby fingers suggested that they'd been taken from a trolljrman. A third arm, this one small and thin, waved about and clutched aimlessly beneath it.

Three arms, Beckett scoffed. Necrology, the Forbidden Science that produced Reanimates, was a heresy in itself, and an affront to Nature and the Word. *But why,* the coroner asked, *do they always think they can improve on it?* To a necrologist, bringing life to the dead was never enough. They always had to add something extra: a new arm, a third leg.

The tangled mass of dead limbs lurched fully into the light now. Blue glints from the phlogiston illumination traced the shapes of the thin copper wires and the glittering silver brackets that provided the electrical charge to the thing's ichor-invigorated muscles. Black gore dripped from its empty eye sockets, as it began to move confidently towards Beckett's hiding place.

A faint pang of fear stabbed at the Coroner — the Reanimate was slow, yes, but huge. Its legs were mismatched, which explained the shuffling; a well-made Reanimate could run as quickly and smoothly as a man. Still, if the thing did manage to catch up with him, its simple bulk would be a huge advantage. And its dead muscles were unconcerned by the limits that they'd had in life. The Reanimate could literally tear itself apart trying to crush Beckett's skull with those huge trolljrman hands.

The fear lanced through the thin fog of veneine-induced anesthesia, only to be throttled and tossed aside as Beckett had done with his fear so often before. *It doesn't matter*, the Coroner thought to himself. The Reanimate swayed its massive, patchwork head back and forth, snuffling like a blood-hound.

Rappa-tap-tap-tap. Skinner tapped another message in code out on the wall, in her complex rhythm. *She's found the necrologist*, thought Beckett. *And he's got behind me somehow.*

The necrologist shouted, and the sudden noise almost startled Beckett into motion. His joints were old, though, and unaccustomed to sudden movement. He managed to stay in place.

"You don't understand," the necrologist screamed. His name was Albert Wyndham, of the Esteemed Wyndham-Vies, and he had a ragged, hysterical voice. "This isn't some random experiment. I'm not just *dabbling…*"

Of course you're not, thought Beckett. *You're a visionary. You're building a better race, improving on Nature.*

"I've begun to build something new here. A new species, a species unencumbered by fear, by pain, by death. A species to lead mankind through a new century!"

Keep waiting. He'll tell you next about how great it is to create life, about how the Word wants us to.

"Don't you see? The Word endowed us with the capacity for science, for reason. We are *meant* to…why would it gives us the science to create life, if it didn't want us to *use* that science?"

Isn't it a crime to squander the gifts of the Word? Beckett resisted the urge to shift his weight. Wyndham's mad enthusiasm for his delusions was strangely energizing. It put Beckett in mind of the heady enthusiasm of his younger days, when he would have come out from the dark shooting, heedless of the consequences. *It's a wonder I made it this far*, he thought, wryly.

"Science is a *gift* from the Word! It would be criminal to squander it!" The necrologist was practically screaming, now. His voice echoed out of the maze of black back alleys behind Beckett; it was impossible to tell from where.

It doesn't matter, Beckett told himself. *Take the Reanimate first. Keep waiting.*

Wyndham was still screaming; he'd gone off the deep end, talking about the dark mysteries behind the veil of life. It was a common delusion among the necrologists: the idea that death was more than the absence of life, but a vital force in itself. He'd talk about the Asphyx next, and the Hidden Heart, the Suspiria, the secret whisper behind the Word. The man's voice grew more and more hysterically desperate as he screamed, as though the Coroner's understanding was as important to him as the science. Despite his decades of pursuing deranged scientists, Beckett had never been able to determine whether necrology drove a man mad, or if insanity was a prerequisite for trying to reanimate the dead.

The massive Reanimate jerked its head suddenly towards Beckett and his hiding place in the dark. It shivered slightly, and a third leg unfolded from beneath its huge, tattered cloak. The creature lunged suddenly towards Beckett, in a ground-eating lope, startling fast for something that size. Its iron jaw worked open, and the creature made a kind of choking sound, as it coughed black ichor from the ruins of its lungs.

Old fears, Beckett knew, are always the strongest, and there's an old, old human fear that reacts to large monsters that move quickly. Instinct called up adrenaline, and the adrenaline pounded at the Coroner's mind, screaming at him to run, just run. Every sense, every primal emotion built into the human nervous system clawed at his nerves and muscles, demanding that they hurry, hurry, hurry. It was all to no avail; Beckett's mind was drug-becalmed by the veneine, and he'd had years of practice standing still when his instincts told him to run.

Beckett snorted, raised his pistol and fired twice. The massive revolver jerked in his hand. Two bullets struck home, right between the Reanimate's legs. The creature collapsed to the ground and began thrashing wildly.

If there was one thing Elijah Beckett could not tolerate, it was incompetence. Reanimation was essentially the easiest, if most time consuming, of the Forbidden Sciences. It involved stitching together body parts, either from fresh corpses or, in Albert Wyndham's case, limbs hacked off from live humans, trolljrmen, indigae, or sharpsies. The necrologist would then saturate the putrefying body with ichor, which preserved it and provided it a kind of vigor. Finally, a complex network of thin silver wires were attached to the major muscle groups, and usually powered by a phlogiston battery. The most expensive

Reanimates usually had difference engines either affixed to the torso, or placed inside a hollowed-out skull. The mechanical thinking-engines were simpler in function than a living mind, but could temporarily stave off the effects of the Putrescent Derangement that was caused by rotting brain-tissue.

The process, while expensive and tedious, was fairly straightforward, and it suggested a few things in terms of design, suggestions that necrologists always seemed to ignore. In their haste to build new, invincible super-men, they seemed to just haphazardly stick limbs together. Of course it was possible to add a third leg to a human torso, and even invigorate it with ichor and electricity, but the Reanimate couldn't use it. It had a spine and a pelvis that was built for two legs. All it could do with a third was drag it uselessly about.

Beckett watched the Reanimate flop around on the ground. It couldn't die, not without being dismembered and cremated – the ichor in its rotten flesh would see to that. But it couldn't get up or chase after anyone with a shattered pelvis. There was simply no structural way for it to support its own weight. Bones, as it turns out, are very important. The thing tried to rise up on one of its burly, trolljrman arms, and, after a moment's thought, Beckett put a bullet in its shoulder, shattering clavicle and scapula. *Just in case.*

"No! NO!" screeched Albert Wyndham; Beckett whirled to see the necrologist framed by the eerie blue light of the phlogiston lamps. The lamps had a tendency to make everyone look sallow and unhealthy, but even considering that, Albert Wyndham did not look good. His ginger hair was greasy and tangled, and the mutton chops and moustache that he wore were shaggy and unkempt. Beard stubble had grown in around his chin. His eyes were sunken and hollow, his clothes sweaty and ragged, like he'd been working in them for days. There were ichor stains down his shirt front. Elijah Beckett's wary, thorough eye noted all of these details as Wyndham moved towards the fallen Reanimate. That same eye did not fail to notice the smallsword that Wyndham carried, loose and casually in his right hand, with the confidence of years of practice with a fencing master.

Albert Wyndham's voice had gone from a self-righteous scream to a ragged whisper as he looked at his fallen creation struggling in the filth of the gutter. "What have you done?" Wyndham whispered.

Rage filled his voice again, and it grew. "What have you done?" Wyndham screamed wordlessly; the necrologist raised his sword and charged at Beckett.

Unlike most things in the world, the smallsword is a weapon that had been perfected by man. Humans had invented them, and had made them thinner and lighter to improve their speed. A modern smallsword was essentially a long, thin spike; it had no edge, and was meant primarily for inflicting deep, deadly puncture wounds. Albert Wyndham's sword was pointed right at Beckett's heart.

Beckett stood very still as the man rushed towards him; at the very last possible second he turned, slapping the slender point of the smallsword away. He didn't turn it quite far enough, and the Coroner felt a hot sting in his shoulder as the tip of the smallsword pierced his heavy coat and tore a narrow runnel in his skin. Beckett grunted and brought the weight of his revolver to bear against Wyndham's head.

Beckett's gun was an old-fashioned Feathersmith model, and much heavier than its name suggested. There was a dull crack as the butt of Beckett's revolver met Albert Wyndham's temple, and the man crashed insensate into the alley wall at full speed. He bounced off the dirty stone, leaving a smear of blood, and collapsed in a heap next to his Reanimate.

Then, because Albert Wyndham was a Heretic, and because it was expected by the Coroners Division, and because it was his prerogative, Detective Inspector Elijah Beckett shot the necrologist between the eyes.

Beckett left the bodies where they were, one dead and struggling, one just dead, and began to work his way out of the maze of dark, covered alleys that the city people called the Arcadium. He double-checked to make sure that he'd wound his watch.

It was almost evening when Beckett emerged from the depths of the Arcadium. The sky had turned from a dull, dark, sooty gray to a duller, darker sootier gray, redeemed only by the fact that looking at it no longer caused migraines. The perpetual cloud of thick, puissant smoke, spewed out by factories that burned phlogiston and flux and coal, hung low over the stony war of parapets, crenulations, buttresses, towers and arches that composed Trowth's skyline.

Beckett's companions in the Coroners were waiting for him in Daior Court, a medium-sized cobblestone courtyard that half-resembled a small island of civilization, floating above and partially-enclosed by the chaotic madness of the lower city. Skinner was there, waiting in a coach that was virtually swallowed by the lengthening shadows. Two trolljrmen, whose names Beckett had never learned and probably couldn't pronounce anyway, thrummed their bone-rattling basso language to their ambulance tarrasque. The giant, two-headed tortoise had a palanquin bolted to its shell. The palanquin would hold medical supplies, and would eventually provide transport for Albert Wyndham's corpse, as soon as someone bothered to retrieve it.

An old man was slumped by the entrance to the narrow stairwell into the Arcadium, and he emitted an alarmingly wet, hacking cough as Beckett walked by. The trolljrmen met the coroner as he approached the coach, baring their huge, slab-like teeth, an expression that they imagined was very friendly. They were eight-foot tall saurians with bright, feathered crests and black expressionless eyes, and each one of their teeth was half the length of a man's thumb. The toothy grins were more horrific than they were anything else. Still, in some, small way, Beckett found himself appreciating the gesture.

One of the trolljrmen gestured with its thick finger to the blood dribbling from Elijah's coat, and thrummed a deep hollow sound to his companion in the virtually incomprehensible language that the trolljrmen used. The second trolljrman shrugged, and produce a hypodermic needle that he proceeded to fill with veneine.

Beckett, who had forgotten entirely about his injury through the twin effects of adrenaline and the heroic amount of veneine already in his system, waved the two trolljrmen off. The wound wasn't so bad. If it turned out to be worse than Beckett thought, he could always stitch it up himself. If he was going to get another injection, he'd inject it himself. The trolljrmen never gave him enough, anyway.

Skinner leaned out of the coach. The fading light glittered on the silver plate she had to wear over her eyes. "Well?"

"Well, what?" Beckett grunted, and began to reload his revolver.

Skinner sighed. If he'd been able to see her eyes, Beckett suspected they'd be rolling. "Is he dead?"

"You couldn't hear it?"

Skinner shook her head. "Something was messing up my clairaudience. I don't know what, a weird echo or something. I heard about a hundred gunshots."

"Four."

"That's it?" She pursed her lips. "Four? That's weird."

"Three for the monkey, one for the grinder."

"Uh. Getting old. Time was, you could have taken a reanimate out with two."

"Not this one. It was huge."

"Sure it was."

Beckett gave his knocker a hard look.

"You know your scary looks are wasted on a blind girl, Beckett." Skinner was grinning from ear to ear.

"It's the thought that counts." Beckett jerked his thumb towards the old man who was slumped in the gutter, still coughing furiously.

"Do you want to tell Valentine he can stop playing 'old Scraver'?"

"Is that what he's doing over there?" Skinner shouted across the courtyard. Her voice rang out on the cobblestones. "Valentine! Valentine Vie-Gorgon! Come over here right now!"

The old man stopped coughing, but otherwise didn't move.

"We know it's you, Valentine," Beckett growled.

After a moment, the old man stood up and crossed the courtyard to Skinner's carriage. He had a resigned air to his walk, which was decidedly not the walk of a sick old man. Once he got closer, Beckett could see the lines where the young Valentine Vie-Gorgon had glued the beard onto his face.

Valentine was crestfallen. "How could you tell?"

"Shoes," Beckett replied. "Regulation spit and polish. Sick old beggars don't have clean shoes."

"'Sword," Valentine smacked himself in the head, then began pulling off his beard. It came away in chunks, still connected to his face by long, sticky strands of glue. "I knew I was forgetting something. I just got very excited. I'd been walking down High Street the other day and I thought to myself, 'you know, Valentine, have you ever really looked at a beggar? I mean looked at them?' And I started looking around and I realized that hardly anyone ever looked closely at the beggars, especially the ones coughing like they had the Scrave, so, you know, I just thought…" he trailed off, and idly picked at the glue still on his face. "I fooled Skinner, anyway."

"You didn't," Skinner shot back. "I recognized your footsteps right away. I didn't even know you were in disguise. Thought you were just being distant."

"Fah, you never did," said Valentine, as he tossed off the filthy blanket that had covered his regulation, charcoal-grey Coroner's suit. "Miss 'I can tell the color of someone's hair by the sound of their combing.'"

"Enough!" Beckett rubbed his temples. The veneine high was wearing off, and the dull ache of his illness had begun to creep in around the edges. "Valentine, I need you to conscript a couple of gendarmes and burn the Reanimate before some kid finds it. Get the trolljrmen to drag Wyndham's corpse out of there."

"Sir!" Valetine snapped off a salute, and then led the two trolljrmen down into the Arcadium.

"Wind your watch!" Skinner called after him. Valetine waved his gold pocket-watch back at her. When the young coroner had left, Skinner spoke to her partner in a quiet voice. "What's wrong?"

"Nothing," said Beckett. "Why should something be wrong?"

"I can hear it in your voice. You sound…ragged."

Beckett shook his head and snorted. He'd only been with Skinner a few months, but had been partnered with one knocker after another for years, and had gotten into the habit of accompanying his gestures with small sounds. A mounting pain at the base of his skull demanded more veneine. "Head hurts." He absently rubbed his right forearm, over the veins that he used for his injections.

"And?"

The Coroner sighed. "What is this, the third necrologist in six weeks? He was taking limbs from *live* people, Skinner. They never used to do that. It was always raided mausoleums and the dead beggars in Rittenhouse field. They were heretics, but they didn't mutilate people."

Skinner shrugged. "Times are changing."

"Yeah, and I don't like it."

"That's because you're an old fart. Now get in the coach, it's cold out."

Beckett climbed into the coach, but had to catch himself as a wave of dizziness swept over him. He threw his lean frame which now suddenly felt so heavy into the coach, and hoped that Skinner hadn't noticed.

"Shall we to dinner, Detective-Inspector Beckett?"

"No," Beckett was shaking his head. "Home."

"Home?"

The Coroner tapped his wrist. "Home."

TWO: BECKETT'S HOME

To understand the city of Trowth, capital of the Trowth Empire, one must first understand the Architecture War. Like virtually every aspect of Trowthi society, the Architecture War was the general product of the bitter internecine conflict between the Esteemed Families of the Empire, and the particular product of the legendary feud between the Family Vie-Gorgon and the Family Gorgon-Vie.

Not long into the reign of Edmund II Gorgon-Vie, about two hundred years before Elijah Beckett's time, Emilio Vie-Gorgon (second cousin to the reigning Emperor) commissioned a tower built in Raithower Plaza. The tower was ostensibly commissioned to celebrate Edmund's coronation, and it was built in a new style extremely popular at the time: tall and thin, covered with jagged merlons and sharp parapets, it looked like a huge crooked finger pointing accusingly at the filthy sky.

Of course, Raithower Plaza stands directly between the great windows of the Imperial throne room and said windows' view of the River Stark, arguably the only good view in the city. The Emperor was not amused. In retaliation, Edmund had a second tower built in the center of Vie Square, directly in front of the Vie-Gorgon mansions. This one was built in a style meant to offend the Vie-Gorgons' penchant for tall, slender, sharp things: it was short, squat, black, and ugly.

This is how the War began. It got out of hand almost immediately. Architecture became one of the weapons that the Families used to lord their status and their wealth over each other. It was not long before the six wealthiest families had developed distinct architectural styles, to make it clear who had claimed which piece of the skyline; Families had their own personal architects, who had their own schools. The schools themselves were violent affairs. Conflicts of design often were resolved with duels, sabotage, or (as in the case of the Crabtree-Daior and Feathersmith-Czarnecki family architects) a one hundred and twenty man street brawl that lasted for three hours and killed six people.

Trowth was a city defined by crowded, complex architectural schemes. Sharp-edged Vie-Gorgon merlons battled blocky Gorgon-Vie crenulations battled leering Wyndham-Vie gargoyles for every available inch of skyline. Houses and towers were built, demolished, and built taller, each one scrabbling for a higher place in the sky.

About a hundred years before Beckett's time, and a hundred years into the Architecture War, an architect from Sar-Sarpek named Irwin Arkady began buying up property on either side of St. Dunsinay's Street, with the intention of walling off either end and expanding his houses into the middle of it. Because St. Dunsinay's Street was a major thoroughfare, the Lord Mayor of Trowth flatly refused this plan; undeterred, Arkday simply built low, beautiful covered bridges between his properties, arching two stories above the street. St. Dunsinay's came to be called the Arcade instead, and a new front in the Architecture War was opened. Within a few years, every street for blocks around the Arcade found itself closed off from the sky with covered bridges, upon which more houses and towers were built. The city itself was ponderously sinking beneath its own weight, so new roads and walkways had to be built on top of the bridges and above the old streets, condemning five or six square miles of streets, squares, and alleys into darkness beneath the mass of the petrified battle of the Architects.

This was the Arcadium, and because the poor, weak sunlight that managed to break through the omnipresent cloud cover above the city always seemed to lack the strength to battle the rest of the way into the Arcadium, there was no way to tell what time it was. A wise gentleman always made sure to wind his watch, lest he lose track of time and inadvertently spend long hours lost beneath the stone mountain of the city of Trowth.

Skinner was in his dream, and she'd left behind the Coroner's charcoal-colored dress and corset, left behind all her clothes, so that she was just pale skin and young, smooth limbs, and she'd wrapped her legs around his waist and her slender hands rested on his cheeks, and Beckett could see his face reflected in the shiny silver band that covered her eyes and framed by the waves of her dark, dark hair, and his face, his face was rotten, full of rotten holes where his cheeks and nose and lips should be, and Skinner opened her mouth and closed it and opened and closed it, so that her teeth made a clack-clack-clacking sound...

...which was really the sound of his old wind-up clock, insistently reminding him that half-past five in the morning was when he should be getting out of bed. A nauseating pain struck him behind the eyes and temples. The withdrawal headache had waited a fraction of a second after Beckett had fully gained consciousness, presumably to hit him with the full effect. The pain often did that; it would lurk somewhere out of the way for a while, only to jump back at him when he turned his head, or stood up suddenly, or when he really needed to be paying attention.

Long, deep, ragged breaths made Beckett feel more like he could resist the urge to take a shot of veneine immediately. He stumbled from bed, moving a little faster than his joints were ready for, in the hopes of encouraging his adrenaline to stimulate his mind awake. The pain in the sides of his knees made him wince, but it worked just as well. Beckett stood and staggered to his washbasin. He looked at his reflection and sighed with dismay.

Elijah Beckett examined in his mirror the bright red hole in his face that gaped between his eyes. He pressed the end of it with his fingers, the tips of which had suffered a similar fate, and was mildly pleased to discover that his nose was still in place. His nose had become completely transparent and, though the purpling skin on his cheeks, the bloody, gaping hole where his nose should have been and which now revealed red muscle and bits of bone all served to dishearten him immensely, at least the nose was still there. The end of his nose was numb, as were his almost-invisible fingertips, but he could still feel the pressure of their contact. It was possible to see just the outline of his nose where light diffused around its curve, giving it a kind of soft colorless edge.

Beckett stretched. His joints cracked alarmingly, and the dull ache that had settled perpetually in them spiked to excruciating levels in his left shoulder and lower back. His body was being ravaged by a disease known as the fades. It was the cause of both the transparent patches and the terrible pains in his joints. He had contracted it in his youth, probably as a boy, trying to earn a little money by scraping ichor-fat from the gutters in the Arcadium that he could sell back to the factories. The disease was mercilessly slow and inexorable. He'd had it since he'd first joined the coroners, barely out of his teenage years. It had manifested then as a numbness in the backs of his hands, and had actually helped him become a bare-knuckle boxing champion. The disease had begun to eat away at him in his thirties, sapping a little bit of the heady pleasure of his glory days. It hadn't started to disfigure him, covering his face and chest with raw bloody patches and cracking his joints and nerves until he turned forty. Everything had gone down-hill from there.

Beckett opened the small chest by his washbasin and removed a little bottle of seven percent Veneine solution, made from the venom of the Corsay dreamsnake, the elixir that the hoodlums called Fang. Small doses would ease the pain; large doses made you see things. Beckett didn't like to hallucinate, but he'd been building up a tolerance to the painkiller, so overdoses had begun to happen more frequently.

When a man first began to taking Fang, he would feel warm and heavy. Pain and fear and anger all vanished, leaving a warm lassitude in its place. Once a man began to take large doses of the drug, he began to see strange things. Every minor thought or feeling suddenly leapt out through the eyes and into the world; life became a menagerie of dueling forks and winged cats and people bleeding from their eyes. If a man took too much he'd feel numb and heavy and he'd want to lie down. If he took far too much Fang, his mind would go places. The first place it went was Cross the Water, which Beckett had seen six times. He had been past it into the City of Brass only once, and it had almost killed him.

Because Beckett's joints hurt him, and because he didn't want to see Cross the Water ever again, he sucked half of his regular dosage into his hypodermic. Beckett grimaced at the small scars on his forearm. It really did look like he'd be savaged by a viper. With a wince, he thrust the needle into a vein and pressed on the plunger. A warm numbness spread from the wound immediately, and began to press the aches away. After a moment's consideration, Beckett packed the hypodermic and the bottle into their leather travel case.

Leaving the rusty washbasin, which stood in a small, dark corner of his small, dark sitting room, Beckett prepared the morning routine of a man who suffered from the Fades. First, check the fingertips to make sure they were not cut. It was tricky because of their transparency, but if he'd been cut he'd be able to see drops of blood, floating strangely on invisible digits. Because the fingers were numb, a small cut might go untreated and lead to infection. Beckett checked his fingers, then his toes. He looked at the three clear patches of skin on his chest, invisible spots the size of his fist that revealed bloody muscle beneath. In one place, the virulent transparency had progressed so far that he could see his ribs. There was a new patch of dark purple like a bruise on his hip. Beckett prodded it and was dismayed to discover it was numb, too. Transparency would probably overtake it in a few days. Secondly, once the inspection is over, wash everything carefully, and rub the faded places with fluxion salts. The little green and gold-flecked granules were grievously expensive, but the Empire, as a reward for years of loyal service, partially subsidized them. The salts are meant to

Beckett

slow the progression of the fades; Beckett had never noticed them helping very much.

Finally, get dressed. Beckett put on his sober-cut charcoal suit, his heavy leather boots, his heavy leather gloves. He put on his belt with his old revolver, and the heavy wool overcoat. Because his clothes were standard issue for the Coroners, everything was charcoal grey; because they were standard issue for people living in Trowth, everything was made of wool. Simple cuts, dark colors, and a gun that had been out of date for ten years. All of which were better than the three-cornered leather hat that topped off the uniform, which had been out of date for closer to fifty years. In the defense of the Coroners, no one had to wear the hat anymore, and Beckett was probably the only one who did. As a gesture of goodwill to anyone that had to look at the raw hole in his face, Beckett wrapped an old red scarf around his nose and mouth.

Beckett took a long look around his room, his eyes glancing off the dusty outlines on his walls and floor where he'd had to sell his things—furniture, kirliotypes, awards, anything that he could—to scrape enough money together for more veneine. There was very little left. It was not comfort, but a cold, wry cynicism that told him at least he wouldn't leave behind a lot of bric-a-brac for someone to sort through when the fades finally got to him.

Long-standing city ordinance in Trowth demanded that all statues, plaques, sculptures and public metalwork in the city be made of bronze. An apocryphal story claimed that this was at the behest of the Emperor Agon VII Czarnecki, whose hatred of all things having to do with the neighboring nation of Sar-Sarpek had caused him to forbid any artwork made from marble. Since bronze was the only other reasonable material with which to make public sculpture, and since Imperial decrees are notoriously difficult to rescind, bronze became the official accent of Trowth.

Unfortunately, the city's harsh winters and salty sea-air turned bronze black and green almost immediately. Not one statue ever survived a Trowth winter without becoming almost completely unidentifiable. And there were plenty of statues. The statues that adorned the squares and courtyards, that stood in front of the towers in Ministry, or in front of the fancy homes in Beacon Hill had become an expanded front for the Architecture War.

The Families of Trowth had great enthusiasm for honoring their heroes, but much less enthusiasm when it came to preserving the memories of those heroes. They had been erecting statues for hundreds of years, in honor of this general or that scientist, sometimes more than once. Poor record-keeping on behalf of the Daior-Crabtrees had caused them to commission no fewer than fifteen statues in honor of Chretien Daior-Crabtree's discovery of the fluxion salt, and over twenty statues in honor of Janusz Vlytze's victory at the Siege of Canth, despite Vlytze's dubious status as a hero of the Sar-Sarpek nobility. This was not altogether uncommon, as most of the Families of Trowth had been at least second-cousins with the massacred aristocracy of Sar-Sarpek, and to be cousins with Janusz Vlytze, who had led the immortal Last Ride of the Saaghyari, was an enviable privilege.

Being cast in bronze was by no means a ticket to immortality in Trowth. The constant feuding between the Families meant that the creation of new statues always received priority over the maintenance of old ones. Trowth was a city full of worn, green memorials, hundreds of thousands of faceless sentinels, standing guard over forgotten honors.

One such statue stood in the center of Queen's Riot Close, which was a small courtyard off of Westbridge Street. Queen's Riot was bordered by small town houses which were generally let out to reliable but poorly-paid civil servants like Beckett. The tall green-bronze figure in the center of the Close was pointing off to the east, its face and clothing eaten away by years of salty winter weather. It stood on a pedestal upon which someone had thoughtfully mounted a plaque, explaining who the eastward-pointing hero was and, perhaps, why he was pointing. Sadly, the plaque had also been eaten away by time and was completely illegible. Beckett called the statue Cuthbert, because it suited him to do so.

"Another ole' morning, Cuthbert," Beckett said, as he stepped into the cold gray winter air. Snow had fallen overnight, and the Close was covered with a layer of pristine white. "Enjoy the snow now. It'll be black with filth come evening," he added. This was most certainly true: as Beckett stepped out of the Close and onto Westbridge Street, he saw that the snow there was already filthy and disgusting.

The sun had not yet risen, and would not for two or three hours. Winter nights in Trowth were long. The sky overhead was black, but the street was already filling up. Westbridge, while not as important a thoroughfare as High Street or the Mile, was in a densely populated neighborhood. Street vendors had brought their carts, and begun hawking onions and leeks, selling meat pies, eggs, and milk. Men sick with scrave, or the fades, or simple poverty had left the relative shelter of archways and alleys in order to eke out a meager living as beggars.

Valentine was waiting for him, sitting behind the wheel of his ridiculous horseless carriage. It was almost the same shape as a regular carriage, but longer, and with smaller wheels. The thing was powered by a great phlogiston engine that looked like a brass pot-bellied stove. It clattered noisily and pumped little clouds of bluish smoke into the air.

The burning phlogiston smelled like blood, cloying and metallic, but it was a smell that all of Trowth had long since grown used to. Valentine himself wore the driving goggles and white scarf that were apparently requisite attire.

"What's this?" Beckett shouted over the noise of the engine. "Where's Skinner?"

"She's at the scene already!" Valentine shouted back. "I'm to take you there immediately! Come on, I've got a meat pie for your breakfast!" He handed Beckett something wrapped in parchment. It smelled like meat and onions, and Beckett found his mood, if not soaring, at least picking itself up out of the gutter, and maybe dusting itself off a little. His nose might be gradually fading away, but at least it still worked.

"How can you stand to drive this thing?" Beckett shouted, as he unwrapped his pie. "It sounds like someone murdering a hundred suits of armor with a wrench!"

"What?" Valentine shouted back.

Beckett resisted the urge to punch him, and instead began to eat the pie.

THREE: THE CRIME

Valentine drove them at a reasonable, if stinking and shuddering pace, to North Ferry, a neighborhood close to the clean end of the Stark, farther up from where the collective sewage and offal of the city began to run into it. It was home to mostly merchant-class families, and some of the less-esteemed Families. The houses were done in Feathersmith-Daior style, which favored simple, peaked roofs tastefully accented with bronze metal work, but they were gradually losing ground to the innumerable gables and the armies of grotesque gargoyles that the Wyndham-Vies were putting everywhere.

Outside of the house at 612 Bynam Lane was a carriage with the crest of the Coroners on the door: the silhouette of a two-headed eagle on a bronze shield. The cab was parked directly in front of the small bridge that led to the house; the front door had clearly once been a third-storey window before Bynam Lane had been built above the crumbling Thurgood Street. There was a gap between the Bynam and the fronts of the houses that it faced. The gap was fenced off by tall, greening bronze pickets. Leaning against the pickets were half-a-dozen rough-looking gendarmes, more than a few sporting the facial brands that marked them as "reformed" thieves or perjurers.

"Well, who invited the goon squad?" Valentine cut the engine on his carriage, and coasted to a stop about twenty feet from the gendarmes and the coach.

One of the gendarmes, a tall man with a large, drooping moustache, was standing at the coach and shouting at someone inside. Like his fellow hooligans, he wore a long black coat with several torn strips of dark blue cloth tied around his right arm. He had a truncheon in his right hand and, Beckett suspected, at least a sword at his belt, possibly a revolver.

" —don't care *who* you work for, you silly twat—" The man shouted.

" —I will not permit you to disrupt the crime scene—" came the muffled reply.

" —I'm going in there—"

" —you have a responsibility of service to the Crown—"

Harry, the coachman, a rail-thin man with grizzled mutton chops, sat tensely in his seat during the shouting. Beckett could see how much he wanted to take a shot at the gendarme, and found himself sympathizing.

It was Skinner's voice in the cab. Beckett recognized it as they approached, and his temper flared. Like many men of his generation, Elijah Beckett took it poorly when he saw slimy, malodorous, tobacco-chewing thugs shouting at young, blind women. Furthermore, he liked Skinner. "Gentlemen!" He called, putting a reasonable amount of effort into making his voice friendly, and still failing miserably. "Beckett" and "friendly" could only under the best of circumstances by the kindest of observers be called more than passing acquaintances. "What's the problem?"

The gendarme whirled on Beckett, took in his leather tricorn and his long coat, and eyed the red scarf around his mouth, then spat sullenly. "Who're—"

"Detective Inspector Beckett. Coroners." Beckett brushed past the gendarme and opened the door of the coach. Skinner sat primly in her seat, lips pressed together in a thin line.

The gendarme muttered something unintelligible, then, "I'm Captain—"

"I don't care." Beckett interrupted. "Take your men and cordon off the street. They'll have to stay until at least noon; we may need them to canvass the homes around here for witness statements."

The captain snorted. "Folks around here like their privacy..." He trailed off in the face of Beckett's icy glare, then spat again. "If the sharpsies broke into a man's *home*, I've a right to know—"

"You'll be updated regarding our investigation when and if we deem it appropriate."

The captain's face was red and he was practically foaming at the mouth. The red number five branded into his cheek had flushed a dark crimson. "North Ferry is my territory, *Inspector*. I don't care who called you but you've no business in my town."

"The entire empire is within the jurisdiction of the Coroners, captain," Beckett told the man very quietly. "Valentine."

The young man stood behind him; he'd pushed the driving goggles up on his head, but at least he'd had the foresight to take off that ridiculous scarf. "Sir?"

"What does 'coroner' mean?"

"Sir," Valentine began unbuttoning his heavy coat, then shook it to reveal the pearl-inlay handles of the revolver in his belt. "Literally 'coroner' means 'agent of the crown.' In our case, 'Coroner' refers to an elite division of the Imperial guard given a mandate by the Emperor both in his capacity as secular and religious commander of the Empire, and answerable only to him and the Minister of Internal Security."

Beckett turned to his companion and feigned surprise. "Really? Answerable only to the Emperor?"

"And the Minister of Internal Security."

"But not to any filthy militia-man that stumbles into my crime scene and can't keep his truncheon in his pants?"

"Not that I am aware of, sir."

There was a long pause, as the captain looked from Valentine to Beckett, and clearly mulled over some choice words. Words about what they could do with their mandate, about what he'd do to them given half a chance, and, perhaps, a few words about their mothers. Words that he was prepared to deliver to devastating effect. Finally, he leaned forward and pulled his coat aside, revealing the walnut grip of a heavy revolver. "I'm not afraid of you and your coroner bullshit."

Beckett said nothing, just stared right in the captain's face, letting the tension build. There is an art to the intimidating glare, and thirty years of working for the coroners had given Beckett plenty of practice. The captain's mouth began to twitch. Beckett, his face concealed by his scarf, appeared as still as a bronze statue. The stillness made him even more intimidating, and the captain began to feel that he was trying to stare down a stone. The man narrowed his eyes, only by the tiniest fraction, and dropped his shoulder a quarter of an inch. It was enough. *This is it*, thought Beckett. The captain took a swing at the old coroner, a right cross aimed straight for Beckett's invisible nose. Though age and illness had sapped much of the strength and mobility from the body of Beckett's youth, there were still a few things he knew how to do.

One of those things was what boxers call a slip. He shifted to the side, bending from the waist, and moving his face just barely out of the way of the oncoming blow. Then, without missing a beat, twisted with his hips and threw a left hook right into the captain's mouth. At the same moment, he reached out to grab a hold of the man's revolver. The whole thing from right-cross to left-hook took less than a second, and suddenly Captain Whoever of the local gendarmerie found the inside of his mouth shredded by his own teeth, and the pain erupting from his lips sending him to the verge of unconsciousness.

The gendarme staggered to the side, crashing against the bronze fence, blood pouring from his mouth. There was a stunned look on his face. He clutched uselessly at his belt, trying to draw his gun, only to find that Beckett had it now. The other gendarmes rushed forward to come to their captain's aid, but were forestalled.

Valentine had drawn his pistols. The gendarmes found themselves staring down the barrels of two gleaming silver-plated revolvers. "Don't," the young coroner told them, with the wry, malicious grin that said he'd probably really enjoy it if they did.

"Clean him up," Beckett told the men. "Then set up my cordon. I'm keeping this," he added, and stuffed the revolver into his pocket.

With what was unquestionably a great reverence for Beckett's authority, the captain spat a wad of blood out onto the snow. One of his men helped him to his feet, and the captain began shouting orders.

As the gendarmes began to set up their cordon, a young boy approached Beckett and his companions, carrying a letter. He looked at Beckett wide-eyed, then thrust his arm out, offering his missive. Beckett took it, and tossed a copper to the boy, who snatched it greedily from the air, and promptly sprinted off down the street.

"Who's it from?" Valentine asked, as he held Skinner's cane while she climbed out of the cab.

Beckett opened the yellow envelope, marked with his name in neat, block print. "Letter shows up for me at the precise moment I get here? It's from Stitch."

"Mr. Stitch? Is…is he here?" Valentine's eyes widened.

Skinner shook her head. "He was. Looked around inside for a little while, then left me here, told me not to let anyone in."

Valentine tried to glance over at the letter, as he passed Skinner her cane. "What's it say?"

Offering the letter to his companion, Beckett told him. "It says 'Not Sharpsies.'"

"That's it?"

Beckett looked back at the letter. "It says 'Not Sharpsies.' Space, dash, 'Stitch.'" Beckett shuffled around the cab and started across the bridge. Skinner followed directly behind him, her cane waving precisely back and forth in front of her.

"Well," Valentine came last. "Well, what the hell does *that* mean?"

The parlor of 612 Bynam Lane was comfortably small, clean and neat. The walls and floor were dark wood, there was a dark red rug with a complex pattern on it, and a small mat by the door on which travelers could wipe their feet. The hall was lit by old-fashioned candles that gave the place a yellow glow. The candles had melted nearly down to the nubs.

"Who lit the candles?" Beckett asked as he and his companions entered.

"Unless it was Stitch, it must have been the family."

Beckett nodded. "Valentine, put them out. Don't knock any of them over."

It was not uncommon for Valentine to receive orders whose purpose he didn't quite understand. Was it easier to examine a crime scene in the dark, for instance? Would smoke from the candles corrupt...something, somehow? Maybe the light hurt Beckett's eyes. Valentine found a little brass candle snuffer and immediately began snuffing the candles in the parlor.

"Where are we looking, Skinner?" Beckett asked the knocker.

She shrugged. "I haven't been inside, yet. Stitch said the bodies were in the sitting room." A sharp rapping sound at about shoulder height worked its way along the walls; this was, Beckett knew, a knocker's way of 'looking around.' "Probably downstairs. These old houses have all the living rooms at the bottom." She pointed at a door. "Stairs are behind that one."

"What's his name?" The dead man was sprawled on a red couch. Thick, sticky puddles of blood were congealing around him. A woman and two children, presumably his wife and children, lay in tangles of limbs around the room. They looked as if they'd been picked up and just tossed haphazardly about, like a lazy child with its dolls. Blood pooled around them, and stuck to Beckett's shoes as he entered.

"Herman Zindel. Wife Isabel, children..." Skinner swallowed hard. "David and Michelle."

"Who called us?"

Skinner shrugged. "I don't know. The milkman found them. He said they hadn't put their old bottles out, so he rang the bell. When no one answered, he got worried. Door was unlocked. He said he didn't touch anything, just ran out into the street, screaming about the sharpsies. Mr. Stitch must have gotten word of it, somehow. He was the one that called me down here."

"We've got a statement from the milkman?"

"Not yet. But I've got his address."

Beckett nodded, and then turned his attention back to the corpses. Somehow, the fresh blood made them more nauseating than the dead flesh of the Reanimates. A twisted, hollow feeling thrummed in the coroner's stomach, accompanied with a buzzing behind his ears. He badly wanted another veneine injection. "See anything, Valentine?"

The young man had just come into the sitting room, studiously snuffing candles on the way. "Uhm. Throats are...torn out, I'd say. Shredded, like with something sharp. Lots of blood. Hm." If anything, the young man was understating the fact. The entire lower half of each corpse's face had been torn away, all the way down to their collarbones. The woman and children had their bones picked clean, but someone had simply torn out Herman Zindel's entire lower jaw. Valentine turned away from the bodies and looked at Beckett, who met his gaze. They took a long moment to avoid looking at the corpses. "Could be sharpsies."

Beckett watched Valentine make the exchange. Beckett had been doing it himself for years, ever since he first saw a dead body hacked apart by a greedy necrologist. The exchange was this: you learn a little bit more about what the world is really like, and in exchange, you give up a little bit of your ability to feel. Beckett had been surrendering tiny bits of himself to the job for three decades. He knew a lot about what the world was really like. He could see the change happening on Valentine's face, an exchange prompted by necessity. The young man's face goes pale, his eyes widen, he starts to feel a little sick. Then he swallows and sets his jaw, determined not to let the mess get to him. When Beckett was a young man, he'd always thought that it was a good thing, being able to grit your teeth and look right down onto a broken, bloody body like Herman Zindel's without feeling that knot in his stomach. Valentine probably thought it was, too.

"Stitch says no, and I'm inclined to agree with him." Beckett turned back to the corpse of Herman Zindel, and knelt beside it. "Look at his arms. What's wrong with them?"

Reluctantly, Valentine followed Beckett's attention. "Uhm. Nothing?"

"Right."

"So?"

With an exasperated groan, Skinner filled in. "So, if a sharpsie comes into your house and wants to bite you in the face, or something, what do you do?"

Valentine looked at her, then back at Beckett. "I don't...uh...I guess, shoot it?" He looked around the room. "But there's no gun. He could have grabbed that poker, by the fire, for a weapon. Handsome piece of ironwork there, too." Blinking quickly, the young man looked around the room again. "Hey, that's funny. There's a lot of nice things here. The gramophone over there, it's still got all its cylinders, even. It'd fetch a few coppers, at the least..."

"Valentine." Beckett struggled to keep his voice even. "Focus."

The young man shook his head. "Right. So, no gun, let's say he couldn't reach the poker. I guess, I guess he'd try and fight them off with his hands, right?" There was a long pause. "But...but if he did that, how come there's no marks on them? There'd have to be bruises on his wrists at least, where the sharpsie held him down, marks from his fingernails. Bite marks, probably, too."

Beckett stood. "Not sharpsies." A twinge of resentment slithered around in his voice. *It's not like I wouldn't have figured it out.* "My guess is that these people were dead before their bodies were...mutilated."

"And someone wants us to think it was the sharpsies?" Skinner asked. "Why?"

"I don't know." Beckett added that question to the list of Several Other Things He Didn't Know, but Would Really Like To: namely, who killed Herman Zindel and his family? Why did they do it? *How* did they do it? How did they get into and out of the house without breaking a lock or a window? And, perhaps most pertinently, why had the coroners been called in to investigate?

Questions needed answers, answers needed information. The three coroners began a thorough search of the house. They found no unusual footprints, broken windows, broken locks, dirt that happened to only come from one part of town, or matchbooks with a tavern's name stamped on them that had been conveniently dropped by the murderer.

In fact, while Beckett and Valentine gingerly made their way throughout the house, searching through cabinets, checking underneath tables and desks and beds, they found nothing at all of note. Skinner was a different story. While Beckett and Valentine examined, Skinner simply followed them from room to room, her telerhythmia bouncing off the walls with a consistent knock-knock-knock, and listening closely to the sound, trying to parse out whatever meaning was hidden in those hollow raps that all sounded the same to Beckett.

"Here," Skinner finally said, at the end of an unusually short hall.

Valentine glanced at her. "You're sure?"

Skinner nodded.

"Try...grab the candlestick there," Beckett told the young man. Valentine did, and nothing happened. "Try pushing against the wall." Again, nothing. "Hm. Wait. There. Is that a bust of Harcourt Wolfram?" On a small table at the end of the short hall was a small, marble bust of the famous scientist. Valentine attempted to pick the bust up, and found it attached to a small cable. There was a clicking sound in the walls, and the end of the hall became a door, and suddenly swung open.

"Paydirt," Valentine said, grinning.

In a city like Trowth, whose heart was a maze of back alleys and labyrinthine passages, a city where a man could be arrested and executed for practicing the wrong kinds of science, where a hundred Ministries and royal Families plied their Byzantine politics at all hours, hidden rooms and compartments like the one in Herman Zindel's house were actually very common. Knockers, while they were useful for relaying information around the city, and keeping track of enemies in the dark, found that the primary need for their employment was locating secret doors.

The tiny room behind the door yielded a wealth of information, though Beckett, for his life, could not have said whether or not it was useful information.

"What is all this?" Beckett asked. The small, cramped room was jammed with large slate chalkboards, and the ground was littered with crumbled sheets of paper. Everything was covered with numbers, diagrams, formulae, all in the same sloppy handwriting.

Valentine pursed his lips and let out a low whistle. "Not like any math that I've ever seen." This was no idle statement of fact; Valentine Vie-Gorgon had the best education money could buy.

Beckett agreed. "I think we know why they called us. This has to be Aetheric Geometry."

FOUR: THE SHARPSIES

From a distance, a sharpsie—whose scientific name was "omphaloskepsis," and whose name in their own language was something utterly unutterable—looked much like a human being. They were the same height, though generally much thinner, and they always either crouched or loped with a springing jog; never anything in between. Upon closer inspection, however, numerous and deeply unsettling differences became apparent. For starters, sharpsie skin was dark and pebbly, very thick and rough. Their eyes were flat, black, and expressionless. And then, there were the *teeth*. Sharpsies were carnivores. They had long jaws and mouths filled with sharp teeth: long, curved incisors in the front, molars like huge meat shears in the back. Their thin, leathery lips, which were only barely able to close together in the front, seemed incapable of any expression except curling back to reveal those gnashing jaws.

There had always been a few sharpsies in Trowth. Like their mortal enemies, the trolljrmen, the sharpsies had brought unusual crafts and trade specialties that the Empire found useful. Sharpsies were, for instance, excellent butchers and superb cooks. Never fully integrated into society, the sharpsies had carved a small niche out for themselves on the fringes.

Starting around 1840, a wave of omphaloskepsis immigrants inundated the Empire. They were fleeing their own lands, west of Sar-Sarpek, and had been settling anywhere that would take them. This did not amount to very many places, and the sharpsies soon became a gypsy race, carrying their own possessions on their backs, always trying to drive their herds of horses and reindeer to new pastures, always finding themselves more and more unwelcome. By the time the Emperor offered them amnesty in Trowth, there were no herds left, and the Sharpsies were desperate.

They accepted the amnesty and attempted to settle in the Empire's capital city. Thousands, male and female, were immediately pressganged into the war with the ettercap. They died beneath the mountains of Gorcia, far from their own homes, from their families, and far from the city that had offered them its feigned sanctuary. Only the old, recognizable by the thick tufts of wiry, yellow hair that they grew on their forearms and shoulders, and the very young were left in Trowth, to eke out a meager existence as best they could, unwanted, untrained, and uncertain.

The young sharpsies that managed to avoid the pressgangs grew into angry young men. No one wanted to hire them. They couldn't communicate their needs effectively, except to other members of their species: the sharp teeth and thick tongue of a sharpsie made learning Trowthi all but impossible. Their own language sounded to Trowth ears like a man choking on a fishbone, which only served to drive a wedge of ridicule in between the city men and the sharp-toothed strangers.

While Elijah Beckett and his coroners searched the house on Bynam Street, most of the sharpsies were doing what they did every day: lounging by the docks on the Stark, trying to find work as day-laborers. Some worked unloading ships or laying stone or in the chilly back rooms of the butcher shops carving meat. It was illegal to hire them, and if the pressmen found that a merchant had employed a sharpsie, the worker was at once sent to the front. Despite the danger, sharpsies could still find work as unskilled laborers—so long as they sold their services cheap enough.

The sharpsies that couldn't find work that day spent it dodging pressgangs or picking fights with trolljrmen. Half past noon, a dozen gendarmes from North Ferry—or, perhaps only six from North Ferry who'd found a few likely fellows on the trip down—appeared in Mudside, the sharpsie shanty town on the Stark. They came with their blue armbands prominent, heavy truncheons ready, riot shields hanging from their wrists. They'd come to find the murderers of the Zindel family, they said, and they'd break the bones of every sharpsie in Mudside if they had to. They screamed and kicked in doors. They threatened to start fires.

If a Trowthi man was able-bodied, it was almost a sure thing that he'd be taken by the pressgangs. The gendarmerie was no protection, but the criminal brand was. Gendarmes were sometimes clever, sometimes old, sometimes lame or sick, but most often they were men with the number three or five branded on their faces. The first indicated that the branded man was a thief, the second that he was a murderer.

The gendarmerie was poorly-supervised and badly trained. It was not an organization of honorable men, but of hard angry ones. The gendarmes that showed up in Mudside were very, very angry.

Fifteen young sharpsie men came out to meet them, black eyes always flat, but faces sullen. They growled their unintelligible language, and they looked like they were spoiling for a fight. They threw rocks and old bottles. The gendarmes attacked, and bore the young men to the ground. The brawl lasted only ten minutes before most of the young sharpsies ran, leaving behind only five: four were beaten too badly to move. One was dead.

Beckett read all about the first action against the Sharpsie Threat in the broadsheets the next morning. He and Skinner were in his office in Raithower House. The building had become the head-quarters for the coroners ever since the Vie-Gorgon family had abandoned it for a bigger one that didn't have Edmund Gorgon-Vie's ugly, lumpy tower looming over it.

"We have nothing," Skinner was saying. "No witnesses saw anything. Zindel's friends had seen him the day before and he seemed fine. His children had been in school, his wife had done the shopping. Nothing."

Beckett tossed the broadsheet onto his small, rickety desk. "Not nothing. Riot in Mudside. Gendarmes."

"I'd heard about that." Skinner was very quiet for a moment. "You don't think...?"

"No." Beckett's head was buzzing. There was a pain in the corner of his right eye, like it was trying to roll around inside his head. He rubbed his temples. "Nothing from the witnesses. Nothing..." It was too hot. He'd thrown off his coat and, because Skinner was the only one there and she couldn't tell the difference, he'd pulled off his scarf, revealing the gap into his face. It was still too hot.

"Elijah? Are you all right?"

She could hear something in his voice. Beckett rubbed his hands over his face, and took a deep breath. "Fine." Another breath. "No witnesses. Nothing in the house...except for the geometry. Which we don't understand." He jerked his head as a thought struck him, then winced at the pain in his neck. "Ow. Co-workers. Who does he work with?"

Skinner shook her head. "He's independent. A thousand crowns a year. Some old prize from the Academy of Sciences, or something. Everyone we talked to said he spent his free time at the public houses."

The buzzing in Beckett's head had grown stronger, and it was now accompanied by a ringing in his ear, and a sickly-sweet taste in his mouth. *Shit,* he thought. "Excuse me."

Briskly but carefully, Beckett rolled up his sleeve, and wrapped it tight around his elbow, then opened the leather traveling case for his hypodermic. The veins in his arm began to bulge. *Not much. Quarter-ounce.* Beckett pulled a small amount of fang into the hypodermic, then quickly jabbed it into his arm and pressed on the plunger.

It was too much. He could tell immediately.

The pain receded; it didn't leave, it just didn't bother him any more. The taste in his mouth was suddenly satisfied. But the world jumped alarmingly, and his vision distorted. It looked like a kirliotype that had been heated with a match. The walls of his office bubbled and turned black.

"Elijah?" Skinner's voice echoed off his inner ear. Six Skinners, scattered around him, spoke softly in his ears.

"Sh!" He blinked rapidly, in an effort to restore his ordinary vision. In the split second that his eyes were closed, he saw water: a vast, churning ocean under a black, stormy sky. Rushing waves filled his ears, saltwater ran up his nose.

His eyes opened, and it was gone.

Blink.

The ocean tossed him back and forth, knocking the air from his chest and filling up his lungs.

Blink.

He was back in his office, panting heavily. He could feel snot on his upper lip, running from his nose. His eyes seemed to have settled down, and the buzzing in his head had vanished.

"Elijah, are you all right?" Skinner's voice was clear, but sounded like it was coming from very far away.

"I'm fine." He said. *Too much. That was Cross the Water.* "Fine." He took a long, slow ragged breath, and wiped off his mouth.

Her voice heavy with concern, Skinner pointed out, "You're not fine. You've been using more, lately."

"It doesn't matter." *Nothing matters.* He had a job to do, and he would do it. If that meant shooting his veins up with fang every five minutes, then that's what he would do.

"But..."

"Doesn't. Matter." Beckett's voice was stone. He rubbed his temples and tried to settle his thoughts. "If. Even if someone had hired sharpsies to hide the murder..."

"Or someone else. Anyone with a..." Skinner broke off. "Well, I imagine there are probably tools for...for doing that."

Beckett nodded. "How did they get in? No broken windows, no broken locks."

They both sat for a moment, and considered. "Let's be logical." Skinner said. "If someone got in, and no locks were broken, then they must have come in somewhere there wasn't a lock. Either another entrance to the home, which I would have found…"

"Or a door that we know about, but was open." There was one conclusion readily available; it made sense, in itself, but didn't help him make sense of anything else. "Our milkman said the door was unlocked when he found it. No one in North Ferry leaves their doors unlocked. So, someone let the murderer in. A maid?"

"No. Maid works every third day. She was off the day before and the day of."

"One of the Zindels, then."

Skinner rolled her cane around in her hands while she thought. "Someone they recognized? Someone they were comfortable enough with to take into the sitting room. Who also had reason to murder them all."

Beckett nodded again. "His collaborator."

"You think so?"

The coroner shrugged. "Maybe. We don't know enough. We don't even know what he was working on in there. Who's our scientific contact for Aetheric Geometry?"

Skinner snorted. "You're joking? Only half a dozen people understood it when the church forbid…forbade? When they had it forbidden. Even then, I think it was only ever Wolfram that got it. And when he died…we don't have a contact for Aetheric Geometry, Elijah."

"Next best thing, then. Charterhouse."

"He's a psychometrist."

Beckett began wrapping his scarf around his face again. "And a cartographer. We can't have Aetheric Geometry, at least we can get regular geometry. Besides, I want him to check over the scene. We need more information." Beckett pulled on his coat and hat. "Where's Valentine?"

"He's watching the cordon, making sure no one gets in and disturbs something."

"Good." Beckett grunted. "Maybe he'll shoot that damned gendarme."

FIVE: ALAN CHARTERHOUSE

Alan Charterhouse's hands were moving almost of their own accord. They quickly used the draftsman's tools on his desk: compass, stylus, t-square, triangle, and his favorite, the intricate brass slide-rule. His pen moved in smooth, steady, straight lines as he copied the map in front of him. He'd divided it into small sections, and his eyes focused intently on each one, making sure he didn't miss a single line or degree. Despite the amount of concentration it took, Alan found his mind wandering.

He was alone in the drafting room, a room in the basement of his family's house that would have been quite comfortable if it hadn't been jammed full of heavy slanted drafting desks, piled up with books, bundles of paper, old broadsheets, and, of course, maps. There were maps everywhere. Rolled up maps lay in bundles on the floor, or were piled up on shelves. Maps of the Rowan-Harshank Corridor, made of folding steel plates, stood in a neat stack by the door. There were copperplate maps, hide maps, and at least one map that his father had made of Corsay on a wide piece of tree-bark.

Alan Charterhouse had woken up that morning with a fantasy about his father coming home; maybe his father would wait until after breakfast, letting Alan think that today wouldn't be the day, and then surprising him during the meal. When that didn't happen, Alan had reconsidered; probably, the old man would wait until lunchtime, and surprise him then. The weak afternoon sunlight was beginning to fade now, and Alan fought hard against the hope that his father would surprise him with his return after a hard day's work in the drafting room.

Alan's mind struggled to interpret the faint sounds he heard. Was that scratch on the cobblestones a random passerby, or Ian Charterhouse setting his rucksack down by the doorstep? Was the rattle of keys his father's, or his neighbors? The thumping footsteps upstairs, were they just his great-uncle Malcolm stomping around?

It was a certain fact of his life, Alan knew, that the second he came up with a dream like this one, one in which someone went to the trouble to surprise him, it would almost certainly not ever happen. He recalled vividly the three years between seven and ten in which he desperately wished for a surprise birthday party, only to realize himself disappointed the second he thought of it. *How do I know something amazing won't happen?* Alan though, as he tried to get his mind back into the work. *Because I want it to.*

"Alan!" Uncle Malcolm's voice startled him, and young Alan Charterhouse nearly spilled his ink. This would have been disastrous; Mapmaker's Ink contained large amounts of nitric fluxate-23, a compound made from volatile flux, and could be extremely dangerous.

"Alan, come up here, boy! There's someone to see you."

Alan's heart skipped a beat. *No. Don't think about it. It isn't dad. And if it is, you want to be surprised. Don't think it.* Alan forced himself to be calm as he stoppered his ink bottle and neatly stacked up his tools and pen. *Be surprised. Don't think about it.*

He tried harder to remain calm as he climbed the steps to the parlor, but found the urge to hurry irresistible, and after a moment he took them three at a time. "Alan!" His uncle shouted again.

Uncle Malcolm was waiting for him at the top of the stairs. He was actually Alan's father's uncle, and probably at least seventy years old. He had been a big man once, and still had a barrel-chest, though his arms and legs and become spindly. A fringe of white hair grew in tufts around his head, and generally got less attention than the huge moustache that covered most of the lower half of his face. Malcolm had slowly been moving out of touch with reality as the years went by. He wore his dressing gown and slippers all day, every day, and never left the house.

Like most people that worked with Mapmaker's Ink, Malcolm's fingers had succumbed to flux-induced necrosis. They'd been removed and replaced with mechanical brass fingers that looked like metal skeleton hands held together with brackets and wire. They clicked and scraped as Malcolm flexed his hands impatiently.

"In the parlor," Uncle Malcolm said. "Come on." He put a cold brass hand on Alan's back and gently shoved him into the sitting room. Alan's heart was practically in his throat; he was ready to leap up and embrace…

The man waiting for him was not his father. He was a lean man with a heavy, charcoal-covered overcoat and a red scarf wrapped around his face. He held a leather tricorn hat in his hands, and was standing very patiently, the way an oak tree or a boulder might stand if it expected to be waiting for a very long time.

"   Tell you he's too young to be messing with this," Malcolm muttered to the stranger. "Twelve years old, shouldn't be touching no dead things."

"Thirteen," Alan said.   "I'm thirteen Uncle Malcolm, remember?"

Malcolm looked at his nephew with mad blue eyes. "Twelve. Your birthday was last week. Twelve candles, twelve years. Remember? I remember. Your daddy came home from…from…" He trailed off and began to squint, as though trying to get a better view of his memory.

"That was last year. Dad was in Gorcia. He's in Corsay, now."

Malcolm snorted and shuffled out of the room. "Too young, too young," he mumbled as he left.

Alan turned to the stranger.

"Let me see your hands." The man said. His voice had a hoarse, raw edge to it, but it was strong and authoritative. Alan held up his hands; he was still wearing his special gloves, made out of cartographic vellum. "Necrotic?"

Alan shook his head.   "No.   Not yet, anyway.   Just hypersensitive, like…like my father's."

The man nodded. "Alan Charterhouse. I'm Beckett. I work for the coroners. Do you know what that is?"

I'm thirteen, Alan thought. *I'm not stupid.* "Yes, sir. You catch people that practice heretical sciences. Like necrologists and oneiricists, and that."

"Yes. Do you know anything about geometry, boy? Have you ever done psychometry on a crime scene?"

"Uhm.   Well, I've been an apprentice mapmaker since I was seven, sir, so I know a fair bit about geometry." He could not hide the indignation in his voice. "I've never been…to…to a crime scene, sir. But I can read objects by touch better than my father." He dropped his hands and held his chin up defiantly.

"Good," Beckett said. "You're going to come with me. The coroners have put you on retainer. Go get whatever things you need for psychometry, and a change of clothes in case we have to keep you overnight. Bring something to read, too."

"Uhm. What?"

Beckett cocked his head to the side. "You. Are. Coming. With. Me. Go get your things."

Trying to read while the coach bumped along George Street was making Alan Charterhouse nauseous. He looked up from his book—a yellowed, dog-eared copy of *Ted East and the Canthi Chanteur*—and considered the man and woman sitting across from him. Beckett sat still as stone, looking out the window. Skinner, a pretty young woman with a silver plate fixed across her eyes, was idly tapping her foot. Alan chose to take the foot-tapping as a sign of a friendlier nature than her partner's.

"Do..." his voice was startlingly loud in the relative quiet of the coach. Alan lowered his voice to practically a whisper. "Do you know Ted East?" Alan held up his book, then lowered it sheepishly when he remembered that Skinner couldn't see it. "It says...in my book it says he's a real coroner, that all these stories are true."

Beckett snorted loudly, and Skinner tried to hide a small smile behind her hand. "Well, Master Charterhouse, you shouldn't believe everything you read."

"Oh, I know...I mean, I know it probably never happened like this. Like in the books. I mean, I'm sure it didn't. There's a spot in...I think it was in *Ted East and the Ectoplasmatists* where he shoots eight people without reloading his revolver." Alan folded the book in his lap.

"I just thought that...maybe, you know, maybe it was based on a real person, you know? Like maybe he sold his story, or something."

Beckett snorted again.

Alan leaned away from him and towards Skinner. "Have you ever seen...I mean...have you ever met a cult of ectoplasmatists?"

"There are no cults," Beckett cut in. "Of ectoplasmatists. And they can't do any of that nonsense like in your penny-books, like conjure knives and axes and things out of the air."

"You've read about Ted East?" Alan asked, his voice suddenly brightening.

Skinner struggled to keep her face neutral. "Oh, Elijah," she said, softly. "I didn't know you could read."

Beckett glared at her. "I know about things. All kinds of things." He turned back to Alan Charterhouse. "Real ectoplasm isn't hard at all. It's kind of like thick smoke, or glue. And there's no such person as Ted East."

"Oh." The young cartographer's voice was glum.

Beckett did not add that the seemingly limitless series of cheap, two-penny books about Ted East, Coroner, which were making a fortune for their author, actually were based on a real person. Beckett also did not add that he'd sold the stories to that same author so that he could buy more fang.

There was a long silence in the coach after that, and Alan Charterhouse spent the rest of the trip looking out the window.

George Street skirted the River Stark for about a mile before it crossed the St. Edmund's Bridge into North Ferry. The Imperial Palace loomed high on Alan's left the whole time; it was a great mountain of a building, and the most vicious battleground of the Architecture War. Every Emperor since Agon Diethes considered it his personal responsibility to add a hall or a tower or something to the palace, and so it had become a sprawling mess of a hundred and fifty Emperors' worth of additions. Merlons and peaked roofs, flying buttresses, gargoyles everywhere, huge towers that rose high into the air and clutched at the dirty sky, the Palace might as well have been a city unto itself. The Bastion, the squat black keep at the center of the Palace, was practically lost in the thicket of sharp towers and stony gray arches. Alan Charterhouse could only see it for a few moments as they crossed the bridge into North Ferry.

The coach pulled down Bynam Lane after that, and the view of the palace was blotted out by the North Ferry front of the Architecture War. A smaller skirmish than the castle, but still just as visible. The coach began to slow almost immediately.

"What's the problem?" Beckett growled up to the driver.

"The crowd, gov. Can't go any farther." Harry's disembodied voice seemed irritated. "Want me to push through?" Harry had been working as a coachman for the coroners since before Beckett's time, driving his two horses which he insisted were descended from Saaghyari devil-mares. He always seemed to be looking for an opportunity to show off what they could do.

"No, Harry." Beckett turned to Skinner. "Crowd?" She shrugged. Beckett grunted and hefted himself out of the coach. Skinner followed directly and Alan, after waiting for an uncertain moment in the empty coach, followed her.

Bynam Lane was filled with people, a hundred at least, all wearing the sober-colored suits and tall hats of well-established businessmen. They were mostly middle-aged men, well-dressed and with well-groomed mustaches and mutton-chops. Occasionally, Alan spotted young women, who he assumed were the wives of the men. Around the edges of the crowd lounged disreputable looking gendarmes, some leaned in alleys or against bronze lamp-posts, others squatted in the street and played at dice or cards.

The crowd was not unruly, except for the man standing at its head. He was up on an old wooden crate in front of the Zindel house, and he was shouting lustily at the men and women who surrounded him. Behind the man, and blocking the entrance to 612 Bynam Lane, were half a dozen Lobstermen.

"I can't hear him from here. What's he saying, Skinner?"

The knocker opened her jaw slightly, and her breathing slowed. "That's Edgar Wyndham-Vie," she said, after a moment. "Adjunct to the

Vice-Minister for the Committee for Public Safety. I heard him speak in Parliament once. He's talking about sharpsies, now. I'm not sure if he's trying to quell a riot or start one."

Beckett took a long look around at the fat, satisfied men in the streets. Some of them were old enough to have avoided the press, but just as many had probably bribed their way out of the war. "I don't think these are the rioting type. Come on." The old coroner began to shoulder his way through the crowd.

Skinner put her right hand on Alan's shoulder, an action which caused a fluttering feeling in his stomach. She smiled at him, then, which caused the fluttering to get worse. Knockers, he knew, had virtually supernatural hearing. Could she hear the butterflies in his stomach? Could she hear what he was thinking now? Alan put his head down and tried to lead Skinner through the path that her partner had made.

"Where the hell is Valentine?" Beckett growled as they approached. "I thought he was watching the cordon."

"He was supposed to be," Skinner called over Alan's shoulder. "He's not here?"

"No. His carriage-thing is, though, so he must not have gotten far." Beckett finally pushed his way past the men in the very front of the crowd. They were holding small blue candles. "What the hell is going on here?" Beckett shouted, as he approached Edgar Wyndham-Vie and his men. The Adjunct did not look at him, but continued to shout out to the crowd.

"...assure you all that the Empire is doing everything in its power to ensure the safety of all of its *human* citizens..."

One of the Lobstermen stepped forward. The insignia on his breastplate marked him as a captain. "No one goes in. Orders."

Beckett considered the captain. The Lobstermen were the Empire's elite troops, drawn from the ranks of the Royal Marines. They were fanatically loyal and obedient. Through extensive and costly trolljr surgeries, bone plates had been grafted to the bodies of the men, in a fashion that resembled the old-fashioned, segmented *lorica* on their chests, saw-edged plates on their arms and legs, and a heavy, crested helmet on the skull. A thin patina of blood continually dribbled down the plates, making them crimson and sticky. Beneath the armor, a network of thin tubes carried ichor-derived chemistry that made the men stronger and faster than even an athletic human. It would also kill them after five years of duty. Fanatically loyal.

"...this foreign threat to our stability, especially now during wartime, can not, and will not be tolerated..."

"Whose orders?" Beckett asked.

"Committee for Public Safety."

The coroner pulled his credentials from his pocket: a flat square of leather with a shiny brass shield affixed. The shield had the two-headed eagle crest of the Coroners Division. "Coroners. We outrank CPA."

The Lobsterman shook his head. "Sorry, sir. Orders. No one goes in."

Edgar Wyndham-Vie had finished his inflammatory sermon to the gathered business men, and climbed down from his box. "Who are you?" He demanded of Beckett. "What the hell are you doing here?" He turned to the Lobsterman. "This area is to be *sealed*, captain. Take these people out of here."

"Detective-Inspector Beckett," Elijah Beckett said. "Coroners Division. And this is my crime scene. Tell the Lobsters to back off."

Wyndham-Vie looked closely at Beckett; the man had a familiar shock of ginger hair, and familiar taste in facial hair: moustache and mutton-chops. "Beckett. Beckett." He said the name to himself as though trying to recall its provenance. His eyes suddenly widened. "You. You're the one." Edgar Wyndham-Vie leaned in. "You killed my cousin," he spat through clenched teeth. "I'll see you *hanged* for it."

Beckett was unmoved. "Your cousin was a heretic. He had to die. But I don't publish my reports."

"You think that matters?" Edgar sneered. "You think they don't know? The rumors have started already. In a year, the Wyndham-Vie name won't be worth *spit*."

Beckett's voice was a deadly whisper. "You misunderstood me. I don't publish my reports. But I could start." He leaned in close. "A year? Your name won't last a fucking week."

The two men stared long and hard at each other: Edgar Wyndham-Vie's cheek twitched, and a vein bulged at his temple. His face had turned very red. Beckett stood as cold and still as the gray city around him, never blinking, never turning his eyes from Edgar's face.

The Adjunct broke first. He turned away, and then waved at the Lobstermen. "Let them in." He turned back to Beckett and his companions. "You have an hour." The coroner walked smoothly past the Lobstermen, and Alan hurried to keep up. He distinctly heard, as he passed Wyndham-Vie, "Hanged."

He also heard Beckett, as they crossed the short bridge over Thurgood Street, mutter under his breath. "Not today, jackass."

Six: Herman Zindel's Home

The mathematics that covered the walls and floor of Herman Zindel's office was, as far as Alan Charterhouse was concerned, extraordinary. As enthusiastic as he was, however, he had to be careful; Aetheric Geometry was a heresy, punishable by death. A scientific heretic didn't even get the benefit of a trial. If Beckett suspected that Alan had been dabbling in higher-plane geometry, he could simply take out his revolver and shoot him in the head.

"This is...well." Alan swallowed hard. He was looking at a group-theory proof that went a long way to solving a harmonic symmetry equation he'd been working on for a year. It was just as well his uncle was going mad. He'd have been furious if he'd recognized the mathematics scrawled in Alan's journals and on the backs of old maps. "Obviously, my father knows...knows a lot more about this sort of thing..."

"We haven't got your father." Beckett was nothing if not blunt. "We've got you. Tell me what you can."

What am I supposed to say? Alan thought. *That Zindel was coming close to re-creating Wolfram's translation formula?* He had a sudden vision of his brains splattered all over the chalkboard, smearing Zindel's brilliant proofs. "It's definitely... definitely Aetheric Geometry. I mean, you don't...don't see anything like this in...in standard cartographic or engineering applications."

"Are you sure?"

"Oh, yes." He pointed to a formula. "See that? That's using..." *Too much. Don't tell them too much. They'll kill you if they find out.* The certainty of that danger clutched at his belly. "Well, uh, I don't know the word for it, obviously. But in standard cartography we usually use a twin-variable axis. For holographic cartography, a triple variable. My father once built a transformative map that could use a quaternary variable grid, but this…if this is right, he's trying to describe something using a nine-dimensional system."

The old coroner nodded. Skinner remained silent, but Alan found his eyes unconsciously drawn to her. She had very smooth, pale skin, he thought, and wondered what it would be like to touch her cheek.

Beckett cleared his throat, and Alan practically jumped out of his skin. "Why?"

"Why, sir?"

He gestured at all the formula. "Why all this? What's it for?"

I don't even know how to describe it with regular words. I could only explain it with math. Math that I'm not allowed to know about. "What…what is Aetheric Geometry ever used for?" Careful. "He was trying to break the translation barrier."

Alan swallowed hard, as Beckett gave him a long look, but the coroner abruptly grunted and turned away. "All right. Take off your gloves."

"Sir?"

"Psychometry, boy. I need you to check the scene."

"Oh." *Whew.* "Right." Alan pulled off the special vellum gloves. His fingers, stained black with Mapmaker's Ink, tingled immediately. He could now feel the tiny variations in temperature, miniscule changes in air flow as the three of them drew breath. "Where…I mean, what do you want me to check… for? First?"

Beckett shrugged. "How good are you?"

Alan considered that for a moment, then went out into the hall. Very gently, he touched the bust of Harcourt Wolfram..

Sensory overload came almost immediately. He could feel hundreds of thousands of textures from a hundred years of hands all vying simultaneously for his attention, grease and oil and dead skin and whatever they'd been touching last, all jittering through the nerves in his fingers and up his arms and into his brain…

Focus. Alan closed his eyes and took a long, deep breath. *Just the last week. Feel the freshest textures.* "Three people have used this door in the last week. One woman. I can feel the residue from her perfume. It's…it stings a little…" A half a dozen other sensations crowded in at that point, what Alan suspected were different varieties of perfume. He blocked them out. "The two men…I can feel the chalk, so I assume at least one was Herman Zindel. The woman…her skin is not as dry, less…" *Not enough words. There are never enough words for texture.*

"Young. She's younger."

"Probably his wife."

Alan nodded. "I think I could recognize them again, if I had to."

"Anything else about them?"

Focus. Find the texture, trace it. What else besides skin did it leave behind? What did it touch last? "Chalk. And not a lot of dirt. Gentlemen, then. One of them...the other man, had expensive gloves. Soft tarrasque-hide, I think." Alan took his fingers from the doorknob, and the sensations immediately subsided. "That's all I can get from the door, I think."

"Downstairs, then."

Alan followed Beckett down the narrow stairs of the Zindel house, with Skinner's hand on his shoulder. At the bottom of the stairs was a framed kirliotype of Herman Zindel, his wife, and their children. They were all looking very somber, because it was hard to smile for the five minutes required to effectively expose film.

"Have you ever seen a corpse before, Alan?" Skinner spoke quietly in his ear. Her voice was serious, but her breath was very warm and distracting.

"Uhm. No."

She squeezed his shoulder gently. "Breathe through your mouth. It helps."

Alan nodded, his eyes lingering on the photograph, particularly on the little boy. He looked so intense, despite his short pants and neatly-combed hair. There were no photographs like that in the Charterhouse home. Did the little boy have trouble standing still for that long? *You're stalling*, Alan told himself.

"Shit." Beckett called out from the parlor. "Shit, shit, shit."

"What is it?" Skinner's voice was faintly tinged with alarm. A sudden rapping—the knocker's natural telerhythmia—moved rapidly across the walls in the hallway and into the other room. "What's wrong?"

"The bodies," Beckett said as he returned.

"What about them?"

"They're gone."

Skinner shoved past Alan and into the room. Alan followed quietly behind her. "What happened?" The knocker asked.

"Someone moved them. There are streaks of blood on the floor."

"Do you think it was the Committee?" The two coroners continued to discuss the issue in low tones, while Alan looked around the room. It was an ordinary-looking parlor, furnished brightly but not garishly with red and gold. There were large bloodstains on the floor and couches. It was easier than Alan thought it would be to distance himself from that fact. His hands itched; there was a strange texture to the air, something he'd never felt before. He knelt down, and lightly touched his fingertips to the rug…

Sensory information began pouring in. There were sharpsie feet; he recognized the leathery texture of their skin. There were human feet, lots of human feet. Children's feet. *The children*, Alan thought, as he imagined them running through the door to climb onto the sofa with their parents. He almost lost his focus then, but shook the image off. There was something here he was missing, something new but elusive. He tried to clear his mind, to blot out the other textures. He narrowed his field of touch to that one, strange texture…

…and almost cried out. There it was: something… something awful. He couldn't say what it was, or even what it felt like. It was not just unfamiliar, but alien — completely alien. He'd never felt anything like this: something not just unknown, but *unknowable*, something completely dissimilar from the million textures he'd ever experienced. The horror of this thought grew as did the sense that the floor was covered in something that was completely impossible for him to comprehend. Alan snatched his hand up.

"…must be trying to hide something…Charterhouse. What's wrong?" There was more curiosity than concern in Beckett's voice. The weight of his attention suddenly seemed very heavy.

Alan realized he was biting his lip. He consciously stretched his jaw and puffed out his cheeks for a moment, before releasing it with a "puh" sound. "I don't know, sir. There's… there was something here. Something…" Alan shook his head and backed into the corner, inadvertently banging against the gramophone. "I can't…I don't know what it is."

"Was it a person?" Skinner asked him, her tone worried. "A sharpsie?"

"N-no. No. It wasn't made of…of what people are made of. Or of what anything's made of." Alan sank to the floor. The sense of the alien presence was fading, and nervous energy was making Alan's hands twitch.

"What does that mean?" Beckett asked him.

"I can't explain it." Alan snatched up one of the cylinders from the gramophone and began to fiddle with it. "I've never felt anything like it."

Beckett looked at him appraisingly for a moment. "All right. Take a minute for yourself, then I want you to check the rest of the room."

Alan nodded. "There were sharpsies, here, sir. I'm having trouble sorting out the chronology, because of all the people that have been in and out. I'd say yesterday, or the day before."

Beckett turned back to his partner. "That puts them here about the time of the murder."

"So Stitch is wrong?" Skinner asked.

"Maybe. I want to know why there's no struggle."

"Poison? Maybe the sharpsies had access to the house. That would explain the unlocked door. They could have gotten in, slipped something into the food..." Beckett grunted, but didn't say anything. "I know, I know. Why?"

"Sir?" Alan Charterhouse said querulously.

"We should question the maid, again," Beckett said. "Maybe they got a hold of her key, somehow."

"Sir?"

"What is it, now?" Beckett asked without looking up. The boy said nothing. Beckett glanced to where the young cartographer had sat down in the corner, then did a double-take that practically snapped his neck. The boy had gone as white as a sheet, and his eyes were bulging like they'd fall out of his head.

"What is it?" Skinner asked. "What's wrong?"

Alan had one of the cylinders from the gramophone in his hands. He was running his super-sensitive fingers over the grooves in it.

"Have...have you listened to these, sir?"

Beckett approached and knelt beside him. He's knees creaked violently as he did so. "No. Why?"

"I can read recording cylinders, by touching them." He looked down at the wax cylinder in his hands. "This...it's not music sir," he turned to the coroner, clearly terrified. "These are from the flight recorder on the *Excelsior*."

SEVEN: THE EXCELSIOR

Beckett wasted no time. He immediately grabbed Alan Charterhouse by the collar of his coat dragged him outside at speed, through the crowd that was still milling in the street, and practically threw the young man into the coach.

"Forget it," he said, over the extended finger that he jabbed in Alan's direction. "Forget everything. Forget what you saw here. Forget that we even came for you." He slammed the door shut. "Take him home," Alan could hear the man shout to the coachman.

The ride back home seemed even longer. Alan watched the crooked shadows that haunted the streets of Trowth grow longer and deeper. The city still made Alan uneasy, despite his years living there, and his familiarity with it. It was the cold late afternoons that were the worst, when icy night air had yet to dispel the perpetual murky overcast of the city, so that everything seemed unnaturally dark. It made Alan long for the summers he'd spent south, in the low counties, pacing out distances between rocks in his cousins' fields, or trying to build sundials in the garden.

Trowth was a cold city, and dark, but above all it was a frighteningly still city. Even in the country, miles away from the crowds and population, there seemed to be more noise, more movement, than in Trowth. It was a city whose every narrow window and crooked shadow seemed to hide invisible eyes, threatening eyes that gave the city's lonely inhabitants cause to pitch their voices low, to keep to their homes and public houses and to stay off the chasm-bordered streets at any dark hour.

Even the parades and markets, or the angry muttering crowds that followed men like Edgar Wyndham-Vie were subdued. Above all in Trowth there was a sense, even among the oldest families that had lived on the shores of the Stark for a hundred generations, of having stumbled into a private garden late at night. The sense of being one loud noise away from attracting the garden's owner. The Trow, the legendary giants that had abandoned their homes on the Stark at least a thousand years before human beings had come, seemed to have never fully left.

That eerie feeling of presence was the first thing that travelers to the city remarked on, and it was so ubiquitous that the residents of Trowth hardly seemed to notice it anymore. There were still times, though, when the sense of sharing a place with—or worse, having usurped it from—something awesome and terrible was very strong, and it could set the entire city's teeth on edge.

Alan turned back to his book, and tried to read in the failing light. The truth was that he was getting tired of the Ted East stories. He'd discovered them a year ago, when his father had bought him *Ted East, Agent of the Crown* for his birthday. Alan had torn through the twenty-two two-penny novels in six months. He practically worshipped the fictional Ted East, with his old-fashioned ways, his out-of-date bowler hat and turn-of-the-century revolver. Ted East protected the Empire from the gravest threats that heretical science could produce: cults of ectoplasmatists, mad necrologists and their armies of the undead, Khadavri spies and invasions by the Leech-Fingered Men. In one of the novels, *Ted East and the Szarkany Rend*, he'd actually fought all of those and more. But it was starting to become boring.

The novels were really very formulaic: they all started with a locked-room mystery, that Ted East would somehow miraculously guess the solution to; often, as Alan was starting to notice, with highly dubious reasoning. Then, Ted East would harass and intimidate his contacts in the criminal underworld until he had enough information to track the criminals to their secret underground layer. This was usually because the criminals were importing some rare chemical for their insane experiments, or because they'd had some kind coal-dust on their shoes that could only be found in one particular factory in the city. In *Ted East, Coroner* the clue had actually been a wrapper for a pat of butter left behind when the villain had eaten dinner with one of Ted East's contacts. The wrapper had the name of the hotel that the man, an ambassador from Canth who was actually an ettercap spy, had been staying at.

Ted East would track the villains down to their lair, and proceed to shoot them all. Sometimes, he'd contrive to blow something up first, if there were too many to be reasonably dispatched with a revolver. Sometimes, sometimes not: Ted East's revolver often carried a little more than six bullets.

Alan wondered if the author of the Ted East novels, a man named Geoffrey Holland, thought his readers were stupid, or if he was just careless. It was possibly a little of both. Alan's cousin had recommended that he start reading Phillip Crowe's work, but Alan had never found much appeal: the novels were too slow, too atmospheric. It took too long to get to the point of the story, and by then he'd lost interest.

Night had fallen about two-thirds of the way into the trip, and Alan found it impossible to read by the intermittent phlogiston-blue streetlamps. He thought instead to what he'd seen in Herman Zindel's house. Of course, Beckett had told him to forget everything, and of course Alan would if he could have, but it was impossible. Alan Charterhouse had a frustratingly perfect memory. He could recall virtually every piece of the formulae he'd seen in that house.

There were some things about the equations that were highly disturbing. It was one thing to theorize, mathematically, about the nature of higher-plane geometry. Harcourt Wolfram, the brilliant scientist who had virtually single-handedly invented the modern world over a hundred and fifty years ago, had journals filled with hypotheses about planar mathematics. It was something else, however, to actually be experimenting with them.

What Alan couldn't reveal to the coroners, because it would reveal too much about his own knowledge of the heretical subject, was that Zindel's equations were using experimental data. They weren't just theories; they were getting information from somewhere. And that meant that Herman Zindel had access to a working translation engine...

The Excelsior, Alan thought, then shook his head. It was impossible. The *Excelsior*, the final brainchild of Harcourt Wolfram and Chretien Daior-Crabtree, had only been used once. The consequences of that experiment were...Alan Charterhouse shuddered.

Harcourt Wolfram had developed a theory, based on the fundamental principles of the Church Royal: that the world as human beings understood it was the product of a single, infinitely complex Word, and that all matter and energy was an intricate sub-harmony within that Word. Wolfram had taken it a step further. A word, he reasoned, has not just sound, but meaning. If what the Church says is true, then the world is as much made from information as anything else. And information was easy to store. You could write it on a piece of paper and lay it flat on your desk.

You could then write more information on a second piece of paper and lay it on top of the first. There they were: two whole universes, right next to each other but unable to interact. Wolfram hypothesized an Aether, a second universe that existed in the same time and place as the human universe, but fashioned in such a way as to be untouchable. The same Word, but in a different language. The information was there, but human beings couldn't apprehend it.

He and Daior-Crabtree had built the *Excelsior*. It was a ship whose engines, instead of carrying it across the sea or through the air, would translate itself and its crew into the Aether, and then back again.

The launch of the *Excelsior* a century and a half ago had annihilated a square half-mile of the city. The crew, including Wolfram himself, had all been killed, as had three hundred spectators. No one from the Royal Academy of Sciences had been able to get close enough to the wreckage of the vessel to retrieve it for weeks. There had only been eleven heretical sciences when Wolfram and Daior-Crabtree built their aethership. After the *Excelsior*, the Church Royal added a new one for the first time in a hundred years.

The recording cylinders had been nothing but screams. Charterhouse had heard five men, screaming desperately, terrified beyond their capacity for speech, their voices filled with pain and horror. The *Excelsior* had been outside the universe for five minutes, and its recording cylinders held nothing but screams. The process of translation had destroyed their minds, their bodies, turned the *Excelsior* into a mangled wreck, and sent a shockwave through Trowth that leveled buildings.

Herman Zindel had been using the *Excelsior*'s translation engine.

Elijah Beckett sat on his bed in the corner of his small room, and rested his head against the wall. He'd achieved a perfect balance of veneine and consciousness: there was just enough in his system to keep the pain out of mind, but not so much that it was clouding his judgment, or threatening to send him to Cross the Water. It was an ideal time to be thinking about the Zindels.

If it hadn't been for Mr. Stitch's assertion that Herman Zindel hadn't been murdered by sharpsie hooligans, the case would be open and shut. Zindel was a heretical mathematician, yes, but the odds were just the same that a random murder by sharpsie housebreakers would hit Zindel as they would anyone else. There were probably dozens of armchair heretics in Trowth, even a few with the funds to bribe the Academy of Sciences for access to the *Excelsior*'s flight recorder. Maybe it was just bad luck for Zindel.

The flight recorder had been almost a dead-end. Beckett had gone immediately that afternoon to the headquarters of the Royal Academy of Sciences, to see the wreckage of the *Excelsior*. He'd been denied entry.

"By orders of the Crown," the clerk had told him, while the Lobstermen assigned to guard him had loomed monstrously. Their bone armor had glistened red and wet in the candlelight.

"Coroner," Beckett had told the skinny, pinch-faced man. "I *work* for the Crown."

The clerk had shrugged. "Unless you're the Emperor or the Minister for Internal Security, I'll need written consent before I can let you in." He had a bored expression on his face; there was no malice in him, just a stubborn need to follow the rules. "Besides, we don't keep the…we don't keep *that* here. It's in one of the Vaults in Old Bank."

The process for getting a Search Writ from the Minister for Internal Security was a tedious one. Beckett had to have a message sent to Mr. Stitch, explaining what he wanted. Stitch would pass the message on to the secretary for the Vice-Minister of IS, who would determine whether or not it was important enough to pass on to the Minister's Adjunct's secretary, who would show it to the Adjunct, who would then probably just sign the Minister's name to it, on the grounds that the Minister was very busy having lunch with Someone Important.

What all that meant was that Beckett wouldn't be able to get his writ for at least a day, maybe more. Not that he expected to find much, even with the delay. Certainly, no one was going to cart off the two tons of wreckage that used to be the *Excelsior*. Beckett liked to be thorough, though. Maybe someone had come in to make copies of the flight recordings, and had dropped a matchbook or something.

On the surface, the simplest solution was a sharpsie break-in, which is precisely what made Beckett distrust it. If Stitch hadn't been there, hadn't called Beckett in right away, then there wouldn't have been a search of the home. No one would have brought in a psychometrist, no one would have found Zindel's equations, or the recording cylinders. The investigation would have just stopped, and the gendarmes would have headed out to kill sharpsies.

If you were trying to throw someone off the trail, the sharpsies made a perfect target. That gendarme captain wouldn't have worried about unlocked doors, about lack of struggle. He'd find the answer he liked, and stop looking. Beckett liked sharpsies as an answer, because they were easy. But he couldn't stop looking. Thirty years in service, trading away the better parts of himself as he steeped in the horror that human beings were capable of, and it seemed like the obdurate refusal to stop searching was the only thing that Beckett had left.

Someone had killed Herman Zindel, and Beckett would give two-to-one that it had something to do with geometry. Beckett closed his eyes for a moment, to rest them, and to try and focus.

A sharp pain stabbed through his head and all the way down his spine, jerking him awake. The candle on his desk had almost burned down; it was just a lump of smoking wax. His joints no longer ached, they shrieked, and it felt like he was crushing shards of broken glass in his knees every time he moved.

Panic struck, when Beckett realized he couldn't move his right hand. There was a horrible cramp in it, it felt like the tendons in his fingers had been twisted around each other, like his fingers were out of place. The hand had curled up like a claw, and wouldn't respond when he tried to move it. It just twisted up harder. It hurt, but it was more terrifying than anything else.

Beckett stumbled around in the dark towards his medicine chest, with his right hand pressed hard under his left arm. The pain was unbearable; a hundred jagged snares of it, behind his eyes, in his arms and legs. The coroner had a brief vision of himself curling up with pain and dying on the floor, inches away from his medicine. He managed to snatch up a hypodermic and a new bottle of veneine and tore off the top with his teeth. Not bothering to measure, he filled the syringe with fang, ripped open his right sleeve, and rammed the drug into his veins.

For a single heart-stopping second nothing happened, and then the relief hit him like a sledgehammer. Beckett barely had time to yank the needle out of his arm before his legs turned to jelly and he collapsed on the ground. He cracked his head on the bedpost as he fell, but barely noticed it. The veneine wrapped its warmth around him, and all the pain and cold in the world seemed a hundred miles away.

Then his vision distorted. His room bulged and shrank, twisted like he was looking at its reflection in the back of a spoon. He blinked, and his nose and mouth were filled with salt water, his ears with the sound of rushing waves.

He was in the stormy, midnight-black ocean that fang-addicts called Cross the Water. It tossed him relentlessly, rolling him in the salty black breaking waves, so he couldn't tell which way was up or down, couldn't even try to swim, as his legs and arms were hammered by the force of the waves

And then it was gone. The water rushed away, and Beckett lay gasping for air on a hot, golden surface. His stomach abruptly rejected the brackish seawater, and he vomited it up, struggling to catch his breath over the violent retching.

Beckett looked up, and saw shattered buildings all around him, all made of shining, red-gold metal.

The City of Brass.

EIGHT: IN THE ARCADIUM

The narrow, twisting alleys off of St. Dunsany's Street, beneath the topside neighborhood called Red Lanes, were the eeriest section of the city, at least as far as James Crowell was concerned. Not only was Dunsany's Street, like all places in the Arcadium, strangely resistant to indications of time, but the labyrinthine alleys and lanes seemed to confuse space and direction as well. If Crowell hadn't made this trip ten or fifteen times already, he could easily imagine himself getting lost; the first time, he'd returned to the same street three times without recognizing it, because he'd come at it from three different directions. From different angles, Quarter Down Street had a different play of shadows, and different light seeping in from Red Lanes. The single phlogiston street lamp, clearly visible when he came at it from Sower Street, was blocked by a verdigris-defaced bronze sign when he came at it from Exeter Street. The bronze equestrian statue, probably a representation of Janusz Vlytze, had the disturbing quality of looking like three heavyset men when viewed from the angle of Short Lane.

He regretted not being able to keep the coach and horses that he drove, but horses generally didn't care to go into the Arcadium. Moreover, Crowell's employer at the livery stable had strict rules about taking coaches for personal use. Which meant that James Crowell had to walk through the increasingly frigid air as night settled over Trowth.

If he'd been topside, in Red Lanes, the coachman would have seen the murky overcast slowly chill and sink to the ground, turning into a dense fog that would drain through the gaps in the upper streets, and begin to fill the Arcadium. The sky would become painfully clear as the atmosphere, which had the effect of blotting out the sun during the day, and kept baleful stars still hidden behind its dirty clouds, had the reverse effect on the moon: magnifying the cold, pale disc so that it hung heavy and bright over the pulsing blue lights of Trowth's phlogiston streetlamps.

Beneath Red Lanes, James Crowell only saw the fog creep in, and kept as close to the center of the cramped arteries of the Arcadium as he could. Vrylaks, the yellow, vampiric foglets that had come to Trowth with the wave of sharpsie immigrants, tended to lurk close to the ground along the walls. They were generally no trouble for a healthy adult man, but if that same man stumbled into a pack of them, they could crawl down his throat and drain the blood out through his lungs in seconds, leaving a red cloud of tiny droplets suspended in the air.

Crowell shivered and tightened his scarf around his mouth. He was on his way back home from Printer's Close, which was the only Close that was still used for the profession it took its name from. Fishery Close, for instance, hadn't been a fish-market for twenty years, and the small courtyard of Advocate's Close hadn't been full of law firms for close to a hundred. Fleshmarket Close was likewise no longer full of butcher shops, but it had been filled by brothels, so almost everyone agreed that the name was still appropriate.

He'd managed to get the first chapter of *Tower of Brass* in to Flood, Cheetham, and Crabtree Printers just before they closed up shop, which meant the pages would be on display the next morning for publishers to look at. If they found it interesting enough, they could put up the funding to have Flood et al. print it. And Crowell had to admit that this one was good.

Tower of Brass wasn't his, of course, but his son's. James Crowell didn't really approve of the boy writing about the kinds of things that the lurid, pulpy two-penny novels addressed, but it was his own fault. James hadn't been able to afford to send his son to University, so all that talent went unrefined and uneducated, wasted. The young man that might have been remembered by history as the next Silas Ennering, the great Poet Laureate under Edmund II, would instead be barely recalled by history at all, and if he was, as a footnote when someone mentioned cheap horror stories.

Still, the boy's first novel, *Ice House*, had sold well, and Crowell rightfully felt that he could claim a piece of it. After all, it had been Crowell who'd given his son the kernels of truth that the boy had spun into an elaborate tale of terror. Elaborate enough, Crowell hoped, that no one would recognize it for what it was. *Shouldn't have told him*, the notion had been haunting him for months, but he dismissed it. He and the boy had barely had anything to talk about since Mrs. Crowell had passed on. Besides, it was too late for regrets.

The coachman warily eyed the filthy shape curled up in the corner of Quarter Down and Backstairs Streets. He was almost positive that the man had been following him, but it was hard to say with the degenerate poor in Trowth. They were all covered in filth and soot, and many of them, like this one, had the scrave—another disgusting gift the sharpsie immigrants had brought with them. The filthy man kept coughing up wads of luminescent green phlegm. If the beggar hadn't smelled like an open sewer, Crowell might never have recognized him. As it was, the stench of sewage was both frighteningly familiar and highly unpleasant; Crowell took the stairs in Backstairs Street two at a time.

Backstairs Street could hardly be called a street at all, as it was really a dark covered staircase that led up out of Quarter Down Street. The single lamp that someone had thoughtfully fixed to the wall had burned out, and puddles of gray, spent phlogiston covered the slippery stairs. The walls of the narrow stair were covered in cheap bills, affixed with the new "stichor" that the Rowan-Czarneckis had patented. The bills were barely visible in the light that seeped in from the streetlamps at the top of the stairs, and they were mostly about sharpsies: lurid images of the sharp-toothed humanoids making off with babies, or wallowing in their own filth, accompanied by mottos like "Protect Yourselves from Predators," and "Clean Streets Win Wars." There were two more bills showing copperplates of men being pleasured by tiny homunculi that read, "Culies Destroy Families!" Presumably, there were several posters encouraging young men to enlist in the Royal Marines, but they'd all been pasted over.

Fear fluttered in his belly as he emerged from the Arcadium into Red Lanes. The tall, high-peaked Ennering-Crabtree houses leaned out over the relatively wide street, leaving the icy moonlight to fall in a narrow strip down the road. *Stay calm. No one recognized it. They'd have come for you when it was published.* Still, he couldn't help thinking about Herman. *Just sharpsie hooligans. Doesn't mean anything.* It was a shocking coincidence, nonetheless.

The filthy, stinking man that the coachman had seen in the Arcadium now emerged from Backstairs, and now Crowell was certain he was being followed. He picked up his pace, and tried to think of the nearest public house he could get to. It didn't matter which, just that it was crowded and nearby. Whoever the stinker was, he wouldn't try anything serious if there were other people around. *The Quarrel,* he thought. *Two blocks from here.* Crowell was practically jogging now, as he came around the corner onto Cleaver Street.

There was something waiting for him there, something strange. It was all wrapped up in a black coat and cloak, with a black hood over its head. It crouched in the middle of the street, then stood, then crouched again, as though it couldn't stand being still. It was as tall as a man, but a deep, terrible dread filled Crowell as he realized that the thing in front of him was not a man at all. It twitched weirdly, rolling its head back and forth like it was looking for something.

"Who..." Crowell's voice cracked. He tried to work some moisture into his throat, while he stood frozen at the intersection. "Who is that?"

There was no apparent change in the thing's movements, but the coachman was suddenly aware of its attention. James Crowell practically jumped out of his skin. He pulled a small roll of bills from his pocket: the day's pay. "I...I haven't got much." He tossed it on the ground. "But...take it, if you want." He swallowed hard.

The thing, still fifteen or twenty feet away, was abruptly very still. In the blink of an eye it was five feet away, almost close enough that it could reach out and touch Crowell. It hadn't moved so much as...slithered, or slipped. It crossed the space strangely, like its joints weren't put together right. It swayed back and forth like a snake, then craned its head towards Crowell. It's face was masked by black robes and shadow, but Crowell could see it turning, could hear vertebrae clicking as it twisted its head almost all the way around. There was a hideous wet slithering sound that came from beneath the thing's tattered black cloak.

Without warning, the thing snapped its head around to look up and off, at a precariously slanted upper storey to Crowell's left. There was a loud, sudden crack like a gunshot, and James Crowell felt a hot knife jab through his chest. Puzzled, he looked down to see blood pouring from a hole in his shirt. *Funny. Thought I had that hole fixed...*he twisted around in time to see the filthy man lunge towards a deep doorway on the opposite side of the street, glittering silver in his hands. James Crowell's legs suddenly felt very, very tired, and it was astonishingly easy to let them fold up, and to lay his face on the ground. Stunned, he closed his eyes. Blackness gripped his head like a vice.

"Coroners!" Crowell heard someone call out, as though from the end of a long tunnel. "No one moves!"

That same evening, between the time that Beckett began to see the City of Brass and James Crowell met with misfortune in Red Lanes, a young sharpsie male found himself walking back to Mudside from the shipyards alone. The next day, the broadsheets would say John Sharpish — which was the name that all the broadsheets used to refer to sharpsies, rather than try to transliterate their guttural native names — was swaggering brazenly, with a cruel look in his eye, shouting insults at women and threatening to eat their babies. At the time, however, the witnesses that had so conscientiously made their reports to the broadsheets would have been hard-pressed to say that the sharpsie was doing anything out of the ordinary, except perhaps walking very quickly.

Whether John Sharpish had been hurrying because he was eager to be home or because he was nervous about being in human-dominated neighborhoods will remain a mystery, but his concerns about his environs were certainly borne out. As he passed through River Village, a quaint neighborhood that consisted almost entirely of public houses, warehouses, and extremely cheap brothels, John Sharpish found himself accosted by four men.

Two of the men were gendarmes; two were dock-workers that had either volunteered or were conscripted for the task of eliminating the vermin from River Village. The surviving gendarme would later say that he'd been doing his solemn duty, to protect the health and well-being of the good people that had hired him. One of the two dock workers would say that he'd just been defending himself when the sharpsie had come at him, all teeth and murder on its face. The fourth man would remain stubbornly silent, asserting only that he'd "done what he had to."

The sharpsie had been moving at a quick clip through River Village, which represented a shorter but potentially more dangerous path back to Mudside. Sharpsies were no less welcome on the other side of the Stark in Bluewater, the indige ghetto, but there were fewer there with the means or the interest in physically removing them. The indige didn't care for the sharpsies, but didn't especially hate them either. Bluewater was safe, but River Village was faster; to safely traverse it, however, a young sharpsie needed to be quick.

It didn't help. The four men caught up with John Sharpish right at the foot of Old Williams' Bridge: the stone road that led over the Stark and into Mudside. The bulk of the conversation between the four men and the sharpsie was never accurately reported in the broadsheets. Some people said they heard only shouting, some said they heard insults, others said that the sharpsie had made vicious threats in its own guttural language. It was not uncommon that those living around the few sharpsie communities should be familiar enough with the language to recognize threats and profanities; besides, witnesses asserted, they could tell by its tone.

The humans and sharpsie apparently continued their heated discussion at some length before one of the dockworkers had enough, and smashed a bottle of whiskey over John Sharpish's head. The sharpsie staggered and nearly fell into the river, but came back angry and out for blood. While the four men had certainly seen sharpsie jaws before, and abstractly recognized the danger presented by long, curved sharpsie teeth, they had certainly never seen those teeth put to such ferocious use.

This particular John Sharpish managed to sever the gendarme's cudgel-hand at the wrist with a single bite, and then nearly took the head off of the second. He bit almost deep enough to sever the spinal column, but certainly deep enough to kill the man instantly. The dockworkers, apparently armed with cudgels of their own in addition to bottles of liquor, immediately fell upon the sharpsie, beating him severely with clubs and fists.

The two men did not stop until the sharpsie had been ground to a pulp on the cobblestones by Old William's Bridge. Only after he was dead did they make an attempt to find help for the two gendarmes.
The man without a throat was clearly lost. The man who had lost his hand was taken in at a trolljrman hospital the instant it was revealed that he'd lost the limb to a sharpsie. In an act of startling generosity, Hahd Khat, a clutch-mother at the hospital, offered to pay for both the surgeries and funeral expenses of the gendarmes.

NINE: THE CITY OF BRASS

Seeing the City of Brass wasn't the same thing as being awake in a strange place. It was more like dreaming a familiar place; the City of Brass had the quality of a half-submerged memory, but it was like no place that Beckett had ever visited. It was a fragment from an imaginary childhood, and a person only ever saw it deep in dreaming.

Like a dream, there was no stability to the vision. Background became foreground, and the brass towers twisted to resemble whatever idle thoughts crossed the mind, or else they slipped away like water through clenched fists. Beckett could see through his own eyes, and also see himself standing among the shifting towers. Sometimes he wore his heavy coroner's overcoat, sometimes he wore nothing. Sometimes the Fades were worse, making large tracks of skin and flesh invisible, disappearing his hands; sometimes, the Fades had completely vanished. The tall golden towers loomed over him, sometimes very far, sometimes very near. The only constant was the blank black sky overhead, and the huge, yellow-green moon that cast its sickly light on the brass towers. Somehow, Beckett could also see the dark, wooden corners of his room, the intricate whorls of plaster on the ceiling above him as he stared at it.

He was in the city, though Elijah Beckett could not have said how he knew it was a city. The brass towers had no doors or windows, nothing that resembled architecture of any kind. They were clearly made of metal, but in many places they looked like melted wax. The city did not extend forever; it was surrounded by empty black space on all sides — an island of shiny towers beneath the foul moonlight.

A shape moved in the shadow of a brass spire, and Beckett found himself suddenly closer to it. Not close enough that he could see it clearly, but close enough that he worried about attracting its attention. The shape was hunched and black, snuffling close to the ground.

The Reanimate, Beckett thought, the idea clear in his mind as ideas in dreams sometimes are. *I'm dreaming about the Reanimate. No...* it couldn't be the Reanimate, because it wasn't really black at all. It was a kind of blue-purple, like a bruise. Was that a robe that it wore, or skin that hung from its limbs in saggy folds?

Then he saw an arm extricate itself from the hunched black shape, an arm that ended in a nest of slimy, black, boneless ribbons of flesh that twisted and rolled and looped around each other.

Sounds trickled in to Beckett's dreaming ears. There were hundreds of muttering voices; wet, slurping voices that clacked their teeth most vigorously. And there was another sound, a deep rasping noise, metal being drawn along metal, but from very far away.

Bruise-black shapes were all around him now, faces low to the ground and snuffling. Beckett wondered if he was still dreaming, or if all the dreams before had been dreams, but this one was somehow real. He looked up at the yellow leprous light of the moon, and felt it tugging on his eyes. He heard the sound of a door opening, and wood scraping on wood, and the moon seemed suddenly very near.

"Elijah?"

The yellow light filled his vision and for a brief moment their positions were reversed, and it was Beckett that floated high above the moon, where black basalt cities crept across its face like an infection.

"Elijah!"

The moon was gone, and then he was in the City of Brass, empty again like it always was, an island of red-gold metal in a black sea that was really his own room. It was his own room, but he couldn't see it right, because the venom had done something to his eyes, had changed them so that they saw cities and leeches.

"Elijah!"

Whose voice is that? I should dream alone, Beckett told himself, and then he was choking on black seawater again, buffeted by titanic, stormy waves.

Blink.

Beckett was in his room, lying on the floor, coughing ferociously. His lungs felt bruised, but it felt good to draw in long, shuddering breaths. There was still enough veneine in his system to keep the pain out of his joints. The back of his right hand twitched, but the cramp seemed to have gone.

Skinner was standing over him. "Elijah, are you all right? What's happening?"

Beckett groaned and tried to get to his feet. "Fine." His head spun, and he reached out to grab the bed-post. "Nothing, I mean. I'm fine. Nothing's happening."

"You sounded like you were choking." There was a white bird perched on her shoulder, cocking its head back-and-forth in a weirdly mechanical rhythm. He tried to blink the bird away, but it was a stubborn hallucination.

"I'm not." Beckett touched his forehead, and his invisible fingertips came away bloody. *Shit.* He went to the mirror over his washbasin. There was a small purple lump above his right eye, and a shallow cut that had leaked blood all down the side of his face. He ran the tap, and cold, brownish water streamed into the basin. He dabbed at his face with a washcloth. "How did you get in?"

"I knocked."

"Are you serious? I didn't know you could do that."

Skinner shrugged. "The telerhythmia isn't much good for moving things, but there's some force behind it. Enough to rattle the pins in a lock, anyway."

Beckett tried to clean up his face. The cut wasn't as bad as it looked — cuts on the scalp rarely wore — and he'd taken worse bumps to the head. "What are you doing here?"

She handed him a small, folded piece of parchment. "Mr. Stitch sent me. He wanted you to read this. What does it say?"

Suspiciously, Beckett took the note and unfolded it. "Beckett," he read. "You need to get out more. Stitch."

"Hah." Skinner said.

"Why 'hah'?"

"Because those were my thoughts exactly. Come on," she tapped her cane on the floor. "You're taking me to the theatre."

"Have you eaten?" Skinner asked quietly, while they were in the coach.

Beckett shrugged. "Not hungry."

Skinner nodded but said nothing. For a few moments, they listened to the rhythmic creaking of the carriage's wheels.

"Skinner…" Beckett said, eventually.

"Yes?"

"I don't." He shifted uncomfortably. "I haven't really got a lot of money…"

"It's all right." She produced a second envelope. "Two tickets to *The Bone-Collector's Daughter*, a new play in the style of Canthi Pantomime by…somebody. I don't remember who." She handed the envelope to Beckett. "It probably says so on the tickets."

The coroner extracted and examined them. Using his keen eye for detail, he eventually spotted the author's name. "Bertram Sitwell. Never heard of him."

"Do you see a lot of plays?"

"No."

"Well," Skinner said, snatching the tickets back. "That explains that then, doesn't it?"

"Hnf." Beckett was silent again. Then, "This isn't going to be like what's-his-name, right? Elias Warrant?"

"When have you seen Warrant's plays?"

"Didn't. Had to read them in school." He made a disgusted face that Skinner couldn't see, but presumably could hear in his voice.

"You didn't like him." This was not a question.

"Rattling on and on about the nobility of wealth and all that? About how the best thing in the world you could be was a merchant? Selling lard to the natives and making off with their phlogiston or gold or what?" Beckett grunted. "Couldn't stand him."

"You probably liked the plays with all the murders and ghosts and things." The bird had vanished from Skinner's shoulder, but Beckett could now see centipedes moving around in the shadows.

"Didn't get to read much of them," Beckett replied. "Didn't you go to public school?"

"Not once I'd manifested as a knocker." Skinner tapped the silver plate over her eyes. "They send us to special schools."

"Oh. Lucky you."

Silence again.

"When did you manifest?" Beckett asked.

"I was thirteen. Just come from seeing…Capale. That's another Canthi Pantomime. I used to love those when I was a girl. I read them all. I'd seen all sixteen of the canonical pantomimes, and a couple of the newer ones by the time…" She smiled ruefully. "Well, let's just say I'd have paid better attention to Capale if I'd known it was going to be the last thing I ever saw."

"Hm." Beckett struggled with his words, trying to find something both sympathetic and supportive to say. He settled on changing the subject. "At school, everything they had us read was a moral lesson. Always something about the Word, and how we could apply it to our lives."

Skinner said nothing, then leaned forward. "Elijah," she whispered, her voice amused and scandalous. "You sound like a man that doesn't believe."

"Heh."

"How does that happen? How does a non-believer end up hunting down people for committing heresy?"

The old coroner shrugged. The centipedes had started crawling down the back of his coat, but he ignored them. It was easier to ignore

58

things that he was sure were hallucinations. "There's steady work in it, for one." He paused thoughtfully. "The Heretical Sciences are dangerous, Skinner. Really dangerous. They never work the way people want them to, and someone ends up dying. That's why the church made them illegal."

"So, you hunt down heretics out of what...civic responsibility? Concern for your fellow man?" He was a liar, and Skinner knew it. It was a delicate process, teasing Beckett's motivations out of the iron trap he kept them locked in. He deflected questions away from himself by old habit, and had probably spent little time considering the why of his life. The tone of his voice shifted, slightly, to the gruff-but-jocular tone he used as a shield, and Skinner realized that she'd lost this round. "You could say that. Really, it's just for the money." He shifted around in his seat and tried to squish the centipede between his shoulder blades.

"Where did you get these tickets, by the way?"

"Stitch. He gave them to me when he sent me to find you."

"Did he, now?"

"What?"

"Nothing." Beckett pursed his lips. "It's just...well. It's just interesting."

Beckett was silent then, and Skinner considered the sound of his voice. It wasn't just cold, or gruff. There was a ragged pain to the sound of him, and there had been for the months that Skinner had known him. That had come as a surprise. Beckett didn't know it, but Skinner had specifically requested the opportunity to work with him, once she'd been inducted into the coroners. The sour, wounded, sick old man was a legend in certain circles. Old Adelwulf Vie-Gorgon, who'd led the department before Mr. Stitch took over, had only ever spoken of Beckett with the utmost respect. Elijah Beckett was a man who had sacrificed everything for the purpose that he'd chosen for himself: defending the Crown from its strangest and most dangerous threats.

If Skinner had been a little more honest with herself, she'd have admitted that she was a little in love with Elijah Beckett, but if she'd been brutally honest, she'd be forced to admit that she was really in love with the *idea* of Elijah Beckett. There always seemed to be a noble, poetic soul lurking beneath the damaged, brittle exterior, but the fact was that there was probably little left of Beckett except for that infallible devotion to his task.

She had a sudden vision of the old man in his youth: a bare-knuckle boxer snatched up into the service, with fire in his eyes and a chip on his shoulder, ready to take on all comers.

"What?" Beckett snapped.

"What, 'what'?"

"You're listening at me. Stop it."
"Sorry."
They rode the rest of the way in silence.

TEN: THE THEATER

The two coroners arrived at what would eventually be known as Sitwell's masterpiece well before the show. Since the beginning of the war with the ettercap, Trowthi citizens had begun to work later and later hours, both to support the weakening Trowth economy, and to be off the streets when the pressgangs came by. Later work hours meant later mealtimes. Later mealtimes meant later shows. And the one thing that was not diminished by Trowth's agonizingly long war with the ettercap in Gorcia was its appetite for entertainment. The Trowthi Theatra Popula in Red Lanes, a privately-funded theatre that was known for doing works much more risqué than those performed by the more staid and conservative Royal Theatre in Old Bank, was packed to the rafters when the coroners arrived.

Beckett showed their tickets to an usher, who took them up a wide, marble-banister staircase to the mezzanine seats. Beckett and Skinner's seats were in a small box all the way to the side of the theatre house, giving Beckett a terrible view of the stage, but an excellent view of the boxes directly across from him.

"These seats are awful," he complained. He had a small vial of veneine cut with brandy, and took a sip from it. The bitter taste made him shudder, but it was warm at least.

"Hush."

Someone dimmed phlogiston lamps in the house, and bright yellow light flooded the stage. Beckett had to crane his neck and lean a little bit over the railing in order to be able to see it at all.

"I can't tell what's happening," he said.

"Sh!" Skinner chided him.

"What?" He lowered his voice. "It's a pantomime. It's not like we're going to miss anything if we talk."

"It's a *Canthi* Pantomime," Skinner whispered. "You're thinking of Thranc mime-shows. They talk in Canthi Pantomime."

"Oh." He leaned back in his seat. "Do...do you need me to tell you what's happening?"

"No. Just be quiet."

Good. Beckett thought, then wondered how Skinner could appreciate a play that she couldn't see. It didn't take long to figure out; the characters announced virtually everything that they did. They came on in pairs and did short scenes together to introduce themselves, and then proceeded to enact an intricate plot. Beckett had trouble following it.

The characters were old stand-bys from the Canthi repertory, back when they did all of their plays with the same seven characters, who all behaved the same way every time: the Young Master enlisted his Servant to help him win the Young Girl, who was courted by the Captain and the Doctor, while the Miser plotted with the Loogaroo. In the end, the Young Girl and the Young Master end up together, the Servant, if not free and rich, is at least shown to be clever. The Captain and the Doctor are embarrassed, the Miser robbed, and the Loogaroo is banished. Sometimes, the roles were switched around, and the Young Master and the Captain spoil the plans of the Servant, who was secretly working for the Loogaroo. Sometimes, the Miser is replaced by the Old Widow, who longs to wed the Doctor. In the end, the stories all turn out happily: good people discover they have secret fortunes, bad people are hanged with their own ropes.

In *The Bone-Collector's Daughter*, Sitwell had positioned the Doctor with the Loogaroo, which was practically unheard of. The Doctor was traditionally a doctor of theology, not a medical doctor, and so his relationship with the Loogaroo, the King of the Bogeymen, would have been heresy. Certainly, Sitwell would have been hanged already if his play had premiered in Canth, where the Convocus ruled the Goetic Church. But the Trowthi Church Royal was a little more relaxed about fictional heresy. Still, the play was shocking and scandalous. It would provoke reviews in every broadsheet in the city, ranging from the vitriolic: "...repetitive, inane tripe..." to the luminous "...spectacular, a work of genius!" *The Bone-Collector's Daughter* would briefly turn Bertram Sitwell into the most popular playwright of the era, before it became apparent that, if this one was a masterpiece, poor Mr. Sitwell didn't seem to have any left in him.

All in all, Beckett would one day regret not paying attention for more than the first fifteen minutes. Still, after hearing, "What are you saying? Let me approach, so I can hear more clearly," three times in the first scene, Beckett found his attention wandering.

"These are terrible seats," he whispered to Skinner. She didn't respond, and Beckett realized that she was using her knocker talent to project her hearing right onto the stage. As far as she was concerned, they might as well have been front row center.

Beckett sighed, and let his eyes meander around the theatre, while he sipped from his veneine-brandy. The Theatra Popula was richly appointed; its walls and ceilings were covered with ornate plaster sculptures of leaves or fruit or something; Beckett had a hard time seeing them in the dark. Along the walls were small box seats; little alcoves that could fit four or five people, and keep them well away from the riff-raff sitting shoulder-to-shoulder in the floor seats. The boxes were angled towards the center of the theatre, not the stage; presumably, this was because having a box seat at the Theatra Popula was more about being seen than it was about seeing anything. Some of the boxes even had family crests emblazoned on them. There was the apple and feather of the Crabtree-Feathersmith, the three bees of Ennering-Vie...

The lantern and staff of the Wyndham-Vies. Edgar Wyndham-Vie's box seats were directly across from Beckett's, and Edgar himself was there, along with another man. It was hard to see from where he sat. He nudged Skinner.

"What?" She snapped at him.

"The box, straight across from it. It's Edgar Wyndham-Vie and someone else. Can you tell who's with him?"

"Why?"

"Just do it."

Skinner sighed. She tilted her head and pursed her lips in the gestures that Beckett knew bespoke concentration. "No."

"You don't recognize him."

"It's not that..." she shook her head. "There's a weird echo. I can't get a bead on any of the voices."

"All right." Beckett stood up.

"Where are you going?"

"Stretch my legs. I'll be back."

The coroner slipped out through the curtains in the back of the box, and down the great staircase to the lobby. In his defense, his legs did ache. It happened sometimes if he sat for too long. He took another sip of veneine, and found an usher.

"How do I get to the Family boxes?" He asked the man, who looked to be about ten thousand years old.

"Family boxes are..." the old man said, his voice a dry rattle that came between deep breaths. "...private..."

Beckett took out the brass shield that had the coroners' crest on it. He held the double-eagle under the usher's nose. The old man stared at it blankly for a few moments, then his eyes suddenly widened.

"Official business," Beckett said. "You understand."

The old man avowed that he certainly did understand, and if Beckett wanted to get to the family boxes he need only take the stair all the way to his left, go to the very top, and turn right at the end of the hall.

The Family boxes all had little brass plaques with their names on them above the red curtains that served as doors. Beckett wandered down the hall until he found the one that said "Wyndham-Vie," then leaned against the wall and waited.

His patience was rewarded. The boxes began to empty at intermission. Pairs and trios of the well-dressed, highly-esteemed citizenry of Trowth strolled down the hallway, taking the opportunity to stretch their legs, and to see who had come to the theatre with whom. Wyndham-Vie and his friend left their own box in the midst of conversation.

Edgar, as he stepped through the curtains: "...don't care what you say, I still think it's tedious..."

His friend: "...but you have to understand, it's a comment on the style of modern...oh. Hello."

Edgar Wyndham-Vie was glaring furiously at Beckett. "What the fuck are you doing here?"

"Language, Eddie. Whose your friend?"

"Robert Rowan-Harshank," the man said, extending a hand. "I work at—"

"Shut up, Robbie," Wyndham-Vie snapped at him. "He doesn't care who you are." Edgar took a step closer to Beckett. He was taller than the coroner by a few inches, but not as blocky. Beckett wasn't sure his joints could handle it if the gentleman was spoiling for a fight; they felt like someone had crushed had filled them with jagged metal splinters. Edgar clenched and un-clenched his fists. "Do you think your little brass shield means anything to me, junkie?" He practically spat the words into Beckett's face. "I am a *Wyndham-Vie*. My Family has the ear of the Emperor..."

No way, Beckett told himself, as his choler rose. It was old and the pipes were rusty, but that black-and-red fury of his youth still clutched at his heart. He pushed it down. No anger. No fear. *I am too old to fight young kids nowadays. Look at him. He's too tall. I'm too old.*

"...I could have you stripped of your authority..."

Too old, he insisted, as recklessness surged again.

"...and thrown into a cell in Old Bank so fast..."

Too... aw, the hell with it. Beckett balled up his fist and punched Edgar Wyndham-Vie in the face. Beckett's withered body remembered the old ways, and for a fraction of a second Edgar's cheekbone was connected by a line of force that passed through Beckett's fist, shoulder, and hip, straight to the ground. The blow was hard enough to send Wyndham-Vie crashing against the wall, and painful enough to keep the man from getting up right away. It was hard enough to split Beckett's knuckles, too, but between the veneine and the numbness in his fingers he hadn't felt it. All in all, Beckett found the experience to be extremely satisfying.

The Esteemed Family members moved quietly back into their boxes, pointedly not noticing the altercation in the hallway. The only thing worse than being involved in scandal was being seen to take too much of an interest in one.

While Edgar Wyndham-Vie was still stunned, Beckett whirled on his companion.

"Now, hang on a second here, friend..." Robert said, backing away. He held up his hands. "I don't...just...I mean... who do you think you are?"

"Beckett. Detective-Inspector, Coroners." He thought about flashing his shield again, but his hand had gone completely numb, and Beckett didn't want to spoil the effect by dropping it.

Robert Rowan-Harshank blanched, and his eyes grew very wide. "Oh. Oh. I see. Well, look..." he smiled weakly, and tried to help Edgar to his feet. "I mean, look. Eddie...he's got a bit of a temper, that's all. I'm sure he didn't mean any-thing..."

"Shut up Robbie," Edgar muttered thickly to his friend. A dark purple swelling was beginning to grow beneath his eye, and blood trickled from his nose. He jabbed a finger at Beckett. "You don't know what the fuck you're doing, junkie..."

"Come on, Eddie," Robert whispered. "Let's just go back inside." He turned back to Beckett. "He didn't mean anything. Really." Robert dragged his friend back into the booth.

Beckett turned away thoughtfully, and came face-to-face with Skinner. "What the hell was that about?" She asked.

"You heard it?"

"I kept trying to listen from across the way. I could hear once you got outside. What's going on?"

Beckett took her by the arm and led her back down the stairs.

"Did you recognize the man with Wyndham?"

"No. What did he say his name was? Robert some-thing?"

"Rowan-Harshank. I suppose the name doesn't mean anything to you?"

They emerged into the lobby. "Nothing. Elijah, we need to leave before Eddie calls the authorities."

"We are the authorities."

"You know what I mean."

Beckett nodded, and took her outside into the cold night air. Their coach waited with a long line of carriages by the side of the road. "You'll have to miss the play," he told Skinner as he knocked on the coach's door. Harry, the coachman, was asleep inside.

"It's all right. I'll see the whole thing some other time. Beckett, why did you hit him?" Skinner waved off his arm as she climbed into the coach.

"It was extremely satisfying."

"Elijah…"

"Stitch. He didn't want me to see the play."

"Right. That's why he sent you theatre tickets."

"No. He wanted me to see the booth. The man with Wyndham-Vie."

"The man that neither of us recognize." Skinner paused. "Why would he do that?"

"I don't know, but I mean to find out."

Skinner heard the certainty in his voice, and nodded. "Tomorrow, though. We're both tired. Let it wait until tomorrow."

"Right." Beckett agreed. "No, wait."

"What?"

"Do you have any money with you?"

She produced a small roll of bills from a pocket in her skirt. "Some. Why?"

"Lend it to me. Have Stitch pay you back. This is a business expense." Beckett took the money and closed the door. Skinner could hear his footsteps receding in the distance.

ELEVEN: THE ASSASSIN

The bullet nailed the coachman right through the chest, and his assassin rolled away from the window. He leaned against the wall in a dark room in an abandoned house and began counting. The idea was to stay down for a full minute, in case the coachman's death caused some kind of ruckus.

The assassin didn't need to count. He could hear the effects almost immediately. There were pistol-shots, and someone started shouting. The only word the assassin caught was "Coroners." *Shit*, he thought. He worked the slide on his rifle, and loaded another round, then slowly leaned over to look out the window.

A filthy man was standing in the middle of the street, a few yards from the coachman's corpse. He was shouting at someone, the assassin couldn't see whom, and waving a pair of shiny revolvers around. *Doesn't see me. Just wait it out*, the man thought to himself too soon; the filthy man in the street abruptly turned towards the assassin's window.

He thought *Shit* to himself again, because his inner monologue did not have an expansive vocabulary. He aimed at the man in the street, fired, and missed. The man jumped as chips of stone flew from the wall behind him, and started shouting again. The assassin started to load another round, when he heard something.

There was a crash in the room next to his. Someone had broken a window. *They're coming in*, he thought. The assassin made a break for the door, his stomach fluttering as he realized he'd have to cross in front of the window to get to it. There was nothing for it though, and he was relieved when no hail of gunfire shattered glass and perforated his skin. He made it out into the hall. There was a room directly across from him, one of the three escape routes he'd planned in case things got tight. A door opened at the end of the hall, and a tall man lurched from behind it. Things had gotten tight. The assassin dove through the door across from him, across the dusty, empty room it led to, and climbed out the window that he'd left open. Slinging the rifle over his shoulder, he quickly shimmied down the rattling drainpipe into a small courtyard.

The courtyard had been built on top of an arch that covered another street below the house; it had maybe once been covered with grass, but the grass was all dead. The assassin sprinted across it to a gap between the next house and the top of the arch, then jumped down into the swirling fog in the Arcadium.

The blue lamps barely cast any light. The assassin could only just see them through the dense fog, but he'd prepared well. *Fifteen paces, then right. Keep your hand on the wall, then left.* He maneuvered through the twisting streets, practically blind. He ducked into a doorway, and waited, listening intently.

After a moment, he heard footsteps slapping the cobblestone street. "I said, don't move!" Someone shouted.

The coroner. How the hell did he find me? The assassin put his shoulder against the door and pushed hard. It gave a little, but stayed closed. The footsteps got closer. He tried again, and this time the lock gave way. The assassin practically threw himself inside.

He found himself at the top of an iron balcony, stairs leading down into an enormous factory of some kind. Heavy metal machines hung silent overhead. The floor was filled with people.

The assassin gasped, and almost had a heart-attack. There were hundreds of them staring right at him. He struggled to make out details in the gloom. Why was no one moving? He could hear the coroner practically outside the door. The assassin leapt down the stairs and into the factory.

The figures he'd thought were people on the factory floor were mannequins. Or, at least, they were the heads of mannequins. Row after row of bald, plaster heads stared at him with thoughtful eyes that had been painted on. The assassin moved as far in as he could, then hunkered down to wait. There was a plaster head right by his ear and, after a moment, he turned it around backwards. Its false eyes made him nervous.

"I know you're in here," the man shouted. His voice echoed off of the machinery and bounced around in the dark. "It's no good hiding. Surrender, and I'll go easy on you."

Not likely, the assassin thought. The coroner stood in the doorway, framed in silhouette by the blue light seeping in from the street. The assassin, as quietly as he could, loaded a bullet into the breach of his rifle, and slowly closed the slide. *Stay there, moron. Just one more second*...he lifted the rifle.

A faint, dry rustle reached his ears, and the assassin quickly turned. A tall man in black had somehow got behind him. He fired his rifle into the tall man's chest. The flash from the muzzle was bright enough to blind him momentarily, and the sound of the gun was like a cannon, resounding over and over in the factory.

The man before him was unmoved. He stood silently for a moment, and then lunged forward, fast. He was too fast, faster than anyone the assassin had ever seen. The rifleman found him-self snared by arms that wrapped around his wrists like chains and confronted with...teeth...

Small white teeth, glittering in glistening red, meat...the thing had a mouth that stretched and stretched and drew in air with a painful, ragged gasp...

The man felt like he was choking, like someone had reached down his throat and made a fist in his lungs, and was dragging everything up, ripping his life out by his lungs. He kicked out at the thing but its flesh flowed like water. It clamped an iron hand around his jaw and brought its gaping red mouth closer, breathed deeper.

Like someone had flipped a switch, the light abruptly vanished.

TWELVE: THE HOUSE ON CORIMANDER STREET

Edgar Wyndham-Vie and Robert Rowan-Harshank left the theatre while the actors were still doing encores, in order to beat the rush. They climbed into the coach with the Wyndham-Vie crest, Edgar holding a handkerchief over the bruise on his face.

"The Windmill," Edgar called to the coachman. "Then knock off. We'll get a hansom back home."

"Sir," the coachman replied, his voice muffled beneath his red scarf. The scarf was new, but Edgar Wyndham-Vie and his friend didn't notice it, because rich people very rarely look at their servants. The coachman clicked his tongue at the horses, and drove them towards Sara's Windmill, the oldest *duetti* club in Trowth. He guided the carriage out of Red Lanes and along the Royal Mile, which led from the Imperial Palace to the Stark.

Traffic was not heavy, this late at night, but there were still plenty of coaches on the road, still women and old men trying to sell flowers or sausages or coal. Topside, the fog was light: just a swirl of dingy yellow-gray clouds around the ankles. Downside, in the Arcadium, people were probably choking to death and dying, sometimes from the vrylaks that lurked in the mist, sometimes from the simple density of sediment in it.

The coach came to a stop in front of an ordinary-looking building, built in the Ennering-Rowan style: plain walls, square windows. The only sign of the club's identity was the square bronze sign about the door, with the image of a windmill pressed onto it in enameled red steel. Inside, young gentlemen of the Esteemed Families of Trowth would watch the *duette*: a slow dance in which two young women would mime at dueling each other with long, slender knives. In Sar-Sarpek, when the *duette* had been invented a hundred years earlier, it had been a bloodsport. Now, it was an excuse for wealthy bachelors and married men to see women dressed in the skin-tight duetta's outfit, instead of the heaps of skirts and bustles that Trowth women were expected to wear.

It was not uncommon that a man like Edgar Wyndham-Vie should dismiss his coachman after arriving at a place like the Windmill. He might go on from there to engage in any number of scandalous activities; following one of the dancers home to a cat-house, or going with his new acquaintances to a hotel room, rented for the sole purpose of doing things that young men ought not to be doing in their homes. Edgar and Robert left their carriage and went into the club.

The coachman drove the Wyndham-Vie coach around the corner, just far enough out of sight that no one could see it from the door, then climbed down and headed back to the Windmill. He stopped a half a block from the entrance of the club, arriving just in time to see Edgar and Robert leaving again. They'd either watched an unusually short dance, or they were off to engage in business of their own.

The coachman tipped his tall black hat down and followed after them, trying to keep a discreet distance behind the two men. New Bank, where the Windmill made its home, saw less traffic than the Royal Mile did. There were few people left on the street here, and it would do no good to be spotted, but a man would be surprised at just how much practice this particular coachman had at being discreet.

He followed the two young gentlemen back down the steep streets of New Bank, then back up the not-quite-as-steep streets of Old Bank. They stopped in front of a familiar building, decorated with the sharp, organic-looking Vie-Gorgon merlons and guarded by a pair of red-glistening Lobstermen. The coach-man coughed and turned away, leaning against a cold buttress, trying to reproduce the look of an inconspicuous gentlemen, out for a brisk walk, taking a rest for a few moments.

The two men were not inside for very long. The coachman wished he recognized the building, but it was un-marked. He noted down the address, filed it away in his memory as the men emerged. Edgar had something square and bulky under his arm. The coachman was prepared to follow them both again, when Robert Rowan-Harshank saw him.

The young man nudged his friend and pointed towards the coachman; Edgar Wyndham-Vie squinted to get a better look. *He can't see me from across the street,* Beckett thought to himself. *Just behave naturally.* He wrapped his coat tight around his waist, shoved his hands in his pockets, and started to walk away.

"You!"

Aw, no...

"You!" Wyndham-Vie started screaming at the Lobster-men. "The man there, with the red scarf! Arrest him! Now, you idiots!"

The scarf. Right. Stupid. Beckett turned, and contemplated drawing his weapon. He thought better of it almost immediately. One of the Lobstermen had raised a rifle, while the other had sprinted in a long, curving arc to the side, staying out of the first one's line of sight and still closing on Beckett faster than he could possibly move.

The Marine with his wet-blood armor crashed towards him at speed, nearly as fast as a racehorse. Beckett raised his hands to show that they were empty. *Shit.* He thought.

"Lie on the ground and put your hands on your head." The Lobsterman shouted as he thundered to a stop, his own rifle held like a spear.

Shit, shit, shit.

The pressgangs raided Red Lanes even before news about the attack in River Village had hit the broadsheets. Men with boiled-leather breastplates and collars, heavy cudgels, and shriek-grenades bullied their way into the back rooms of every shop and restaurant. They found sharpsies working as butchers' assistants and cooks, or just engaging in the untrained labor of carting inventory around. The sharpsies were dragged into the street, beaten and chained, and immediately packed off to the ironclad warships bound for Gorcia.

If a shop owner was insistent about protecting his privacy, the pressgangers would through down their shriek-grenades; a special tympanum, treated with ionized flux, would begin to reverberate with a deafeningly loud, high-pitched wail, combined with a deep, stomach-churning moan. The dissonance between the two sounds was enough to bring the average person to his knees, gasping for breath and vomiting on the floor. The pressgangers, with the specially-treated counter-tympanum in their helmets, were immune. While shopkeeps and customers curled up on the ground in agony, the pressgangs kicked in doors and tore up floorboards.

If a man had employed sharpsies illegally in Red Lanes, the pressgangs found him that day. If he had never done so, the pressgangs rarely apologized for destroying his shop and making him and his customers bleed from the ears.

The work crews in New Bank, where the Family architects had been waging a particularly bitter pitched battle about flying buttresses, and which hired numerous sharpsie day-laborers for unskilled positions, were unscathed by the press-gangs.

All told, the pressgangs managed to fill the holds of two ironclads. Sharpsie men and women — pressgangers didn't know how to tell the difference, and wouldn't have bothered to if they did — were chained to each other and then to the floor of the ship. The ironclads would leave for Gorcia with new fodder for the Ettercap War that afternoon.

THIRTEEN: VALENTINE RETURNS

The Vie-Gorgons of Comstock Street are not quite the Vie-Gorgons of Raithower Street, though a certain amount of confusion is understandable. The Vie-Gorgons of Raithower Street, the branch of the family headed by the venerable patriarch James Gordon Vie-Gorgon, were the most affluent Family in all of Trowth. James had wisely chosen to secure a monopoly on the internal railroads of the nation, rather than enjoying control over the phlogiston importation that was disrupted by the ettercap war like the unfortunate Gorgon-Vies. The Raithower Vie-Gorgons were astonishingly wealthy, and had the strongest claim to the Imperial throne after William III Gorgon-Vie, who currently held it. They were known to be ruthless business dealers, and severe but sophisticated dressers. The Raithower Vie-Gorgons held parties only occasionally, and attended them even more rarely, preferring to spend their time deeply embroiled in the intricacies of controlling their vast wealth.

The Comstock Street Vie-Gorgons were third-cousins to the Raithower Vie-Gorgons, and stood on the other side of a relatively peaceable schism. Ever since their mutual great great-grandfather, old Raithower himself, after whom house, street, and plaza were all named, determined that his grandson Albrecht Vie-Gorgon, son of the same Emilio Vie-Gorgon that started off the Architecture War, should receive the bulk of the Vie-Gorgon business interests, while Albrecht's cousin (by coincidence, also named Albrecht) should inherit only an annual stipend. When grandfather Raithower and then father Emilio died, the first Albrecht took his fortune and moved from Raithower Plaza to Rowan Street, which was promptly renamed Raithower Street in honor of the old man.

The second Albrecht took his significantly less-sizable fortune to Comstock Street, which was not renamed in honor of anyone. The second Albrecht was a shrewd businessman, and managed to parlay his small stipend into near total-control of the print industry by the time his first grandchild was born. Roughly sixty percent of the broadsheets printed in Trowth were con-trolled directly or indirectly by Comstock Street, and, perhaps more importantly, nearly ninety percent of the paper milled in Trowth.

In general, the Comstock Vie-Gorgons were known for being not as rich as the Raithower Vie-Gorgons and, as far as fashion goes, both less severe and less sophisticated. Popular opinion had it that the Comstock Vie-Gorgons made up for their sartorial deficiencies by being friendlier; Allisandre Vie-Gorgon hosted an evening party virtually every week, received visitors every morning, and spent her afternoons calling on a number of well-off acquaintances.

The Comstock Vie-Gorgons were also known for being far more eccentric than their Raithower cousins, but this was due solely to the activities of their youngest member: Valentine Vie-Gorgon.

The young coroner arrived in the Vie-Gorgon house on Comstock Street covered in black filth and smelling like an open sewer. He burst through the main doors just as the midmorning sun began to come out ahead in its struggle to warm the ice streets, and handed a disgusting coat that looked like it had been dipped in sludge to his butler. The poor man had not even had time to ask the name of the foul vagrant that had entered without knocking; it goes without saying that Valentine was virtually unrecognizable.

"Have that cleaned for me, Henry," Valentine told his butler. The young man strode with a jaunty, athletic gate. "I suppose I'll need a new one for today. Have I got any other clean ones? Never mind, I shall just buy one!"

"Master Valentine?" Henry the butler managed to croak, his arms filled with the disgusting coat. It was too late. The young man had already gone into the parlor.

"Mother!" Valentine called out as he saw Veronica Vie-Gorgon, sitting with a number of ladies and talking about something that, no doubt, the young coroner would find of little interest. He grinned, showing teeth that were the luminescent green of a man afflicted with the scrave, then leaned over and kissed her cheek. "I've been out, as you can see. I shall have a bath, now, I think."

At the sight of the young man, covered as he was in what seemed to be a malodorous mixture of dirt, tar, coal dust, and horse manure that made his clothes look like they'd been used to stop up toilets and covered every inch of his face with black, two of the ladies in the room were taken with a sudden case of the vapors. Unaccustomed to the youngest Vie-Gorgon's antics, they took him to be the worst kind of ruffian, and immediately perceived that the house had been invaded by some kind of disgusting housebreaker.

Veronica Vie-Gorgon merely sat with a long-suffering look on her face, and permitted her son to kiss her cheek.

The third lady in the room, a beautiful, delicate-featured young woman with skin as smooth as glass and as black as pitch, rose to her feet. This was Emilia Vie-Gorgon, youngest daughter of the Raithower Vie-Gorgons, and not one to be fooled by the simple disguise of sewage.

"Cousin," she greeted Valentine. Her voice was warm and charming, and she had a pristine white dress that contrasted sharply with the color of her skin.

"Cousin!" The young man replied, taking her hands and kissing her on either cheek.

"You smell like shit." She showed him her white teeth. "Moreover, you seem to have covered yourself with sewage."

"Ah, cousin," Valentine smiled his bright green smile, his eyes twinkling maliciously. "I see that your skin is still as black as your heart."

It is unclear precisely how seriously Valentine and his cousin insulted each other, but it turned out to be of less-than-vital importance. Valentine took his leave almost immediately and headed straight for the sumptuously appointed bathroom in the Comstock house. A private heater provided running hot water, a luxury to be found in few homes west of Old Bank. Valentine spent over an hour soaking in soap and water in an effort to scald the filth from his skin.

When he had cleaned himself or, at least, cleaned himself to his satisfaction, Valentine dressed in his neatly-tailored grey suit, belted on his pearl-handled, nickel-plated revolvers, and went out in to the streets of Trowth on an adventurous search for a new coat.

Valentine arrived at the Coroner's Office in Raithower plaza around noon. He was wearing a new coat; it was charcoal grey like everything the Coroners were meant to wear, but with two lines of silver buttons and a fancy black braid looped at the right arm. Skinner and Beckett's secretary, Karine, were the only two people in the main office, which had once been Albrecht Vie-Gorgon's parlor.

Karine was in her own office, adjacent to the main. She'd been hired partly at Beckett's insistence; after years of frustration in his attempts to investigate heresy in Trowth, the old coroner had stumbled on a novel idea: he'd demanded an entire staff of workers whose sole job was to collect and read broad-sheets. Stories about murders, which were plentiful, were clipped out and filed away by date. Stories about people were clipped and filed away according to their names. If a story was about more than one person, or in the case of the murders, a tag was placed in the file for the sake of cross-referencing. The secretarial department would also collect reports from the Imperial Guard and all the local gendarmeries about every single arrest they'd made every day. Few of the gendarmeries were consistent about reporting arrests, and hardly ever noted the freelance beatings they administered, but the Guard was fairly reliable.

Beckett had gone to Mr. Stitch and demanded a secretarial staff. Stitch, in turn, managed to secure enough funding to pay Karine. She was a conscientious and thorough worker, and Beckett had been trying to get her fired since day one. Karine was an indige, and her people had phlogiston in their blood. They were virtually immune to the cold, and they refused to dress properly. Karine wore low-cut blouses, dresses without underskirts or petticoats or bustles, and sometimes with slits in them that went as high as her hip. It was all to the purpose of displaying the silvery tattoos all over her blue-black skin, and was scandalous by modern standards. For Beckett, whose sense of propriety had been established thirty years earlier, seeing Karine come to work "practically naked" was enough to give him apoplexy.

Stitch had refused to fire her. She was, after all, an excel-lent worker, and Stitch was interested neither in social mores nor in racial tension. Valentine caught a glimpse of the indige secretary through her open office door. He smiled and winked, but didn't think she noticed.

"Valentine?" Skinner snapped, as soon as she heard the young man's footsteps. "Is that you? Where the hell have you been?" She wrinkled her nose. "Augh, you smell like piss."

"I've been...well, it's a long story. I need to talk to Beckett right away. He's in his office?" Valentine opened the door without waiting for a response, only to find the room empty.

"No. He didn't come to work today."

"Is..."

"He's not at home either," Skinner went on. "We don't know where he is. I told Stitch, but we've got no one to spare right now."

"Well, where is he?"

"I don't know, Valentine," Skinner was practically snarling. "In the meantime, where were you? You know Public Safety took the Zindel bodies?"

"What? They what?"

"That's right, Valentine. I'm not sure how. They must have snuck right past you and your cordon. You know, the one that you were supposed to set up to make sure no one got in and disturbed the scene?"

The young man stuttered. "I. Well, look, it's...the thing of it was..."

Skinner shook her head. "I don't want to hear it. Tell it to Beckett when we find him. All I can say is, it'd better be fucking good."

Valentine groaned and sank into a chair.

"Ms. Skinner?" Karine came out of her office, and pointedly refused to look at Valentine. "I think I know where Mr. Beckett is?"

Skinner cocked her head. "And...?"

Karine held up a bit of paper. "It's the report from the Imperial Guard in Old Bank." She passed it to Valentine, still without looking at him.

"Aw, no," Valentine muttered, reading the report.

"What? What is it?"

"He's been arrested. Assault, theft..." Valentine scowled. "Attempted *espionage*. He's being held at Montgomery Square."

"Montgomery Square...?"

"It's the Committee, Skinner. The Committee for Public Safety has him."

FOURTEEN: HERESY

Alan Charterhouse sat on the bed in his room. Papers were scattered about him; they tumbled in piles on his bed, they were balled up and crumpled on his floor, they were pinned to his walls. He used a book for a desk while he sat in his nightclothes, scratching formula after formula in a mathematical language that he could be executed for even knowing about. There was a copy of *The Dangers of Heresy* laying open on the bed next to him. In his feverish rush to understand what he'd seen in Herman Zindel's home, Alan Charterhouse did not notice the irony.

Dangers of Heresy was given to every young boy or girl the first day they came to Sebet-Day school, to learn about the religion and the Word. It was full of terrifying copperplate etchings of Reanimates, of people that died of dream poisoning, of the hideous creations of chimeratists and ectoplasmatists, followed with page after page of descriptions about how terrible heretical science could be. The last two chapters were devoted to the *Excelsior*.

The pictures of the *Excelsior* were actually cheap kirlitotypes, so they were much more detailed than the copperplates. The first pictures were of the whole *Excelsior*, looking like nothing so much as a great brass shark with a huge, piston-driven phlogiston engine protruding from its back. There was a copy of the famous kirliotype of the *Excelsior*'s launch, with the Lord Mayor of Trowth smashing a bottle of sparkling wine against its brass hull.

The rest of the pictures…it wasn't always possible to get kirltiotypes. Something was left over in the air after the launch that disrupted the flux-membranes used in the cameras. There were big black spots obstructing the view sometimes, like someone had burned the photographs with a match. Sometimes, the spots looked like they had fingers.

What could be seen was awful. The area directly around the launch, when the *Excelsior* had returned to real-space, had been completely annihilated. There was just an empty scoop out of the ground that was covered with ash. The mangled ship sat at its center. All around the central crater were twisted, burned-out buildings. Doorways or chimneys sometimes stood where houses had collapsed. Towers were burned and covered in black soot.

The people who had been nearest to the Excelsior had died almost instantly; vaporized along with the ground they were standing on. It had happened so fast that they'd left their shadows behind. According to the book, the few people daring enough to live in the Break insisted that they could still see those shadows moving about. Still, those were lucky ones. The people around them were less fortunate. They were sometimes fortunate enough to be burned alive for a few seconds; if they survived that, the Aether would get to them.

Somehow, the *Excelsior* had brought a wave of meta-physical space back with it. It erupted out from ground zero, wrenching space and reality out of alignment. People died as their bones sprouted thorns, veins turned to glass, skin shattered like stone. One man was torn apart as his muscles came to life like snakes, and tried to rip themselves free from his body.

Not everyone died immediately. There were survivors at the very outskirts of the explosion, and others who tried to move into what came to be called the Break shortly afterwards. They did not last long. They choked on extra teeth growing in their throats, or went mad as their limbs slowly began to split in half.

It was not the lurid photographs of the victims of the *Excelsior* that Alan was interested in. There were no blueprints or schematics available for the machinery on the Aethership; the kirliotypes in *Dangers of Heresy* were the closest he could come. He needed more information. The young cartographer felt starved for it.

There was something unsettling about the equations that Zindel was using, though the idea that someone had gotten access to the *Excelsior*'s translation engine and had been using it was certainly unsettling enough. Something else, though, nagged at Charterhouse's mind, and he couldn't say what it was. So, he plotted through the equations, copying down everything he could remember from Zindel's walls, reconstructing formulae where he had to, improving on them when he found it necessary.

"Got yer lunch, boy," Uncle Malcolm called to him. "Hungry?"

"No, Uncle Malcolm," Alan called back automatically. He could hear the panic in his own voice. "Not right now, thanks."

There was silence from the old man. Then, "Should eat something. Some soup. I'll leave some in the kitchen."

Alan said nothing. He was staring at the photograph of the *Excelsior*, with its huge phlogiston-powered engine in the back. There were two short antennae at either end of the protruding pistons; Alan was now able to recognize them as a kind of stabilizer. They'd create a sub-harmonic that would allow the *Excelsior* to return to normal space.

Two. He thought. *No. Oh, no.*

FIFTEEN: VENEINE

Beckett tried to keep his breathing normal as nausea welled up in his stomach, crawling up his throat, choking him, trying to drag itself out and into the air...*No. Not again.* His body screamed at him. Icy nails had been driven through his elbows and knees and into each vertebra in his lower back. There was a whooshing sound in his ears, a ringing that made it almost impossible to hear.

He coughed a wracking, full-body cough, then rolled over and vomited. His stomach had nothing left to bring up so the waves just wrenched his body into convulsions. His head... something hammered at his head, and he was sure he was bleeding through his eyes.

Pain was blinding while he retched. It cleared for a moment for Beckett to see the brass beneath his palms, hot under cold moonlight, his knees ached...he closed his eyes and tried to scream at himself to stay calm. Crashing waves broke around his ears and he puked up sea water and spiders that crawled away, skittering on five misshapen legs. The cut on his head had opened again, and there were new cuts on his fingers now. Blood rolled down the skin of his face to the end of his nose, and into the crevices between the stones on the floor, dropping away into space, he could see it falling through and thought it might come out the other side of the world.

More pain came in waves and clenched bony fingers into his muscles. He curled up on the floor and tried to take the pres-sure off of his lower back. Shards of glass in his knees and elbows crunched and slashed his tendons to ribbons and he wanted to scream. He tore at his elbows with his fingers; they'd taken the coat he'd bought off of the coachmen, and Beckett had long since turned his sleeves to rags. A red tumor had grown up inside his elbow, and he saw its long red tendrils snaking down his arm, trying to get to his invisible fingertips.

Teeth bared, he tried to bite it off, but touching it sent sharp needles of pain straight up his arm and through his shoulder; they lanced through his lungs and stabbed at his heart. He choked on bile and tried to vomit again, with a fist clenching in the back of his throat. The fist opened into feathers and he coughed up a black bird whose sharp talons scored the inside of his mouth. The walls of the tower were brass, and he wasn't alone here, beneath the hot moonlight. Something with wet slimy boneless fingers reached out for him.

Beckett rolled away against the wall of the cell, screaming. The fingers were biting at his eyes now, tiny, toothy, jawless mouths. He grabbed at them and tried to pull the leeches out of his eyelids but they were stuck. Their bodies came off in his hands, but their mouths stayed fixed to the inside of his eyes, chewing and chewing. He screamed, his hands filled with swarms of black leeches.

"Beckett! Word and fuck, Beckett!"

Someone screamed at him, and Beckett was sure it was a voice from the City of Brass whose towers now loomed over his head, shining claws reaching at the pale leprous disc of the moon. The moon called out to him and screamed his name.

"Beckett! What's wrong with him? What did you fucking do to him?"

The moon was wide as wide as the sky and he wasn't floating up to it but falling towards it, and there were cities of black basalt teeming like termite colonies across its surface and there were things that lived there.

"Beckett!" There was a hand on his arm, a hard real hand, not soft like the hands in his mind.

The old coroner grabbed a hold of his mind through nothing more than force of will. "V-valentine...?" He rattled, gasping for breath. "Wh-..."

"Elijah, it's all right, we're getting you out of here..."

"Why did you..." he gasped and almost choked again on saltwater. "...leave...the cordon..."

"I'll explain it to you later. We have to get you out of here."

His vision swam and then, for a moment, was mercifully clear. The cold, merciless iron that was the core of Beckett's being seized control. The pain temporarily took a place back-stage, the rushing sound in his head died away, as Beckett grabbed Valentine by his shirt-front. He stared at the young man's narrow, angular face, at his dark eyes.

"No! Stitch will do it." He coughed, and yanked hard on Valentine's shirt. "Wyndham... took...eighteen...."

"Wyndham took eighteen what? What are you talking about? Elijah? Elijah!"

The world was fading the moon swelled up beneath him. "Eighteen twenty." The choking fist was in the back of his throat again. "Corimander Street."

Another wave of agony shook him. Beckett screamed and curled up on the ground, as someone hit him over and over in the face with a hammer, and then: darkness.

Valentine slowly rose to his feet after Beckett had collapsed into unconsciousness. *It's the veneine, flushing from his system*, he thought. *Or else it's the fades. Is that what they do to you? Tear you apart from the inside, while they make your outsides transparent?* The young coroner turned to where Edgar Wyndham-Vie stood at the end of the hall. They were deep beneath Montgomery Station, where the Committee for Public Safety kept its cells. The ceiling was low, and curved all the way to the ground on either side, leaving little room for a prisoner to even stand.

"He needs to be released." Valentine told the other man. "Now."

"He assaulted my *person*," Edgar Wyndham-Vie said. "He stole my family's carriage. I found him trying to break into a restricted-access Vault in Old Bank..."

Valentine bore down on him, and brought his face very close to the other man's. "He said you took something. Eighteen-twenty Corimander Street."

Edgar swallowed. "Perjury. He is the thief. And a liar. He has a vested interest in impugning my character..."

It took every ounce of willpower Valentine had to not draw his revolver and gun Wyndham-Vie down right then and there. This was quite a feat; Valentine was a man used to indulging his whims. "Right. He had to execute your cousin for heresy, and *he's* got the vested interest—"

"Considering the crimes levied against him," Wyndham-Vie interrupted, "I'm petitioning for a full inquest into my cousin's murder—"

" —execution—"

"*Murder*." Wyndham-Vie sneered at him. "Family name notwithstanding, Valentine, you should be careful. I could have you held as an accessory."

This time, Valentine really would have shot the man, despite the red-armored Lobsterman at Wyndham-Vie's back, had not another voice cut into their conversation.

"Unacceptable." The voice was a rasping sound, the kind three voices might make if they'd been crammed together into one big voice and then torn apart a smaller, fourth one.

Edgar Wyndham-Vie blanched. "This...this isn't..."

Mr. Stitch limped slowly down the hallway towards the two men. The steel braces on his lower legs clanked loudly on the stone. His eyes, which looked like microscope eyes, brass mounts with clear glass lenses in them, were utterly expressionless as he stared at Wyndham-Vie, and practically dragged his seven-foot-tall frame towards him. A trolljrman, at least as tall as Stitch, followed close behind. Its gold feather crest was flat, and it wore a shapeless gray robe over its leathery shell.

Stitch drew a long, terrible breath. "Beckett will be. Released into. My custody." His dead muscles creaked as he turned his head towards Valentine. "Valentine. You have. Your orders."

Mr. Stitch was a Reanimate. He'd been built over a century and half ago by Harcourt Wolfram himself, and was the only Reanimate in the history of the heretical science that hadn't eventually gone insane and started randomly murdering people. His brain was an ingenious combination of ichor-invigorated human brains and a whirling, nickel-steel difference engine of such brilliance and complexity that its construction had never been replicated. By some uncertain means, nearly a hundred years ago, Mr. Stitch had secured an official royal pardon for himself as an Abomination before Science and the Word. He not only commanded the Coroners Division, but it had been Mr. Stitch, along with Adelwulf Vie-Gorgon, that had created it.

Mr. Stitch was the only other agent in the Coroners that wore the regulation tricorn hat. Dead muscles creaked and rasped again, as Mr. Stitch handed Valentine a folded piece of parchment. It was not uncommon for Stitch to communicate by written missive; his lungs had seen little use since he'd died. They had, in fact, rotted away. Wolfram had replaced them with a kind of billows sewn into his chest.

"You're interfering..." Edgar Wyndham-Vie took a deep breath as he took in Stitch's huge form and the dead, leather skin on his face. The stitches from which he took his name were black roads that crisscrossed his face. "You're interfering with an investigation by the Committee for Public Safety." The Adjunct managed to gather some fortitude. He pointed imperiously at Beckett. "That man assaulted...he..." his courage seemed to falter. "He was...he stole my *coach*."

Stitch drew in a long, painful breath. "I wonder. Why. Was he so interested. In you?"

Edgar Wyndham-Vie's eyes narrowed dangerously. "You are standing very close to treason, Mr. Stitch."

Another breath. "I am. Precisely aware. Of how close I. Am standing. To treason." His voice was without nuance, and deeply frightening, like the tortured sighs of a dying man.

Wyndham-Vie's complexion went from white to red as the implications of Stitch's statement became clear. "Him. Arrest him. Arrest them all! I am officially declaring the Coroner's Division a threat to the safety of the public of Trowth."

"No. You. Are not."

"Do it!" Wyndham-Vie screamed at the Lobsterman. "Take him, now!"

The Lobsterman grabbed Mr. Stitch's arm, and reached for a revolver at his waist. The chemically-modified ichor that pulsed in his veins made him stronger and faster than an ordinary human. But Mr. Stitch was not an ordinary human, and if the Lobsterman had some diluted ichor in his system, Stitch had been pickling in the stuff for a hundred years.

He drew his arm across his body, yanking the Lobster-man off-balance then swung, hard, his great dead, leathery fist hammering into the Lobsterman's chest. The blow pinned the Marine against the stone wall with a crunch and a hollow-sounding boom. The Lobsterman slid to the ground, a spider's web of cracks on his bone breastplate. He made small choking sounds, and his eyes rolled back in his head.

Wyndham-Vie went for his gun, but Valentine was faster. He pressed the barrel of one nickel-plated revolver just below Edgar's ear. "No. Drop it." Wyndham-Vie pulled the gun from his belt with two fingers, then dropped it on the floor. Valentine kicked it away.

Stitch made a languid movement to the trolljrman, who squeezed by to Beckett's cell. The huge Reanimate took another ragged breath. "We will take. Beckett. He gave you. An address."

Valentine stared. "How did you know?"

Mr. Stitch slowly raised his dead hand, and tapped his forehead, where a hundred thousand tiny gears were spinning. "Go."

Skinner was waiting in the coroner's coach when Valentine emerged from beneath Montgomery Station. "What happened in there?" She asked, as Valentine climbed in.

Valentine looked at her. "You weren't listening?"

She shook her head. "A weird echo. It made it hard to hear anything. It happened with Edgar before." She paused, thoughtfully. "And before that, with his cousin."

"You think there's a connection?"

"It's not important now. What happened?"

"Wyndham-Vie wanted to hold Beckett. Mr. Stitch intervened." He unfolded the parchment Stitch had given him, and read it. "We're meant to investigate eighteen-twenty Corimander Street. Beckett thinks Wyndham-Vie took some-thing important from it." He shouted the address up to Harry, the driver.

"What's that?" She'd heard Valentine fussing with the parchment.

"Stitch gave it to me. It's a Writ of Search. For any and all holdings of...the Royal Academy of Sciences?"

There was a long pause, as the coach rattled off.

"How..." Skinner's voice was very soft. "How was he?"

Valentine grimaced, and was glad that the knocker couldn't see his expression. Still, he supposed she could hear it in his voice anyway. "Bad. I don't...I don't know if it was the disease or the drug..." He took a deep breath and unknowingly let a small piece of himself dissolve away. A tiny vein of iron replaced what he lost. "Stitch will see to him. We've got work to do."

THE TRANSLATED MAN AND OTHER STORIES

SIXTEEN: CORIMANDER STREET

Paper money was introduced to Trowth in the late seventeenth century. Until that time, gold, silver and copper had been the most widely-used currencies, and an individual coin was, literally, worth its weight. The coins were kept in a variety of banks in the neighborhood that was, at the time, called Bankhouse. The banks competed with each other to offer the most secure storage of their patrons' wealth: huge subbasements were dug beneath the buildings, and impregnable vaults constructed. Towards the end of the century, more than sixty banks had built over a hundred thick-walled vaults with great iron doors to store piles of gold.

When Owen I Gorgon took the throne, he immediately had all of the wealth in Bankhouse seized. Patrons were first issued promissory notes, which were gradually replaced by printed bills set to the store of gold in the newly-built Imperial Reserve. Ostensibly, this was because the Reserve was more secure even than the vaults in Bankhouse. In fact, it was because Owen's predecessor, James Agon I Daior, had emptied the Royal Treasury.

The consequence of Owen Gorgon's actions, which would be known later as the Great Forfeiture, were numerous: firstly, Trowth once again had a viable treasury to fund government projects. Secondly, all of the vaults in Bankhouse were suddenly empty. Thirdly, all of the wealthy families that had made their homes in the district gradually relocated to the district called New Bank, where the view was better and the houses were much nicer.

The district was still technically called Bankhouse: a pedestrian would be able to see the name written on every verdigris-covered bronze street sign, had they still been legible. The citizens of Trowth simply referred to it as Old Bank. In the wake of the Forfeiture, a variety of both public and private interests found uses for the extremely secure Vaults in Old Bank. The Vaults under Montgomery Station, for example, would eventually find use with the Committee for Public Safety as holding cells. Some would be used by the Ministry for Internal Security, others by the War Powers Ministry, which was responsible for funding the pressgangs.

The Vault at eighteen-twenty Corimander Street was not marked. It didn't even look like a vault so much as it looked like the town-house of a moderately wealthy family, able to afford to purchase the property but not to invest very much money in its upkeep. The stone walls were dirty, the heavy wooded sills and shutters were black and rotten from salt air. The entire upper stories had a disused look about them, which may have been appropriate; if the building was used solely as a Vault, most of the interest would be invested in the lower-level floor-space.

"Come with me," Valentine implored. He climbed out of the coach, brandishing his Writ.

Skinner didn't move. "I can hear fine from out here."

"Please. I..." The young man tried to bite his tongue, but couldn't. "I'm not...you know I'm not as smart as you or Beckett. I need you with me."

The knocker threw up her hands. "Fine. But if I get shot, or something, you've got to explain how you lost the Coroner's only knocker."

"Heh. I'm sure I could afford to hire a new one."

"You wish."

Valentine helped the young lady down from the coach. "Besides, I can't understand your damnable tapping code any-way."

"It's easy," she said, resting a hand on his elbow and waving her cane precisely in front of her. "There's a heavy tap and a light tap. The sequence of taps will stand for a letter, except when they stand for numbers. Then they'll be preceded by a single simultaneous tap. A simultaneous double tap means yes, a simultaneously triple tap means no..."

"See, you've already lost me..."

"And then it counts. Four light taps followed by a heavy tap is one, or 'A,' three light taps followed by one heavy tap and then one light tap is two, or 'B,' three light taps followed by two heavy taps is three, or 'C'..."

"La la la, I don't understand, la la la..."

"Valentine, you'll never learn if you don't pay attention."

Inside the address on Corimander Street, the two coroners found a heavy wooden desk, behind which sat a young man of rather ordinary features. Valentine estimated that he was a gentleman, owing to his youth and bearing — as a more common young man would have surely been sent to the war already—and that he was of Rowan or Czarnecki relation, owing to the long, straight nose. Behind the desk was an iron door with a little window in it. Standing next to the door were two blood-and-bone armored Lobstermen.

"Hallo, chum," Valentine said to the young clerk. "Can you tell me, what've you got behind that door?"

The clerk looked at Valentine, then at Skinner and the silver plate across her eyes, then back at Valentine. "Well...no. I'm afraid I can't.

"Robert?" Skinner asked, suddenly.

"You two know each other, splendid!" Valentine exclaimed. "Skinner, have him open the door for us."

"I don't..." the clerk seemed confused. "I don't think we do know each other." He shook his head. "This is a highly-restricted area. I'm afraid that if you don't have authorization from the Academy, I'm going to have to ask you both to leave. Immediately."

"Huh," Valentine said. He unfolded his Writ. "The Academy? You mean, the Royal Academy of Sciences? Be-cause it just so happens I have a Writ here...well, you can read it just as well as I can explain it." He handed it to the clerk. "I suppose that'll do. Open the door, chum."
The clerk read the Writ and swallowed nervously, then gestured to one of the Lobstermen, who used an alarmingly dense array of keys to open several locks on the iron door.

"I hope they don't decide to lock us in," Valentine whispered to the knocker, as the door creaked open and the two coroners began to descend a steep, stone staircase. They passed through another iron door at the bottom of the stairs, this one thicker and stronger-looking, but ajar. Beyond it was a very large, round room. At its outside edges burned small phlogiston lamps. They failed to cast enough light on the huge, still shape in the center. Whatever it was, it was nearly two storeys tall and at least fifty feet long. It was covered by a white sheet, and loomed menacingly in the dark.

"That..." whispered Valentine. "Is that what I think it is?"

"What?" Skinner asked. Her telerhythmia moved quickly along the walls before it found the shape in the center and began rattling on the sheet. Each rap threw up a tiny cloud of dust and made a faint, metallic ringing sound.

"The *Excelsior*," the clerk told them, his voice hushed. Valentine hadn't even realized they'd been followed.

"He took something..." Valentine said to himself. "The cylinders from the flight recorder. Where are they?"

The clerk gestured to yet another iron door, set into the curving wall. Valentine ran to it and threw it open, only to find that it was indeed full of etched copper recording cylinders.

"Instrumentation is on the right. Those," the clerk pointed to five neatly stacked cylinders, "are the audio recordings."

Valentine turned to him. "You keep a record, right? A list of everyone that comes in? They have to sign a...a book, or something..."

"The logbook, yes."

"I'll need to see it."

The clerk shook his head. "I can't."

Valentine started waving the Writ around. "You misunderstood me. By order of the *Crown*, I am *seizing* your log books."

"No, sir," the clerk said. "*You* misunderstood *me*. I can't give you the logbook. It's already been taken."

"By whom?"

"The Committee for Public Safety," Skinner said, her face thoughtful. "Right, Robert?"

Robert Rowan-Harshank nodded.

With a growl, Valentine grabbed the young man and threw him against the wall. He drew his revolver, and pressed it against Robert's cheek. "Someone came in here and copied those recording cylinders. Who?"

"If you shoot me, the Lobstermen will be down here before you can draw a breath..."

"I'm sure that'll be a great consolation to you when you're *dead*. Who copied the cylinders? Was it Wyndham?"

Robert Rowan-Harshank shook his head. "No. I can't tell you..."

"I. Will. Kill. You."

"Valentine," Skinner interrupted. "We need to go."

Robert's face was deathly serious. "If you kill me, you'll never find out."

Valentine paused, then thumbed back the hammer of his revolver. He removed the gun from Rowan-Harshank's cheek, and pointed it at the man's crotch. "I can keep questioning you after I've shot your balls off."

"You'll hang..."

"Valentine!" Skinner shouted.

"Not me," Valentine sneered. "I'm a Vie-Gorgon. I won't even get Transportation."

Robert Rowan-Harshank snorted. "A *Comstock* Vie-Gorgon. You might as well be a Wyndham. Or a Crabtree."

"Who made the copies?" Valentine screamed at him.

Skinner grabbed his arm. "Valentine. We need to leave. Now."

For one long, desperate moment, Skinner was afraid that Valentine was going to shoot the young man in front of him. Then, he took a deep breath, gently lowered the hammer back into position, and put the revolver in his belt. "You may think you're doing someone a favor," the coroner told him. "But right now, you are in. Over. Your. Head."

He led Skinner back up the staircase. "What is it?"

"Gendarmes. A lot of them. I can hear them coming up the street."

"Oh. Do you have any idea what's going on here?" Skinner was quiet as they passed the Lobstermen, who stood at their posts with the placid disinterest of career sentries. Then: "No. I don't." The street, when Valentine and Skinner arrived, was empty. "Skinner, I don't see anyone. Are you sure…oh. Never mind." The young man practically threw her into the coach. "In, get in. Go back to the office. Wait for me, or Beckett, or someone. I don't know. Go."

"Valentine —"

"Listen, I really feel that, of the three people investigating this situation, at least one of us should not be in prison. I nominate you. Second! All in favor, aye! Good!" He slammed the door of the coach, and shouted to Harry. "Go! Back to Raithower!" Then turned to meet the approaching gendarmes.

These were ordinary human beings, outfitted only with the same riot armor that the pressgangs wore: boiled leather breastplates and collars, greenglass goggles. They carried swords and cudgels. One man rode a horse; a big draft horse that he probably used to stomp on criminals.

There was little question that these men had been sent by Edgar Wyndham-Vie in his capacity as Adjunct to the Vice-Minister of the Committee of Public Safety. His authorization for deploying Lobstermen was no doubt quite limited. Un-questionably loyal fanaticism was expensive, after all.

There were half a dozen different organizations with Imperial mandates to operate in the city of Trowth. The management of these organizations was a delicate balancing act, all designed to keep the major Families constantly at each other's throats. The organizations all had different jurisdictions, and limited budgets. The Imperial Guard, and the Coroners Division by extension, for instance, was responsible directly for the protection of the Emperor. The Committee for Public Safety was technically only responsible for the safety of the city of Trowth. The War Powers Ministry was empowered only to act within the city limits when it came to recruiting. The Ministry of Internal Security was empowered to override the jurisdiction of the Committee for Public Safety in circumstances when the larger safety of the Empire was at stake.

This made determining priority a tricky business, especially when it came to the Coroners, which were technically a joint venture of the Imperial Guard and the Ministry of Internal Security. The Committee for Public Safety could override the activities of the Coroners, and even arrest its members, if their actions didn't directly protect the Emperor or the Empire but were endangering the safety of the city. None of this included the gendarmerie, either: they were commissioned and employed by individual neighborhoods and were essentially autonomous, unless they were conscripted by one of the government agencies.

All of which meant very little to Valentine as he watched the gendarmes approach. The only really relevant aspect was this: he had no case, which meant that if Edgar Wyndham-Vie could show that he was a legitimate threat to the safety of the city, Valentine would have to show that Wyndham-Vie was a legitimate threat to the security of the Emperor. Or the Empire. Or something.

Aw, damn it, Valentine said to himself, as the nine pedestrian and one equestrian gendarmes fanned out around him in the street. If he was lucky, only the man on the horse was carrying a gun. *Think, Valentine. What would Beckett do?* He'd probably say something mean, and punch someone in the face. And maybe shoot someone. On the other hand, Beckett had got-ten himself arrested. Valentine was almost certain he could not beat all ten men in a fist-fight and, despite his posturing with Rowan-Harshank, he suspected he really would be hanged if he shot someone unlawfully.

"Gentlemen," Valentine said, as he pulled out his revolver. "I'm sure we're all eager to resolve this peacefully." *Can't get arrested. Okay. Pretend you're Beckett.* Beckett was in jail. *Pretend you're Beckett before he was in jail, the Beckett from the old days that was too crazy to be arrested for doing crazy things.*

The men had moved into a reasonably tight circle around him. "Valentine Vie-Gorgon," the man on horseback said. He had a number five branded on his cheek. "You are under arrest. Drop your weapon, lie down on the ground, and put your hands on your head."

"Sorry," Valentine tried to smile his most charming smile. Beckett would have glowered, or glared, or done something equally sinister, but allowances had to be made. Valentine did not have an especially intimidating glare. "On whose authority am I being arrested?"

The men shifted uncomfortably. "You're under arrest..."

"You said that already. If you're going to arrest me in the name of the Committee for Public Safety, you've got to declare it." He thumbed the hammer back on his revolver. "That's how it works. Say, 'I arrest you in the name of the Committee for Public Safety,' or something like that." He shrugged. "Not that it matters. Under the circumstances, I've no intention of going with you. My authority supersedes yours."

"We're here in the name of the Committee…"

"Right, but you're not actually *employed* by the Committee, you've been *conscripted* by the Committee," this, Valentine knew, was almost certainly true, "which technically means that I can lawfully refuse arrest until I'm approached by actual agents of the Committee." This was almost certainly not true. The gendarmes, however, didn't seem to know that. "You need to get out of here," Valentine told them, "before I start shooting you."

Trying to make a convincing argument to the men about to arrest him was not a very Beckett-like thing to do. Threatening to shoot them was. Valentine felt the two gestures balanced each other out.

"Huh." One of the gendarmes said. He had a long scar under his right eye, and a three branded beneath the left. "You can't shoot all of us." Ten men, six shots to a revolver; the man was, mathematically speaking, correct.

Almost. Valentine drew his second revolver, cocked it. "Sure I can."

"Some of us will get to you…"

"What is this?" Valentine snapped. "A pissing contest? Fine, I can't shoot all of you. Maybe I can only shoot five of you. Maybe I can only shoot two. Who wants to go first?" Trying to threaten his way out of the situation did not seem to be working. Maybe they knew he wouldn't really shoot. Maybe the men behind him were planning on rushing him. He needed a new plan.

Aw, Mr. Horse, I'm sorry. There was no way he could let the man on horseback draw a pistol.

There was a loud crack, as Valentine fired a shot right between the horse's hooves. The animal screamed, reared, lost its balance and fell, but Valentine had already turned to charge the men directly behind him. He ran as fast as he could, roaring at the top of his voice, waving his revolvers in the air.

In the excitement, the gendarmes forgot that Valentine probably wasn't going to shoot them. They dove out of the way, their instincts to "Avoid the Raving Maniac" overriding their rational desire to "Arrest that Man." Valentine ran past them and up the hill.

They were in Old Bank. Raithower Square wasn't far. If he could get to it, he'd be safe. It was no fun trying to run up hills, but there was some small satisfaction in knowing that the slope would give as much trouble to his pursuers as it gave the young coroner. At least, until the equestrian got his horse back on its feet. Valentine put on speed.

Seventeen: Valentine's Story

Harry the carriage-driver had led Skinner into the Raithower office of the Coroners. He was concerned for her safety, which is why Skinner held back the urge to kick him in the shin and say that she was perfectly capable of finding her way into her own office, thank you very much. Once they'd gotten inside, Harry had breathlessly explained to Karine about the hundred men who'd come to kill Valentine, and how he was facing them down even as they spoke, and surely soon a whole battalion of Lobstermen would be crashing the gates of Raithower House. Karine immediately took charge of Skinner's protection, and with all concern helped her find a comfortable seat on the couch.

Skinner growled inwardly, but was pleased to note that she kept the sour expression off of her face. The indige arrived with tea; Skinner heard the silver spoon clink on porcelain as Karine scooped sugar into a mug.

"Karine," Skinner asked, gently taking the hot cup. "Would you please look out the window and see if Valentine is coming? I think I can hear his footsteps."

"He is, Miss Skinner," Karine said after a moment. "There's some men chasing after him. He's running for the gates now. The guards are opening them..."

"Does it look like he's going to make it?"

"I think so...wait. He tripped! No, he's up again. He's past the gates now, and the guards have closed them. They are yelling at the other men. Harry's on top of the coach, waving his rifle around and shouting. I suspect he means to shoot some-one."

"I can hear them, Karine, I just can't see them." She took a sip from her teacup. "What's Valentine doing? He isn't saying anything."

"He's lying on his back, miss. On the flagstones."

"Oh." They waited. Skinner drank some more tea. "Is he still there?"

"Yes."

It was several minutes before Valentine burst through the office door, face flushed and still panting. "You..." he said. "...wouldn't...believe. How far I had...to run."

"I would," Skinner told him. "I came the same way. In the coach."

"But I had to *run*. Fast. The...men. They had...sticks and things."

"I'm sure it was very hard. Do you want tea?"

Valentine was silent for a long moment. "No." His voice was sullen.

After a moment, Skinner heard him sit, and the tell-tale clinking sound of porcelain teacups. She smiled.

"So," Valentine asked between gulps of tea. "Do we know *anything*?"

"Not unless you found out something spectacularly interesting on the run up here. Or when you disappeared..."

"Oh!"

"Yes?"

"No," there was a sound of more clinking teacups. "Burned myself." He paused. "I did find...well, something. I was going to wait until I could tell Beckett, too..." He cleared his throat. "So, I was setting up the cordon around Zindel's home..."

"Like you were ordered to."

Valentine groaned. "Fine. Right. Like I was *ordered* to. And after about an hour, I see this coach pull up. The driver looks at the house, looks at the cordon, he seems like he's con-fused. Then he goes real pale, and he turns the coach around and drives off. So, naturally, I followed him."

"You followed him? Valentine, the cordon was *important*. Public Safety took the bodies..."

"He was acting suspicious!"

"That's—" Skinner got a hold of herself. "Never mind. What happened?"

"Well, I recognized the livery stamp on the coach. Tanner's, it's called. We used to send them after my brother when he'd been out debauching himself, so as not to sully the name and that..."

"Valentine. Focus."

"So, I knew where the livery stable was. I took the auto-carriage there and parked it in an alley. Then I put on my disguise." She could practically hear him grinning. "I remembered what Beckett said, about my shoes being too clean, so I found...well, there was this filthy gutter. I mean, really filthy. There was all this black sludge, you know? I don't even know what it was. And I just covered myself in it. Head to foot. I took special care on the shoes."

"Is that why you smell like piss?"

"Probably. So, I'm all covered in filth, I've got my scrave tobacco—that's this custom tobacco I had made. They...I don't know how they do it, something with flux and gametes, or something, they make the tobacco bright green and luminescent, so it lights up your spit like you've got the scrave. There I am, all covered in filth, spitting my green spit, and I follow this man. I think that he was supposed to meet Zindel at the house. Any-way, he doesn't have any more jobs. Just errands, and things. Buying groceries, right?"

"That's it? You left your post and covered yourself in filth so you could follow a coachman while he went to the grocer?"

"No! I followed him when he went into the Arcadium. He was dropping something off at Printer's Close. When he came out of Backstairs, there was somebody waiting for him. In the street. I thought it was a man, at first. He looks like he's about to do something. Then...*bang*!"

"He shot the coachman."

"No, right, that's what I thought. No, someone *else* shoots the coachman. Coachman falls to the ground, and this man in the street, he turns and *runs up the wall* of a house. I don't know what's going on. I pull out my guns, tell everyone to stay still, and someone from the house takes a potshot at me from the window. Misses. But the man from the street...I'm thinking he's a reanimate, at this point, crashes through the window. I think...I don't know what he was going to do. I head around the back, I think maybe he's going to come out the other side, and I see him dropping down into the Arcadium.

"So, I followed."

Skinner almost choked on her tea. "Naturally. There's a man with a gun—you don't know where he is—and a reanimate that can run up walls. What does Valentine Vie-Gorgon do? He runs after them into the darkest, foggiest place he can find. It makes perfect sense."

"Oh, all right. It was stupid. But listen. I chase the Reanimate, I keep yelling at him to stop. Nothing. He ducks into this factory...I don't know what kind of factory. There were these plaster heads everywhere. The Reanimate is doing some-thing, I yell at it again, it doesn't listen. So, I shoot. A lot. Nothing."

"You missed."

"Oh, no. I hit him. Hips, shoulders, base of the spine, just like Beckett says. *Nothing*. And I don't mean it didn't go down. It didn't even flinch. Like I was shooting air. I get to thinking, 'Maybe this isn't a Reanimate.' Anyway, I can't hurt it with bullets, so I run. I'm not sure if it chased me, I wasn't thinking about it. I just ran towards the river, and hid in an open sewer until the sun came up. Then I went back."

"You went back? Valentine..."

"I know, I know! But I had to see what it was doing in the factory. There was a man there, I don't know who he was, but he had a rifle. I figure he was the one that took the shot at me. And his whole neck and jaw are just one big, purple bruise, and his eyes are all bugged out. There's blood coming out of his mouth, right, but get this: ectoplasm. Sticky little strands of it, dribbling all over the ground." Valentine lowered his voice to a dramatic whisper. "The thing had...somehow...ripped the life out of him."

"What about the coachman?"

"Gendarmes had found the body by the time I got back to it. I was in less of a hurry; I knew how he died."

Skinner was silent for a long moment. What Valentine had done had been, on many, many levels, astonishingly stupid. Or at least, it would have been astonishingly stupid if it had been someone other than Valentine, whose ridiculously irrational decisions came so regularly that they'd lost all power to astonish. On the other hand, what he said was...well, it was something. "What do you think it was?"

"I don't know. Not human, definitely. And not a Re-animate."

"Could it have been khadavri?"

"I don't think so. Not a lich. Maybe one of the Princes. But they...they drink *blood*, don't they? Or something? They don't suck the life out of people."

Actually, popular wisdom had it that the Dragon Princes had to *bathe* in hundreds of gallons of blood to preserve their monstrous existence. It was probably not worth running down a lone gunman. "You think this is connected to Zindel."

"It's a weird coincidence if it's not. Man gets murdered, the next day his coachman gets murdered by a sniper, who is then murdered by some kind of a monster. Also, I was thinking. The wounds from the sharpsies...on Zindel's family? All over the throat and jaw? That's right where this rifleman had his bruises." Valentine sighed, and Skinner heard the creak of the chair as he leaned back in it. "I really wish Beckett were here."

Skinner nodded her quiet assent, and sipped at her tea.

The raids in Red Lanes had petered out by mid-day, when Valentine found himself running for his life in Old Bank. In fact, the men that had been conscripted to chase him had been serving double-duty: both as pressmen for the War Powers Ministry, and in the gendarmerie in the New Bank district. They had stumbled into Wyndham-Vie's way while on their way back to their home turf from the shipyards. When they failed to persuade the guards at Raithower House that their borrowed authority gave them the right to enter and arrest Valentine, the gendarmes decided to knock off back to New Bank.

They had forgotten about, or else were unconcerned by, the fact that they were still wearing the gear that they used for pressganging. This proved to be a most unfortunate oversight on the part of the gendarmes-cum-pressmen. The ten men, one on horseback, slouched down the hills in Old Bank until they came to Hightower Square.

The edifices on Hightower Square had been in the Crabtree-Daior family for over a hundred years, and were a securely-held beachhead that the Family had long been attempting to use to break into the Vie-Gorgon-controlled New Bank district. However, as part of a piece of legislation served through the Committee for Public Safety, the Wyndham-Vies had managed to get the rights to supplant the intricately-carved floral downspouts characteristic of Crabtree-Daior design with the leering gargoyles that the Wyndham-Vies themselves favored. They had been replacing a great deal of stonework over the last few weeks, and had hired twenty sharpsie day-laborers to do it.

Word of the pressgangs had preceded Valentine's pursuers as they stumbled into Hightower Square. The sharpsie workers panicked when they saw the boiled breastplates and greenglass goggles. The sharpsies, frightened, moderately organized, and armed with hammers, chisels, and chunks of stone, determined that they would not be sent to Gorcia that day.

The ten men thought to put up a fight, but they were exhausted and outnumbered. They didn't stand a chance. The sharpsie workers pelted them with rocks first, knocking the horseman from his mount — the animal ran off, back towards Old Bank. One of the sharpsies, an angry young male, leapt in and lodged a chisel in one man's eye. A second sharpsie knocked a gendarme to the ground, then pulverized his knee with a hammer.

They beat the men to death, then bit off limbs, heads, and genitals, and scattered the bloody pieces throughout the square, in an orgy of unleashed rage at their oppressors. Hightower Square looked like someone had gone at it with buckets of red paint. Women and children screamed. One cool-headed old gentleman thought to call for the gendarmerie, all unaware that the ten men dressed like pressgangers were the only gendarmes on duty. By the time additional authorities had shown up, the sharpsie laborers were gone.

The broadsheets all had their own sensational headlines for the incident. "Massacre at Hightower!" "Gendarmes Murdered!" But the *Observer* took in the most readers with a single word: "War."

Eighteen: Psychestorm

Wolfgang Rowan-Czarnecki had once been a great statesman. He'd served in Parliament for twenty years, and had served two memorable terms as Minister of the Exchequer. Never quite as charismatic as his brother Montgomery, who'd become Trowth's youngest and most celebrated general, Wolfgang had been the quiet, competent, authoritative man that Trowth could turn to in a time of crisis. It had been Wolfgang Rowan-Czarnecki that had stabilized the Empire's economy when the war with the ettercap threatened to bankrupt it. It had been Wolfgang that stood against the Corsay Trading Company when the financial giant had tried to wrest political control of the nation. The erstwhile Minister of the Exchequer was never going to have seen his face printed on the money, but he had done well for his country in his own intelligent, patriotic way. Ministers of the Exchequer were never remembered by anyone but historians, but if a historian that specialized in Not Especially Glamorous But Still Very Important Government Positions ever decided to compile a list of the finest Ministers of the Exchequer that Trowth had ever seen, Wolfgang Rowan-Czarnecki would have definitely been on his way to the top.

Then, his brother had been killed. This was during the second Riehl Valley Action: Montgomery Rowan-Czarnecki had moved into the valley with his staff, thinking that the occupying ettercap had been eliminated. It had been a trap. Three thousand men had been killed trying to evacuate the command staff, and for nothing. The ettercap had sealed the valley. Suicide troops detonated their poison-sun weapons. Ironically, it had been the marines left behind to secure the retreat that managed to survive.

The life had drained out of Wolfgang after he'd lost his brother. He became listless, uninterested in politics, leaving important decisions to Vice-Ministers and Adjuncts. He no longer challenged the party leaders when they proposed ill-considered plans. Wolfgang Rowan-

Czarnecki had become completely disaffected with the Empire, his primary political attitude be-came one of passionate unconcern.

The Emperor, concerned still about showing favor to the Rowan-Czarneckis, who controlled the production and distribution of that supremely useful panacea called ichor, offered Wolfgang the position of Director of the Royal Academy of Sciences. The position would serve to remove Wolfgang from any position of real influence, without actually removing him from public life.

At the Royal Academy of Sciences, Wolfgang Rowan-Czarnecki could be allowed to slowly die a quiet death, uninvolved in any decisions where his apathy might directly harm the Empire.

He sat at his desk, waiting for his guest, and stared up at the ceiling. He felt that he spent more and more time lately with nothing to do but wait. He'd been taking more naps, just letting the quiet weight of his loneliness and loss bear him down into sleep. It gave him something to do while he waited for the next meal. Or visitor.

Wolfgang took the small brass device on his desk and wound the key. A low, faint humming came from the flux membrane in its center. To his ears, and any ordinary, human ears, the sound was nothing more than that. If, on the other hand, someone attempted to spy by clairaudient means, they would find their hearing scrambled: words all lost in a cascade of reverberating echoes. The device had been the invention of a bored clockmaker who'd thought of it as a clever practical joke to play on knockers.

There was a faint rap at the door, and Wolfgang's secretary put his head in. "Sir…"

Wolfgang nodded. "Send him in."

The secretary nodded. Moments later, Edgar Wyndham-Vie swaggered into the room, slammed the door shut, and flopped into a seat opposite Wolfgang's desk. He had not waited for an invitation. Wolfgang was willing to chalk that up to the impetuosity of youth. "Well?"

Wyndham-Vie shrugged. "Stitch got Beckett out. There was nothing I could do. But he's out bad…" the young man tapped a finger on his temple. "…delirious. I don't think he'll be investigating anything for a while."

The older man grunted. "And?"

"And nothing. Beckett's the only danger. His man is incompetent. I've sent a few gendarmes out to take him in."

Wolfgang groaned and rubbed his eyes. "You haven't got the authority to keep arresting people, Edgar."

"I had to. He was going after the log at Corimander Street."

There was a long silence, then, and Edgar began to fidget nervously.

"Why was he at Corimander Street?"

Edgar shrugged, but he still seemed nervous. "I don't know. I assume...Beckett must have said something to him. He...spoke to him. In the cell for a few minutes. I thought Beckett was delirious, but..." Wyndham-Vie tapped his fingers on his knee. "Maybe he told him the address. It doesn't matter. The log wasn't there. Robbie didn't say anything. There's nothing to connect you..." he trailed off.

Wolfgang had stood, and for a moment, the shadow of his fire-eyed brother was visible in the old man's paunchy face. "They are too close to this. The Coroners have been practically breathing down our necks..." he seized Edgar by the front of his shirt. "Do you understand that if we're exposed, we could all hang? That's if Beckett doesn't execute us on the spot. Do you understand that?"

Trying vainly to slither out of Wolfgang's grasp, Edgar replied, "I do. I understand. And I'm in this as deep as you are, so don't think I'm not trying to keep it all under wraps. And it *is* under wraps. The gendarmes will pick up Valentine for interfering with a Committee Investigation. Beckett's out of his mind on fang..." Wolfgang let the young man go, straightened his own coat, and went over to his window. There was a psychestorm brewing above the forest of stone towers and bronze chimney pots; verdant green lightning played across dark, gray-green clouds that grew black as the hidden sun set. Already, people were closing up their doors and windows as tight as they could, to protect themselves from the dementia-inducing winds.

Edgar watched the old man, bitterness roiling in the back of his throat. It's not like he didn't know the danger they were in. The danger that they were *all* in, and that Wolfgang Rowan-Czarnecki was responsible for. The Wyndham-Vies, Edgar spat to himself, had been serving the Empire for decades before Wolfgang's upstart family had risen to prominence. Hadn't it been Harcourt Wyndham that had advised Owen I Gorgon? Hadn't it been Dikaios Vie that had served Agon Diethes before the Second Reconciliation? Edgar Wyndham-Vie had half a mind to tell the old fart off once and for all, let him know where the real power in this situation lay.

Instead, he said, "What about the pilot?"

Wolfgang shook his head. "Lightman. It'll go after Lightman, next. Then...then everyone it knows will be dead." *Just another bit of nastiness crawling around the city.*

"You're not going out," Valentine insisted. "The storm's almost started. You wouldn't get farther than Red Lanes."

"There's enough copper in the coach..." Skinner insisted.

"To protect you, yes. And Harry? Going to give him a copper top-hat, or something?"

Skinner snorted and sulked in her chair while Karine and Valentine bustled about, closing the copper shields over doors and windows. The psychestorm had essentially trapped her at Raithower House for the entire night. *At least there are beds upstairs.* Though Mr. Stitch did not require sleep, he had at least been thoughtful enough to provide a row of narrow, uncomfortable cots for his employees in the event of emergency.

The psychestorms usually blew in out of the mountains far to the north, from the area around the Castle If. They picked up volatile, sublimated flux from the clouds that the great Trowth mining-engines threw up, and then proceeded to rain it all back down on the city. The storms had been extremely dangerous, at first, but the Committee for Public Safety had been instrumental in setting up their "Program of Preparedness" to help citizenry cope with the mind-poisoning weather.

The storm would roll over the city in a few hours, and then crash to pieces on the enormous sea-wall around the harbor. In the meantime, anyone caught out in the street could be swept up in dangerous whorls of synaesthesia or delirium tremens. In wealthy neighborhoods, like the Banks or North Ferry, heavy copper shutters that had been corroded green with time and salt were fixed over doors and windows. In poorer neighborhoods, people gathered to wait out the storm in pubs that often had better shielding. During a psychestorm, even the poor and de-generate were admitted, if reluctantly, behind the copper barriers. The only poor souls refused entry were the dangerously contagious scravers, who were revealed by their coughing and their virulent green mucous.

The Brothers of the Mad Wind, who believed that the psychestorms were the purest reverberations of the Word, would choose one among their number to stand out in the streets in Fishtown. They prayed that the wind would deliver divine secrets; usually, it just delivered another madman.

In places like Mudside and Bluewater, sharpsies and indige would huddle under large sheets of copper that the Committee had been passing out for years. It was a compromise between the need to protect even the undesirables from the psychestorms — because a lunatic sharpsie was even more of a threat to public safety than a sane one — and the need to not spend very much money. The sheets worked: the sharpsies had built large, makeshift shelters out of theirs, the indige had lined their roofs. As a general rule, they were far less susceptible to the dangers of the psychestorm than humans or sharpsies.

In Lantern Slope, where the Indige Shipping Concern flew in the limited amounts of phlogiston while the major pipe-lines were disrupted by the ettercap war, indige and trolljrmen stevedores reigned in the huge, copper-hulled airships. The levitite at the cores of the airships could not be deactivated, instead slowly decaying over time, so the ships had to be brought to ground by huge iron chains attached to complex block-and-tackle systems. Somewhere in the shimmering, indigo-stone homes of the few wealthy indigea in the city, the headmen of the Shipping Concern gnashed their teeth and clenched their fists as they suffered the unavoidable delay in their business.

In South End, Philip Crowe sat in his bedroom, with the copper shutters on his windows open just a crack. He could see flashes of green from the flickering lightning spill onto the floor, and thunder rumbled. The wind began to pick up, screaming, bringing the sound of ruptured senses with it. Philip sat patiently, and waited for the madness to come to him.

When Valentine and Karine had finished with the windows, Valentine returned to his chair. Thunder boomed out-side, and echoed strangely in Skinner's thoughts.

"Do you want to play a game, or something? Do you...I mean, can you play chess, or anything like that?"

The thunder was followed by a strange echo in her thoughts. "Not now, Valentine. I'm not in the mood." The thunder echoed strangely.

"We could play The Minister's Cat, or something."

"No." Strangely. "I need to go upstairs." The upstairs room that Stitch had put the cots in didn't have any windows, and there was copper piping in the walls. It should be better shielded from the psychic reverberations of the storm.

"Do you need help...?"

"No." Skinner got to her feet and went upstairs, using her knocks to find her way.

Because Raithower House had first been the home of one of the wealthiest families in Trowth, its construction was exceptionally grand. It featured the traditional Vie-Gorgon design: everything was tall and narrow. Tall, narrow windows. Tall, narrow doors. High ceilings, narrow halls. In an effort to both create a sense of space and to give the viewer a sense of being in the middle of a forest of (tall, narrow) columns, many of the walls were open arches.

The tendency of the Vie-Gorgons to fill large rooms with tall pillars made navigating by way of telerhythmia tricky; Skinner had to sweep the knocks out in wide arcs in front of her, and listen carefully to screen out the double-echoes. Still, she knew her way around the building, and eventually succeeded in finding the small sleeping chamber that Stitch had set aside for emergencies.

Green lightning flashed, and Skinner could see it behind her eyes. It was common knowledge that knockers, at least the ones strong enough to be employed by the Coroners, were blind, but this was only partially true. In fact, Skinner's eyes were extraordinarily sensitive: seeing with the unbearable clarity of her eyes was actually excruciatingly painful. She, like most knockers, wore the band of silver over her eyes to make sure that her vision was completely eclipsed.

It didn't help during the psychestorms. Despite the silver plate and the copper shielding in the walls and roof of the building, the green lightning was always visible. She could be a hundred miles underground, and still see those eerie pulses of green. More thunder rumbled, but the mental echo that accompanied it was mercifully faint.

The wind began to pick up, and then the clouds broke. Huge globs of snow fell in the screaming winds; Skinner could hear them hitting the copper-sheathed roof, despite the fact that it was another storey over her head. The sound of fat snowflakes on the copper roof stabbed delicately at her inner-ear, a sharp violent sound that she could never hope to explain to the ordinary-of-hearing.

She made her way to a cot and sat down on the edge. It creaked and groaned, and threatened to collapse beneath her weight, but held firm. Skinner sighed and set her cane down next to her. She was beginning to regret leaving Valentine downstairs. His conversation might be inane, but at least it was better than sitting quietly by herself while the storm moaned around her, buffeting her throbbing head.

Lightning flashed again, and in the psychic afterimage in her mind, Skinner could see the city, its merlons and spires and chimney-pots black silhouettes limned with dull green. The snow fell in a horizontal wave of black spots. The image was gone almost immediately, but the thought of it lingered in her mind, a peculiar aspect of the psychestorm. Skinner shivered, and wished she had some music to listen to.

Beckett has a phonograph in his office, she thought briefly, then discarded the idea. She'd have to leave the room then, and her sensitivity to the strange effects of the psychestorm would make that unpleasant. *He probably only has old Corimander symphonies anyway.* Like most of the Trowthi, Skinner recognized Edmund Corimander as the greatest Trowthi composer in history, and she'd heard *The Siege of Canth* enough times that she knew the movements by heart, but that was about as far as her interest in the epic, brassy sounds of Corimander's orchestra went.

Another flare of lightning threw the whole city into stark relief again. It was followed swiftly by a sharp clap of thunder whose echo penetrated the copper in the walls. *There had been a man on the roof,* she thought, climbing over a forest of small bronze chimneys, when the thunder echoed. *He'd been on the roof next door.* The sound of the thunder rolled in her mind still. The man had been climbing through the storm....

"Valentine!" There was no response. Skinner tried to project her clairaudience outward, but recoiled as soon as she got past the door. The sound of the maddening snow and wind of the psychestorm had lashed out at her, for a brief instant trans-forming all the sounds into smells. There was a second of disorientation as she pulled her mind back, reeling with the synaesthasia, listening to the acrid, bitter sound of the storm. "Valentine!" She called out again.

Another flash of lightning and a deafening thunderclap, and she turned her head straight up and could see the man crawling across the roof now, while the thunder slammed against the inside of her ears. He was slithering down the eaves of Raithower House, head-first. The thunder rang insistently in her ears, the thought of it demanding her full attention.

"Nnf," Skinner muttered, as she tried to get to her feet. Her thoughts were distorted, her hearing still disrupted by the synaesthasia from the storm. She sent out a wave of white-sound knocks, which came back all manner of strange red and gold colors, and the man, she'd seen a man on the roof. "Valentine!" She screamed at the top of her lungs, certain now that the man was making his way towards an upper story window.

She could not risk projecting her clairaudience out to listen, but she was certain she could hear the faint scratching of fingernails against the green-copper shutters. The creaking sound of hinges as he threw them open, the shattering of glass as he crawled inside...

"Skinner?" Valentine's voice drifted towards her from the hall, and she could hear his footsteps now, roughly textured like the sound of burlap. The synaesthasia cleared, and the sounds were sounds again, as Valentine entered. "Skinner? What's wrong?"

"There's...there's someone on the roof. Trying to get in." Skinner heard Valentine draw his pistol.

"Where?"

"Third storey. I think, second window in from the right."

"All right. I will be *right back.*" His footsteps rang on the stone floor.

I'm blind, I'm not a child. I'll be fine. As a gesture of goodwill, Skinner chose not to snap her acid remarks after the young coroner. She took a deep breath, and tried to project her clairaudience again.

The disorientation was immediate as the information that reached her ears was scrambled, but not unbearable. She tracked her hearing up to the third floor, into a large room on the east side. Her telerhythmia scattered a wave of white-hot knocks, and the shiny, acrid-colored echoes returned. They gave her a picture of a room only a little larger than the one she was in, with a few cabinets, a desk, and a chair.

Valentine's sharp-edged footsteps clattered into range. The wind of the storm eased for a moment, and Skinner's hearing began to return to normal. "Skinner? Can you hear me?"

She rapped twice on the floor by his feet.

"I don't see anything here, Skinner. Is this the right room?" The wind blew hard again, making his voice red and blue. The clairaudience shifted suddenly, as though it had been dislodged by the heavy wind, and shook her mind about, threatening to cast the sense out into the street.

She screwed up her face and tried to concentrate, keeping her clairaudience under control. She rapped twice again. *Yes, that's the right room.*

The icy sound of Valentine lighting a match actually made her chilly. She threw another wave of knocks out against the windows. They burned when they came back, their echoes painful in her ears, but the copper shutters were still closed.

Hallucination, Skinner told herself. It's the storm, it's screwing all of my senses up.

"Skinner, I'm going to open a shutter."

Three raps. *No.* It was hard enough to keep her mind together behind the copper shutters. If Valentine opened one…

"I need to see if someone's outside."

Three raps again. *No.*

"I think there's someone there." *No.* "Can…can you not hear that sound?"

Skinner paused, and fear fluttered in her stomach. Instinctively, she responded with the complex double-rap she used to communicate with Beckett. *What sound?*

"I don't understand that, Skinner. There's a kind of scraping sound, by the window." *No.* "You don't hear it?" *No.*

Gently, Skinner pushed her hearing towards the copper shutters. The storm set up a kind of turbulence that kept pushing her thoughts around, robbing her of focus and clarity. She bit her lip and concentrated.

There. A faint green sound, that glistened in her mind. Now that she'd found it, she didn't seem to be able to tune it out. It slithered around all the other sounds in the room, moving beneath and behind them, echoing weirdly on the walls.

"Skinner, I need…shit. Shit, the window, the lock's opening." She heard him cock the revolver. "The lock…the lock on the window…"

Lightning and thunder split the air, illuminating the city with eerie green light and sending Skinner's clairaudience spinning away from the window. She could briefly make out Valentine in silhouette, staggering back from the shutters, and the shape of a man standing on the windowsill, shutters swinging behind him.

Exposure to the storm had twisted her hearing beyond recognition, the sounds from the room reached her distorted by whirling Doppler effects and synaesthetic scrambling. Was the man in the window screaming a black, oily scream? The strange echo of the thunder tried to blot her thoughts out. Were rattling heavy hard sounds thunder, gunshots, thunder...? *Why can't...* the thunder strangely struck her ears...*why can't I think...*green light and a strange man standing before a city beneath a storm of madness, and that awful thunder pounding at the inside of her mind...

"Skinner?" Valentine's voice was quiet and close. A brief flicker of red accompanied it, and was gone.

"What..." she gasped. She was lying on her back on the cot, and immediately bolted upright. "The man, we've got...he's trying to get in..."

Valentine's hands were firm on her shoulders. "He's gone. It's all right, he's gone."

"What...?"

"You fainted, Skinner. You've been unconscious for an hour."

"Fainted...what happened? The man?"

"He...it. I think it...I shot it, Skinner. Four times. It didn't even notice. Like I was shooting smoke. I think it would have killed me if..."

"What? Damn it, Valentine, what happened?"

"The psychestorm. It was struck by lightning. I saw it fall three stories to the courtyard, and then run off towards New Bank."

Skinner shook her head and began to relax. She began shivering, suddenly, and nausea welled up inside of her. "I... what was..." The shivering got worse, as her body finally found the time to be frightened. She felt Valentine's arms wrap around her, and she wanted to smack him. But they were warm and comforting, so she let him get away with it. He was shivering, too.

Nineteen: The Hospital

Skinner was in his dream again, and he could see the white, smooth curve of her hip. He reached out to touch her skin with invisible fingertips, but they weren't transparent; they were missing, and the fades crept along his fingers as he moved so that his hands were disappearing as they approached her body and his arm sank away into nothing up to his elbow at her hip...

Beckett awoke, to find himself surrounded by white. He was in a white bed, with white curtains, and, for some reason, wearing white pajamas. The pain was gone from his limbs, and the cotton that the veneine packed around his head was absent. He got to his feet, and pulled the curtains aside.

Beyond the white curtains, Beckett saw row after row of white-curtained beds. He heard a voice: a low, muttering voice growled behind the white. Beckett approached, and he could begin to make out words. Another few steps, and he could clearly hear a strange glossolalia whispered in a harsh, tormented tone, obscured by the white curtains which were stirred by a gentle, hidden breeze.

The man said, "...and if I walked by icy walls of warring wisdom, cracked by the simple discipline of psychic strangeness, all the stone attractors of that ancient emblem of the world, that screaming tower of melted bronze..."

Beckett snatched the curtain away, to see the man whose voice he heard.

There was a terrifying moment of disorientation when Beckett awoke again, as his mind tried to identify his surroundings: not his home, not his cot at the office, not the cell he'd been locked in, where was he? He tried to move his arms, but found he could not, and a kind of strangled panic pushed past the haze of waking. He desperately tried to move, to do some-thing, to find a weapon that he could use, even to lift his arms, to turn his head, but his muscles weren't responding.

After a moment, his brain accepted the fact that he was in a new place and began, in the meticulous fashion of which Beckett's mind was eminently capable, to catalogue the details.

There were not many. He was undressed, on a small bed with clean sheets. By his head was a wall with large, square stones and dirty white mortar. At three sides of his bed hung white muslin curtains. Beckett felt very, very heavy, and the pain of his illness had returned. Mercifully, the veneine buzzed warmly in his mind, and kept the sharp, shattered-glass aches in his joints far away.

Slowly, as the last shreds of disorientation were banished, Beckett found that he could move. He began by clenching his hands and fingers, which cracked loudly in the silence, then by flexing his elbows and knees, which also creaked and cracked. There was a stabbing pain in his right knee, but it was brief and vanished quickly.

Beckett's body shook as he climbed out of bed. He recognized the fatigue in his stomach muscles as being the product of extensive vomiting, and tried to remember when he'd engaged in something like that. Withdrawal had riddled recent memories with holes, but given that, Beckett supposed it fairly likely that he'd been sick repeatedly. The quivering in his arms and legs was familiar, and usually meant he hadn't had enough to eat.

He managed to find clean clothes — not his — folded up under his bed: a white shirt and a grey suit. Beckett dressed and threw the white curtain aside. He found himself surrounded by beds similarly partitioned to his own, an eerie reflection of his dream. Judging by the silence, the beds were either empty or filled with sleeping men or women. There was a quality, an emptiness, to the silence, though, that suggested the former.

A sound sprang suddenly in the quiet: a low, faint muttering, emanating from one of the beds. Warily, with an un-pleasantly strong sense of déjà vu, Beckett approached the mumbling. He had a sudden, irrational fear of being trapped for-ever in an infinite cycle of white curtains, muttering voices, and sudden jolts into wakefulness.

Beckett pulled the curtain aside, and saw a man sitting on a low, iron-framed bed, his knees pulled up to his chest. The man had a haggard face, with wide, bloodshot eyes. His hair was graying, and some great terror had etched its lines into his face so that fear was stamped perpetually on his brow.

The man was speaking. "...did the sun rise over cracked peaks and great glass mountains, far away on the edge of the moon, where black basalt cities crawl slowly in the dark, and red teeth clutch wearily at hollow-eyed men..."

"You've seen them?" Beckett asked. His voice was hushed; awe had pressed it to a whisper. "The cities on the moon?"

The man's strange verbal emission halted. He turned his terrible, red, staring eyes on Beckett, and said nothing.

"Tell me. Tell me if you've seen them." Beckett lunged forward and grabbed the man by his shirt. "The cities on the moon, the towers of brass," he screamed, "You've seen them, haven't you? Tell me!"

The man worked his jaw, and Beckett could see that his tongue was black. "Are my eyes open?" The man asked. "Is this awake, to see the other side of eyes and dreams, where the world is pulled away by the wild whirling weary ways of wretched infamy..."

Beckett felt a heavy hand on his shoulder, and heard a voice that was impossibly deep, a bass rumble that made his bones shiver. "Dream poisoning."

The coroner turned, and came to face a great trolljrman, his thin lips curled back over tombstone teeth, black eyes glittering dispassionately. "He is sick," the trolljrman went on, in that stomach-churning *basso*. He spoke without moving his lips; the trolljrmen used a complex web of membranes in their throats to mimic human sounds. "He suffers from dream poisoning. Oneiristry."

Oneiristry was a science forbidden by the Church Royal, and under other circumstances Beckett would have questioned the sick man's exposure to it. Instead, he found himself preoccupied with what the man was saying. "He told me about towers," Beckett said. "There's something familiar about it."

The trolljrman shook its great, reptilian head. Its feathered crest rose and sank in a gesture of dismissiveness. "There is no sense," it rumbled. "He speaks words he knows, over and over, without reason."

Because it had no lips, the trolljr had to make "r" sounds with its tongue. The word came out "uhdeason."

"I had a dream about him," Beckett said. "Just now. I dreamt I heard him speaking."

The trolljrman nodded. "His dreams," this sounded like "duhdeams." The trolljrman gently but firmly guided Beckett away from the bed and into the room. "His dreams are wounded. Bleeding. We must keep him away from others. But your..." The trolljrman hesitated, and rumbled something in its deep, nearly-subsonic language. "Clutch-father? War-father? Captain." It seemed satisfied with this word choice. "Your captain wanted you somewhere private."

That must have been Mr. Stitch. Beckett tried desperately to remember what chain of events had brought him here, but it was all just black. The previous...hours? Days? "How long have I been here?"

"You have slept for twelve hours."

That wasn't especially long, but Beckett did not relish the idea that he was losing time on his investigation. Flashes of the last day bloomed from the dark. Valentine and Skinner were going to go to the address in Old Bank. Had they found any-thing? And what was Stitch up to? "I have to go. I have to get to Raithower House. Where am I anyway? What is this place?"

"Ghahat Dhu Hospice. We are in North Ferry, but I cannot let you leave."

Ghahat Dhu was a tolljr brood-mother, and known throughout the city as a surpassing surgeon, among a species whose capacity for surgery was held to be miraculous. "I'm fine, really." Beckett's knees wobbled dangerously. "I just need something to eat. I'm in the middle of an investigation, I have to go."

"No," the trolljrman thundered. "It is dangerous—"

"—just give me my gun—"

"There is a psychestorm." The trolljrman showed Beckett out of the dream-sick man's room, and into a small parlour. Its walls had tall windows cut in them that were now covered with burnished copper shutters, and it was furnished with a few stuffed chairs and a small table on which rested a covered dish. A sweet, spicy smell wafted to Beckett's nose, and his stomach growled. He was suddenly conscious of how very hungry he was.

The veneine addict walks a fine line through his sensorium. Too much of the drug shrouds the mind and eyes and skin with thick cotton. It's warm and it mutes the pain, but it divorces the man from himself and the world, eventually leading the mind away to that strange, *other* destination that lurked at the extremity of fang. Less veneine enables a man to feel, to keep his mind sharp, to stay in touch with the world, but it also leaves him vulnerable to the constant, intolerable anguish of his life.

This was the line that Beckett vacillated across as he sat down to his meal. There was just enough veneine to keep his joints from aching, but not quite enough to keep him divorced from himself. The terrible enormity of what he faced, of a murder he couldn't solve, a city gutted of its youth and industry, racial tensions that were threatening to explode, of the rest of his life—a few long years gradually being eaten away by his disease—settled on his shoulders like a mountain. The soft tissue around his eyes shriveled and his breath caught. It was too much. He wanted to sit, to lie down, to weep, to tear his ravaged face from his skull. It was too much.

Beckett imagined just staying at the hospice. He could stay there and find a bed among the other sufferers of the fades—mostly children and young men and women who'd spent too long in the workhouses refining flux—their faces hideous and patched with blood and gristle and bone looking out from the inside, their skins turning transparent even as the broken-glass pain of the sickness ate away their organs from within. They would give him veneine and he would sleep a blissful sleep, troubled only by occasional glimpses of Cross the Water.

Forty years, he thought. *Forty years of service.* No one could say he didn't deserve it. No one could say that Elijah Beckett had been anything other than absolutely dedicated to the Crown, though he'd never been given a medal, never seen any reward but the simple satisfaction of having a job and doing it well. He had earned the right to spend his last remaining years (how many? Two? Three?) in a quiet, narcotic stupor. If three decades of indefatigable determination didn't bestow upon a man the right to give up, then what did? How much more could the Crown expect from him?

Beckett's breath came in ragged gasps and tears, he realized, were streaming from his eyes as he collapsed into the chair. Hours without a drop of fang had left him vulnerable, and now the utter hopelessness, the meaninglessness of his time of service had forced its way into his mind. Despair, now a house-breaker, burgled him of the last bit of energy that had kept him on his feet.

Done. This was the only thought left behind. *Done,* and an image of himself, warm and safe and full of drugs, gently letting go of those last few ties that kept him connected to his city. Like the corona of a dying star, all that was left of Beckett boiled away, a brief flare, then nothing but cold, dark iron.

This iron was the essential core of Beckett's being: hard, brittle, unyielding. As the years had passed by, the old coroner had found himself giving up more and more of all of the peculiar idiosyncrasies that delineate a man who lives a life from a man who simply has one. Again and again, in the face of terrible threats to his homeland, it had been only Beckett's unflagging tenacity that stood between life and death. Even as he realized he didn't believe in heresy, even as he came to learn that his efforts mattered little to the Empire, he remained tenacious.

So it was out of the habit of personality more than any-thing else that Beckett clamped down on his despair. He gritted his teeth and took a deep breath, and pushed it all away. *No.* He clenched and unclenched his fists. *No.* He closed his eyes and bit his tongue. *No. There's work to do.* With an act of will so long habitual that its extraordinary power was forgotten, an act that Beckett had become so accustomed to that he had no real inkling of the strength it took, or what it cost him, the old coroner willfully seized upon his despondency and cast it out from his mind.

He looked up at the trolljrman, who had remained an expressionless spectator to Beckett's existential crisis. "Do you have paper? A pen?"

The trolljrman flicked its crest in a gesture of assent, and then glided ponderously out of the room. Beckett's stomach growled, more insistently this time, and so he regarded the covered dish on the table before him. Beneath the cover he found a game hen, cooked in the fashion of Corsay mudlark; it was stuffed with fruit and pepper.

Beckett took the small knife and fork provided for him, and set about devouring his food with a less miraculous but no less vital act of will; in what would surely be an insult to the meal's cook, Beckett did not at all notice the subtle interplay between mango, Corsay *djang* fruit, and white pepper.

TWENTY: CHARTERHOUSE'S DILEMMA

While the psychestorm raged across Trowth, Alan Charterhouse sat in his room, on his bed, shuddering while his mind slowed back down to normal speed, after being virtually consumed with the obsessions that mathematics represented to him. It was not an altogether uncommon phenomenon that, as he worked, the essential details, the basic needs of daily life, should fall out of his perceptions until every spark of delicately functioning neurological machinery was devoted solely to theory.

There was a bowl of soup sitting on his nightstand. It was cold, but as Alan looked at it, he realized he was so hungry that he didn't care. He slurped it down, and considered what he'd found. He was, firstly, sure that he'd inadvertently invented a new kind of dimensional analysis—he'd had to in order to effectively get his head around a tricky couple of equations that he'd seen in Zindel's notes. He was secondly sure, beyond the barest shadow of the tiniest doubt, that he was dealing with heretical science. He'd been deep into discovering precise mathematical rules for leaving the four walls of nature and leaving the language of the Word behind. It was unquestionably wrong, it was dangerous, it was blasphemous. The horror, formerly displaced by the power of his obsessive intellect, was now beginning to seep in.

Alan Charterhouse had, with Herman Zindel's help, found the cracks in the edges of the world, and they terrified him. There was a whole, second universe, separated from his own by no more than the breadth of an atom, yet so far away it might as well be on the other side of the moon. And the rules that this second universe followed...Alan wasn't even sure there *were* any rules to it. It could simply be a place of utter, squalid chaos, where nothing like light, matter, or life could survive.

Worse than all of this was the third thing that he had discovered about Herman Zindel's equations. They were a schematic, he was sure of it now, for a theoretical translation engine that was manifestly different from the *Excelsior*'s. But there was something else, something that had been bothering him since he'd first glimpsed the formulae in Zindel's house.

Thunder rumbled outside and echoed in his mind, echoed. The Charterhouse home had good, solid copper shutters and copper insulation in the walls, but still, the eerie insanity of the psychestorm tended to seep in, thunder echoing strangely. Alan Charterhouse rubbed his eyes. His heart fluttered, and he felt his breath catch in his throat.

I have to tell them, he thought. The consequences, though, of revealing what he knew, were deadly. *I can't help it. It's not my fault, I can't just stop thinking about it.* Alan was getting hysterical, and tried to keep himself calm. If he told the Coroners about what he knew, they'd execute him, without question. He already knew more about Aetheric Geometry than anyone but Wolfram himself, and that made him a terrible threat to the entire Empire. He could try writing a note and delivering it anonymously, but Beckett would have to be pretty stupid not to connect the note about Aetheric Geometry and the young man that he'd called on to discuss it, and the old coroner didn't seem like a stupid man.

Besides, Alan wasn't sure he'd be able to explain Zindel's theory effectively in a letter. That meant that he'd have to go to the Coroners directly. That meant that Elijah Beckett could execute him on the spot. *Maybe he won't*, Alan thought. *I could just tell him...I can show him that I can help him...*he remembered all of his Ted East novels. The heretics were always trying to convince Ted East that, yes, their sciences were dangerous, but this time, *this time*, it was okay. They'd discovered it by accident. They'd never use it. They could help him in his work, tracking down other heretics. It never held up. Ted East was never fooled. He would shoot them on the spot.

And if I don't tell them? The thought was a lead weight in his belly. The danger presented by Zindel's theories was astronomical. A real, bona fide threat to the Empire. To the world. *I have to. I have to tell them.*

Alan Charterhouse lay down on his bed, while the psychestorm buried Trowth in snow and madness. He wanted to cry.

Twenty-One: Mudside

The psychestorm cleared up shortly after noon, breaking apart into tattered wisps of iridescent green clouds that disappeared over the top of the great sea-wall in Trowth harbor, while a thicker, blacker cloud cover replaced it. Still, only the most foolish or desperate citizens would dare for several hours to venture into the drifts of icy snow that glowed gently blue beneath the streetlamps.

Elijah Beckett supposed he was both foolish and desperate. There was no chance that he could find a coach, so he tromped through the snowbanks and hoped his boots would hold out. They were good boots, stiff and lined with wool, so he was optimistic. The fact was, he had little time. As soon as it was safe, Wyndham-Vie and his men would be out and scouring the streets, trying to arrest Beckett and his coroners and trying to eliminate the last remaining leads that remained.

During his enforced stay at the hospice, Beckett had puzzled out where he had left to go. He suspected that Valentine had found nothing at the house on Corimander Street; whatever Wyndham-Vie had taken, he'd probably gotten away with it. Beckett had missed his chance to find out who Wyndham-Vie was working for. Zindel and his family were dead, and there was no sure way of finding out who killed them.

That only left one lead: someone had tried to throw him off by making the murders look like they'd been done by sharpsies. As near as Beckett could figure, that meant one of two things: either they'd had some kind of tool that could mimic a sharpsie bite — in which case there wasn't a lot he could do to find them — or someone had hired actual sharpsies to do it. And if Beckett wanted to find sharpsies, that meant going to Mudside.

The sharpsie ghetto was south of Red Lanes, and about half an hour's walk in the bitter cold. Beckett was protected only by his boots, his heavy coat, and the dose of veneine that the trolljrman had given him before he left. The drug was warm in his limbs, and steadfastly kept the cold at bay. It was entirely possible that a man could freeze to death while on veneine, and never notice it.

Mudside spread out by the south bend of the Stark. The river rolled out of the mountains in which Trowth nestled, and had cut a long channel through the impenetrable bedrock on which the city had been built. By the south bend, thick, oozing mud and sediment were thrown up by the swiftly flowing river, leaving a layer of shifting, unstable soil in a smooth fan by the riverside. This unsteady foundation made the construction of any kind of substantial buildings cost-prohibitive, and so Mud-side was routinely overlooked in the Architecture War. It had historically been the habitat of the dirty and destitute; land there was cheap, because no one of any importance wanted it. The neighborhood had been a natural home for sharpsie communities.

For a moment, as Beckett looked out at the sharpsie shantytown, he was daunted by the task, and the old despair took a moment to rear its ugly head. The population of Mudside numbered in the thousands, and he couldn't even speak their language. Still, he didn't have a lot of options. Beckett muttered to himself as he trudged down the snow hill into Mudside. When all this was over, he was going to Stitch and demanding more changes in the way the Coroners was run. From now on, they were going to see every murder, every theft, every breaking and entering first, and no one else was going to touch *anything* until Beckett himself said that he was satisfied.

Beckett found a trolljrman shoveling snow from in front of his shop at the lower end of Red Lanes. It would be a risk, bringing him into Mudside, but the coroner found himself hard put for choice.

"You, trolljr," Beckett called to him. "You speak sharpish?"

The trolljrman flexed the feathered crest on his head straight up, and rumbled something incomprehensible in trolljr.

Beckett showed his bronze shield to the trolljrman, and offered him ten crowns if he'd help the coroner in Mudside.

The trolljrman cocked his head to the side, then rumbled, "Yes. Speaks sharpish." He pronounced it "shaduhpish." He set down his shovel and crunched through the snow towards Beckett. "Twenty crowns, and I will help."

Beckett agreed, and he and the trolljrman set off into Mudside. The sharpsie hovels, completely ignored by the Trowth Architecture War, were built in a style called "Arkwrights' Mansion." It was named for the Arkwrights' Guild in Sar-Sarpek that, for reasons various and sundry, had found itself bankrupt and criminalized. The guildsmen had been forced to relocate to shanty-towns much like this one, and build their homes out of scraps and driftwood, and the occasional hollowed-out hull of a salvaged ship.

The sharpsies in Mudside had likewise built their homes out of whatever they could find, in whatever place or order they could, completely unmindful of preserving streets or public squares. The neighborhood was a warren of blackened wood, where thin wisps of smoke rose from peat and dung fires, and unemployed, shiftless sharpsies sat curled up against the wooden walls of their homes. They sat with their knees pulled in, and their long faces resting against their chests, giving the impression that they were staring at their stomachs.

Beckett realized his mistake almost immediately. Upon sight of the trolljrman, even the most apathetic sharpsie snapped its head up, eyes glittering warily, and then slunk off into the shadows. Beckett and his translator traveled well into the neighborhood, but with every step more sharpsies deserted the public places, and it became a ghost-town. More troublesome was a suspicion that snuck around in the back of Beckett's mind: that the disappearing sharpsies weren't running away, but were *regrouping* somewhere.

After ten minutes in the eerily empty, snow-covered and filth-smelling Mudside, a brazen-looking sharpsie youth appeared and blocked Beckett's path. He was not taller than the coroner, but was leanly muscular, and his great, sharp teeth arranged in a nasty-looking grin certainly suggested formidability.

The sharpsie coughed and growled for a few moments, and the trolljrman translated. "He say we not belong. We should go."

Beckett shook his head. "No," he told the sharpsie, "Not until I find out what I want." He pulled out his gun and his shield, and showed them to the youth. "Listen to me..." The sharpsie coughed something again, but Beckett kept going. "Listen. I know that, three days ago, at least one of your people was hired to mutilate the bodies of three people in North Ferry."

The sharpsie growled and spat indignantly. The trolljrman spoke, "He say he don't know about it."

"I don't care," Beckett said. "Someone knows. I am *not interested* in arresting a sharpsie. At all. I know that the man in North Ferry was *not* killed by sharpsies. Whoever did it was set up. Your people were set up. Do you know what that means?"

The sharpsie eyed him, but said nothing.

"The gendarmes, the pressmen are about to fall on you," Beckett insisted, his voice low and steady, his manner serious. "They are going to tear you apart, because they think you murdered this man. I can stop them, but only if you help me find the truth."

The youthful sharpsie cocked its head to one side, in a gesture that Beckett couldn't positively translate, but was nonetheless put in mind of a man, weighing his options and leery of deception. For a moment as the sharpsie did nothing, Beckett's frustration nearly boiled over into fury, and he came close to knocking those great sharp teeth out with the butt of his pistol.

Abruptly, the sharpsie nodded.

"Good. I need to find the sharpsie that was responsible, because I need to find the man that hired him. I need to know who hired him, and I need to be able to prove it, so that I can hang him. You understand?"

The sharpsie grunted, and then said a few more words in its native language.

"He wants to take us to his…." The trolljrman paused. "I do not know this word. It is 'head man.' It is like, a brood-father?"

"Like a priest?"

The trolljrman scoffed. "Sharpsies not have priests. They worship bones and sticks. He probably take you to his pet shark."

The sharpsie growled and coughed at the trolljrman, and the intent behind the sounds was unmistakable. The trolljrman thrummed something back in its own bone-rattling voice, and it flattened its crest against its head.

"Enough!" Beckett shouted at them. "Or I will shoot the both of you. You," he pointed at the sharpsie. "Take us to your headman. You," he said to the trolljrman, "I paid you to translate, so cut the commentary."

The sharpsie spat a gob of yellow spit into the snow at the trolljrman's feet, but then nodded curtly. It led Beckett and his translator deeper into Mudside.

The headman's home was, by far, the largest of the shoddy wooden dwellings in Mudside. It appeared to be the hulk of an old clipper-ship, turned upside down and half buried in mud. The inside was hollowed out to make one, large room, and the walls were covered in sheets of hammered copper; Beckett suspected that his was one of the few places to which sharpsies could retreat in order to shelter from psychestorms.

There were a dozen sharpsies hunkered up in filthy blankets, barely illuminated by the reddish light of a great fire in the center that poured suffocating black wood smoke into the air. Beckett's guide slipped into the flickering shadows and leaned close to one of the curled-up sharpsies.

This one was old; yellow clumps of hair tufted at his elbows and chin, and his skin was a deep, leathery brown. He uncurled himself from his place by the copper-covered wall, and Beckett could see that his chest was wrapped with leather straps, from which hung fetishes of bones, feathers, teeth, claws, and bits of fur. The sharpsie shuffled towards the coroner, his normally-rapid gait slowed to a bare crawl by arthritic age.

"My name is Elijah Beckett," the coroner told the ancient sharpsie. "I work for the Emperor. I know that one of your people was hired to do something...something pretty terrible." The sharpsies, Beckett knew, were not naturally predisposed to cruelty, despite what their vicious grins suggested, but desperation could drive anyone to great lengths. "I am not after you or any of yours. All I want is the man that hired him."

The old sharpsie's black eyes were covered with a blue-gray film; Beckett couldn't tell if it was staring right at him, or completely blind. It stood stock still for several moments before gurgling something in sharpish.

"He wants to know how he can trust you," the trolljrman said.

Beckett shrugged. "You can't. But I'll tell you this: the Committee for Public Safety is about to fall on Mudside like a hammer, all because of the murder in North Ferry. If I can find who set you up, there's a chance we can stop it."

The old sharpsie was still and silent for a long time. So long that Beckett, fearing the old creature hadn't heard him, drew breath to repeat himself. Even as he did, the sharpsie nodded, then coughed a loud chain of glottals to another of his nearby people. This one uncurled himself from its spot by the fire, and practically bounced on its springy legs to where Beckett stood. The old sharpsie and the new one spoke quietly in their choking, growling language for several minutes. Finally, the old headman turned to Beckett's translator and spoke.

The trolljrman interpreted. "He says, this one, they keep her nearby when they find out what happens. She tells, say she was on a work-crew in North Ferry, lengthening the arch-windows on Sansome Street. She hears a man banging on a door, then finds door unlocked, goes inside. He comes out, come to her, offers her money to bite the bodies up."

"Does she know the man's name?"

The old sharpsie nodded. "She heard him call out when he banged on the door," the trolljrman said. "They don't know how to say it in Sharpish," he added. "It sounds like Hoh-ooash Uhhaechngung." The old sharpsie muttered something else. "He says...Sun-Man?" The trolljrman asked. "No. Light-Man."

"Lightman?" Beckett asked. "Is that his name? Light-man?" His last name. The man's first name was something that the sharpsies could only pronounce Hoh-ooash. "Do you know anything else about him? What he looked like? Where he was from? What…"

There was a sudden commotion outside. The sharpsies, even the ones that seemed asleep, immediately sprang to their feet in the dark room, eyes alert. Someone started banging on the door, and the wary sharpsies began growling.

"Wait!" Beckett shouted at them. He held up his shield and gun. "Wait. Let me handle this. Okay? I'll take care of it."

Beckett immediately threw open the copper-banded door, and was met by a small army of gendarmes with greenglass goggles and blue armbands. Surprised, both at the appearance of a human being and, no doubt, by Beckett's fades-ravaged face, the men fell away from the door, leaving a relatively large semi-circle into which Beckett stepped.

"Sir," one of the gendarmes grumbled. "You'd better get out of here. We've come to make arrests."

"You're not arresting anyone." Beckett brandished the bronze emblem of his rank. "I'm with the Coroners. I am conducting an investigation here, pertinent to the safety of the Empire. You don't get in until I've finished."

The gendarmes looked at each other. None of them seemed to have firearms, but there were plenty of cudgels, short swords, long knives, and bronze knuckle-dusters to make Beckett nervous. "Coroners. You Elijah Beckett?" One of them asked. "We've got standing orders to bring you in, too." He tapped his cudgel on his thigh. "Regardless of condition."

"Haha." Beckett offered by way of reply, grinning meanly. He drew his pistol and fired all six bullets into the man's chest, a succession of gunfire that sounded almost like a single peal of thunder.

The Feathersmith revolver that Beckett carried was huge, at least the length of his forearm, with a barrel as thick around as his thumb, and almost ten years out of date. The barrel wasn't rifled, so the huge bullets that it fired would tumble end over end through the air, shattering bones and punching holes in men. It made a sound like a mortar when it fired. Beckett liked it because the amount of incidental trauma the bullets caused was enough to bring down a Reanimate, and because the gun was big and heavy enough that he could easily beat a man senseless with it.

The suddenness of Beckett's attack, which left the gen-darme slumped bonelessly in the snow and bleeding from great rents in his chest, caught all of the gendarmes off-guard. They backed away, hesitant and uncertain.

In the few moments that he had, Beckett slowly opened the revolver and dumped out the shells. His mind knew that it wouldn't be long before the men realized his weakness and would simply rush him, but he was counting on their fear and confusion to give him enough time to reload. He forced himself to remain calm, slowly taking each bullet out, carefully pressing it into its chamber. His numb fingers were a liability; if he dropped a bullet, or showed even a moment's hesitation, he'd be dead. So he took his time, and loaded the gun carefully. His nerves thrummed against the clamp he kept them under. They wanted to make him sick. They wanted to make his hands shake with fear and excitement. He didn't let them.

One of the men decided that he'd had enough. He rushed Beckett, who managed to close the revolver at the last possible second, allowing him to club the man across the face. The massive weight of the Feathersmith knocked the gendarme senseless, and Beckett had his gun up and aimed at the remaining men.

The implication was clear: the gendarmes could rush him, but whoever went first would die. Ultimately, because the gendarmerie represented the dregs of Trowth's citizenry, those too weak or too cruel or too petty to be taken by the pressgangs, Beckett was surrounded by cowards.

Almost immediately, the men in the back of the group slunk off into the Mudside labyrinth, already looking for easier prey. The rest fled after one vicious, "Fuck off."

Beckett turned back into the sharpsie home. He could hear, in the distance, more men shouting, sharpsies screaming, and the sound of gunfire. "You need..." he said, but couldn't think of anything. What were they supposed to do? If Mudside was crawling with armed gendarmes, if the Committee for Public Safety had sent a substantial force in to the sharpsie neighborhood, what could they do? They had nowhere to run to, no armaments to defend themselves with.

The trolljrman brushed past Beckett. "Leaving," he said, on his way out. "Will come for my money."

The old sharpsie grunted something to the coroner, then began gesturing to a spot on the floor, which was made of wood. He pulled up something that looked like a trapdoor, and Beckett looked down to see a wooden set of stairs leading off into the dark. The old sharpsie was grinning, because that's all that sharpsies ever did, but it seemed that the old man was pleased to see Beckett's surprise.

Of course, Mudside was built on mud. Old buildings sank slowly into it, new buildings were built on top. It would take regular work to maintain the old buildings, replacing rotting wood, building supports and struts. But it could be done; the sharpsies could have built themselves an entire network of tunnels beneath Mudside. *Just like the Arcadium*, Beckett thought, wryly.

The sharpsies had begun dropping through the hole in the floor. The old man waited until the last of his people had dropped in, then cocked his head quizzically. Beckett considered the dank, dark, claustrophobic wooden tunnels of Mudside, piled over with tons of mud and ramshackle wooden homes.

"No," he said. "You go. I'll find my own way out."

The Imperial Committee for Public Safety had come in force to the sharpsie shanty-town on the shores of the Stark. Despite the recent violence, the sharpsies appeared unprepared for the attack. The Committee came with a thousand gendarmes, their blue armbands prominent. They'd enlisted another half a hundred pressgangers, and had apparently bought enough greenglass goggles to outfit the entire army, enabling it to see clearly in the poorly-lit neighborhood even after night had fallen.

Panic spread through the community, as frightened youths sprinted down narrow alleyways and crawled into narrow bolt-holes, fleeing the gendarmerie with desperate terror. Though the Committee had caught the sharpsies unprepared, the omphaloskepsis were well-practiced at avoiding authorities. Within an hour, Mudside had been almost completely abandoned, with only a few, scant possessions left behind. Somehow, thousands of sharpsies managed to disappear into the city. The gendarmes brought great barrels of phlogiston, and set the ram-shackle wooden homes on fire, in the hope of smoking out any remaining inhabitants.

Roughly a hundred fled the flames and ran into the waiting leg-irons of the Committee's soldiers and pressgangers. Another hundred burned to death beneath their own homes, but their deaths were not noted. Mudside took approximately six hours to burn to the ground, leaving acres of black ash next to the Stark. The thousands of remaining sharpsies were nowhere to be found.

The Committee for Public Safety suspected that they'd fled into the Arcadium, and advised all citizens without urgent business there to avoid it. It did not suggest what the poor squalid citizens that actually lived there ought to do. The Committee for Public Safety assured all the moderately- and very-wealthy citizens that lived topside that the Sharpsie Threat would soon be contained, and that John Sharpish would no longer terrorize the streets of Trowth, murdering innocent families in their homes.

TWENTY-TWO: THE COACHMAN'S SON

"The storm's been clear for hours," Valentine said that evening, as he peered through the crack between the shutters. From his vantage-point in Raithower House, he could not see the lurid, ruddy glare of Mudside burning. "Do you…do you want me to take you home?"

Skinner shook her head. The events of the previous night had upset her immensely, but after a few hours sleep, and with-out the psychestorm and its traumatic effects on her senses, she was itching to do something. "We should….I don't know. We need to keep going. The longer we wait, the more steps Wyndham can take to cover his tracks."

The two coroners were in the parlour-room office on the first floor. Valentine flopped into one of the overstuffed chairs. "I wish we knew where Beckett is."

"We can't wait for him. If he was as…," she paused, as though the word was stuck in her throat. "If he was as sick as you said, it could be days before he's ready for work again." *If ever.* "So. What do we know?"

Groaning and rubbing his eyes, Valentine attempted to recount what they knew about Zindel's murder. "Zindel is a geometer. He's at home with his family…we're assuming that he's locked his front door, because everyone in North Ferry does." He raised his head. "Should we be doing that? I mean, if the door was unlocked, then anyone could have gotten in and just done it. It could just be a random murder."

"Right. In which case, we'll never find who did it. Let's assume, for the moment, that the open lock is something important, because it gives us somewhere to look."

"Okay. So, someone came to the Zindel house, and un-locked the door. He murders them, then maybe gets some sharpsies to cover it up, or maybe he is a sharpsie and does it himself. So, why does Zindel let the sharpsie into his house? It must be because he's dead, so someone must have hired the sharpsie. But then, why didn't he just hire the sharpsie to kill Zindel in the first place? If he had access to the house? Maybe he did, but I still don't understand why a sharpsie would come in and murder someone and then not bother robbing them…"

"All right." Skinner's voice was firm. "All right. Let's skip that bit. Whatever happened in the house, we haven't got enough information about it. Tell me about the coachman again. He came to Zindel's house…"

"The coachman saw the cordon and left. Suspiciously. I followed him. After he went to Printer's Close, someone shot him. That same someone was then killed by a…by a something that I'd rather not think about."

Skinner leaned back in her chair and started tapping her fingernail on the plate across her eyes. "You know his name? The coachman's?"

Valentine nodded. "James Crowell. Works for a private livery stable in New Bank. He lives right about where Red Lanes turns into River Village."

"So, that's easy. We talk to his boss, find out what jobs he took."

Valentine shifted uncomfortably. "Ah. I tried that, actually. Right after I found it. The company usually lets cabs out for…hm. Trips to Fleshmarket, things like that. They pride themselves on being discreet."

"We'll demand their records…"

"They don't keep any. I mean, they do. But cabs are all paid for in advance, and anonymously. Drivers are given an address, often not the home address of their passengers. Passengers are never identified by name and the drivers never keep a record of where they've gone."

"So, his boss doesn't know who hired him, or where he took the coach?"

"Correct."

Skinner started tapping her eye-plate again, for several seconds. Valentine found it decided creepy, and was about to ask her to stop when she said, "Hnh. Well, I guess we'll go to his house."

"Do you think he left notes?"

Skinner shrugged, and got to her feet. "He might have. Right now, it's the only thing we can check that we haven't got conclusive answers about. Karine," she called to the indige secretary, "have Harry get the coach ready."

The trip to River Village gave the two coroners a much better view of what was happening in nearby Mudside. The shanty-town was burning fiercely: blue phlogiston flames turned to red and orange as they spread to the wooden homes. Men were shouting, dragging struggling, tooth-gnashing sharpsies out into the street, occasionally shackling them and throwing them into the backs of reinforced prison-wagons. More often, the gendarmes, who generally outnumbered their opponents at least five to one, were simply beating the sharpsies bloody, sometimes to death.

One such group dragged a young sharpsie man right into the path of the coach, ignoring Harry's shouts as he demanded that they clear the street. The men screamed at the sharpsie as their cudgels rose and fell, blood splattering on their faces, days' worth of fear and anger finding free expression in their violence.

Valentine climbed down from the coach. He fired a few shots into the air and the gendarmes, who rarely could afford comparable firearms, ran off. Valentine examined the body of their victim, but found that he was already dead.

"Leave him." Skinner's voice was cold. "We have work to do."

After a moment's thought, Valentine decided to at least move the sharpsie to the sidewalk, and attempted to arrange its limbs in a restful position, instead of the tangle of broken arms and legs that the gendarmes had left. Reluctantly, Valentine returned to the coach.

The two coroners found James Crowell's house without difficulty. They were surprised, however, to discover that it was not empty. Skinner had opened the front door of the small, single-story dwelling. She leaned in close to the lock and there was a tinny, metallic rapping. After a few seconds something clicked and she turned the knob.

There was a young man in the house, sitting in an overstuffed chair next to the woodburning stove. He was thin and pale and lank-haired, and his eyes had the glazed-over look of a habitual fang user.

"Who the hell are you?" Valentine asked, as he entered.

The young man required a moment to regain his focus, but once he had his eyes were suddenly sharp. "This is my house. I think it's perhaps customary that you should introduce yourselves, first."

"Coroners." Valentine showed the brass double-eagle shield. "Also, this is James Crowell's house."

Eyeing the badge suspiciously, the young man replied. "We share...shared it. I'm Phillip Crowell. His son."

"Oh. Ah. Yes." Valentine put his badge away. "Sorry... well, sorry about that, we didn't realize that there'd...I mean, that he'd had, or that...you know."

"We'd like to talk to you about your father," Skinner said calmly and, if not soothingly, at least dispassionately. Her cane, swiftly swinging back and forth, discovered a second chair, not quite so well-stuffed, which she sat in without invitation.

"You would? The Coroners?" He shifted uncomfortably in his chair. "Please sit, by the way. No need to wait on my account." Phillip fumbled with a small bottle that he'd had set on the floor, finally pouring a measure of amber-colored liquid into a tiny glass and then sipping from it. "My father was a coachman, not a scientist. I can't see that you'd be interested in him at all."

"You don't think it's possible," Skinner asked, "that he might have been involved with some people in whom we might take an interest?"

Phillip shrugged. "My father didn't talk about his work. He believed in being discreet."

Valentine snorted, but said nothing, choosing instead to prowl around the room. It was dark, and small, with only a few pieces of mismatched furniture. There were no pictures, but there were many books, piled in corners, stacked up on book-cases, standing in place for one of the chair legs.

Skinner ignored the other coroner. "So, you've no idea at all why someone might want to kill him?"

Philip smiled cruelly over his little glass. "I have a number of ideas. A hundred ideas. I am full to the brim with ideas." He downed the remainder of the amber liquid, and winced slightly. "That is not the same as knowing something."

"You don't seem very upset," Valentine put in. "About your father being murdered, and all."

Philip shrugged. "I'm not." After a moment, he added, "My father and I...did not get along very well. I suspect he imagined more affection from me than really existed. I didn't hate him, but I didn't especially care for him."

The two coroners were silent for a long time. "That is...shockingly cold, Mr. Crowell." Valentine said. Philip only shrugged a second time.

"What was your father doing in Printer's Close?" Skinner had begun to tap her eye-plate again.

Philip Crowell seemed suddenly uncomfortable. "He was...dropping something off. For me."

"That was nice of him." Valentine was practically sneering. "Suppose it was because of all that imagined affection."

"My relationship with my father is none of your damn business," Philip spat at the coroner. He seemed angry but petulant; mad enough to shout, but not mad enough to get to his feet.

"What was he dropping off?" Skinner interjected.

"Pages from my book," Crowell said, offhandedly. "*The Tower of Brass.* It's about a hallucination I had while on veneine. I find the visions are fantastically consistent. Of course, I had to rework them somewhat to make an interesting story out of it all..."

"Phillip Crowell..." Valentine pursed his lips. "Your name's familiar..."

"I usually write under Philip Crowe. You might have read one of my earlier works. I've had stories published in a few of the papers, the *Observer* and the *White Star* and that. My most popular story was obviously 'The Doom of Michael Lightman.' It's..."

"*The Ice House,*" Valentine interrupted. "You wrote *The Ice House.*"

Philip Crowell seemed suddenly, unaccountably shy about his work. "That...was also one of mine."

"Heh. I read that one. It's good." Valentine turned to his partner. "You should read...er. I guess, I mean if you had someone read it to you..." he trailed off.

Skinner ignored him. "So. James Crowell had taken the first pages of your next book to the Close, and was murdered shortly afterwards. And you have no idea why, because he never talked about his work anyway, and it doesn't especially bother you, because you never really liked him anyway. Is that right?"

"Yes," the young man said. "That's about it."

"And you don't think his murder had anything to do with the trip to Printer's Close?"

Philip paused. "N-no. No. Why should it? He often went to the close for me. My lungs are weak, so travel is often....what are you suggesting?"

"I am suggesting nothing, Mr. Crowell." Skinner smiled. "Excuse me. Mr. Crowe. I just find it a strange coincidence that your father's assailants should have such certain knowledge of where to find him."

"Are you suggesting that I had something to do with this?" Outrage filled Crowell's voice, but something else, as well: the sharp bite of hysteria. Skinner said nothing, perhaps in the hopes that Crowell's uncertainty might force him to reveal something pertinent. She was disappointed. After a moment, he appeared to compose himself, and once again began to glower over narrowed eyes and grin slyly. "You don't know anything. You have no idea who killed my father, or why. You're fishing." He poured himself another drink and down it immediately. "I think, my dear Mr. and Mrs. Coroner, that if you've nothing else to ask, perhaps you ought to leave."

Valentine stepped up behind Crowell's chair, and loomed over the young man. "I think that we'll decide when we ought to leave. How about that?"

"Valentine." Skinner got to her feet. "It's all right. We're done here."

The knocker and her companion left Philip Crowell to sit in his hovel and drink. They climbed back into the coach, and Skinner had them head back to Raithower.

"That was unproductive," Valentine said. "And a little creepy. I mean, he's a creepy writer. He writes creepy things. But I didn't think that *he'd* be creepy."

"It wasn't completely unproductive," Skinner mused. "He knows something. And it's something to do with Printers' Close."

"How do you...oh. No. Are you serious? You can hear when someone's *lying*?"

"Not always. But there are clues, if you know what to listen for. Changes in pitch, in rhythm. Unfortunately, it's not enough for me to figure out what the truth is."

"Oh." Valentine was silent for a moment. "Hah. That...that was pretty funny, when he called us Mr. and Mrs. Coroner, right?"

"What about it?"

"Well, nothing. Just. What about that, right? Hahah."

Skinner cocked her head to the side. "You are so strange."

They rode without speaking for a while, the only sounds the creaking and rattling of the coach, and the distant shouts and screams from Mudside. Valentine often shifted his position in his seat, crossing and uncrossing his legs, leaning against the window, thrusting his chin into his hand. He wanted to *do* something, to get up and shout that the sharpsies weren't responsible, that they were after the real criminal already. He wanted to catch someone, to chase someone, to *find* someone, to do something to forestall the ominous threat to his city that was building.

"Harry!" Valentine shouted abruptly, shifting in his seat and pounding on the ceiling of the coach. "Harry, stop here!"

"What is it?" Skinner asked as the carriage creaked to a halt.

"Bookshop," he said, climbing out. "Wait here, I'll be right back."

TWENTY-THREE: QUESTIONS. ANSWERS.

Valentine and Skinner returned to Raithower to find Beckett already there. There was something, Valentine thought, that was appropriate about that. Beckett had been gone for days, he'd been sick and out of his mind when Valentine had seen him last. And now he was back in Raithower, sitting in the parlour-office in his charcoal gray suit with his red scarf wrapped around his nose and mouth and glaring at Karine.

It was exactly what he did every day. Right down to the sullen cast of his eyebrows, the way he gingerly crossed his legs to avoid the pain in his knees. Beckett sat in the parlor in Raithower House as though nothing had happened.

"Where the hell have you been?" Beckett snapped.

Really, exactly the same as every other day. "Around," Valentine replied. "Uhm..."

"Valentine found us a lead," Skinner put in. "He followed a coachman away from Zindel's house." She went on to explain the coachman's murder, and the murder of his assailant, the incident during the psychestorm, and the interview with Philip Crowe.

Beckett was silent for a long moment while he took this in. Valentine knew the old man, and he knew what was going through his head: Beckett was methodically going over each and every word that Skinner had said, tying every event to every other and working it over again and again, so that he could ask exactly the right question.

"And you think this is connected to Zindel's murder?" He asked, finally.

Well, thought Valentine. *They can't all be winners.* "Maybe." He held up the parcel that he'd bought on the drive over. "This is Crowe's last book. I read it before but…" A sheepish expression skittered across the man's face. "I don't really remember it. I'm going to go over it again, look for…you know…"

"Clues?" Beckett asked, eyebrow raised.

"I was going to say 'anything of value,' but I guess 'clues' works just as well."

Beckett nodded curtly, and Valentine adjourned to the adjacent office to read. Beckett turned to Skinner. "Does the name 'Lightman' mean anything to you?"

"In what context? Is it a person?"

"I think so. Harris Lightman, maybe? Harcourt? I met a sharpsie in Mudside who claimed that someone with a name like that hired her to…to mutilate the Zindel bodies."

"Is it Horace Lightman?" Karine piped up suddenly from where she'd been hovering in the room behind Beckett.

"Well, I don't know," the old coroner snapped. "If I knew his name was 'Horace,' I'd have asked if she knew a 'Horace,' wouldn't I?"

"I'm sorry, sir," Karine mumbled, as she disappeared into her file-room. A moment later she came back with a thick sheaf of papers. "When you started investigating Herman Zindel, sir, I did some research. I know you like information, so I pulled up copies of all the broadsheets I could find with Herman Zindel's name in them." She handed Beckett a small clipping. "Zindel knew a man named Horace Lightman. This is from when they both won the Royal Academy of Sciences Order of Distinction, three years ago. They were colleagues at the University, in mathematics and engineering."

Beckett took the article, and began to scan it. "Horace Lightman. We need to find him. Karine, I want you to get me an address…"

"I've already done it, sir," Karine said, offering another paper from her sheaf. "The Ministry of Revenue's tax records. But it won't help."

Beckett looked up. "Why not?"

Karine handed the coroner a final page. "It's a report, sir. The gendarmes in New Bank, you know, they're very conscientious about your request for….for reports on arrests and….he's dead, sir. Horace Lightman. He was found dead yesterday, his…"

"…throat bruised and his lungs crushed," Beckett finished, reading from the report. "In his home, no visible means of entrance or exit."

"Oh!" Valentine looked up from his book. "Bruised throat, that's like the fellow…"

"We know, Valentine," Skinner told him. "Hush."

Slowly, Beckett handed the articles back to Karine. "Nothing. They've taken his body already and burned it, cleaned his house. We couldn't even bring a psychometrist on." A dreadful certainty was growing inside him. "We have nothing. No idea who murdered these men..." *Some idea*, he though, but it was an idea he'd rather not have had. "No way to connect them to Wyndham-Vie. The log at Corimander Street is gone. The only two people we know that came to Zindel's home are dead. Unless there's something good in that book..."

"Nothing so far," muttered Valentine.

"Then we have nothing." He leaned back in his chair and steepled his numb fingers. He shook his head. "I'll stay here, tonight. You two are welcome to do what you like."

Alan Charterhouse packed his papers into a small satchel. He put on his Primeday clothes, the dark blue suit and shiny shoes that his father had always made him wear when they went to church. There was something a little ironic about that, thought Alan, that he should be wearing it when he confessed to heresy. He left his room, which still looked as though a tornado had whirled through, leaving papers and detritus scattered in his wake. He closed the door and locked it.

That's it, thought Alan. *That's the last time I'll see it.* After a moment's hesitation, he opened the door again and looked in. He tried to take everything in. The bed with the tall wooden posts and the burgundy curtains. The writing desk with the comically-small chair that accompanied it—his father had bought if for him when Alan was only ten, and he'd never gotten around to getting a new one. The washbasin, ceramic white with little blue flowers around the outside, in the dark-wood carved stand. His bookcase, which still had the old picture books that Ian Charterhouse had read to his son—Benjamin Walpole's *Anything Stories* with their crudely-illustrated fables about leopards and tarrasques and therians, Gunther Molnar's *Tales of the Trow*, stories of epic majesty accompanied by beautiful copperplate etchings—all the dog-eared copies of Ted East novels, Wolfram Harcourt's *Principles of Mathematics*.

There was paper scattered everywhere. Alan had thought that perhaps he'd tidy the place up before he left, because it didn't seem fair to leave all of that to his uncle, who'd surely be full of grief when he heard about his nephew's execution. The fact was that there just wasn't enough time. Alan was, he realized, sitting on top of a grenade whose fuse was still burning, one that could go off at any time.

Alan closed and locked his door again and hurried downstairs. Uncle Malcolm was asleep in the sitting-room, and Alan looked fondly on him while he tried to fix the old man's features in his mind. *Last time.*

Goodbye, Uncle Malcolm. The young man slipped out the front door and into the cold night.

The air was still cold and raw, and it had been raining all morning and afternoon. The downpour had helped to put the fires out in Mudside. Alan pulled his coat tight about himself and slung his satchel over his shoulder, plunging his free hand as deep into the wool pocket of his coat as he could.

A deep sense of loss and loneliness washed over him, as Alan Charterhouse left his life behind. He knew what he had to do, and that it was right that he should do it, but the knowledge that it would bring his execution seemed to crowd out all other thoughts.

There was a tension in the air as Alan approached Old Bank, and he was at a loss to explain it. There were sharpsies, many more than usual, lurking in shadows and corners, gathering in small groups by the crevices in the street that led down to the Arcadium. Alan had not read the broadsheets in several days, and so was not aware of the events that had taken place in the sharpsie ghetto; he was moreover unaware of how remarkable a thing it was that he should be seeing any sharpsies, let alone in the numbers that now wandered Old Bank.

It was not long before he realized that there were two sharpsies following him, springing along with casual, athletic strides on their bare toes. Alan tried to keep his head down and mind his business, walking as fast as he could without showing fear. He tried cutting through Exeter Street, to move around Old Wall Square, but that turned out to be a mistake.

As soon as Alan had left the main street, the sharpsies leapt at him. They were quick, much quicker than he was, and soon each one held one of Alan's arms in an iron grip. Alan screamed, and all fear he'd been damming up inside exploded out, shivering through his muscles, welling out his eyes, covering his face in tears.

The one on his left sputtered and hacked something in sharpish.

"I don't understand!" Alan practically screamed. "I'm not...I'm not...please, don't hurt me! I'm just trying to...I have to see the Coroners!"

The two sharpsies snapped and guttered at each other this time, then the one on Alan's right leaned in close, slowly working its long jaws with those nasty, huge, hooked teeth. Its breath smelled like raw meat. It rasped something in the back of its throat.

"Please," Alan whimpered. "It's important. I need to see the Coroners."

The sharpsie rasped something again, and this time it sounded vaguely familiar. "Ghehkek."

"I don't..." Alan tried to understand. Was the sharpsie trying to tell him something? Something in Trowth? They'd reacted when he mentioned the Coroners. "Do you...you mean Beckett?"

The sharpsie nodded slowly.

Alan was now left in the unfortunate position of trying to guess whether or not the sharpsie was favorably disposed towards the old coroner. If it was, there was a good chance it might let Alan go. If it wasn't, then there was an equally good chance it would bite the young man's face off. Alan swallowed noisily. "Yes. I need to see Beckett. It's important..."

The sharpsie snapped something vicious-sounding at his companion, then turned back to Alan, and curtly nodded again. The two long-jawed men released Alan, then made a gesture indicating that he should be off. Warily, and still sniffling, Alan backed away from the two sharpsies towards Raithower House.

They followed, but at a distance. When Alan passed another small group of sharpsies past Old Wall Square, the two following him shouted something guttural at the others, and Alan found himself unmolested. The sharpsies disappeared about a block away from Raithower House.

Strangely, the terrifying encounter with the sharpsies seemed to have purged Alan of his fear. He knew he ought to be jittery and stammering as he approached the guard at the coroners' headquarters, but he found his stride confident, his voice strong.

"My name is Alan Charterhouse," the young man told the waiting guard. "I need to speak with Detective-Inspector Elijah Beckett regarding the murder of Herman Zindel."

The guard said nothing, but retreated into a small guard-house. Past the bars of the main gate and through the tiny window of the guardhouse, Alan could see another man, this one wearing the silver plate over his eyes that signified a knocker. The knocker cocked his head to the side as if waiting for an answer, then nodded, satisfied. The guard returned from the house.

"You can go in," he told Alan. "Through the front door, right at the main stairs, into the parlor at the end of the hall." For a moment, all of Alan's concerns vanished from his mind as he thought about what it meant that the knockers could communicate over distances like that. Was there a way to replicate their telerhythmia? To transmit code through space without a knocker at all? Anyone could send messages, then. You could...

The iron gate swung open with an ear-splitting shriek, startling Alan from his musings, and he walked across the dark courtyard to where to phlogiston lamps burned blue and un-earthly by the doors.

They, too, swung open, and out spilled golden candle-light from the interior. Alan followed the guard's directions, and soon found himself in the red-and-gold appointed parlor.

Beckett was nowhere to be seen. Skinner was seated primly on one of the couches, while another man, tall, thin, and rakish sprawled on his back—nearly upside-down—in one of the chairs and read.

"Alan," Skinner said, as his footsteps reached her ears. "What are you doing here?"

"I..." The young cartographer found his voice caught in his throat. "Uhm. I need to talk to Beckett." He pulled out a sheaf of papers from his knapsack, the formulae that he'd been unluckily unable to forget. "About Zindel's mathematics."

There was a sudden growl from behind him, and Beckett stumbled into the room. He was not wearing his coat, but he still had the red scarf wrapped around his mouth and nose. He had no gloves, either, and his right sleeve was pushed up. Alan could see that the tips of Beckett's fingers were invisible, and there was a livid, glistening blood-red spot on the inside of his elbow where the skin had become transparent. Beckett tugged the sleeve down as he entered. "Why?" He grunted. "I told you to forget about all this."

Alan took a deep breath. "I can't, sir." He opened his satchel, and took out all of his papers. "I remember everything I see. Almost everything. When it comes to math, anyway. And I wasn't completely honest with you when I told you what I saw in Zindel's home." He spread the papers out on a small coffee-table. "I know what the equations were. I mean, I didn't know a hundred percent, at the time. But I know a lot about Aetheric Geometry. I mean, a lot. I can do the math. And I've figured out what these equations mean."

"Don't tell me that," Beckett said. "I don't want to hear that. You *know* what I have to do, *don't* tell me..."

"Arrest me," Alan said. Tears welled up in his eyes again, and he heard his voice quavering. "Execute me, if you have to. I know, don't think I don't know. I know exactly what...you have to kill me. I used to do equations like this, I found them in *Principles of Mathematics* when I was a kid, and I never thought anything of it. I figured no one would ever find out. But last night I realized that I have to tell you. I can't keep it a secret anymore, because it means the safety of the entire Empire. This is more important than me." Alan was weeping openly now; salt tears dripped onto his formulae. "So if you have to execute me, then you have to, but let me tell you what I found out."

Beckett was silent for a long moment. Then, "All right."

Alan sighed, and began to explain. With each word, he drew farther away from his fear and into the simple science, the pure mathematics with which he had always been most comfortable expressing himself. "Zindel's equations are the mathematical schematic for a translation engine."

"We know," Beckett said. "The *Excelsior*."

"That's what I thought," Alan replied. He knelt down and spread his papers out on the floor. "But it's not. See here? This matrix, that's the arrangement of those six numbers, that's using a triple-pronged stabilizing system, when the *Excelsior* only used a double-prong. I think it has to do with the way the coordinates are expressed in our space. The *Excelsior* disaster happened because the engineers that built her engines were only accounting for her transition into real space in two dimensions. It's a catastrophically stupid error, when you think about it, but I guess it must have been easy to overlook at the time. Since they didn't imagine they'd be going up or down, they must have figured that two coordinate pairs would be enough. But this..."

Alan gently spread the pages out, until he found the one he was looking for. "See, here's where Zindel was going to rebuild a different kind of interlocutor, with a three-prong stabilizer."

"So, Zindel and his partner were designing a new kind of translation engine?" Something was nagging at Beckett, now. Was it Valentine's story that bothered him? Was it his own memories of the kirliotypes in *Dangers of Heresy*, of the hideously-malformed bodies that had been the victims of the *Excelsior*'s launch?

"That's the bad part. That's why I had to come to you." Alan found another page. "See this? These columns of numbers? This is data. And it's not data that he made up. It's too precise, it all fits together too neatly. This is experimental data. Zindel wasn't designing a translation engine. He'd already *built* one."

And suddenly, Beckett understood. The answers snapped together so powerfully in his mind that he, for half a moment, suspected that Skinner could hear the click of interlocking facts. He knew who, really *what*, had killed Herman Zindel and Horace Lightman, and why. He knew why they'd had to kill the coach-man, and what had killed his murderer. And he knew where to go for the last answer that he needed.

"So," Beckett said. "Where did they build it, Valentine?"

The thing young man looked up from his book. "What?"

"The answer's in there."

Valentine looked startled, then looked closely at the book. He flipped through the pages, checked the imprint. "I don't understand. Is there a code?"

"What's it about, Valentine?"

He set the book down. "Oh. Well, it's a kind of, it's like this: what if the royal family had had this horrible, monster off-spring, and they wanted to get rid of it, but they couldn't kill it? So, they take it up into the mountains and it lives up there in this house on a glacier, right? And it's told from the perspective of the monster's keeper, and he has to keep riding up the mountain to...to...what?"

Skinner was smiling. "Think about it. Why did they kill the coachman? The book's about the royal family having a terrible secret, and a man that has to go out into the mountains to care for it. A terrible secret, like Zindel's engine."

Understanding dawned on the man's face. "Huh. And you think...you think James Crowell gave his son the real location, and that's why...? But it's not real. The house. It was supposed to be a Gorgon-Vie summer home on..." he checked the book. "Mount Hood. Trust me. I know all of the Gorgon-Vie houses, and they haven't got anything that far into the mountains."

"Not Gorgon-Vie," Alan said, startling everyone. "Rowan-Czarnecki. It's called Gotheray Castle." He met their incredulous stares with his own open face. "It's on one of the maps. Uhm. Ministry of the Exchequer's Taxable Land Estates of 1686."

Beckett sighed. "Well. I guess you're going with us."

"I..." Alan began.

"We need to find the house, boy, and you know the way." Beckett crossed his arms. "Or maybe you'll tell me that you don't remember what the map looks like."

Alan sighed. At least it meant they couldn't execute him. Yet. "No, I do. I remember — "

"Everything, I know. Wait here. We'll leave shortly."

Valentine came into Beckett's office while the old coroner was shrugging into his coat.

"Beckett."

"What?"

Valentine shifted uncomfortably. "I...I can't go. Not now."

Beckett said nothing, just stared at him with an obdurate, unreadable expression.

"You've seen...you know what's happening out there," Valentine told him, passion warming his voice as he grew enthusiastic about his subject. "The city is ready to explode. The riots we've seen...it's going to be worse than that. Whatever happens is going to be worse. I know it, I can *feel* it. I don't know how to explain...it doesn't matter. I know what's going to happen. I can't leave now. My Family is here, they'll need..." he trailed off.

"Need?"

"Me. They'll need me. I can't just...I can't just go..."

"What do you think they'll need you for, Valentine?" The younger man was silent. "What do you think you're going to do? If there's a riot, if the sharpsies decide to lay siege to Comstock Street? Are you going to shoot them?" Silence, then, as Valentine looked down at his finely-polished shoes. "You want to help, I understand that. You want to protect your city, I understand that to, but listen to me, and listen very closely: there is only one way that you can help your city. There is only. One. Way. You come with me, and we find out who did this. We find the truth. We do our jobs. And if we're lucky, we can stop this."

"Do you really think we can?" Valentine asked after a moment. "That it'll be enough? Even if we do find out..."

Beckett sighed. "I don't know. You never get to know. You just do your damn job. Because *someone* has to do it. This is what you signed up for, this is what matters. Now, go get your coat."

Skinner was waiting for them, seated in precisely the same position and location as when they'd left her, only now wearing a long gray overcoat—giving the appearance of having miraculously apparated the coat onto her person. Karine was busy explaining her cross-referencing system to Alan Charterhouse, who listened with wide-eyed fascination. Beckett could practically see the wheels turning in the young man's head.

"All right," Beckett growled. "Let's get on with this."

TWENTY-FOUR: MOUNT HOOD

It was almost a relief to leave the city that night. The strange feeling to which Valentine had confessed, the electric urgency, the overwhelming sense of immanence was palpable to all and sundry. Sensible men claimed that, with the destruction of Mud-side, the sharpsies had probably simply fled the city, now to find some new nation that might tolerate them, and good riddance. But the sensible men, sensible as they were, were quite unable to deny the sense of danger that walked the streets that night. Alan Charterhouse and the three coroners left in a heavy, closed, weather-beaten coach pulled by a team of strong but docile horses, hired from the same livery company for which James Crowell had worked. Harry had insisted that his own horses were good enough for the climb up Mount Hood, but Beckett had been resolute.

The coach took them out of the city and to the west, away from the huge, looming forest of stone architecture and bronze statues. They passed the Sentinels: two great statues that, according to legend, had been erected by the Trow. The work of the pseudo-mythical giants had been unearthed nearly two thousand years earlier, when the city was first founded. They were each a hundred feet high, devoid of any mark that might have suggested tool-use, and vaguely human in shape. Yet, there was something eerily alien about the cast of their shoulders, the faint details of their features.

The royal family claimed that these statues were Gorgon and Demogorgon, the two giants that were the founders of the imperial line in Trowth. They represented one of the few places in the city exempt from the Architecture War: no family would build anything less than twenty yards from where the statues stood along High Street as it ran straight as an arrow out from the heart of the city. Gorgon and

Demogorgon stood on two bare islands of stone on the line between the city and its ever-widening suburbs.

Though legend claimed that the statues had been gradually, slowly, glacially moving over the course of the last two-thousand years, they appeared quite still as the coroners' coach passed by. It took another hour and a half before the coach had left behind the last of the suburbs on the west. The road followed the Stark up into the mountains.

The route of the Stark was one of long, gentle curves. Fed primarily by mountain springs and runoffs, the river Stark was a deep, swift, wide river, ice-cold and treacherous. It never froze, not even during Second Winter, but any poor soul that fell into the black waters would likely die of hypothermia within minutes. The Stark led the road past the farms that managed to scrape a living out of the rocky soil; there was a sea of corn and wheat stubble everywhere, dotted with the occasional low, dark-windowed farmhouse, sullenly leaking woodsmoke into the air.

The harvested fields bespoke a great desolation, some-how more profound than the ordinary sense that First Winter left in the mind. For miles and miles, there was simply nothing but flat, stony plains and the knotted remnants of the year's harvest. It was late, and cold, so naturally no one would be about, but there was still a terrible loneliness to this place.

Eventually, the thick, smoky fog of pollution that hung over Trowth gave way to a clear sky, with the moon bathing those bleak fields in a harsh, pale blue-green light. As the blue glow from the lights of the city faded behind the coach, the stars became apparent: tens of thousands of baleful white eyes, watching with undisguised malice.

Is it any wonder that the citizenry of Trowth should fill the air with filth, when faced with those glaring stars, with that foul, leprous moon? Is it surprising that they should not raise a hew and cry about preserving their atmosphere, but rather breathe a sigh of relief knowing that the plumes of bruised black-and-blue smoke served as a shield between them and the malicious, terrifying night sky?

The farms gave way to forests that had long since been on the receiving end of the woodsman's axe: field after field of corn stubble became rolling hills of gnarled tree-stumps, all worn and blackened by the weather, as though the last of the trees had been cut down a hundred years ago. The coach followed a dirt road that pulled away from the river and began to work its way in bumpy, shuddering switchbacks up Mount Hood, all around surrounded by those acres of sundered forest, while moss and black weeds tangled their way up and out of the mountain slopes.

Eventually, after hours in the chilly coach, beneath the malevolent sky, the tree-stumps grew fewer and fewer, the ground harsher and colder, so that the evidence of living things began to disappear. Weeds grew sparse and rougher, mosses vanished completely. The stumps remained, but grew thinner and fewer between. Occasionally, a low shrub or tree had escaped the devastation; invariably, it was twisted and gnarled, a clutching claw rearing up from the ground.

These last signs of life disappeared as well, as the coach crossed the tree-line. The road petered out over the permanently-frosted earth, and eventually had to come to a stop.

Beckett led the way out of the coach, climbing down as quickly as possible to stretch his legs and arms; they cracked and creaked as he did so. While his companions left the coach, the old coroner treated himself to another veneine injection from the traveling case he kept with him.

Valentine took two phlogiston lanterns from the coach and lit them, adding to the light already cast by the lanterns that hung from the coach itself. Alan looked up at the sky, and tried to gain his bearings according to the constellations.

"We're still about…a mile or two away." He turned up-wards on the gentle slope of the mountain. About a hundred yards away was the very edge of a glacier, a vast plain of ice that stretched to the mountain's summit. Someone had, some time ago, courteously erected a kind of wooden walkway that left the stony slope of the mountain, and served as a bridge onto the ice. "Up that way." He squinted in the dark, but couldn't see any-thing.

Beckett nodded. He had brought heavy, over-stuffed coats, crammed into the luggage compartment in the coach; now, he'd begun to unpack them and pass them out. "We'll have to climb. And by we," he added, as he handed Alan a coat, "I mean me and Valentine. I want you and Skinner to stay here."

"What?" Skinner and Alan spoke almost simultaneously.

"I won't be able to hear you from here…" complained the knocker, while Alan said, "You won't be able to find it…"

"Enough." Beckett shrugged into his coat. "Alan will point us in the right direction. If the house is up there, we'll find it. And, no offense, Skinner, but I can't trust either of you on the glacier. Stay here with the driver. Besides, if something goes wrong, I want at least one of us alive enough to report back to Stitch."

"Elijah…" Skinner began.

"No arguments. Understand?"

She nodded.

"Good. Valentine, put your coat on, and give me one of those lanterns. We're going up."

TWENTY-FIVE: GOTHERAY CASTLE

As it turned out, finding their way up the glacier was not going to be as difficult as Alan had suspected. Beyond the little wooden bridge, Beckett and Valentine found a number of iron spikes driven deep into the ice, connected by a long, hempen rope. The rope and spikes led up the glacial plain much like the road had led up the mountain: in long switchbacks. The temperature dropped a full ten degrees as soon as Beckett and Valentine stepped onto the ice, and grabbed hold of the guide line. They trudged slowly, exhaustingly across the waste, while the frigid air clutched at their muscles, draining them of strength, and snatched their breath away until all they were able to breathe in were desperate gasps.

The blue lanterns illuminated only a small circle around them, and they soon felt that the glacier had become a huge wall, rising infinitely high into the darkness, first on their right side, then on the left, as they passed back and forth over the gradually-increasing slope. It was dangerous; Valentine slipped several times, and was spared a frozen trip back down the mountain only because of his death-grip on the robe. Beckett, who was mindful of how age and illness had made him much less agile than his partner, took only slow, measured, careful steps, despite the chill that threatened to murder him.

Two miles in a straight line was five miles along the zig-zag trail that had been left in the glacier, and the two coroners almost cried with relief when Gotheray Castle appeared out of the darkness; unlit, it was illuminated suddenly when they grew close enough to cast the weak light from their lanterns on it. The mountain of ice rose up immeasurably high behind the castle; it looked like the glacier had washed down the side of the mountain and half-buried Gotheray in ice.

There was another, frustrating half an hour of being able to see the castle in the darkness, but being forced along the indirect path across the glacier to reach it. When they finally obtained the castle's stone landing, Beckett and Valentine found the doors — ponderously heavy but unlocked — which were at the top of a stone stair leading right out up from the glacier. Unlocked doors stood to reason, Beckett supposed, as Gotheray Castle's location made it an unlikely target for burglars.

Gotheray Castle, hunching on the glacial mountainside like a tired predator, was built during the fifteenth century, long before the Architecture War in Trowth. It reflected the spirit of the times: before the Second Reconciliation of the Continental Powers, Trowth was in a perpetual state of war with its innumerable neighbors like Thranc, Sarein, and Sarpek. Castles, even castles that were meant to be summer palaces, were built first as fortresses, and Gotheray was certainly that. It was squat, with narrow windows that had recently been fixed with glass panes and copper shutters. Its walls were thick granite; the main door led through a tunnel into the house proper, a tunnel that could potentially be defended indefinitely by only a handful of men. Beckett and Valentine walked down the long tunnel, rubbing their hands and chests, trying to work blood back into circulation.

The two coroners found the castle stiflingly hot. Though none of the lamps were lit, a wave of dry heat poured down the entrance tunnel of the castle. By the time they reached the end of the tunnel, Valentine had stripped down to his shirtsleeves, and Beckett had tucked both winter coat and his overcoat under his arm. The two men left the excess outerwear in a pile in the main hall.

"Have they installed a furnace, do you think?" Valentine asked, trying to make out the details of the main hall in the places where the faint blue phlogiston light touched on them.

The heat shimmered across Beckett's eyes, and for a moment he found himself unaccountably reminded of the gleaming, melted towers in the City of Brass. "No," he replied, curtly.

Valentine stood in the center of the huge, hollow empty hall, surrounded by the circle of light cast from his lantern. His shadow was thrown long on the floor. "So...what do we do? I don't think there's anyone here."

Beckett nodded. "It doesn't look like it. So. We start looking. You know anything about castles like this?"

Valentine scratched at his chin. "Well, in the old days, there wasn't a lot of consistency to design. I'd guess that most of the living spaces are near the center of the building. And there's probably a basement."

"Down. Sounds about right. Let's see if we can find a stair."

They began to search, hands out and lightly resting on the walls, as they opened doors, and explored down hallways, always in a pair. Even though Gotheray appeared to be empty, Beckett didn't like the idea of splitting up. Especially because of the buzzing numbness he felt in his hands, the pins-and-needles effect that sometimes accompanied veneine overdose.

It took several minutes, but they eventually succeeded in locating a narrow spiral stair that extended both up and down interminably into the dark. "I'll go first," offered Valentine immediately, and enthusiastically. Beckett might have been resentful of the offer if not for two reasons: firstly, Valentine always offered to go first, especially if it meant going somewhere dangerous. Secondly, Beckett noticed a weakness in his knee, and he didn't want the younger man to see him struggling with the stairs.

The staircase seemed impossibly deep. As they descended deeper, Beckett's ears began ringing. It was a strange, distracting but not painful sound that grew stronger with every step, and made a journey of what could not have been more than minutes seem like it took hours. The heat grew worse towards the bottom of the stairs, though it was now occasionally interrupted by a strong gust of icy wind. Beckett was finally obliged to take off his suit coat.

The stairs ended abruptly on a stone landing. The phlogiston lanterns showed the two coroners a hall that appeared to be covered with ice, in defiance of the waves of dry heat washing over them. Beckett noticed something along the wall, a brass knife-switch. He groped towards it, and threw it.

Immediately, a string of dim, yellow, electric lights blossomed into view, running off down the long, ice-covered tunnel, above a floor made of heavy flagstones. Runnels along the sides of the tunnel collected water that dripped from the walls and the ceilings, draining it to somewhere out of sight.

"Put out your lantern," Beckett said.

"Why?" Valentine asked, even as he turned the agitator at the bottom of the phlogiston sphere all the way down.

"Electric lights? These are expensive. Why wouldn't you use phlogiston?"

Valentine shrugged. "I don't know. Why not?"

"I don't know, either," Beckett replied. "But until I do, I don't want to chance doing something stupid." He began to make his way down the icy tunnel; the sound of his boots on the flagstones was very loud, compared to the faint, constant sound of water dripping from the ceiling. "You notice something weird about the tunnel?" Beckett asked.

Valentine hurried after him. "Well, it looks like it's covered in ice. I'd call that pretty weird."

"No." Beckett shook his head. "It's not covered. I think they dug it through the ice. All this," he pointed to the slowly-melting ice above them, "all this is glacier."

"Oh." Valentine gulped, as waves of dry heat continued to assail them. "What do you think holds it up?"

"I don't know. A kinetic engine, maybe?" If Beckett was concerned about the prospect of a hundred tons of ice crashing onto their heads, he didn't show it.

The tunnel ended at the top of a huge, round chamber, that sank even deeper into the glacier. The chamber was ringed with a series of wooden platforms and narrow stairs, and crudely divided with partitions and more platforms throughout its volume, raised on scaffolding made out of the same, dark wood. The sheer scale of the construction was remarkable: the cave was at least two hundred feet across, and descended several stories into the ice, and the wooden constructions seemed to occupy as much space as a whole second castle.

The platforms and partitions obscured whatever rested at the bottom of the chamber, but Beckett was sure he knew what it was. That dry, infernal heat wafted up from the bottom, burning his eyes; he closed them, and dreamed about swimming in a great, stormy black sea…

"What is this?" Valentine called. He'd climbed around the wooden platforms ringing the upper-most level of the cave, and had found a small room. Beckett carefully picked his way around the not-especially-sturdy-looking platforms. "It's some kind of control center, I think."

The young coroner was right. The small room—not really a room at all, only an area blocked off on three sides by walls made of the same dark wood as everything else in the vast cave—was full of brass levers and dials, massive gear-boxes, and tangles of fat cables that snaked past the walls and down into the dim expanse of the ice-chamber.

"We should go down," Beckett said, after studying the controls for a few moments.

Valentine nodded. "I'll go first."

Of course you will, thought Beckett. He followed the younger man down the narrow wooden steps. They had no railing; Beckett kept one hand resting on the wet, slippery wall on his left, still mindful that, if he did fall, the ice would afford him no purchase. The dim, electric lights led them deeper and deeper in to the heart of the ice, past more small rooms filled with enigmatic machines, past narrow wooden bridges connecting to more platforms whose use remained obscure. All the time, the heat grew worse, and Beckett's mind wandered deeper and deeper into the waves and storms of the black sea.

At the bottom, half-eclipsed by the tall wooden walls, was a vessel. It was made all of dull brass, and in the shape of an airship or a submersible. There were no propellers, no visible means of propulsion; from the back of the ship sprouted gears and pistons, tall antennae, and three stubby prongs, glowing white and pouring dry heat into the air. Stenciled in black along its hull was the word *Montgomery*. The aethership.

"How long as it been since they used it?" Beckett mused aloud. "And it's still hot. How can it even be that hot?"

"Uhm, Beckett?" Valentine, ever the victim of his erratic attention span, begun exploring the other chambers at the bottom of the cave. "I think you'd better see this."

The young coroner had found a small room packed to the brim with crushed ice. There, preserved by the cold, were a number of cots, and three bodies. The bodies were, or had once been, human. Something had changed them now, some force outside the stability of the Word had disrupted the essential laws which all matter in nature was bound to follow.

The men's bodies, though clearly dead, were hideously plastic, shifting beneath the eye, avoiding natural classification. They changed from black to white to red, giving the impression that, at the same time Beckett was seeing their outsides, his eyes were struggling to cope with the fact that he could see their insides as well, continually blossoming out from the deepest recesses of the body to the edges of the skin and back again. Limbs, twisted at angles that seemed impossible not only by the limits of the human body but by the limits of normal space, were strangely manifold: sometimes a corpse would have only one arm, sometimes twenty, sometimes a hundred legs and no arms at all, and somehow all at once. It seemed as if each man was made of a thousand men, some half-faded from view, some horrifyingly clear, and all superimposed upon each other. Through-out that hideous panoply of pain-wracked corpses only the faces of the men remained constant: three rigid screams of agony, all untouched by whatever force had mutated the bodies.

Just looking at them caused a foul terror to sprout from Beckett's stomach and crawl up his throat, a terror that not even the veneine could keep at bay. He felt sick, a dark tunnel began to close in at the edges of his vision, and the awfully melted towers of the City of Brass sprang up behind his eyes, clawing frantically at a leprous moon covered with black basalt cities.

"Nng," Beckett groaned as he staggered from the room and leaned against the wall of ice. The cool radiating from it helped to restore his senses.

"Are you all right?" Valentine asked, his face painfully white. He, too, seemed unsteady on his feet. "There's...there's four cots in there, Beckett, but only three bodies..."

Beckett nodded. "One of those things survived."

"How do you...oh, no." If it were possible, his face grew even paler in the dim light, almost luminescent. "That thing, it's loose in Trowth."

"No." Beckett pushed himself away from the cold wall and composed himself. "I don't think it is, anymore. I think it's come back *here*."

TWENTY-SIX: A VISITOR

Fatigue held Alan Charterhouse in its ironically tireless grip. He stared out the double-paned window of the coach, while the small phlogiston heater kept the cold mercifully at bay, and Harry the coachman, who had come into the coach to warm himself, spoke in an almost-constant stream of anecdotes about old adventures he'd been on with Beckett.

"...of course, that's the thing about the ectoplasmatists. All kinds of fancy arms and what, but a bullet between the eyes is a bullet, right?" Harry's storehouse of problems that bullets could solve seemed inexhaustible. Alan blinked and struggled to keep his eyes open. His mind had been wandering far afield over the last...*How long have we been here?* He thought to himself. Earlier, he'd been sure that he'd seen a tiny, black shape making its way slowly across the field of ice. He'd followed it with his eyes as it moved out of sight, towards Gotheray Castle, and then became convinced that he'd only imagined it.

"Now, I know it was none of Mr. Beckett's fault," Harry went on, crooked teeth gleaming beneath the wiry forest of his moustache and mutton-chops, "I'm sure he told that fellow what happened just the way it did, but I think it's a crying shame that ol' Harry never made it in to any of those books."

Alan blinked again. "What books?"

"Why, those...oh, what do you call 'em? Ted East." The loquacious coachman seemed incredulous. "Don't tell me, a boy your age, and you never heard of Ted East."

"No," Alan said. "I mean, yes. I have heard...I mean, I read them. All of them. What do they have to do with Mr. Beckett?"

"Why, they're his stories," Harry replied. "Oh, I mean, they've been spiced up a bit, especially the saucy parts with all them foreign ladies. I know he's sick now, but even when he was young Mr. Beckett weren't much of a looker. Besides, there never was any time for dilly-dallying like that, if you know what I mean..."

"Beckett is Ted East?" Alan's voice was soft.

"Well, after a fashion, yes."

"Harry," Skinner interrupted suddenly. "Sh." The coachman was immediately silent and attentive, while Skinner, her face largely inscrutable behind the silver blindfold, pressed her lips together with concentration. "There's..." She twitched slightly. "An echo. Someone, a coach, coming up from the North..."

"Not the North, miss," Harry whispered. "That's up the mountain."

"I know. The South, I mean. The South." She shook her head. "I can't seem to...to hear it very clearly..."

"Well, all right," Harry said cheerfully, pulling on his heavy gloves, hat, and coat. "I'll have a look, I will." He grinned at Alan. "Back into the cold again. Make sure the heat stays on, right?"

A blast of frigid air accompanied Harry's exit, and Alan pulled the door closed as soon as he deemed it polite. After a few moments, the door opened, bringing more cold air with it, and Harry climbed back inside.

"You're right, miss. A coach is following the trail up from the south. Big one, got the Rowan-Czarnecki crest on it. Should be here in a few minutes, I'd think."

Skinner nodded. "All right, Harry," she told him. "You know what to do." Though she didn't appear to move her head, Alan was somehow certain that she'd fixed her attention on him. "Well, it is their house, right?"

"Do you think they're..." Alan began, unsure how to finish. "I mean, it's their summer home. Are they coming to...?"

"It's hardly Summer, is it?" Skinner replied. "No. They're not here for a visit, I think. They're probably here for us."

"So, what do we do?"

"Right now, I think we should wait here where it's warm."

Alan nodded. "That's a good idea." After a moment, he added, "Is Mr. Beckett really Ted East?"

"Yes," Skinner told him. "He sold his life story to a potboiler novelist so that he could buy his medicine. I wouldn't say anything to him about it, if I were you."

"Oh."

They waited in silence for several minutes, while Alan's anticipation grew. His young mind, possessed as it was of a fearsome capacity for reason, desperately conjured plans and contingencies. Would they have to fight? How? What weapons were there? What about moving onto the glacier? Could they use it to escape? Were the horses of Harry's coach faster than the ones coming up? Except for Harry's sudden silence, which Alan barely noticed, Skinner and the coachman both seemed completely unperturbed.

The sounds of another coach, rumbling up along the stony trail, reached their ears, and Skinner winced. The coach brought a strange echo with it, one that disrupted her ability to accurately identify sounds. She tried to clear her mind. "Well, let's go and meet our guests, shall we?"

She opened the door and climbed out, while Alan followed behind. The Rowan-Czarnecki coach, a beautiful black vehicle drawn by a team of beautiful, if tired-looking, horses, pulled to a stop, and Skinner's discomfort intensified. The doors of the coach opened, and three men emerged: one was fairly tall and heavy-set, older, with a paunchy, tired face but with an intensity in his gaze that spoke a fiery certainty. The other two had the bored expression of professional men; they wore dark suits, and each carried a revolver.

Skinner leaned on her cane, and put a hand to her ears.

"Excuse me," the older man said. He drew a small device from his pocket, a collection of brass rings that whirled rapidly around a nugget of polished, soapy green flux. The man did something to it, and the rings abruptly stopped and folded up. "Something new we developed at the Academy. To stop eager ears from overhearing what they shouldn't."

Once the device had been deactivated, Skinner seemed to recover almost immediately. "Thank you, sir, for your consideration. May I ask what you're doing here?"

"This is the road to my house," the older man replied. He had a deep, sonorous voice, and Alan felt certain that he'd seen the man somewhere before. "I should ask you the same question."

"We are here as agents of the crown," Skinner told him. "Conducting an investigation." She took a step closer to the three men, and the two guards raised their pistols immediately; there was a moment of tension, but the guards relaxed, a little sheepishly. Skinner was clearly blind, after all.

"I understand that it's appropriate to inform a party if the coroners intend to investigate their properties. I received no such notice." The man told them.

Suddenly, something fell into place in Alan's head. "Wolfgang Rowan-Czarnecki," he said, and the older man looked startled. "You're in charge of the Royal Academy of Sciences. My father took me to one of your lectures, about using flux tympanum as an energy source...." He trailed off. "Uhm. Excuse me, sir, I didn't mean to interrupt. Please, continue."

"We weren't saying anything important, Alan," Skinner smiled. "It's traditional, under circumstances like this, to be cryptic with each other, and vaguely threatening. There's really little point to it, if you ask me."

Wolfgang smiled ruefully. "Agreed. This situation comes down to two essential elements: I do not intend to be hanged, and I will not let you stop my experiments."

"But...they're dangerous," Alan pointed out. "And heresy. The *Excelsior*..."

"If you've come this far," Wolfgang interrupted, "Then you know that Zindel and Lightman have solved the problems with the *Excelsior*. Not only can we return effectively from aetherspace, but the stabilizers can be adjusted so that engine can return to any place in the world. Think about that, before you try and stop me. Near-instant transportation."

"The war," Skinner said her voice softening in sudden sympathy. "You want to end the war."

The pain in the old Rowan-Czarnecki's voice was clear; it throbbed in his throat, brought tears to his eyes. "Fifteen years. Fifteen years sending our young men, our best and brightest off to die fighting that filth. Why? To preserve the phlogiston pipelines. You take a look around our city, hollowed out by war, nothing left but the crippled, dirty dregs that escaped the pressgangs, and you tell me that this wasn't worth the risk."

"A pretty speech, Mr. Rowan-Czarnecki," Skinner replied, her voice firm again. "You should save it for your trial."

Another rueful smile. "We both know that this is never going to go to trial. Where are your men? Beckett and that Vie-Gorgon pissant."

"They're at the Castle already," Skinner said. "Gathering evidence."

Wolfgang glanced over Skinner's should into the coach. "Well. Why did they take the coachman?"

Skinner only smiled.

Twenty-Seven: Vlytze Square

The weather of First Winter in Trowth often vacillated between damp, raw, chilly days and damp, raw, considerably warmer days, unlike Second Winter, which simply plunged the city into a deep freeze for two months. After the psychestorm's cold front had broken up in the treacherous air-currents above the Trowth sea-wall, the rain came in from the south.

A heavy, steady downpour fell from black clouds that were mercifully lacking in the terrible psychological effects that came with the green clouds from the north. The rain muted the fires in Mudside, enabling the Committee for Public Safety to look out at the plain of muddy ash and pat themselves on the back for a job well done. The afternoon following the raid, Edgar Wyndham-Vie would announce to a small congregation of umbrella-clutching gentlemen victory over The Sharpsie Threat.

The Committee for Public Safety had, in fact, spoken too soon. Based on the information gathered from the raid at Mud-side, they simply presumed that they had vastly overestimated the number of sharpsies living in Trowth. This was not an unreasonable assumption, since sharpsies rarely paid their taxes and humans could neither distinguish one sharpsie from another by sight, nor recognize their guttural native names. Moreover, the fires that the gendarmes had started served to obscure the wooden tunnels that had sunk into the mud by the riverside. Nearly two thousand sharpsies had fled through those tunnels, and it would eventually become clear that those who remained had allowed themselves to be arrested on purpose, to give their fellows time to escape.

After Wyndham-Vie's speech, which would be lambasted in the broadsheets for months to come, but before night had fully fallen on the city, a massive explosion rocked Old Bank. The method and elements of that explosion would never fully be determined, because immediately following it a wave of sharpsies boiled up from the Arcadium and seized the twelve square city blocks at the top of Old Bank hill.

Some had brought barricades with them, perhaps old pieces of their homes. Others raided offices, shops, and houses on the hill for desks, chairs, tables, bookcases, anything that could be piled up in the streets, choking off the narrow lanes and alleys that made up the neighborhood. They carried weapons; sometimes they used the tools of their trades: hammers occasionally, but usually meat cleavers and long butcher's knives. Others had improvised weapons: broken chair legs, long coils of rope with iron hooks or pulleys on the ends, sometimes even the stone downspouts that the Crabtree-Daiors used for their gutters.

The barricades were constructed and manned by sharpsies that hurled rocks from their slings and bottles that they'd filled with phlogiston at any authority foolish enough to approach; meanwhile, a smaller but still sizable group of sharpsies staged raids on the three Vaults where their fellows were being held. The few Lobstermen that had been set as guards were caught unawares by the suddenness and size of the attack, and despite their strength and speed, they were rapidly overwhelmed by the sharpsies, who now demonstrated a speed and agility, especially in close-quarters, that seemed to catch everyone unprepared.

It took little more than an hour for the sharpsies to take control of the top of the hill, and murder anyone that even looked like a gendarme or a pressganger. It did not take much longer for them to break out their fellows and arm them.

The gendarmerie in neighboring New Bank and North Ferry responded fairly quickly. They gathered their members together, a few thousand strong all told, and attempted to breach the sharpsie barricades. They staged a simultaneous attack on the barricades at Rampling and Czarnecki Streets, and another at the barricade used to wall off Old Wall Square. The men came on with the greenglass goggles, rarely bothering with their armbands; in fact, many of the members of this rag-tag militia were not gendarmes at all, but the few able-bodied, relatively young men left in the city that had avoided the pressgangs.

A handful of the gendarmes were equipped with rifles or pistols, but their attack was characterized by the single most prominent characteristic of the Trowth gendarmerie: disorganization. Riflemen and pistoleers were spread out randomly throughout the attacking mob, firing at whim, choosing targets almost randomly. They did little damage as they approached, as it was generally assumed that the weight of their numbers would overwhelm the sharpsie blockades with little trouble, and the men could use their swords and clubs once the walls were breached.

Unfortunately for the gendarmes, the narrow alleys in Old Bank made the approach to the barricades difficult; they were forced into a large mass as they were fed into a kind of bottleneck, and then showered with phlogiston bottles that exploded in blue and red flames — a weapon that would eventually be called Sharp Brandies. The sticky phlogiston adhered to the men as it burned; they attempted to run screaming from the walls, but found themselves trapped by the men behind them, and succeeded only in setting more people on fire.

At Rampling Street, the makeshift army managed to attack quickly enough that twenty or thirty men actually reached the walls. They attempted to drive the sharpsies away, but were unequal to the staggering agility the sharpsies displayed with their knives. The attackers were neatly butchered, and a row of brandy-throwers raced to the top of the wooden-furniture barricade to throw their incendiary cocktails at the remaining men.

While the first assault by the gendarmerie was a complete disaster, it did give the militia throughout the rest of the city time to mobilize. Men were called up, armed with short swords from the armories; every fifth man was given a rifle with three bullets. They were brought together under the tactical leadership of Edgar Wyndham-Vie, largely because of his family's prestige.

Just as Wyndham-Vie prepared his assault on the Old Wall Square barricade, fires appeared in Red Lanes. A handful of socialist radicals, who had consigned their criminal meetings to the duetti clubs of Fleshmarket Close, assumed that the sharpsies were starting a revolution, and so they decided to start one of their own. They set ablaze two government offices and an armory that they'd raided. Wyndham-Vie was obliged to send a third of his men to Red Lanes to put that neighborhood to rights.

As the men reached Red Lanes, they found themselves immediately set upon not by the radicals there, but by a small force of indige from Bluewater, armed as well with improvised weapons. They had been on their way to attack the Indigae neighborhood, using the sharpsie riots as cover for their own assault on the "race-traitors" who hoarded the wealth brought by the phlogiston industry. The attack on the gendarmes was an unfortunate accident, but it turned what should have been the rout of a few disgruntled radicals into a protracted, three-way brawl that lasted for hours.

Down a third of his army, Wyndham-Vie attempted a subterfuge. He sent the bulk of his remaining forces towards Old Wall

Square, in what he hoped would appear to be over-whelming odds. Meanwhile, he would take a smaller group, well outfitted with rifles, to the barricade at High Street. They would take the smaller barricade, and then take up position on the north side of Old Wall to lay down cover fire.

As his smaller force moved into position, another problem soon became apparent. There was another Vault on his side of the barricade; it had been used to hold the notorious gang leader that the broadsheets called Anonymous John, and his own men had seized the opportunity to attempt a jailbreak. They managed to take control of the entire Vault building, and had set up their own men—all of whom had rifles and plentiful amounts of bullets—in the windows of the upper floors.

While John's men, largely smugglers know as the Dockside Boys, were both racist and nationalist, the only thing they could be said to hate more than sharpsie foreigners were the gendarmes. Consequently, when an opportunity presented itself to not only interfere with the Committee for Public Safety's plans *and* to kill the blue-armed men that so often disrupted their own operations, they leapt upon it. While Wyndham-Vie led his men down the narrow alley, the Dockside Boys immediately opened fire, sniping first at anyone that wore a captain's hat.

The riflemen among the gendarmes found their attention divided between the snipers in the Vault and the sharpsies with their incendiary grenades on the barricade. Unable to mount a concerted attack on the barricade, they found themselves pinned. Only a handful of men, among them Edgar Wyndham-Vie himself (who had chosen to lead from the rear) managed to escape the ambush that would eventually be known as the High Street Slaughter.

Of course, without Wyndham-Vie's men laying down cover, there was nothing to keep the sharpsies off the top of the barricades at Old Wall Square. When the bulk of the gendarmerie approached, they found themselves faced with a hail of stones and broken glass and bottles of explosive phlogiston that detonated in their midst, showering them with fire and razor-sharp shrapnel. The gendarmes were forced to retreat.

After half an hour of fighting in Red Lanes, the indige faction retreated back across the river, leaving the remaining gendarmes to break down the radicals. The men were arrested and then, because the Vaults in Old Bank were presently a war-zone, summarily executed. The now-diminished force of gendarmes headed back towards Old Bank, only to meet the Dockside Boys halfway, and found themselves pinned down at Thurston Square.

The indige of Bluewater had mostly given up on their revenge, except for a small mob of about twenty that found its way to Indiga, broke into the home of Loren Hoge, who con-trolled most of the air-ship importation of phlogiston into Trowth, and dragged the man and his family out into the streets. Loren, his two wives, and his three oldest children were bludgeoned to death with paving stones. The two youngest children, both girls, had silver stars tattooed on their faces, and were left to wander homeless and anathema, according to indige tradition.

After the Committee's disastrous assault on the sharpsie barricade, the Emperor stepped in. He ordered five hundred Lobstermen to an assault on the Rampling street barricade, accompanied by a small force of trolljrman artillery.

The Lobstermen, possessed of superhuman speed, raced beneath the hail of grenades towards the barricade, while the trolljrmen brought their cannons, bolted directly to the shells of their great, two-headed tortoises, into position. The Lobstermen drove the sharpsies down from the walls, and the trolljrmen began to demolish the barricade with the irregular thunder of their cannon-fire.

With the barricade breached, the Lobstermen pressed into the center of the sharpsie-controlled area, with the gendarmes pouring in behind. Despite their preparation, they still found themselves hard-pressed to deal with the knife-wielding sharpsies. The agility of the snaggle-toothed inhumans was astounding; they leapt from low windows and walls to land on the broad backs of the Lobstermen, slashing wherever they could find unarmored flesh, and then springing away again to catch overhanging eaves or downspouts before a return attack could be made. They dropped into the midst of rushing gendarmes, heavy cleaver-knives whirling, huge jaws snapping, severing the soft human limbs with ease.

The attack into Old Bank was slowed by the vicious assault, and a handful of sharpsies took the opportunity to attack the trolljrmen tarrasques that had been left behind after the initial rush. They ran along rooftops to catch the trolljrmen by surprise, and then hopped down directly onto the backs of the giant tortoises. The sharpsie ambushers managed to fire the cannons off of three of the tarrasques; one shell crashed harmless into a heavy, Gorgon-Vie style turret. A second exploded in the midst of the gendarmes. A third actually detonated among the Lobster-men, further slowing the marines' assault.

The trolljrmen, who had been caught off-guard by the sharpsie attack, managed to bear the ambushers to the ground, hammering at them with heavy fists and relying on their thick, scaly skin to protect them from tooth and knife.

While the assault had slowed, it had not stopped. Lobstermen led the gendarmes through the narrow streets of Old Bank, while sharpsies abandoned their makeshift barricades to engage in half-hearted flanking assaults on the large force. They brought their incendiary grenades with them, but the riflemen, using their flux-ground greenglass lenses, could spot them with ease, and were generally able to pick them off before any of the phlogiston explosives could be thrown.

The Lobstermen pushed on against what appeared to be a flagging enemy force. Sharpsies were sniped at distance, ground down beneath the hammering of cudgels and tromping feet of the marines and gendarmes, or hacked to pieces by their swords. After the first initial attempt to hold the invaders, the sharpsies panicked and fled through the streets of Old Bank, while the Committee's army pursued, roaring with victory.

The rout was another ambush. The sharpsies weren't retreating; they were regrouping, leaping out of the street and scaling the complex, Gorgon-Vie architecture onto rooftops. They consolidated the bulk of their number on the roofs around Vlytze Square, where High Street met Corimander, and when the gendarmes and Lobstermen reached it, they fell on their attackers with the reckless abandon that only the knowledge of impending doom could bring.

Gendarmerie soon found themselves hemmed in on all sides by the towering buildings of the district, while slashing knives and sharp teeth dropped on them en masse from above, a wave of hundreds of sharpsies, furious and full of bloodlust. The gendarmes defended themselves with swords and cudgels, with rifles and pistols, but they found themselves trapped, packed in, unable to maneuver.

The sharpsies, with so much experience as butchers and herdsman, had turned Vlytze Square into a slaughterhouse. Their dexterous feet gripped heads and shoulders as they ran about *on top of* the flailing crowds, hurling themselves teeth-first at the most likely targets. The Lobstermen attempted to rally, but soon found themselves as equally disadvantaged as the gendarmes. Their own speed and strength was of little use when they had nowhere to move, and the nimble sharpsies had pegged them as targets immediately. They attempted to overwhelm the bone-armored men, using their own bodies to tangle up weapon arms while their fellows brought knives to bear on the joints between bleeding bone plates.

Still the sharpsies found it difficult to gain advantage, as more gendarmes appeared from every street, freed up from their battle with the Dockside Boys. The sharpsies were also unable to use their favorite weapon—their incendiary grenades—now that they were locked in close-combat with their adversaries. The battle had become a bloody, brutal stalemate; two opposing forces, equally matched and unable to retreat, attempting to simply grind each other down.

That was when the first shells landed. There was a whistling scream, and a deafening explosion as a house by the square collapsed, hurling rubble among the fighting men. Another scream, and another explosion, this time in the square itself, and men and sharpsies disappeared in an explosion of blood and limbs.

Edgar Wyndham-Vie had commandeered the Imperial frigate *Revenge*. He had maneuvered it up the Stark, and had turned the long guns on the ship's deck towards Vlytze Square. His men had reluctantly begun to fire on their own city, chilled by the knowledge that Wyndham-Vie would surely murder as many humans as it took in order to kill all the sharpsies that he could. They primed the cannons and kept firing, while Edgar Wyndham-Vie stood at the helm, red-faced and mad-eyed, leering with ecstatic glee at the devastation he was causing.

It was after the first volleys from the *Revenge* fell on Vlytze Square that the unthinkable happened.

The men and sharpsies fighting in Vlytze Square, if they were not deafened by the cannon fire from the *Revenge*, all stopped as one and listened to an eerie, impossible sound that shrieked in their ears and reached down their throats to wrench at their stomachs. It was a supernormal wail that grew and grew, and imposed a silence over the combatants. The sound ended abruptly with a sudden, echoing crack.

For a long moment, nothing happened; men and trolljr-men and sharpsies all held their breaths in an extended, desperate pause.

Then, there was an explosion. A huge, deep, heart-stopping bone-rattling thunder spread in a wave across the square as a massive column of blinding, blue-white light tore shrieking into the sky. The north half of the square vanished, collapsing into a sinkhole and dragging men and sharpsies with it to be vaporized in the blinding inferno. The rest of the square began to follow it, and, unmindful of their previous enmity, sharpsie, man, and trolljrman began running. A wash of dust, smoke and fire followed after them, claiming the slowest runners and hurling more to the ground. Three-quarters of Vlytze Square disappeared into the dark, and as much an area to the north. The center of Old Bank had become a bloody hole of devastation.

Later, after the dust had settled and someone had time to work out what happened, it would be assumed that the sharpsies were responsible; seeing their intended revolution fail, they'd done the only thing they could think of, and accepted a kind of mass-suicide.

Of course, this hypothesis left a number of disturbing questions unanswered. How did the sharpsies know about it? How did they know where to find it? How did they get in, and know how to use it?

Was it really the sharpsies, preferring to kill themselves rather than lose to the humans? Or was it someone from the Committee, fearful that the *Revenge* might level even more of the city? Or was it someone else, with a purpose more devious?

Someone, deep beneath the house on Corimander Street, had activated the engines of the *Excelsior*.

TWENTY-EIGHT: THE PILOT

To alien-adapted eyes, Castle Gotheray was a vast inverted labyrinth, a latticework of rooms stacked upon rooms, a strange pattern of outer walls beneath inner walls that could still be seen. Deep beneath the castle, and simultaneously in its center, always at the center, no matter what flowers of past and future bloomed before those eyes, was the beacon, the still glowing white-hot engine of the *Montgomery*.

The distorted shadow of its limbs, now only fractions of a greater whole, gripped the surface of the ice, and also under and within it, as it made its lurching way up the glacier. The blue-green moonlight was not light, but the shadow of something brighter, something that these new monstrous eyes had come to see. In shadows of the brighter-than-light lurked more and more shadows, strange forms that twisted into and out of space at every moment, and went all unnoticed by human vision. The ice reared up and sank down again, and every step brought it closer to the Castle.

The Castle. The doors were open, but now the thing did not need doors. It moved straight on towards the wall, revolving itself through material space and finding a place on the other side. The latticework, the dragonfly-eye collage of visions transformed to a view of a hundred thousand staircases, all leading down, down to the ship beneath the ice. It chose a stair at random; the near ones all led the same way, and most of the future stairs were crumbled and unusable.

Down the stairs and through the ice, to the great white gap in the cold, where only the barest flecks of the brighter-than-light could filter through, long since leaving its shadows behind, and where it could see dancing waves of electricity slithering in columns up and down.

There was breath down there, and voice, and the thing changed its perspective so that it was now at the bottom of the cave, and could stand comfortably on its ceiling. Voices spoke, but they were fractions of the sound its ears had come to hear, and so unintelligible. None of this mattered. It had come for its home, and no voice or breath would stand in its way.

The Pilot had returned for its ship.

"What are you smiling about?" Wolfgang demanded of Skinner, but she said nothing. He gestured to his men, and they raised their guns. "There's no way out of this for you. You know that. I can't let you stop me."

Dust leapt up in small explosion at this feet, at the same time Alan heard an echoing *crack* from up the slope of the mountain. Wolfgang stared at the ground in disbelief for a moment, then he and his men all leapt to the sides, their eyes scanning the horizon.

Splinters exploded from the coach. The driver stood up, fumbling under his seat for a weapon. Too late; something hit him in the chest and he tumbled over the back.

While the guards were occupied looking for the sniper, Skinner leapt forward, her telerhythmia whirling around her in a circle, rapping fiercely on men and carriages alike. She snapped her cane down on one man's revolver, sending it flying from his grasp, then pulled the cane apart...

A *sword*, Alan thought, *she's got a sword in there!* The second guard had turned back towards Skinner as soon as sword was drawn, but it was too late. A flower of blood blossomed in his shirt and he fell back. Wolfgang immediately went for his gun.

Alan sighed, set his shoulder, and charged as hard as he could into the older man's stomach. Alan was not a large boy, and he could not run fast, but he managed to catch Wolfgang low in the gut and unprepared. The older man gasped and fell back against the carriage, his gun slipping from stunned fingers and clattering away down the mountainside.

Skinner slashed with her sword at her opponent: two strokes, precisely aimed. The first was low, and caused the man to throw his hips back, pulling his stomach out of the way of the blade. The second was at his eyes, and he quickly snapped his head back out of range. The combination of movements — which Skinner must have learned by rote; it was impossible that her telerhythmia was that precise — threw him off balance, and Skinner's third attack, a thrust directly at the center of his chest, landed home. Five inches of sharp, slender blade sank into his flesh, just below the sternum. The man shivered and convulsed, but the thrust had paralyzed his lungs, and he couldn't scream.

Wolfgang threw Alan bodily aside; the young man cracked his head against the wheel of the coach, and the world swam for a moment before his eyes. The older man jumped towards Skinner and grabbed her sword-arm. In one smooth motion, he wrenched her around, arm locked up behind her back, and wrapped his free hand tight around her throat; she made a gagging sound, as he pushed her in between himself and where he suspected Harry was shooting from.

"No!" He screamed. "No! Tell him to back the fuck off! Tell him!" Skinner tried to speak, but Wolfgang's iron grip on her throat choked off all the words. "I know you can communicate with him. Use whatever signal you have to tell him to stand the *fuck* down before I break your neck!"

No, no, no, thought Alan Charterhouse, as the scene swam back into view. His head throbbed, but his adrenaline was chasing the pain from his system. He crawled away, under the coach, desperately trying to think. He tried to shout at Wolfgang, but the words only came out as a harsh whisper. The older man didn't hear him anyway; he was too busy whispering furiously in Skinner's ear. Alan tried to work his voice back into his mouth, while he looked desperately around for something, some weapon that could be hurled against Rowan-Czarnecki's broad back.

Harry appeared out of the dark. Alan thought he must have run directly from the coach as soon as he and Skinner had gotten out; now, the coachman had a long rifle held up over his head. "It's all right," he called. "It's all right."

"Put it down!" Wolfgang screamed at him, his hand tightening further around Skinner's throat. Alan could not see her from his angle beneath the coach; he wondered if she was even still conscious.

"Here. I will, see?" Harry slowly began lowering the rifle to the ground.

Alan licked his lips. *I have to do something…*his eyes found one of the revolvers, lying on the ground. It must have spun away when one of the guards had fallen. Alan grabbed it with both hands, surprised by the weapon's weight.

He found his voice, and shouted, "Let her go!" Even as he realized with a sinking feeling that if he fired, the bullet might go right through Wolfgang and into Skinner.

Rowan-Czarnecki half-turned. His eyes widened when he saw the gun. He opened his mouth to speak, then shouted as Skinner threw her head back into his jaw. In the same moment, she tore his hand from her throat and tried to twist away; Alan heard a sharp snap from her shoulder, but she managed to duck down.

Alan raised the gun and screwed his eyes shut. There was an explosion, a gunshot thundered in his ears, and he could smell burnt sulfur. There was, however, surprisingly little recoil. Alan opened his eyes; Wolfgang stood, a baffled expression on his face, with his shirt-front soaked with blood. Alan looked down at his gun, horrified. There had been no recoil at all; it wasn't even smoking, *No,* he thought, *oh, no, I've killed him, I've killed him...*

There was another gunshot, just like the first, and the air was filled with the smell of gunpowder again. Wolfgang's head snapped to the side; he crashed against the coach and fell to the ground. Alan could only stare.

"You all right, boy?" Harry was shouting at him. He had his rifle raised, smoke curling from the tip. Alan could only nod, quiet and stunned. Harry immediately knelt next to Skinner, who had collapsed into the snow. "Are you all right, miss?"

Skinner's face was pale, and she tried to speak, but only coughed instead. She indicated her shoulder, where her arm hung limply by her side.

"It's dislocated," Harry told her. He grabbed her upper arm and shoulder. "This is going to hurt, a lot." The knocker nodded and gritted her teeth; Harry took a deep breath, and wrenched her shoulder back into place.

Skinner screamed, and half-collapsed into the snow again. Harry made to help her up, but she waved him off, breathing heavily. "I'm fine," she managed to gasp. "Fine."

Harry nodded and stood, then turned an appraising eye back on Alan. The boy was still beneath the coach, his face white, his eyes wide. "I killed him..." Alan said.

The coachman shook his head, and gently took the revolver from Alan's hands. "You never did. Look. It's not even hot. You never fired. It was just me." He tossed the gun into the snow, and tousled Alan's hair. "You did good, though. That was quick thinking that was, and it sure saved us all. What's say we get you and the miss back into the coach and warmed up a little, right?"

He began to help Skinner to her feet, when a peal of thunder shook the ground beneath them. They all looked up and immediately turned their eyes towards Gotheray Castle. There was nothing to see.

"What was that?" Alan whispered.

"Something bad, I'll wager," Harry muttered under his breath. "Come on. Into the coach."

Twenty-Nine: The Translated Man

"What do you mean, it's here? How do you know?" Valentine asked.

"I can feel it." The Brass Towers loomed in his imagination, and the ringing, buzzing sound in his ear intensified. Over the last few minutes, he had become more and more certain that this was not an effect of the drug; or, rather, that what the drug did was not so much cause a hallucination as it made him sensitive to certain other things — things that his mind was forced to interpret as hallucinations.

"Well," said Valentine. "Well, we should leave. Right? Let's go."

"No," Beckett told him. "Not yet." *Patient*, he told himself. *Be patient.* The thing had come back to the castle, he knew, and he was sure it would return to the ship. Where else did it have to go? "We can't let it loose. We've got to stop it here." *It'll come to the ship. Be patient.*

"All right," Valentine muttered. "Hope you've got a plan, is all..."

Beckett snorted. He did not mention that he could see a black shape, creeping down the wall on the far side of the chamber. Head first, it slowly slithered down the icy walls, somehow folding under or around or through the wooden plat-forms in the way. *Wait, wait, wait. Wait until it gets to the bottom.* The shape moved out of sight.

"Now," Beckett said, softly. "Start up. Slowly, quietly. Right?"

"What?" Valentine practically shouted. He dropped his voice to a whisper. "What? You mean...it's here? I mean, *here*, here? Like, in this room?"

Beckett nodded, and gestured to the stairs. The young coroner started to back up the wooden steps, his hands hovering near the grips of his revolvers, though he knew bullets wouldn't stop this adversary. Beckett waited for a few seconds, then he, too, began the ascent.

The two men could now hear a strange noise from behind the maze of wooden partitions on the floor of the chamber. It was a wet, sticky noise, like someone was pulping fruit.

"Go!" Beckett shouted, suddenly. "Run!"

Valentine didn't hesitate. He tore up the stairs, Beckett close on his heels. They'd made it less than a hundred yards before Beckett turned. He could see the thing now, crawling up the stairs after them.

If the corpses of the translated men had been awful, this living specimen was a thousand times worse. It was a mess of shifting limbs, some fading grotesquely from sight, others appearing and disappearing at random; it's flesh not only blossomed and turned itself inside out again and again, but it slithered across the bones, sometimes leaving the skeleton behind, rearing up like a clutch of snakes, only to return to that hideously shifting body. Coils of blood and gristle darted out from its body and dropped back in, or they waved like an insect's antenna, lightly touching the wood and ice around it. It's face was the only thing that never changed, and it was even more awful for its stillness. The thing's face was just like the faces of the dead men: locked in a rigid, unchanging, terrible scream, its jaws stretched and mouth open, its eyes rolled back in its head. The head rolled lifelessly on its neck, in movements seemingly unrelated to those of its bizarre agglomerations of real and phantom limbs.

Beckett drew his weapon as the thing approached. It was moving slowly, perhaps because it didn't feel threatened, but the coroner suspected that would change once it heard gunfire. *Have to make this count.* He aimed carefully, not at the monster before him, but behind it…

"Beckett!" Valentine whispered desperately. "What are you doing? Bullets don't hurt it!"

At the sound of the gunshot, the thing froze, or it froze as much as it could. Its millions of arms and legs still blinked in and out of existence, its weird, lifeless head still rolled about on its shoulders, but it had stopped its approach.

Missed, Beckett thought. *Try again.*

The thing began to move towards him, this time more quickly. After the second gunshot, it began to charge up the wooden stairs.

"Shit!" Shouted Valentine. He drew his revolvers and opened up on the translated man, which paused beneath the hail of bullets. Flesh exploded out of its back, then splashed right back into its skin; each bullet left a tiny whirlpool in the rapidly mutating body of the creature.

"Done," Beckett said. "Go, go, go!"

The two men turned and ran up the stairs, all thought of care and safety abandoned, despite the rickety wooden construction and the lack of guardrails. That weird, pulping-fruit sound followed them, keeping distance easily.

Beckett was almost breathless when they reached the top platform. He made straight for the control-room. "Get out," he told Valentine.

"What are you doing?" The younger man screamed at him.

"Go! Get out of here!" Beckett stood before the brass switches in the little room. "Go!" He screamed at Valentine. "That's a fucking *order.*" Reluctantly, with a glance back at the monstrosity that was still methodically make its way up the stairs, Valentine disappeared down the icy tunnel.

Which one? Beckett thought. Then: *There is no way this is going to work.* He looked at the biggest switch he could find, a great knife switch set into the wall, and threw it. The coroner was rewarded almost immediately with a low hum, deep enough that it seemed to emanate from the very walls. *Now what?* There was a dial, something that looked like a timer. He set it to the smallest increment that he could, something that looked like a little less than a minute. It began to tick. Blue lights on the panel began to flash.

Judging by the wet squishing sound, the creature had reached the top platform. Beckett stepped out of the control room, praying that there was nothing else to do. He began to back away towards the tunnel. The creature's head rolled in a wide circle before hanging towards him. It began to follow.

No. Beckett thought. *It'll follow me out. Shit.* He'd reached the opening of the tunnel, and the creature was still following. Beckett sighed. *I've got to stay.* He drew his gun and fired the remaining four bullets, right at the thing's head.

Blood and meat exploded into a beautiful, strangely-symmetric flower before reconstituting themselves exactly into that awful, screaming, dead-eyed face. The thing had not even slowed it's pace. *Can't let it leave.* Beckett steeled himself, and prepared to charge.

Something began to scream at the bottom of the cave, an unearthly wail at the highest pitches the human ear could perceive. The thing paused for a second, then resumed that steady, terrible approach.

Suddenly, Beckett felt a hand on his shoulder; Valentine shoved him out of the way and, roaring, hurled one of the phlogiston lanterns directly at the feet of the monster. Ordinarily, this would have simply sprayed burning phlogiston everywhere, but for some reason, some effect of the kinetic engine that held the ice together, or an effect of that terrible machine at the glacier's core, the lantern exploded.

The blast was thunderous. It threw the two coroners back against the wall. It threw the translated creature clear across the cave like a flaming comet, tearing wooden scaffolding apart with it. The thing wailed, its limbs consumed with blue and red flames that burned in strangely symmetrical patterns.

Beckett found himself tangled up with Valentine on the floor, head resting against the icy wall. His ears were ringing now, and he could barely hear anything except that horrific scream from down below. He pulled himself to his feet and took quick stock; once he'd ascertained that his limbs were all intact, he tried to wake Valentine.

"Oh, you fucking idiot." The man was bleeding from the head. He was breathing, but unconscious. "Stupid, stupid. Wake up! Get up, now!" The younger man didn't move. *No time, there's no time.* The wail had grown louder, and now the creature clutched the wall on the far side of the room. It still burned, but seemed unconcerned by that fact.

Crap. Beckett bent down and, grunting, managed to pull the younger man onto his shoulders. *No fucking TIME!* He half-staggered, half-ran as the wail rose to an ear-splitting pitch, following the dim lights down the hall towards the remaining blue lantern. That creature began to follow them into the tunnel. Beckett had just reached the staircase when the wailing sound abruptly ceased.

The translated monster paused. Then, without warning, it turned and leapt back into the icy cave. *No time,* Beckett thought to himself. His heart and lungs were pounding, screaming for air as he dragged Valentine up the stone stairs. His thighs felt like they were about to explode.

No time.

The Pilot changed its perspective again, so that it stood on the wall and could run straight forward towards the ground. Wood and ice spiraled out of the way, as it revolved itself through material space. Its beacon had vanished, the beautiful brighter-than-light heat was gone, the ship was gone, it wanted its *ship.*

Space adjusted itself again as the Pilot climbed onto the floor, staring at the gap where the *Montgomery* had been. It's translation out of space had removed it from all the creature's eyes, the thousand honeycombs of vision that opened up the world to it all saw that it was gone, gone. A feeling that was like fear, and like rage, but also the product of an alien heart to which such feelings were meaningless, rent its chest in two, and then smoothed itself back together.

The ship would return. The ship always returned. It never left for long. The creature looked down at the ground, where heat swirled up in curling spirals of squares. There was brass on the floor, and the creature folded itself in half so that its arms were low enough to touch it. It was a piece of brass, the length of a human hand. A part of the Pilot's mind, untouched by the hideous transformation that had translated its body, spoke. *That was one of the harmonic stabilizers,* it said. The Pilot was unconcerned.

The man had shot it off. The voice insisted.

The pilot didn't care. The ship would be back soon.

Shit.

The *Montgomery* lurched back into normal space.

THIRTY: DOWN THE MOUNTAIN

They were only halfway up the stairs when the explosion came, and this time Beckett really was deafened. It crashed against his ears, reverberated against the walls, and brought with it a flood of images. He was choking in the sea, now looking at the City of Brass, now he saw the moon, looming strangely in the sky…

"No!" Beckett gripped his mind with an iron fist. "No," he said, though he couldn't hear himself. The floor of the castle had begun to tilt. Slightly at first, but the angle was becoming alarming. "Out."

Beckett counted his steps with gasps. *One-two-three breathe. One-two-three breathe. Keep moving. Keep moving.* The floor of the great hall was at a forty-five degree angle by the time Beckett reached it, and he could feel knives stabbing at his heart.

"Wake up, Valentine!" He threw the younger man to the ground and began slapping his face. "Fucking wake up!" It was no use. The man was completely unconscious.

Grimacing, Beckett found their coats, still piled by the main doors. He dressed himself and then Valentine, as quickly as he could without slipping; his senseless, stupid fingers betrayed him again and again as he fumbled with the clasps. Then, he took out the travel case for his veneine. There were two ounces of the drug left. Beckett drained it all into the syringe, then thrust the needle into his carotid artery and mashed down on the plunger.

The world was covered with a blanket almost instantly. The pain in his legs and back and arms wandered away, his heart pounded from the end of a very, very long hall. The ringing in his ears receded, and there was nothing but pleasant warmth engulfing all his senses.

You're not done, yet, a voice told him, but Beckett ignored it. The sound of rushing water was coming to him, the great sea that would lead him to the city, and he didn't mind at all; light and warmth suffused his being.

The voice spoke again, now with a strong and furious tone. It was his father's voice, the voice of the overseer on the factory floor, the voice of his sergeant from the Royal Marines. *I said that you are not. Fucking. Finished. Get up.* Beckett didn't move. *Get up!* His body refused to respond. *GET UP!*

He lurched to his feet. All sense of his body was muted by the drug. It made him unsteady as he pulled Valentine onto his shoulders. The floor had canted to a frighteningly steep angle as he ran down the hall, legs now insensitive to the pain and exhaustion he had to work through.

Likewise, the cold touched him with only the barest hint of an edge. The veneine kept it all at bay, as Beckett gripped the hemp rope down the glacier in his iron fist. He could tell that his glove was being worn away as he dragged himself faster and faster down the hillside. He suspected that it eventually eroded the grip on the glove and started to burn the skin from his hands, but he couldn't feel it.

He could feel the regular shivers that were beginning in the ice. Tremors, emanating from massive and still-growing sinkhole about Gotheray Castle, were beginning to shake the glacier loose.

Beckett's frustration screamed at him from beneath the haze, ordering him to go faster. He ignored it. It swore at him to forget the curves of the switchback and cut straight down the side of the mountain. He ignored it.

A huge, shivering wave passed through the ice beneath his feet, rocking him as he walked, and for a moment everything vanished, and he was rolling in the black waves of a stormy sea, beneath a black sky. Saltwater filled his mouth and nose, cleansed the filth from his eyes and lungs tossed him up and down so that he lost all sense of direction...

Stay here! The voice in his head shouted, and he was back on the glacier. He began to focus on the ragged cold breaths that scraped his lungs, and the broken glass that was slicing the inside of his knees to ribbons. He tried to find a balance between the drug and the pain, using his agony to keep his mind from drifting off.

Time was distended. He had no idea how long he'd walked, if it was faster or slower than the time it had taken them to climb. All he could think of was the pain of his body and the warmth of the drug, and the weight of Valentine on his shoulders, crushing the breath out of him.

And then, there was the promontory where they'd left the coach. There was the wooden bridge that led from the glacier. There was another terrifying shudder in the ice, and thousands of tiny granules began to shower past his feet. *Almost there!* He told himself. *Almost!*

The bridge. He'd made it to the bridge. Halfway across. And then his legs gave out. Pushed to the brink of exhaustion and beyond, his legs simply stopped working. He collapsed beneath the weight of his friend, halfway to safety. The ringing in his ears began to fade, replaced now with a great, rumbling sound, the huge, earth-shivering thunder of an earthquake.

Too late, he thought to himself, even as his inner-sergeant bellowed and tried to bully him to his feet. It was no use. His will was strong, but there was simply no strength left in his body. He heard the thunder bearing down on him, and felt the cold creep in past the drugs. His arms and legs were numb, well beyond feeling. The cold was a terrible fist, slowly closing around his heart. Beckett snatched what ragged breaths he could; his lungs felt too tired to breathe. The thunder rolled closer and closer, and Beckett closed his eyes. *Well, Valentine,* he thought in the dark. *Guess we didn't make it, this time.*

Beckett was so tired that the cold was beginning to miraculously transmute itself into warmth. Real warmth, not the fiction of the veneine. Real warmth, and the thunder had become the rolling waves of the sea, and Beckett let himself go to Cross the Water...

"Grab his feet, there, boy!" A rough voice spoke, and rough hands gripped Beckett's arms. "Hurry, we haven't got time to dawdle. That's it!"

Hands, voices, all vanished into the sound of the sea. There was a cough, and Beckett imagined he heard Valentine. "Owww. Did...what happened?"

"No time for that, Mr. Valentine. Get on your feet if you want to live." Was that Harry's voice?

It didn't matter. Sleep claimed him, and an enormous sea of ice and snow swept the wooden bridge away into the darkness.

Thirty-One: A Conclusion

The coroners returned to Trowth in the wake of the sharpsie riots. Beckett remained unconscious for the entire trip, pushed beyond the limits of human endurance by his heroic trip down the mountain. Valentine, who had regained just enough of his wits to climb onto the stone promontory from the bridge before it was swept away by the avalanche, remained addled for a little while, but soon was back to normal.

The city, on the other hand, had been completely transformed. Almost all of Old Bank had been destroyed; Raithower House was one of the few buildings untouched by the second disastrous launch of the *Excelsior*, but dozens of government offices, including the headquarters for the Ministry of War and the Committee for Public Safety, had been utterly destroyed. Records were lost, chains of command disrupted, and the organizations were thrown into disarray.

Strangely enough, the people of Trowth seemed to feel a renewed sense of unity and cooperation in the face of such a terrible disaster. Since the last of the sharpsies had disappeared from the city after the explosion, there was no need to form armed mobs. Instead, groups were formed to look for survivors of the disaster of Vlytze Square, gendarmes committed them-selves to rebuilding as much of the destroyed city as possible, and the wealthiest families, but especially the Comstock Vie-Gorgons whose home in Old Bank had also managed to weather the disaster, opened their doors and their coffers to support the survivors in any way.

For a short time, the quiet, melancholic city was not held in the grip of raging passions or roaming pressgangs. They were not consumed with hate for their enemies, they did not feel the desperate horror of their own loss, the loss of their young men to the war, that had found outlet in so much violence. For a short time, there was nothing to do but rebuild.

Edgar Wyndham-Vie was tried for his illegal commandeering of the *Revenge*, and for his overwhelming incompetence in handling the "sharpsie situation." Beckett's testimony would eventually prove instrumental in his conviction for threatening the public good, both because Wyndham-Vie had tried to cover up heretical sciences, and because in so doing he had caused the escalation of tension that led to the sharpsie riots. True to the Beckett's prediction, the Wyndham-Vie name became worthless in a matter of months; everywhere the characteristic gargoyle-downspouts of the Family's architecture were torn down and thrown into the street.

Wolfgang Rowan-Czarnecki was tried posthumously, and found guilty of heresy. Only an impassioned plea on his behalf from coroner Elizabeth Skinner prevented the Rowan-Czarnecki name from suffering the same fate as the Wyndham-Vies. She argued vehemently that, for all his faults, Wolfgang had been motivated not by personal gain or greed, but by an abiding love for his lost brother, by a powerful sorrow for all that his city had suffered through the war. One of the judges, who had himself lost a son to the war with the ettercaps, had been moved to tears by Skinner's words. It was determined that, given the trying times that now beset the Empire, Wolfgang Rowan-Czarnecki would be pardoned of his crime by the Emperor himself, and his body, once recovered, would be buried in Vie Abbey.

The *Excelsior* was publicly dismantled. The elements of its engines were taken to half a dozen sites across the city, and melted down. Many people attended. Most of them cheered.

Alan Charterhouse was quietly placed under arrest and held at Raithower, and given a comfortable room there while the Coroners decided what to do. Like Rowan-Czarnecki, it might be possible to receive a pardon, but only after he'd been executed. Especially in light of the disaster in Vlytze Square, it seemed unlikely that anyone with knowledge of Aetheric Geometry could possibly escape capital retribution.

Young Mr. Charterhouse found himself spending most of his time lying on his back in the bed that the Coroners had provided him. He would lie perfectly still, his hands resting over his eyes, trying to sleep, but finding it impossible with his nerves jangling up and down his body. He waited for days, and was well-cared for. Beckett's men provided excellent food, clean sheets, books when Alan asked for them. Valentine was permitted to visit occasionally. Both were voracious readers, and they talked enthusiastically about books, always studiously avoiding the subject of the Ted East novels that had once been Alan's favorites. The days blended together into a long stretch of gloom, as Alan awaited his execution.

One day, Valentine knocked on Alan's door, a few hours before dawn. This was alarming—though the coroner had been a regular visitor, he only ever came in the late afternoon. "Alan," the young coroner called, softly. "Are you awake?"

"Yes," Alan muttered. Understandably nervous about his impending execution, he'd been unable to sleep again. "What is it?"

"Get up, get dressed," Valentine said. "You're leaving."

Alan sat bolt upright. "What? Now?" His heart sank deep into his stomach. "I thought...don't I get a last meal, or something like that?"

"Not to the gallows," Valentine grinned. "Come on, I'm busting you out." He tossed the young man a satchel, stuffed almost to overflowing with clothes.

"W-what?" Alan said, not daring to let his hopes up.

"Can't execute you if you're not here, right? Hurry up, get your clothes on."

Alan quickly began to dress. "Where, I mean, where am I supposed to go?"

Valentine's grin widened, and the young cartographer found it infectious. "Corsay. There's a ship waiting for you by the docks in River Village."

"Corsay?" Alan practically choked on the word. Corsay was halfway around the world, a backwater colony, full of savages and monsters. "What...?"

"You've been accepted at the University there. Corsay University, I'm sure you know, is a long way from Vie Abbey and the Church Royal. They've a little more relaxed view about geometry, if you take my meaning."

"Valentine," Alan protested, "I can't afford university."

Valentine rolled his eyes. "Who'd have thought it'd be so difficult to convince someone to miss their own hanging? Don't worry about the bill. Everything's paid for, courtesy of Comstock Street. And don't worry about your age. You'll have to take the long way around, so you'll be about sixteen by the time you get there. There's a tutor waiting for you on the ship, though I'm sure you won't need one." He handed a number of sealed letters to the young man. "There's your letter of acceptance, thanks to the recommendations of certain highly-placed members of the Trowth civil-service," Valentine winked, "And a letter of introduction to a boarding house in Ennering Village there. Also paid for. Tell my aunt Helena hello, by the way."

"Valentine..." Alan Charterhouse found himself speechless.

"Oh, one more thing." Valentine drew one of his pistols, opened it, dumped the bullets into his hand. He stuffed the beautiful, pearl-handled revolver and its ammunition into the satchel. "Never know when something like that will come in handy." He tousled Alan's hair.

The young man didn't move. After a moment, he said, "Beckett."

"Trust me," the young coroner told him. "This is exactly what Beckett wants. He can't say it, because he can't know about it, because if he did know, he'd have to stop it. But you saved Skinner's life, Alan. You saved all our lives, potentially even the Empire. We owe you." He grinned again, and Alan found himself grinning so widely that he felt his face would crack. "Besides, what good is being rich if you can't throw money away? Now," he took Alan Charterhouse by the arm, "Let's get you out of here."

"That's my report," Beckett told Mr. Stitch. The huge, hideously leathery Reanimate regarded him without expression, his brass eyes immutable. "I don't know who activated the *Excelsior*. Anyone I might suspect was otherwise engaged."

Skin and muscles creaked as Mr. Stitch finally nodded. He sat behind his great wooden desk, its surface bare, his hands folded before him. "It is. Unfortunate. I will. Take over. That investigation."

"You don't want me to look into it further?" Beckett asked, slightly appalled.

Stitch slowly cocked his head to the side, and Beckett shivered. He had never trusted the Reanimate, despite what amounted to a century of loyal service to the Empire. "Tragedy. Has strengthened. Our city."

Beckett stared. Was Stitch really saying what it seemed like?

"I will. Look into it." The Reanimate's voice was strangely emotionless, and yet it still held a note of finality. "You. Would not like. The answers." Slowly, Mr. Stitch raised its dead hand, and dismissed him.

Outside of Stitch's office, Beckett found Valentine and Skinner sitting on the couch in the parlor, whispering softly to each other. It reminded him of other business.

"The boy's gone," Beckett grunted. "Wonder how that happened."

Valentine nodded, his face studiously ingenuous. "I don't know, sir. We were watching him closely."

"I'll bet," the old coroner replied, his face hidden by the red scarf. After the incidents at Gotheray Castle, the fades had proceeded to further ravage the old man's features, making it a gruesome, skeletal visage of grinning teeth and blood-red muscle. Beckett was quiet for a few seconds, while Valentine practically held his breath. "Well. We'll get him if he turns up again. No time to worry about it now." He tossed a folder of clippings and arrest reports to Valentine. "We've got work to do."

Other Stories

THE HANGMAN'S DAUGHTER

Choking, she thought. *I'm choking.* Something was in the air. It was dark, and she couldn't see it, but it was thick and hot and sticky like tar, and it filled her mouth so wide she couldn't scream, and it filled her throat and tried to crawl into her lungs, even as it sat on her chest and squeezed the life out of her pressing her ribs so much they hurt, stabbing her eardrums like she was deep underwater, dry and burning in her eyes, so heavy, she couldn't breathe, couldn't breathe…

And then she was awake. Not with a start, but suddenly. Cresy opened her eyes, and she could see the slanted corner of the ceiling above her bed. She was breathing shallowly, but the fear was still with her, curled up in a ball in the center of her chest and peeling out like a piece of jagged, sticky twine. Something was pulling a harsh string out of her chest, pulling a piece of herself away, and Cresy couldn't see it. She couldn't tilt her head, or turn it to the side, or even let her eyes flick down. All she could see was the spot above her bed, faintly lit by moonlight.

But there was something here. In the room, with her. She could hear it breathing, harshly, through wide nostrils. She could hear it fumbling at the foot of her bed, a shuffling like bare feet on wood. *There is something here,* she thought, and Cresy was afraid of it. There were no other sounds; her room, her bed was an island in a black void, and she was afraid that if she could turn her head, she'd see only blackness. Cresy was alone here, with something.

She tried to move, tried to do anything, to lift her hand, to look out the window that she knew was right next to her face. She shouted silently at her body to *get up, move move move,* as that…thing shuffled at the foot of her bed, and a terror, a terror overwhelming in its intensity, crawled up and down her spine and hammered at her eyes, and made her want to just cry, and hide, and turn her mind off, and run away deep into dream as far as she could, and *oh gods its getting closer* and she screamed at her body again to just *get up*.

Cresy snapped upright. There was nothing on her bed. She looked around her weirdly canted room, with its slanting ceilings and the skewed window next to her bed. The grain of the wood was faint in the pale light; strange faces and weird creatures leered at her from the timbers, but there was nothing moving, nothing breathing harshly. Her father's sword, stuck half into the floor, glinted coldly at her like it always had. The sounds of the city had returned: the incessant, dull thrumming and pounding of the enigmatic machines in New Town. The shrieking steam whistle of the train to Outcrop. The hooting language of therians, as they bickered and quarreled with each other. Birdsong.

The sudden sounds of the city, and the sudden absence of that dread, that certainty that there was some living, breathing (awfully breathing) thing, half-convinced her that this too had been a dream. That she'd only just woke up from a nightmare in which something had been in her room.

Pulling her knees in close, and looking askance at her window, Cresy wished that she and her father could afford candles. She'd love to light one, and look under the bed, and out in the staircase. To search the bare walls of her room thoroughly, to make sure that there was nothing here. But she could not. All she could do was huddle under her blankets, shivering despite the tropical heat, and stare at her crooked window, which now hung open. The thick, wooden shutter swayed freely in the faint breeze, though Cresy knew she'd latched it before she went to bed.

Gods, she hated being afraid.

John Gyre was quiet as he hunched over his breakfast, working on his rice and fish-eggs with the practiced efficiency of a soldier at mess. Cresy stared at him, his pale eyes downcast, his short, white hair stirring slightly as he moved. *It'll need to be cut, soon*, she thought. Her father liked his hair very short. So no one could grab it, he'd told her by way of explanation, right after he'd taken his knife and roughly hacked her own red pigtails off. It was the first thing he'd said, the first thing he'd done, when Cresy came to live with him, two years ago. She had been eight, and John Gyre had thought that she would cry. He'd been surprised. Cresy's mother had always crooned over the girl's hair, and twisted it into complex braids, but, quite frankly, Cresy was disgusted by the whole mess.

She knew her father had been proud of her, when he cut her hair and she didn't say a word. Cresy loved her father, and she couldn't look at his hard, cold face, and not want his respect. He was a person that she wanted to be proud of her. Sitting at the table, picking over her own breakfast, she opened her mouth to speak.

And then reconsidered. She looked down at her rice and eggs, and spooned a little of it into her mouth. What would he think of her, if she told him? Told him what? That she had had a bad dream? That she was scared by nothing? John Gyre was not a man who was ever afraid, Cresy thought. He'd think she was a silly little girl. Like her mother. Cresy was defiant. *I am not like my mother. I am strong.*

She looked up at her father again, and squeaked, unintentionally. He was looking at her, his blue (almost clear) eyes, unblinking, fixed on her face with the obstinate single-mindedness that infected everything he did.

"Sleep well?" He asked. John Gyre's voice was stone.

Cresy swallowed hard, and nodded. John Gyre grunted in response.

"I've to the gallows, soon. There's only three today, so if you're quick with the washing, we can go to the park."

Disappointment twitched in her. "I promised Ally and them…I said I'd play, today." She liked spending time with her father, and he was usually very busy. But she had promised.

Nodding, standing, John Gyre gathered his and his daughter's dishes, and took them outside to the water pump that he and his neighbors shared. Cresy sat at the table for a few moments until, chattering and hooting wildly, Fellik careened into the kitchen.

Fellik was John Gyre's house-servant, after a fashion. He was a therian, so it was against the law for him to have a job, but John Gyre treated the creature like an apprentice.

Effortlessly, the ape-like therian leapt up onto the table and leaned into Cresy's face. He widened his huge, human eyes, and pursed his animal snout, and stared at her and stared, until, helpless, Cresy began to giggle. Fellik smiled in response, baring just the lower set of his huge teeth.

"Good morning, miss Cresy," the therian said, hopping from the table to the cabinets, where he clung to the door with his feet, and rummaged through them with his long, strong arms. "And how did we sleep last night? Well, I hope? It's said that you North-born folk have trouble with our heavy southern air, but…" Fellik leapt, twirling, and landed back on the table where he sat down with a thud, "…I certainly've never noticed anything wrong with our air." He started to munch on a piece of thick-rined fruit that he'd found in the cabinet.

Cresy watched him for a moment. "Fellik," she said, "Do you...would you know if something was in my room last night?"

His answer unsettled her, despite being just what Cresy had expected, "Of course, of course, nothing could get in here, and nothing would, not for fear of your father. Snug as a bug in the mud, that's you in your bed." It unsettled her because, for a moment before his words were spoken, his strangely-human, strangely-animal face was quite shocked. His eyes wide, his nostrils flared. Therians were terrible liars, incapable of keeping everything they felt from their faces, and what she had asked had scared him.

Before Cresy could press him further, though, John Gyre returned with the clean dishes, and shouted to the therian, and the two of them left for the gallows.

Cresy finished with the washing around noon, but it was too hot to find her friends and play. Instead, she found a shady spot under a half fallen building, and nibbled at some fruit that she'd found. Shattertown, the neighborhood that she and her father lived in, was one of the poorest neighborhoods in the city. John Gyre had told her that the neighborhood used to be full of wealthy, almost-aristocrats; merchants and bankers, and Men of Property. It had been a rich neighborhood, until a hundred years ago. Until the Quake. Of course, no one alive could remember it, but they told their stories to their children and their grandchildren. A third of the city had been destroyed, and the spot that was now called Shattertown had been hit the worst. Even now, a century later, there wasn't a straight, up-and-down building anywhere. The Men of Property had all left, and the crooked, fallen buildings were just hollowed out, shorn up, and then filled with cheap hovels. Like hers.

Shattertown was poor, but there was nowhere in the city of Corsay where the poor couldn't eat. In the city's tropical humidity, fruited plants grew virtually everywhere. Private orchards spilled over to the streets, gardens grew a hundred different kinds of fruits and vegetables. In places like Shattertown, where the cement and cobblestone ground had been broken apart, sometimes lesh-vines grew right out of the ground. The beggars of Corsay were not like the beggars back on the Continent; they did not beg for food, but for other things that Cresy could not give them—half-naked, they begged for clothes; homeless, they begged for shelter from the heavy summer rains; sick and plague-ridden, they begged for miracles with clutching, outstretched hands.

As the sun approached mid-afternoon, and the yellow and amber and gold colors of the city began to change their tint to the greenish-yellow of summer storms, Cresy sought out her friends. She still had trouble finding her way through the winding intricacies, the rope bridges, stairs, walkways, and fallen heaps of rubble that characterized Shattertown, but she knew how to get to Emmerin Fountain from anywhere in the neighborhood, and she knew that's where the boys would be.

And there they were. Ally (Alistaire), and Dorian, and Denholm. They had such silly names, thought Cresy. The kinds of names that parents give their children so that everyone will be impressed. Cresy — herself named Allisandre — much preferred the nickname that the therians had given her. It was... harsher. Stronger.

The boys were sitting on the lip of the long-dried fountain, its abstract spire-center providing little shade. They were talking animatedly about something that Cresy couldn't quite hear. Nearby, four therians, also in the middle of an argument, spilled out of an alley in a dazzling whirlwind of hairy limbs, hoots, and shrieks. The boys didn't seem to notice. Hardly anyone ever did.

"...it had great, big feathery things on the sides of its head, and they moved up and down when it talked," Ally was saying, "and when it did talk...it was deep. Like, you could feel its voice in your *bones*..."

"What?" Cresy interrupted. "What talked?"

The boys, except for Ally, glared sullenly at her. Dorian and Denholm had harbored dislike for Cresy ever since she'd fought her way into their little circle. "It was a trolljrman," Ally said, breathless; pale, freckled flesh glowing with excitement. "I saw it, I saw it down by the train supports. It was huge," he waved his arms expansively, "twice as big as me, and it had big tufts of feathers, and teeth like big stones..."

Ally went on for several minutes about the trolljrman, describing in surprisingly intricate detail the creature's manner of dress, the way it moved its hands, the sound of its voice, and the startlingly boring adventure that it had been in the middle of: purchasing several bolts of fabric. Ally thought it was fascinating, though, so Cresy indulged him. She knew that Dorian and Denholm barely had time for poor, shy Ally — youngest brother in a brood of shrieking sisters. They tolerated his perpetual exuberance for storytelling only because they both knew that they were better than he at the Manly Pursuits.

So, when the other boys finally did grow tired of the story, they started challenging each other to wrestling matches. Wrestling and kickfighting were the respectable past-times for young men, the Manly Pursuits that their fathers taught them, and Dorian especially enjoyed it. They didn't let Cresy wrestle. They used to; the first time she'd met the boys, in this very same fountain, she'd said something rude to them, and Denholm had tried to toss her to the ground.

He had been surprised to find himself hurtling head-first into the cobblestones. Cresy had spent the first two years of her life in Corsay in the company of therians. Which was fun, and exciting, and more often than not ended in one of the innumerable quarrels that the therians had with each other, which, in turn, became a vast wrestling match. Wrestling one boy, who only had hands at the ends of his arms, and not on his feet, was much easier than wrestling a half a dozen therians. In fact, wrestling three boys turned out to be much easier, which Cresy realized after Ally and Dorian had joined the fight.

In any case, now she couldn't wrestle with the boys, so she just watched them for a while, as the sky grew steadily darker and greener, and the wind began to kick up. The leaves rustled and turned up their pale underbellies as they clung to the countless flowers and vines that crept out of the cracked pavement and up the walls of the surrounding buildings. After about half an hour, Cresy announced that she would go.

"It'll rain soon," she explained, as Ally shouted submission to Denholm, and Dorian, flushed and panting, cheered them on. After a moment, Denholm let Ally up, and they all just sat around, catching their breaths. "Hey," Cresy said. "Have you...have you ever had dreams? That you can't breathe? And then you think that, maybe there's a person, or something, in your room with you?"

The boys looked at each other for a moment, then shrugged.

"Sure," Ally said. "Everybody gets those. It's the bogeymen." He looked away for a moment, then back at Cresy. He seemed hesitant to talk about it, which was rare, and unnerving. "It's...it's not so bad. Sometimes kids die from it, but not usually. Everybody gets it."

Cresy left the fountain, and headed back to the crooked house that she shared with her father. A restless unease stirred within her. The boys had been born and raised in Corsay, at the edge of the world. Maybe everybody they knew had nightmares like that. But Cresy hadn't left the Continent until she was eight. *Everybody* did not have bogeymen.

That night, Cresy stared at her father's sword for a long time before she fell asleep. Buried halfway into the floorboards, her father had put it there himself. The only time she'd ever seen him furious; she'd come after an afternoon of arguing with the boys, and asked if she could get one of the thin, delicate stiletto-knives—the knives that *ladies* dueled with. In a blink, his cold reserve had vanished, replaced with this roaring inferno of anger, not at her, but at the society in which he lived. He'd stormed out of the room, railing at whatever idiot had invented ladies-knives, and had come back with his hanger, from the war. He'd snatched Cresy up by the arm, and taken her and the short, thick, curved saber to her room. There, he'd slammed the weapon deep into the floorboards.

"When you're strong enough to pull it out," he'd said, "I'll teach you to use *this*."

It was a promise. A promise that her father had made to her, that she would one day learn what he knew; that she'd one day be as strong as him. And it was a symbol. Of her father's expectations for her. Of his love for her. It didn't matter that she was a girl, she imagined John Gyre saying, or that her mother was weak. If Cresy wanted to learn to fight, then by the gods, he would teach her the *right* way.

The sword, Cresy thought. *I can have the sword when I'm strong. I won't be afraid.* She drifted into sleep.

Choking, she thought. *I'm choking.* Something was in the air. It was dark, and she couldn't see it, but it was thick and hot and sticky like tar, and it filled her mouth so wide she couldn't scream, and it filled her throat and tried to crawl into her lungs, even as it sat on her chest and squeezed the life out of her pressing her ribs so much they hurt, stabbing her eardrums like she was deep underwater, dry and burning in her eyes, so heavy, she couldn't breathe, couldn't breathe…

Cresy was awake again, and she couldn't move. She could feel; she could feel the weight of the darkness pressing in against her, the humid air suddenly cold. She could feel that sensation, of having something long and ragged drawn from the center of her chest. And she could feel fear, lumbering clumsily inside her, involuntarily tightening her muscles, trying to bring tears to her eyes, trying to get her frozen muscles to make her run away. That fear was a palpable thing now, a real thing, crawling up from her stomach, trying to slither through her throat and out her mouth, trying to choke her.

The Thing was here, in her room again, shuffling softly by her bed. She could hear it, and it made her afraid. And more than anything, the fear made her angry. She shouted and screamed and wailed inside her head, screaming at the fear to go away, trying to make herself be strong, trying to move her arms by force of will if the muscles wouldn't work.

I am the Hangman's daughter, in her mind, her voice echoed from the walls. *I have seen a hundred men die, watched them dance the hanged-man's jig. I've smelt them, when they spewed their guts, I've watched them before the door opens, crying for their mothers. I have seen horrors! I am not afraid! I am* strong. *I am not afraid of you!*

After what seemed like an eternity, Cresy sat bolt upright in her bed, and the sounds of the city came back to her. But this time, this time she saw it. A black shadow by her window, curved, hunched over. It was built like a therian — small, like a child, but with long arms and huge hands, hands built for strangling. Its eyes glowed, featureless yellow orbs. And in the light from those eyes, she could see its face, and she could see that it had no lips. Just skin, stretched across its jaws, as it tried to scream, and couldn't.

The Thing glared at her with hate and malice, and screamed with its silenced voice, and it was gone.

Cresy didn't know what to do. She couldn't move, couldn't think. It had been here. Right here with her, doing...something. Something awful to her. It was a real thing. A bogeyman. She sat for a long moment, dread finally giving way to determination. *I must follow it.* And she clambered out her own window.

In her two years in the city, Cresy had spent a great deal of time with the therians. The simian creatures, disdaining roads, had built scaffolds and ladders, and complex networks of poles and posts all throughout the old neighborhoods. As their friend, Cresy had done her best to follow them where they went. While she was never as quick and sure-footed as the therians, she had done a fine job of keeping up with them.

And so, Cresy was agile enough to get to the roofs. From there, she stood, her eyes adjusting to the dark, and tried to pick out movement. There seemed to be no therians out tonight; maybe they were scared, too. *There,* she thought, as something dark and hunched leapt to a rooftop not far away. Cresy followed. For perhaps half an hour, she chased it, as the thing sometimes vanished into the dark, only to reappear after a few moments. A dark blot in a dark night. When she lost it for the last time, Cresy realized that she'd come as far as the Seam — the narrow strip of straightened buildings that marked the point where New Town spilled down Lirrigan Hill into Old Town.

She stood at the top of a low building, on a shallow-sloped roof, searching the unyielding darkness for signs of her quarry. It was difficult to make anything out; she thought she could see movement, not far ahead, but it could just be therians, or nightbirds, or...something. There was a sense that the night was moving around her. The silhouettes of cornices and scaffolds seemed to shift a little in the subtly dancing shadows.

*Dancing shadows...*Cresy looked around, puzzled. The gas-lamps had all gone out. The only light came steadily from moon and stars. *Why are the shadows moving?* Cresy began to realize what she was seeing. The whole stretch of rooftops seemed suddenly alive with movement. Black shapes, impossible to clearly make out, lurched from chimney to scaffold, through little pools of moonlight. There were so many of them…a hidden, invisible army. They crept, dark and sinister towards…towards…

Something. Trying to find a better view Cresy climbed to the edge of the roof, and reached out to snatch a piece of lattice work. She swung around it, and up to a higher, steeply-sloping shingled roof. There was a figure that the dark, lurching shapes were making their way towards. It was hard to see from where she stood, but it seemed tall and thin, and ragged. Its shape seemed almost human…a man, with long arms outstretched. And at the ends of its arms were…not hands. Twisted things, like claws or…or…*Gods, what's wrong with its hands?*

Understanding began to dawn in her mind. Menace radiated from that ragged shape with its awful, twisted hands. *Oh no. Oh no no no. Not that…don't let it be that…* Cresy felt tears in her eyes as her fear fluttered in her, a flock of crows seeking escape. *No…*she slid gracelessly from the roof, and scraped her knees. She sprained her ankle as she fell to the ground and ran, and tried to find the way back to Shattertown. *It can't be that…*

More tears as panic fought for control of her mind. *I can't find…I can't find the way back, how do I get back? Daddy!* She cried, and tried to stamp her fear down. The unfamiliar buildings loomed and curved above her head, blocking out almost all the moonlight. Pitch-black chasms yawned around her, every corner was a place that could harbor a hunched, lurching bogeyman. Worse, she was sure that ragged figure with its terrible hands was just behind her, breathing warm breath on the back of her neck, ready to grab her, to snatch at her with clutching talons…

Cresy wept openly as a wrong turn took her to a dead-end. She whirled, to confront the enigmatic creature that she knew was following her. The darkened mouth of the alley was empty, but she was sure she could hear something, something moving, some sound just below the blood pounding in her ears, as she ran out of the alley and climbed onto a rope bridge. It swayed mercilessly, and for the first time in her life, she was afraid she might fall. She coughed and choked on her own mucous and ran. It was behind her again, following her with silent footsteps. Cresy dropped from the bridge, and ducked into the narrow passage made by two half-fallen buildings.

And there, moonlight shining down around it like a sign from her own patron god, was Emmerin Fountain. Cresy cried out with joy as she threw herself into its dry basin, pressed her back against its abstract spire, and looked out at the empty courtyard. Nothing moved in the pale blue light of the moon. She sniffed and wiped her nose with the sleeve of her nightdress. She knew her way home from here.

This is not right, she thought, as the mindless panic of her flight ebbed. *I will not stand for this. This can't happen again. I will be* strong.

At breakfast that morning, John Gyre noticed something changed in his daughter. She was pale, and had a harried look to her. "What's wrong?" He asked her, as they ate.

Cresy looked up at her father, and smiled a wan smile. "Nothing. Something was wrong, but it won't be. I'm going to fix it."

John Gyre nodded. A knowing motion. He leaned in, close to his daughter, and whispered. "You're doing a brave thing," he said, "but not everything can be fought with your hands." Cresy blinked, wide-eyed, but her father said not another word. Just cleaned the dishes and left for the gallows.

When she was finished with the washing, Cresy decided to find her therian friends. She climbed the intricate lattice of scaffolding outside her own house, up to the weirdly slanted rooftop, and started shrieking the only words in therian that she knew. The truth was, she didn't actually know what they all meant; they were just the words that she'd heard often enough to be able to repeat, and she suspected that they might actually be swears. It wouldn't matter, though; therians were compulsively inquisitive. They'd *have* to find out who was shouting.

It was only moments before a few, ape-like creatures, curious beyond their capacity to ignore, appeared over the edges of the rooftops. "Shodi!" Cresy called to one of the creatures that she recognized.

Shodi, who Cresy thought might have been Fellik's sister, leapt close, and grinned wildly. "What, oh why are we making so much noise, dear?" Two more therians shambled closer as well. They took a good look at Cresy, and then began hooting and chattering at each other in argument.

Cresy lowered her voice to near a whisper. "Shodi...have you ever seen things on the rooftops?" The two arguing therians were suddenly silent; they stared at Cresy with their wide, strangely human eyes.

As poor a liar as her brother, Shodi was unable to stop her trepidation from slithering across her face. "Of course of course, we see lots of things, little sister. Sometimes birds, or snakes. Sometime our own cousins. But nothing horrible, or scary, or anything that a little girl like you should have to worry about..."

"I know something is out there," Cresy interrupted. "I saw it. Something came into my room last night, and I followed across the roofs, almost all the way to the Seam, and I saw..." Her tongue was tied. She couldn't bring herself to say the name. *It can't be. It's just a wonder-story.*

It's not real. "You have to help me. The... bogeyman is going to come again tonight, I know he will. I have to follow it, I have to...find out where it goes." The two unknown therians began to slink away to the edges of the rooftop, and Shodi eyed them apprehensively. "Please?"

With panicked shrieks, Shodi's friends leapt away, leaving only her and the human child on the rooftop. "I...can't." Her eyes were so sad, so *conflicted.* "I can't help you, little sister. None of us can. We don't go out when *he* is out. When he's hunting." Shodi herself was backing off now, trying to discreetly make her escape.

"Why?" Cresy's voice was soft, but she wanted to scream. "Why?"

"Because...we're scared." Therians weren't like humans, Cresy knew. They couldn't cry; but she was sure that she saw Shodi's tear, before the simian creature slunk away. Strangely quiet.

"You *have* to," Cresy pleaded with Ally, now her last hope. Dorian and Denholm had left, and Cresy and her friend were sitting tight up against a wall, nestled beneath a fallen statue, as the afternoon rain pattered restlessly across the steaming pavement. "Please, Ally? I don't have any other real friends here. Not humans, anyway."

Ally shrugged, and shifted about, uncomfortably. His freckles twitched around his face as it twisted into a grimace. "Come on, Allis — Cresy. Sorry. Cresy. Look, everyone gets those...dreams. And everyone thinks they see the bogeymen, but..."

Cresy shook her head violently. "I don't *think* I saw anything. I saw it. It was there, in my room. It was giving me those nightmares. And it's going to come back tonight, and again and again, and I am not going to let it."

"It's just...it's a natural part of life, you know? Like...I dunno, like sneezing, or wetting the...uhm. Like sneezing. I mean..." He paused, and Cresy let the silence hang. She knew he'd argue himself around in a circle if she let him. "But...I mean...what can *I* do?"

Beaming at him, eyes wide, Cresy was a picture of ingenuousness. "Because, I know if you're there, I won't be scared. Please? You can meet my father. You'd like him."

"Your father." Ally swallowed, a little nervously. "The hangman?" But Cresy knew she'd won. Ally would stay with her and her father tonight.

It was easier to fall asleep with Ally in the room. He was curled up on the floor, next to the bed, on a pile of old blankets. He'd been quiet and nervous when he'd met John Gyre, and a little more nervous when he'd seen John Gyre's (soon Cresy's) sword, rammed halfway to its hilt into the floorboards.

But he'd relaxed a little as they'd settled in, and he and Cresy had talked for a few hours about not much of anything. Ally's mother was a maid for a household on Lantern Hill, and the family she worked for might be moving up to New Town, and taking the staff with them. Ally was nervous about it; he'd heard stories about New Town, about the great, thunderous machines that laboured away around Gorgon Plaza and Vie Plaza, at the top of the lopsided Lirrigan Hill. Machines made him nervous. Cresy told him not to be such a baby, and conveniently forgot why she'd asked Ally to stay the night.

It was not too long before their conversation wandered off into a few, subdued exchanges, and then into a companionable silence, as each child listened to the other's breathing grow slower and more regular. Night was only halfway gone before they both fell asleep, nearly at the same time.

Choking, she thought. *I'm choking*. Something was in the air. It was dark, and she couldn't see it, but it was thick and hot and sticky like tar, and it filled her mouth so wide she couldn't scream, and it filled her throat and tried to crawl into her lungs, even as it sat on her chest and squeezed the life out of her pressing her ribs so much they hurt, stabbing her eardrums like she was deep underwater, dry and burning in her eyes, so heavy, she couldn't breathe, couldn't breathe...

No, no, no! She thought, and was awake, her eyes open and staring, fixed, frozen on the dark spot above her bed. And the fear was back, clutching viciously at her stomach, as she sensed the presence of that bogeyman, as she heard his breathing. Fear lay on her like a metal blanket, like six feet of piled earth, pressing her, stopping her arms from moving, snatching her breath away...

No! Cresy screamed in her mind. *I am the Hangman's Daughter. I am not afraid of you!* And with a jerk, she was upright in her bed. She saw the Thing, the bogeyman, crouched next to her window, taking long breaths through its nostrils, sucking in something that looked like smoke and snot. The creature looked at her with stupid, malevolent eyes, and that voiceless scream seemed loud in Cresy's head. She looked to Ally, intending to spare him only a glance before turning her eyes back to the monster in her room, and then froze.

There was another Thing there. It had long jaws like a crocodile, and a hundred skittering claws, and it was perched on Ally's chest, as he gasped for air in his sleep. He was coughing...something up. Some kind of viscous, almost-vapor, something...

Her eyes flicked back to her own bogeyman, and saw that it had a knife in its hand. A long, curved thing, shining in the moonlight. It stared at her, and held its weapon tightly, and its jaw worked as it tried to speak voiceless words.

Moving away from one creature would only lead it towards the other; in her effort to escape, Cresy could only jump forward to the end of her bed, on the floor, not two steps from the stairs. But the thought of running did not enter into her head at all. She turned back to the two Things that had invaded her home, had tried to choke her in her sleep. The Thing with the skittering claws had scrabbled away from Ally, and with a disturbing cacophony of clicking noises, had crawled up the slanted roof. Away towards the window. The first Thing glared at Cresy, and moonlight shone on its knife.

But Cresy had jumped from her bed not to get away, but to get to something. The sword. Her father's sword, buried in her floorboards, the strength that he one day hoped she would carry. She grabbed the handle and bent her legs, and pulled and pushed as hard as she could, and for one heart-stopping moment it stayed, stuck fast, as the knife-wielding creature inched towards her...

Then the sword was free. And though it was far too long and heavy for a ten-year-old girl to use effectively, still she swung it back and forth, in wide, sweeping arcs. And the bogeymen backed away. They leapt and skittered through the window and out into the night.

Cresy took a long, shuddering breath, as Ally awoke, himself panting, half-choked.

"What," he gasped, "what..."

"They were here," said Cresy. "Two of them." *One for each of us.* She looked at her friend, and there was murder in her young eyes. "I'm going after them."

Cresy took a step towards the window, then paused and considered the weight of the sword in her hand. Her father's hanger was a spearman's sword—a short, curved saber, meant to be used one-handed by a grown man. Her father could swing it one-handed, easily, but the weapon came nearly to Cresy's chest. She'd need a way to carry it...Cresy's eyes lighted on the window tarp.

"Help me with this," she called to Ally, "pull the rope out of it." Ally immediately knelt down and began fiddling with the tarp. Like most families, Cresy and her father couldn't afford glass windows, or even heavy shudders; they had a few pieces of heavy oilskin tarps affixed to their windows with tough chords during monsoon season.

"What are you going to do with..." Ally began, but broke off when Cresy snatched the three feet of cord from his hands. She was still looking out the window, trying to follow the dark shapes of the bogeymen as they slunk across the roofs.

Quickly, quickly, Cresy thought to herself, as she tied the chord around the blade — close to the hilt, so that it would rest below the edge of the weapon. "I can't carry it while I'm climbing," she told Ally, and tied the other end of the chord in a large loop. She slung cord and hanger over her shoulder. "Stay here."

Before Ally could respond, Cresy climbed out of her bedroom window, and onto the omnipresent scaffolding of Shattertown. As nimble as a therian, Cresy climbed up and onto the roof of her house.

She could see the bogeyman, this time, and — even encumbered by her father's (her own) sword, she followed it as fast as she could. It was a nightmarish, breathsnatching trip, over rooftops, across the intricate therian scaffolding. She followed the bogeyman through deep shadows, as the moon hung low in the sky, and fractured her vision with a thousand thick, black fissures. Despite the makeshift harness she'd made, the sword almost killed Cresy twice — first, when it caught on the edge of a piece of scaffolding, and threatened to shorten her jump just enough to miss the nearby ledge.

The weapon almost killed her again on the gables of Mrs. Crowe's house, a run on narrow roofing that Cresy had made a hundred times. She'd sprinted to the edge of the rooftop and paused to try and catch sight of her monstrous quarry, and the sword had swung forward, over-balancing her, and nearly throwing her from the roof. She threw out her hands, arms windmilling wildly as she strove to regain her balance.

Flinging her weight as hard as she could backwards, Cresy landed hard on the roof behind her, her heart pounding in her throat, desperately hoping that she wouldn't lose sight of the bogeyman.

But she had lost it, and now was alone in the dark, nearer to the Seam now than she had been the last time. The night was quiet as she looked about for signs of movement, for anything. Warily, Cresy slipped the loop of chord from her shoulder, and took the sword in both hands...

The shriek of the whistle almost caused her to drop it. The whistle glared ahead of the deafening rumble of the early train from Outcrop, racing across the Sound, shuddering on its elevated tracks. And for a moment, the bright beacon at the head of the engine illuminated Cresy's field of view, as the train rattled by overhead.

The light showed her a sight. She could see them. The bogeymen. Not just hers, and the thing that had tormented Ally. But hundreds of them. Shapeless, indistinct, but still frightening; weird agglomerations of limbs and features. Of claws, wings, teeth. Eyes that shone in the light like great lamps, bat ears that flicked back and forth.

And hands. So many gripping, clutching, grabbing hands. They were crawling and leaping and flying across the rooftops; an army of nightmare amalgams, circling around one central figure, not more than twenty yards from where she stood.

The train passed, and the light vanished, but now that she knew what to look for, Cresy's night-adjusted eyes had no trouble seeing the hordes of shambling, lolling, limping things. Fear snatched at her for a moment, and Cresy could not creep closer to the figure they surrounded, that tall shapeless thing; she marveled that not one of the creatures made a sound. Oh, their feet hit rooftops with flat slaps, and their wings beat the air with soft thumps, but not a one of them called out, or shrieked, or chattered their great teeth.

Gritting her own teeth, and fighting down that growing dread, Cresy forced herself to approach the center of that silent army. She held her sword tightly. She did not know what she would do with it, if the hundreds of Things decided to fight her. But she felt better for having it. She knew what was at the center of that horrible army, but her horror stayed at bay because she could not believe it. And then she saw it, and she believed, and she really did drop her sword, and it clattered loudly on the rooftop.

The Loogaroo, she thought, her mind gibbering at the thought of it. *Oh gods oh gods the Loogaroo.* The King of the Bogeymen. It was standing right there, a tall, gaunt pile of shapeless black rags, its black, three-cornered hat like a crown. Covering the top half of its…face…was a bone-white mask, with a long, sharp nose. *Like a vulture's skull*, some still lucid part of Cresy's mind thought.

Everyone, everywhere, even as far as the Continent knew about the Loogaroo. The King of the Bogeymen. The Nightmare Prince. There was never a more monstrous creature to walk the earth, it was a living fear, a terror that took shape. Children and their parents could hardly believe in it; nothing that awful, that terrible could be real. But there it was. Something shuddered through Cresy's mind as she saw this thing, surrounded by its twisted minions. Something so far beyond fear that she had no word for it. Some driving need tore through her, closing off her mind, saturating her nerves, past the need to fight, or flee, all the way down to her most basic response. *Stand still. Oh gods, maybe it won't see me…*

Her own body unresponsive, Cresy watched as, slowly, the Loogaroo's black-gloved hands (*twisted like claws, like something worse… gods what's wrong with its* hands?) reached up its body, into its chest. It pulled apart its black rags, and exposed a hole just as black, perhaps more so, in the center of its torso. A great hole in the world, a flat, perfect darkness. Cresy saw her own bogeyman, the mouthless ape-thing with its shining knife, crawl up the Loogaroo's body and into that hole, where it vanished. No sign existed that the thing had ever been. The rest of the Loogaroo's robes did not so much as twitch.

One by one, each of the other creatures flew, or crawled, moved by whatever shattered means of locomotion existed for it, into that black pit in the center of the Loogaroo. The hundreds vanished into that space, where there should not have been room for one. And menace radiated out from the statue-still Prince like some invisible light.

As the last of the miserable, malformed things entered its master's body, that quiet, still-lucid part of Cresy's mind began to speak up. *Hundreds of them. One for you, and one for Ally. Sucking something out of you, and then bringing it back to him.* The fear still clung to her, running through her veins like ice. *Hundreds. He sends them out to* hundreds *of children. To your friends, to people you've never met.* The fear wavered now. *He's hunting them. Sucking the life out of them.* Her eyes flicked down to the sword at her feet. *Sometimes they die. He's* murdering *children. Is that what they turn into, when they die? One of those things?*

Cresy looked down at her sword. Her muscles shivered uncontrollably, violently, threatening to paralyze her. *He tried to hurt me. To hurt my friend.* She moved more smoothly as she mastered her body, gave it something to do. She picked up the sword. *This cannot be allowed.* She looked up at the Loogaroo. It stood still as a tree. It didn't seem to notice her at all.

Without another thought, without giving heed to the fear that still slammed against her nerves, Cresy ran at the black shape with the bone-white face. It didn't matter that she was only ten, and a girl, and could barely hold her sword. It didn't matter that the thing ahead of her was as old as memory, and commanded an army of nightmares. Cresy did not care. All she knew is that this thing had tried to hurt *children*, and that if it wasn't stopped, it would try again and again.

Even as she got close to it, the Loogaroo didn't seem to notice her. It didn't move at all, until Cresy swung, wild, full of strength born of terror and desperation and a sudden, volcanic hate for that awesome monster. Then the Loogaroo moved. It moved like water, like wind. *Gods, it's so* fast, *how can it be that fast?* It backed just outside the swing, and then it was in the air, cartwheeling slightly, above Cresy's head. And then it was behind her, and Cresy spun, and swung again.

This time, the Loogaroo caught her wrist with one of its twisted, black...hands, and her throat with the other. It twitched, and pain lanced through Cresy's arms. The sword fell to the ground, but Cresy could not hear it. The King of the Bogeymen had lifted her from the ground, and was staring into her face with that nacreous mask. Its eyes were empty black pits. Its nose was long and sharp, and Cresy wondered if it could cut her.

The nightmare-creature cocked its head to the side, like a curious bird. A sound escaped from somewhere in the folds of black rags. It sounded like a long, drawn out sigh, the last release of breath from a dying man, the sound a yawning cave might make, the sound of dust in a crypt.

Cresy stared at that mask, those empty eyes. Snot and tears ran down her face, and she realized that she was crying. Crying in fear of this thing. *I'm going to die,* she thought. *But I am not going to die like this. I am not afraid of you.* Her mouth was dry as the desert. It took her a moment to work saliva into it. But she did. And then, her face twisted with hate for this monstrous prodigy, Cresy did the only thing she could think of.

She spit in its eye.

The Loogaroo did not react. Did not so much as twitch, for a long moment. Cresy did nothing else. She had made her last act of defiance. She was (or thought she was) ready. And then, without ceremony or sound or any superfluous action, the King of the Bogeymen dropped her to the ground. In her surprise and fear, she hardly felt the impact. She just stared up at the Loogaroo, as it stared back down at her.

And then it was gone. Dust-motes, lit by setting moon, trailed like sudden comets in the Loogaroo's wake. Far away, she thought she saw a scaffold shake, slightly. It was gone. The fear slowly, painfully slowly, drained from Cresy as she sat, trying desperately to catch her breath. The King of the Bogeymen was gone.

Cresy stayed there for several minutes, looking off into the blank night into which that *thing* had disappeared. She took long, deep breaths, as her nerves jangled about inside her arms and legs, her knees still threatening to give way. Then, she collected her sword, looped its cheap harness over her shoulder, and began to make her way home.

The sun was just coming up when she reached her father's house. John Gyre was there, elbows on the kitchen table, hand clasped in front of his mouth. Ally sat with him, his eyes wide, his face white. His hands were folded neatly in his lap, and he just stared off into space as Cresy came in.

John Gyre looked at her, hard, for a moment. His eyes took in everything; the disarray of her hair and nightdress. The flush on her cheeks. The strength she now carried in her shoulders and her back, proud and upright. The sword.

"Well?" he said.

Cresy looked back at him. "Well what?"

John Gyre nodded sagely, then looked pointedly at the sword. "Ready for that, then?"

Looking at the sword in her hand, smiling — slightly at first, then broadly — Cresy replied. "Yes."

BECKETT'S JOB

"How long has she been like this?"

It was very quiet in the Coopers' front room. Their daughter, young Agnes, was in the tiny bedroom she ordinarily shared with her two brothers. She was alone now, and her mumbling could barely be heard behind the heavy door. Her parents — mother puffy-eyed and red-nosed, haunted by fear for her little girl; father stoic in the way of a working man of Trowth, determined as desperation mounted to be more fiercely unavailable to it — sat on their low, shabby couch, and said nothing. Valentine Vie-Gorgon leaned against the wall, arms crossed, doing his best to look serious, but unable to keep the compassion from his face. Two gendarmes crowded into the room as well. Beckett didn't know their names, he'd conscripted them on the way to the Coopers'. The new knocker stood just inside the front doorway.

The room was dense and humid with nervous sweat; hot and almost unbearably quiet. Agnes spoke softly in the other room, unintelligibly, punctuating her remarks with a sound like she was rapping on wood.

"How long as she been like this?" Beckett demanded again. He tried to seem sympathetic. Not because he was sympathetic, but because he knew that sympathy would take him farther in his work. His goals were hindered by his illness; the fades had claimed his right eye, now, leaving it an empty, bloody socket in his face. No man could easily appear sympathetic with a face that was half a skull, wrapped halfway around with a red scarf to cover the more alarming deformities, and Beckett wasn't trying very hard anyway.

"Mr. Cooper?" Beckett asked a third time. "How long?"

Arnold Cooper blinked and looked up, as though the question represented an unacceptable distraction from his business of appearing disinterested in painful situations. "Uhm. I think. A day. Two days."

"A week," whispered his wife. "Since —"

"Shush." Arnold shook his head. "She was always a little. You know. I mean. Pixelated. Not quite here. Two days ago," he asserted firmly, "is when she wouldn't come from her room."

Mrs. Cooper was shaking her head. "It was earlier," she said, softly. "When she —"

"Catherine," Arnold Copper interrupted. He'd settled on his story. "My wife. She isn't. I mean, children do strange things. Sometimes. It's nothing to do with this. It isn't...I mean..."

Beckett said nothing, just stared, and waited for Arnold Cooper to run out of steam. After a moment, there was again no sound but Agnes, whose voice had taken on a hysterical lilt, but whose words were still impossible to comprehend, and the ticking of the heating elements in the family's tiny, free-standing radiator.

"When she what?" Beckett asked. Mr. Cooper looked as if he was about to answer for his wife, then looked as if he had perhaps thought better of it, and said nothing.

Catherine Cooper was quiet, and sniffed, and wrung her hands, and then she spoke. "Last...last Midweek, at supper. She started...she was staring at her food all night. For ten seconds, or twenty seconds, before she would eat anything. I asked her..."

"Cathy, this isn't anything, she was just being. I mean, Cath."

"...I asked her what was wrong. She tried to tell me, I think. She..."

Arnold's face was reddening now, and he chewed the inside of his lip. "Cath —"

"Mr. Cooper," Beckett snapped. "Shut up." He turned back to Catherine Cooper. "Go on."

Mrs. Cooper shook her head, and tears welled again in her eyes. "She was trying to tell me something, but...it was like...like she couldn't think of the words? She opened her mouth, but nothing came out." Beckett and Valentine shared a glance.

Catherine Cooper continued. "She was very upset. I told her to never mind it..."

"And she was fine," Arnold put in. "That night, she was fine, there was nothing wrong. Whatever happened —"

"Mrs. Cooper." Despite the warm muffler of veneine in his system, Beckett found his patience wearing thin. "A week ago. Was your daughter exposed to anything unusual? Did she do anything differently? Besides eating."

Mrs. Cooper looked discreetly at her husband, wiped her nose, and sniffed again. "No," she said at once. "Nothing."

Beckett nodded, then turned to the two gendarmes he'd brought with him. They were eyeing the door to the little bedroom, listening to Agnes' high, sing-song voice. "Toss it," he told them.

"Now see here!" Arnold Cooper was on his feet immediately, prepared to wield his indignation as a weapon in defense of his home. "We've told you everything! We've got nothing we're hiding here!"

"Even the...uh." One of the gendarmes, ignoring Arnold Cooper, attempted to ask, struggling to divert his attention from that door.

"Not the bedroom. Not yet."

"Not the bedroom!" Mr. Cooper repeated. "Not anything! You're not...now, don't touch that! Don't you...don't you touch anything!" His protestations were to no avail; the gendarmes began searching every inch of the front parlor. They pulled cushions from the furniture and books from the shelves, tore into kitchen cabinets and permitted pots and pans to clatter noisily to the floor.

Arnold Cooper seemed on the verge of apoplexy, face red, following the gendarmes around and demanding an accounting. Catherine Cooper had leapt to her feet and had begun to wring her hands again. Valentine put his hands on her shoulders and whispered something to her. Beckett didn't know what it was, but it seemed to keep the woman calm, so he didn't particularly care. After five minutes of thorough searching, the gendarmes returned to Beckett with a small sheaf of pamphlets.

"This is all," they said, while Arnold Cooper spluttered with impotent rage.

Beckett examined the pamphlets over Arnold Cooper's most extreme protestations. The first was titled "Why They Need Us," and appeared to be a tract regarding the value of women in the workplace. The remaining six continued on in this vein: "A New Way to Educate," "Notes from the Working Lines," and so on. "Suffragist literature?" Beckett asked, raising his eyebrow.

"I..." Arnold began. He paused, turned to his wife. "I'm sorry," he told her quietly, then confessed to Beckett. "It's hers. Cath's. I told her. I told her not to bring it into the house. It's unnatural."

"Arnold..." Catherine Cooper looked caught between wanting to scream at her husband and wanting to faint away with shock at his betrayal. That strangled cry was all she managed.

"I'm sorry Cath," Arnold went on, "but if it means helping Agnes. I was just...I was trying to protect my wife," he said to Beckett. "Agnes. She got into it, do you think? It's given her the hysteria, or something?"

"No." Beckett replied. He tossed the pamphlets to the ground. "No, I don't think so. Skinner—" Skinner was gone, he reminded himself. The new man was James. "James, I mean. There's something else here. Probably under the floor. Find it."

The new knocker was a pale young man, with a defect in his silver eyeplate that caused it to leak ichor periodically. It made him look like he was crying thick, gummy black tears. James nodded, wiped the ichor from his face, and began to rattle the floorboards with his telerhythmia, head cocked in the peculiar knocker fashion, listening for discrepancies in the echo.

It was probably an illusion, Beckett knew, that Agnes' voice seemed more intense with the telerhythmia counter-point. She couldn't respond to stimulus, not in her condition. But still, it sounded almost like her muted babbling was growing more frantic.

"Under the chair," James said at last. "The soft one."
Arnold said nothing now. His face had gone white. He chewed on his knuckle. The gendarmes knocked over an overstuffed armchair and located a loose floorboard beneath it. They pried it up, and looked into the cavity beneath.

"Aow!" Shouted one the gendarmes. He stumbled back from the opening and fell to the ground. The other man just stared.

In the opening beneath the floorboards were a few yellowed packets of paper. They had text neatly printed on them, and small diagrams. There was a lump of greasy brown stone, flecked over with gold. Faintly, the stone buzzed, just below the audible range, enough to set the teeth on edge. An almost-imperceptible nimbus of improbable memories swirled across its surface, defying direct observation, but flickering at the edge of vision.

It was a deliaroid, a mineral made from condensed dream material. The substance was extracted in small quantities from the pineal glands of humans, therians, and certain higher-order mammals, then crystallized and treated with a tincture of denatured phlogiston. It was a product of oneiristry—one of the thirteen heretical sciences—it was illegal, and dangerous, and an increasingly-popular drug that its users usually referred to as "Delia."

It was Arnold Cooper's, of that Beckett had no doubt. The man would have shaved thin slices from the rock, then held them under his tongue while he drank a strong solvent, like whiskey or brandy. He would experience a kind of synaesthesia at first, coupled with a mild euphoria. Eventually he'd become convinced he could see ghosts, or the end of time. Or, if his mind was already weak, or if he had been very young, his conscious mind would suffer a schism from his perception of the real world, and he'd succumb to shatterbrain. As had his daughter.

Arnold Cooper said nothing as Beckett picked up the deliaroid and dropped it into his pocket, collected the yellowed pamphlets, and then nodded to the gendarmes. They ushered him out into the frigid night-time air.

Beckett rubbed his blind left eye. It should be senseless, he knew, because the fades destroyed the sensibility of the flesh they made transparent, but he had lately become convinced that it was itching.

"What will they do to him?" Catherine Cooper asked.

Beckett looked at her. She was no longer sniffling, now, but steady, jaw set, eyes firm. Beckett found it difficult to look at her. "He's damaged his mind," he replied, turning away. "The fumes from the deliaroid will have made an ulcer on his conscious-subconscious membrane. Have you been having dreams? Vivid dreams, whose content was unclear to you?"

Catherine Cooper nodded, very slowly.

"He's bleeding out. The damage is irreparable. Worse, it's contagious. Exposure to him could risk an epidemic. Another shatterbrain outbreak."

"So. What will they do to him?"

"They will take him," Beckett growled, "to the isolated ward of the First Hospital of Saint Goetius, where doctors will examine him and conclude just what I told you. They will keep him locked up there until I go there this evening. When I do, I will shoot him in the head." He rubbed his eye again. "For good measure, the surgeons will dissect his brain, to ensure that his pineal gland is thoroughly destroyed. If it is not, they will remove it and burn it. It will be," Beckett told her, "because I have been doing this for a very long time."

"And Anges?" Her voice was barely above a whisper.

If Beckett had been a man of great imagination, he almost could have told himself that he'd heard nothing, that she'd said nothing, and perhaps then convinced himself that he wasn't here at all, that Agnes Cooper wasn't slowly dying from a lacerated psyche, that maybe Beckett had been lucky enough to die during the Dragon Isles campaign so many years ago. But Elijah Beckett, detective inspector of the royal coroners, was not a man of great imagination; he had done his job well for over forty years, precisely because of his dogged refusal to do anything but accept the world the way it was.

"You'll want…" nothing caught in his throat, nothing at all, you didn't work as a coroner for forty years and still have to choke back a sob when it came time to do your duty, "You'll want to speak to her. Then Valentine will have to take you to the hospital as well. And your two boys. Make sure you're unharmed."

"And if we're not? If we're like Arnold?"

Beckett tugged at his scarf. "Then you'll still want to say goodbye to your daughter."

In her bedroom, Agnes Cooper was saying her evening prayers. She invoked the hierologue, as was the custom among young children in the evenings, and asked the Word to keep and bless her brothers and her mother and her father, little realizing that he was the man who'd poisoned her mind. She asked Divine Providence to uphold the Emperor and the Empire of Trowth, and if it wouldn't be too much trouble, she was hoping to get a small kitten for her birthday. Agnes finished her prayers and climbed into bed; the second her head touched the pillow, she jerked upright, crawled out, and began again.

Over and over. Agnes recited her prayers and went to bed, then got up and did it again. She'd been doing it for two days. Beckett knew, from experience, that trying to stop her would be virtually impossible — you could drag her to the other room, but she'd just run back. You could lock her in the basement, but she'd just pretend she was in her bedroom and go through the same ritual.

Agnes was crying; tears were streaming openly down her face. Some people, Beckett knew, were fortunate enough to lose their minds when they suffered from schismatic perseverance; Agnes was not one of the fortunate. She knew what was happening to her, but was equally unable to stop it; she'd become a prisoner in her own body, desperately repeating the same actions over and over again, trapped in a quirk of her psychology. She raised her voice or lowered it, pitched it high, sometimes tried to speak very quickly; these seemed to be the only elements that she could control.

"Aggy?" Catherine Cooper sat on the bed. Agnes still wept, but she let her voice dwindle to a whisper. "It's all right, Aggy. Dad and mum have to...ah. We're going to..." She turned away, and took a deep breath. "Dad had to go away to get some medicine. But I'm going to stay right here. Mr. Beckett here is going to help you, all right?"

Beckett looked over at James, who'd followed him into Agnes' bedroom. Valentine waited outside. "Check," Beckett told the knocker.

"Sir, she's clearly —"

"Just say it, boy. I have to be sure."

James nodded. A tiny thread of ichor dribbled down his cheek again. "There's definitely a reverb. I can hear her voice twice: once aloud, once aetherically."

"How long is the delay?"

"Three-quarter seconds," he said. Catherine clutched reflexively at her daughter's hand, but couldn't hold on to it. Agnes kept pulling it away to clasp in front of her while she prayed. "'Sword and fuck, Beckett, isn't there anything we can do?"

"Yes," Beckett said, his voice hoarse. He reached out to find the empty place inside, and promised he'd let himself suffer for this later on. "There's one thing."

Beckett drew his gun.

CRESY AND THE SHARPSIE

"Augghk. Ughghk."

"What are you doing?"

"Ugggghkh."

"What...Allisandre! Allisandre Rowan-Czarnecki, what are you doing? Stop that at once!"

"Cresy," said the girl, sullenly. She was seated in the very back of the room, as far from her tutor's eyes as possible. There was a bit of a breeze from the open window, and it came very close to alleviating the sweltering, oppressive heat of Corsay in the summer. Cresy's classmates had been dutifully practicing their Sarpejk. Today was verb conjugations, and everyone was, in unison, conjugating declarative-mood verbs.

"Excuse me," replied Miss Ennering, the tutor. She was a rail-thin woman with a pinched face. "Excuse me, what did you say?" There was a fine, downy moustache across her upper lip, which Miss Ennering bleached assiduously.

"My name is Cres—"

"You are in the roll books as Allisandre Rowan-Czarnecki, and that is what you will be called. Now will you please tell me what you were doing?"

Cresy mumbled something, then glared balefully at Miss Ennering. The girl had a terrible stare, one she'd inherited from her father. Her eyes were a very pale, almost luminous green, and deep-set beneath fierce brows. She fixed them like a predator on whatever had attracted her attention, and routinely unsettled both tutors and classmates.

Miss Ennering was, unfortunately for Cresy, quite accustomed to it. "Don't you glare at me, young lady. And enunciate when you speak.

In language class I expect you to at the very least speak your *own* language correctly." There were tiny drops of sweat on Miss Ennering's brow, very nearly a victory of corsets and petticoats over humidity. Most of the other girls in class struggled to sweat so little in such terrible heat.

"I was practicing Sharpish," Cresy said. "The sharpsies don't have no lips, so they've —"

" — don't have *any* lips — "

" — so they've got to make all their words in the back of their throat, like this," Cresy curled her lips back away from her teeth and growled something from behind her uvula. "Ugggghkh. That means 'bollocks,' I think — "

"Allisandre!" Miss Ennering snapped. "That is quite enough. In the first place, sharpsies do *not* have a language, any more than...than apes or therians do. In the second place, today we are practicing Sarpejk. In the third place, I don't expect you to be using profanity like...like what you just said in *any* language. You've not been paying attention, and so I'm going to have to award you five de — "

"I have! I have been paying attention!" Cresy insisted. She was not afraid — never afraid — of demerits, but her fierce pride would brook no criticism of her grasp of Sarpejk, which was her father's native language.

Miss Ennering crossed her arms and pursed her lips, more than mildly irritated by the interruption. "All right," she said, softly. "*Erek*, 'to lie,' in the declarative mood."

Cresy's scowl deepened. "*Erek*," she said. "*Ereki, erekei, erekora, erekoran, erenk.*"

"*Ereki* is the indicative mood, Allisandre, which you would know if you'd been paying attention to the lesson."

"No one ever uses it that way, though," Cresy snapped back, "Which *you'd* know if you knew someone that really spoke it, instead of just getting it from old books. It doesn't even make *sense*..."

"Enough!" Miss Ennering threw up her hands, strode to the door of the classroom, and threw it open. "Out. You're to go to Discipline, and tell Miss Daiorin to give you thirty switches. I will not tolerate this disrespect in my classroom."

Cresy gathered her skirts about her, thrust out her chin and walked haughtily out of the classroom. The door was slammed shut behind her, and she could immediately hear a chorus of girlish voices chanting, "Erek, ereka, erekei, erekora, erekoran, erenk," over and over. Cresy shrugged and took the long-familiar route down to Discipline. As usual, she did not make it all the way.

Mrs. Wyndham-Crabtree's Academy for Exceptional Girls was the finest finishing school in Corsay. It was, without exception, where every Esteemed Family sent their precious daughters, and the wealthiest and most influential Common merchants of Lantern Hill squabbled constantly that the Academy should find room for their own girls in its delicately beautiful whitewashed walls. Cresy had, at thirteen, been enrolled against her will the second her mother had come to Corsay with her new husband. Alliare Rowan-Czarnecki *née* Chretien had married well. Very well. Well enough for her daughter-out-of-wedlock to be accepted into her new Esteemed Family, and accepted also at Mrs. Wyndham-Crabtree's.

But all the good marriages in the world can't buy good breeding, and, by the Academy's standard, Cresy was nothing if not ill-bred. Halfway to the Discipline office, along the broad, airy, stucco hallway, Cresy had kicked off her shoes, untied her suffocating corset, pulled off her skirts and three layers of sweaty, sweltering petticoats, and leaving behind everything but her bloomers and the smallclothes beneath them, climbed out one of the Academy's beautiful picture windows.

The Academy was a series of buildings at the foot of New Town Hill, just above the Seam; the entire complex had, somewhat unusually for Corsay, all been constructed at the same time, and so eschewed the frenetic disorganization so often characteristic of the city. It was built in what had become known as "Native Style" — round arches, smooth, white stucco walls, red ceramic roof-tiles. There were large windows and sweeping patios everywhere, and an abundance of sturdy metal rain gutters.

Cresy especially liked the gutters, and now clambered up one, the metal almost too hot in her hands, as she made her way to the Academy roof. From there it was a short hop to the attached stables, a sprint across an adjoined rooftop, across the Seam and into Shattertown, where the forest of bamboo scaffolding, tumbled buildings, and half-finished construction made her passage faster and easier. She moved fast, then, swinging wildly, sometimes taking to the air for a full second or two, in complete free-fall, before a suitable hand-hold presented itself. A few therians joined her, always eager for the opportunity to race. They, with their long arms and prehensile feet, were better at swinging and leaping than she — *But I'm getting closer*, Cresy commended herself — though she could still beat them when it came to quick sprints. Therians shouted curses at her in their own language, and she shouted them right back, laughing wildly, never staying in place long enough to be embroiled in their ubiquitous quarrelling.

The object of her journey was her father's workplace — her *real* father, not the poncy fop her mother had married — Hangman's Plaza.

John Gyre rarely had to hang anyone these days, so his time was mostly spent keeping the gallows in good repair, and leaving a casual but careful eye on the petty criminals still in the holding cells. When Cresy arrived, he was practicing tying nooses, though he was already expert.

"Is he here?" Cresy called, as she clattered nosily down a bamboo strut. "Is he still here?"

"Is who…" John Gyre said. "What? Cresy! Allisandre. What are you doing?" Though he was surprised, it would take a deft observer of human nature to note anything more than mild interest on the hangman's face.

"The sharpsie, is he still here?"

"Of course he's—Allisandre. What are you doing here? Why aren't you at school?" He stood up, leaving the knotted noose beside him. "Where are your *clothes*?"

"I've been trying to learn Sharpish, so I can talk to him. Did you know that there are therians that speak Sharpish?" She slipped past her father towards the jail—its upper storeys were canted with the strange angles of Shattertown, the residual ruination of the Great Quake, but the basement had been built sturdy; its small, barred windows were just as round as ever. Cresy peered into them, to see which cell held the sharpsie.

"You need to get out of here," her father told her, grabbing her by the shoulder. "Now." His voice was dangerous then, rough and practically a shout. It was a mistake to talk to his daughter that way, and he knew it.

Cresy thrust out her chin and stared him right in the eye. *Almost tall enough that she doesn't have to look up,* he realized. *Oh well.* Cresy Gyre would not be intimidated, not by anyone, not ever, and the harder her father or her teachers or anyone else tried to scare her, the more ferociously she resisted. Two wolfish gazes locked on each other then, and John Gyre knew the sun would go down before his daughter looked away. She would not be afraid.

"You need to go, Cresy," he said again, his voice softer, now matter-of-fact. "Quick, now, before—"

"Mr. Gyre!"

"Too late," the hangman muttered. He turned away to find that Hangman's Plaza was now occupied. Three men, led by a portly fellow with wide mutton-chops, had arrived. The fellow with the mutton-chops, a certain Egbert Rowan-Vie, was dressed far too formally with his suit and waistcoat for the stifling heat and humidity of Corsay. His poor sartorial choice showed plainly on his face, which was florid and drenched with sweat. At his side he held a rifle called a long-pin; it had been built for the war, and used a lump of levitite to propel a slug faster than the sound it made as it split the air. Egbert leaned on it like it was a walking stick.

"Mr. Gyre," Egbert Rowan-Vie said again, his voice genial, as he wiped the sweat from his face with a handkerchief—a fool's errand, as it turned out; the handkerchief was already sopping. "We've come for...your charge." One of the men behind him noticed Cresy, and mentioned something to his neighbor; they snickered, and Cresy scowled.

John Gyre said nothing. He returned to the gallows and picked up his long spade, then slung it over his shoulders, resting his hands lightly on either end.

"You've discharged your responsibilities admirably, of course," said Rowan-Vie, "but the constabulary of New Town has an obligation. An obligation, I think is right. The right way to put it, I mean." John Gyre had said nothing, nor moved, nor given any other indication that he had heard a word the other man was saying. "We're going to...we're going to need him to come with us."

John Gyre looked up, away from Egbert, and squinted into the sun for a few moments.

"No."

Egbert Rowan-Vie patted his face with his handkerchief again; it dripped sweat onto the lapels of his suit coat. He glanced nervously back at the men behind him, a rough-looking pair, wearing the same kind of loose shirt and light trousers that John Gyre wore. Low men, then, and used to the city heat; sailors or inshoremen, probably recruited for their intimidation value, though neither bore criminal brands. "Now, Mr. Gyre, I don't think there's...I think it's better if you cooperate..."

"Law says he stays here 'til he's had a trial," the hangman said. "It's up to me to let him out sooner, if no magistrate comes. Not going to let him out." He whipped the spade around and dug its metal end into the cobblestones with a casual speed and precision that was startling. The metal scrape on stone was loud in the ominous quiet of Hangman's Plaza, a plaza already well known for its oppressive sense of ominous quiet. Distant clouds, heralds of the fast-approaching monsoon season, tinged the light with a strange amber clarity, that somehow made the place simultaneously darker and more sharply-hued.

The quiet persisted. In Corsay the profession of hangman carried with it a natural and powerful respect. And John Gyre's tall, broad frame, blunt features and scarred face betrayed his past as a fighting man. He'd grown up in Sar-Sarpek, served in the legion, and had been called on to kill men with his shovel when he'd run out of gunpowder.

At once, Egbert Rowan-Vie chuckled, seeking to ease the tension, but his face grew redder. "Come, come, Mr. Gyre, no one here wants any trouble. Leastways not me or my boys. Why...why, my goodness. Is that your daughter?" Egbert turned to Cresy and smiled broadly. She could see that he had a brass tooth. He tapped his fingers lightly on the slender rifle barrel, though made no move to lift it. "How do you do, young lady? I notice that you've misplaced your...petticoats."

"Allisandre," John Gyre said, without taking his eyes from the men in the square. "Sprosi. Avandi ec sis. Nem korret eimi opaluk tua sis nikt." *Get out of here,* he told her in Sarpejk. *Do not let me see you here tonight.*

"Alu!" Cresy objected. "Rek menim..." *But! The men...*

"Spros." He turned to look at his daughter. "Avandi." *Please. Go.*

It was the "please" that did it. Though she wouldn't tolerate orders, she still couldn't refuse her father anything. Cresy shot a last baleful glare at Egbert and his leering companions, and scrambled up the scaffolds and out of the square with the reckless agility of youth.

Surely, Cresy thought, as she vaulted lightly to a rooftop, *he didn't mean to go* far. *He'd have said that.* And so she didn't, and rather lurked on a nearby rooftop, struggling to overhear the muttered conversation in the plaza. That it was a tense conversation, Cresy had no doubt. Her father appeared relaxed, always casual, himself as comfortable discussing the severity of the rainy season as he was with precisely how much rope it would take to snap a man's neck with the gallows trap sprung. But he never let his eyes rest on Egbert, instead appearing to look off into the distance. This was, Cresy knew, John Gyre's way of keeping an eye on all the men at once, and a sign that he was expecting trouble. *What if they attack him?* Three men; she knew she should count Egbert, even if he was fat and sweaty. A fat, sweaty man with a rifle was just as dangerous as any other man with a rifle.

I could drop something on one of them. The men were talking quietly and intently. Cresy couldn't make out what they were saying, except for the words "sharpsie" and "menace." *I could drop a roof tile on Egbert, and then jump on the back of the big one with the striped hat. If I bit his ear he'd probably chase after me...*

Egbert was getting more than florid now, and gesticulating wildly. His voice rose, echoing off the crooked walls of Shattertown.

"...until every last one of them is dead! Do you hear me, Gyre?" The man's voice had a hysterical bite to it that Cresy didn't understand, an urgent insistence that seemed to have no grounds. He took a menacing step towards the hangman, gripping his long-pin tightly.

Are they getting ready to rush him? Cresy pried up a ceramic tile and gripped it tightly. *Here it comes...*

The tension nearly snapped then, but Egbert — perhaps wary of John Gyre and his shovel, perhaps simply afraid of the legal repercussions of threatening the hangman — made a great show of regaining his composure, and drew away. There was more quiet muttering, but no attack came. The men grumbled and swaggered, but left without further incident. John Gyre gathered his rope and shovel and went into the jail.

Disappointed, Cresy returned to school.

That evening, after a meal of blandly-boiled traditional Trowth cuisine, Cresy spoke to her friend, Dorum, a therian who liked to hang from her window ledge. The ape-man bobbed up and down, as he quickly and randomly switched grips. Right hand, left hand, left foot, right hand. His calloused palms made a soft, scratching sound on the exterior stucco. There were bars on the windows — hastily mortared on once the school administrators had caught wind of Cresy's easy willingness to exit the school by any available aperture. Verity Daior-Crabtree, who shared Cresy's room with her, kept her blanket pulled up over her head and did her level best to ignore human and therian. It was early to try and sleep; late, red sunlight still fought its way through the stormy clouds in the west.

Cresy looked out at the slowly, violently churning evening sky, and talked in Theria. She'd picked it up, eventually, having spent more time among Corsay's anthropoid, second-class inhabitants than she had with humans. "What did they do?" She asked Dorum. "The sharpsies, I mean."

"Oh, I don't know, they don't tell us anything. I heard there were riots in Trowth, maybe they're afraid? Of riots here? But there's no sharpsies here, anyway, or almost none. Not now." Dorum held himself up on one hand, then did a kind of a half-backflip and dropped out of sight, catching the ledge with his feet. "There was those families living in Trowtheri parish, but they left once someone set their house on fire."

"Someone did that? Why?"

Dorum pulled his face up level with hers, separated now only by the bars on the window. When she was younger, Cresy had believed that therians didn't have feelings the way humans did; now, she understood that they had just as many feelings as anything else — but because they expressed them differently, humans often failed to recognize them. Dorum was squinting now, and softly expelling air between his lips. It was a blubbery kind of expression that made him seem like he was about to cry, but really meant that he was just thinking. "People do stupid things when they're scared."

"Are you done yet?" Verity snapped, her voice muffled from beneath her coverlet. Cresy rolled her eyes. "You've been gabbling at that monkey for hours, and I want to go to sleep."

"Shut up."

"You know he can't understand you. Therians can't really speak, they're like parrots. They just copy words they've heard."

Cresy rolled her eyes again, this time so hard she had a brief but tangible concern that she might sprain them. "Dorum," she said, in Theria again, "we can't let the sharpsie stay in prison. Those men are going to come back and they're going to do something stupid."

"Oh, probably," Dorum replied. "How do you know he shouldn't be in prison, though?"

"If he was arrested properly, how come there was no trial? If he'd done something wrong, papa would have just hanged him. If it was right for New Town to drag him off, papa would have let them. He's trying to protect the sharpsie, and that means the sharpsie needs protection."

"But your father told you to stay away."

"How did you know about that?"

Dorum noisily sucked at his lower lip three times, the therian equivalent of a shrug. "Birds tell stories, you know?" Gossip. Therians loved gossip as much as they loved argument.

"Anyway," said Cresy, "it doesn't matter. He didn't tell me not to go back, he just said he didn't want to *see* me. That's practically the same thing as asking me to sneak in and break the sharpsie out." Of course that's what he'd meant. John Gyre couldn't be sure that none of those men spoke Sarpejk, so he'd had to tell her what he needed in code. He needed her to do this.

Right?

"Can you get these bars off?" She asked her friend.

Dorum pouted and puffed his cheeks out, looking at the spots of mortar at the top and bottom of the bars. "Yes, I think so." He grabbed one with both hands, hefted himself up, and planted both feet on the wall. Dorum grunted, yelped, heaved — and the bar snapped away from the window, and went careening off into to the dark. The therian stumbled and scrabbled for a grip on the remaining bars.

"What are you doing?" Verity squealed, as she shot upright in bed. "What did that thing just do?"

Cresy glared out of the corner of her eye — a less potent form of her day-to-day glare, but also one that would not interrupt her current task — as she rummaged under her bed for her pair of men's trousers.

She'd stolen them one day, when she'd stumbled across three boys swimming in the North Fork River. "I'm going out," Cresy told her roommate. "Don't bother leaving the light on."

"You can't just leave," Verity's face contorted in horror. "You can't..."

"I can." Cresy pulled on the trousers, and stuffed her nightgown into their waistband.

Verity crossed her arms and tried to look grim. "I'll tell."

"So?" Cresy said, and then struggled through the gap in the bars on her window.

"Now what do we do?" Cresy whispered, as she and Dorum peered between the gables of the jail. The roof had once been peaked, but now as the building leaned to one side, it was nearly flat. A small djang tree grew nearby, desperately struggling to build a root system in between the stones. Below John Gyre and another man — a new hire, probably — were standing at the door, keeping a kind of relaxed guard. This was extremely unusual; John Gyre didn't take on extra help unless he really needed it.

Dorum sucked on his lip again. "I don't know. This was your plan." He puffed out his cheeks again. "Wait, I do know. I'll throw something at them, and they'll chase me."

"You'll get in trouble," Cresy said, but Dorum was already snatching small red djang fruits from the tree.

"I won't," he said, taking a bite of one of the fruits, and chewing gleefully on it. "Pinkies can't tell any of us apart, anyway." Before she could respond, Dorum leapt down the side of the building and scrambled into the plaza. Hooting and grunting and cursing in Theria, he hurled the bright blood-colored fruits at John Gyre and the other man; when his hands were empty, Dorum began scooping up stones and throwing them, careful now not to hit anyone.

The two men looked puzzledly at each other, then John Gyre nodded to his companion. The man set off across the plaza towards the therian, who continued to howl and hoot, but backed slowly away, trying to draw the man farther off. Halfway into the square the man stopped, and would not proceed any farther no matter how much Dorum howled.

The therian looked briefly up to Cresy, still hidden on the roof, who shrugged. Dorum sucked his lip, then, without warning, sprang forward and bit the guard on his shin. The man shouted and this time chased Dorum when he ran.

John Gyre, however, remained by the door.

Now what? Cresy thought to herself. *He won't let me in. If he could break the rules to let me in, he could just break the sharpsie out himself. I can't lure him away...*She looked down at her feet, searching for something, some clue to her next course of action...and saw the roofing tile that she'd pried up that afternoon. *This is a terrible idea,* she thought as she picked it up.

This is a terrible idea, she thought again as she hefted the tile, then leaned over the edge of the roof. *Oh, this is a terrible idea.*

It's the only way. Sorry, papa. She looked down at her father, closed her eyes, and dropped the chunk of ceramic.

It made a terrible, sickening crunch when it hit his head.

That was the moment that she realized that she might have killed him; in a desperate panic, Cresy clambered down the wall of the hold, nearly losing her grip twice, and ran to her father's side. He was slumped against the stone wall, blood trickling down from his scalp, his eyes closed. A nasty purple welt had begun to form on his forehead, right below the hairline.

He was breathing.

Cresy let out a shuddering sigh of relief. The blood looked like just a scrape. He was breathing. Cresy debated trying to pat his cheeks and revive him. What if the blow had scrambled his brains? But then, what if it hadn't? What if he woke up and was furious at her, first for hitting him on the head with a roof tile, and then for letting herself be seen when he explicitly told her not to?

Better to let someone else find him, Cresy thought as she stole his keys. She had to get the sharpsie out.

Inside the jail was a kind of receiving room, then down to the sturdy basement cells. They were all empty now, except for the one in the very back. The cells were unlit; the only illumination came from the last weak rays of sun that was now being slowly strangled by the encroaching storm. It was very dark, and the sharpsie in the far corner of his cell was barely visible. He lay crumpled, face tucked in towards his stomach, arms hanging limply at his sides. He wore only a pair of ratty trousers, held up by a frayed hank of rope.

His teeth were visible, though—almost luminescent—and it was obvious why his people were called sharpsies. If a crocodile had dreamed his way free of the muddy wet marshes and into chiseled stone cities, he would fashion for himself a shape and semblance like a sharpsie's. He had great narrow jaws and a lipless mouth with a mess of long teeth. In the front there were jagged sharp spikes; towards the base of his jaw were crooked ridges that looked like meat shears. His eyes were like a cat's; he closed them by squeezing his cheeks together.

Though the sharpsies had been taken into the Empire, the inhabitants of Corsay and its parent city, Trowth, had never lost their fear of those fearsome, gnashing jaws; they evoked childhood nightmares, primal terrors never fully banished from the human psyche. No clear word of the events in Trowth had come through the ships yet — some said that sharpsies had tried to start a revolution, some that they'd simply started butchering people. All that filtered through the tenuous chains of gossip was that old, inchoate horror. Sharpsies were monsters again, just like everyone had always known, deep in the pits of their timid mammal souls. Fear thickened the air in the city as fully as the storm did, and one or the other would soon break.

"Hey," Cresy whispered, while she unlocked the door. "Hey, come on, we have to get out of here." She approached the silent figure and tried speaking to him in Sharpish. "Hey, come on. Hggghk. Friend. I'm your friend, okay? Hggghk." She grasped him by the shoulder and shook him.

Immediately, the sharpsie's eyes snapped open, black eyes with wild white rims as they rolled in their sockets. He gnashed his jaws and snapped at her hand. Instinctively, Cresy snatched it away, cupped her other hand and struck him across the ear with it. The sharpsie yelped and fell back.

"Hey, stupid!" She shouted at him. "Hggghk, stupid. I'm your friend. Hggghk. I'm trying to…" Something was wrong.

She didn't feel right, felt instead a strangeness, a sudden dizziness, almost…Cresy looked down at her hand, her right hand, the hand the sharpsie had snapped at. It was bleeding. There was blood everywhere there was…

Her ring finger was missing.

Raw red panic welled up inside of her, a paralyzing fear that grabbed at her throat and made her feel like she was choking, a pure, animal terror, strong, so strong that it just leapt past every cognitive barrier she'd built against her fear, that roared through her body like a hurricane…

Her finger…she felt the pain, then, a wicked twist of a thing that ran all the way up her forearm and screamed at her.

The sharpsie was grabbing at her, then, had her wrist in a grip like an iron vise, and she struck out, trying to keep her left hand low, beneath those terrible deadly teeth, pushing at his neck, keeping that mouth up and away from her face. She kicked out at his leg and tried to push him away; he was growling and spitting at her now, making a throaty choking noise while he tried to grab at her free hand.   Cresy bucked and twisted wildly, but couldn't break his grip on her wrist, couldn't really hit him for fear that her hands or feet would meet those nasty, deadly teeth.

"Get away! Let go!" she screamed at him. He began grappling at his trousers, then, pulling off the frayed rope that he used as a belt. "NO!" Cresy screamed again. "LET GO!" She kicked out at him then, her toes pointed right at the side of his face, but the sharpsie reared back and she missed. He growled something guttural then, took the rope in his free hand, and bit it in half.

Cresy continued to struggle, but panic had taken its toll. After that first burst of adrenaline, her muscles felt weakened now, shaking, and she still couldn't get her wrist away. And the sharpsie...the sharpsie wasn't doing anything, except holding onto her wrist like he was trying to crush it. The girl's breaths came slower now, as she tried to forcibly seize that terror and keep it under control.

The sharpsie growled again, but this time, Cresy heard it for what it was: words. He was speaking Sharpish; with no lips and thick tongues, the sharpsies' language could only be made of those growling, guttural, glottal syllables. "Ugghkkh. Gahggh. Hggghk."

"What..." Cresy sniffed. There were tears on her face. She couldn't remember shedding them, and their presence made her flush hot with embarrassment. "What did you say?"

"Hggghk," the sharpsie said. It held up half of its rope belt, then tapped her wrist with it. "Ugghkkh. Agh, gah hakkh. Gkg."

Cresy looked down at her hand. It was red, almost black in the failing light, where the severed stump of her finger had been spilling her blood. The bleeding...the sharpsie was holding her wrist so tightly to stop the bleeding. And wanted to use the rope... "You want...you want to make a tourniquet?" Why was it trying to help her?

Fear. People do stupid things when they're scared. She'd scared him, he hadn't meant to bite her. Now he wanted to help. Was that it? Could that be it? Or was it a trick, to get a better grip? To lull her to safety before those jaws snapped shut and tore out her throat...

Do I think that because it's true? Or do I think it because I'm scared of his teeth? Cresy sniffed again. *No.* No. *I am* not *afraid. I will* not *be afraid.*

Cresy met the sharpsie's eyes. "Okay," she said, "okay, do it."

The sharpsie nodded, then let go of her wrist. Cresy had to fight to stop herself from immediately snatching it away; quickly and dexterously, the sharpsie tied the rope tight. Cresy pulled the end of her nightgown from her trousers, and ripped a piece of it off to stick against the bloody remnants of her severed digit. New shocks of agony washed over her as she did; Cresy gritted her teeth and pressed the cloth against it as hard as she could.

The pain and panic began to recede then, and Cresy experienced a weird, distancing sensation, as though she were not in her body at all, but operating it remotely. The pain in her hand, the sick feeling in her stomach, those things were happening somewhere else, to someone else. *Is this what shock feels like?* She thought. *Oh, who cares. We're not done yet.*

"Hggghk," Cresy told the sharpsie. "Friend. You speak Trowthi?"

The sharpsie nodded.

"My name's Cresy."

"Gheghki," the sharpsie replied, then tapped his chest. "Hghg'lkg'ghk."

Cresy stared. "Is...is that your name?" The sharpsie nodded again. "Yeah...that's...good. Get up, we have to go." *I can't believe you bit off my finger.*

The jail's office was still dark and empty. "Stay down," Cresy told the sharpsie. "Quiet. Okay?" Her hand was starting to throb now, but the strange detachment she'd felt before was getting stronger. She crept towards the door into the plaza, but now felt like she was floating above herself, like the walls and floor were the surface of a deep pool, just the reflections of a world, and she could put her hand...her mutilated hand...through that surface and swim...

No. Stay here.

John Gyre was no longer slumped by the entrance. He was standing in the center of the square, facing down Egbert Rowan-Vie, who now carried his long-pin slung against his shoulder, and had twenty men at his heels. Not just inshoremen this time, or a few hired heavies meant to make a statement; these were men that lived in Shattertown and Trowtheri parishes, angry men with makeshift weapons in their hands, scared men with murder on their minds.

John Gyre, despite the black bruise on his forehead and the blood that caked half of his face—or, perhaps because of it—remained extremely intimidating. But there were limits to the peculiar dread of the hangman's glamour, and twenty angry men was more than he could handle.

The men had blue phlogiston lanterns, and angry, lurid red salt-lamps, both kinds heavily sheltered in brass and iron to protect them from the rising winds. Egbert shook his rifle, more confident now with a small army at his back. The lights glimmered and winked around him, turning his fat face into a ghastly cascade of stark shadows. The exchange of heated words was whipped away by the coming storm, which had now raised its voice to a constant howl, and threatened to carry off any small things that had not been nailed down. Some shutters, improperly secured, clattered and banged somewhere far off.

Cresy kept a careful eye on Egbert and his rifle. "We need to run," she shouted to the sharpsie. Could the men in the plaza overhear her? She didn't know, but doubted it. "When I say 'go'…"

Too late—the sharpsie was on his feet with his mad agility, his weirdly-bent legs making him a superior sprinter. Cresy watched him run, with his strange kind of bouncing lilt, each leg a spring that coiled and stretched…but he was going the wrong way. He'd gone left along Ogri Street, towards Mireside. Cresy tore after him, bare feet slapping painfully on the cobblestones, and managed to catch up with him only because he'd paused at an intersection to get his bearings.

"Hey!" Cresy shouted at him, not sure now if he could hear anything over the sound of the wind, which slapped her face with the spray of nascent raindrops. "Hey, you can't go that way! You don't want to go into Mireside! We need…" She considered. Where could she take him? Would the smugglers in the sound even be willing to carry a sharpsie? The score and more of raving men, who now boiled out of Hangman's Plaza towards them, suggested there would be few doors open to a sharpsie tonight.

The sharpsie began to run again, and Cresy took off after him. They headed south of the plaza, into the bulk of Shattertown neighborhood. Here, the crooked streets and labyrinthine alleys, the fallen retaining walls, the piles of debris and strangling clusters of bamboo scaffolding served the two smaller, agile fugitives well. The confused maze of narrow paths was enough to hobble the sharpsie's matchless speed, but it slowed the men behind them even more. Hampered by the use of only one hand, Cresy still managed to struggle over and around obstacles that would force their pursuers to make long diversions to catch up, and the tangle of streets meant they had no sure way of knowing where girl and sharpsie were going.

Not that Cresy had any better idea of where they were headed; she was not altogether confident that the sharpsie did, either. He kept pausing at intersections, looking up and around as though the leaning buildings were unfamiliar to him, then appearing to choose a direction at random. They sometimes came closer to Mireside, sometimes they came farther away, sometimes they back-tracked. *At least it will make us hard to follow,* she mused. Cresy's muscles were getting exhausted now, her breath was coming hard and there was a stitch in her side.

And her hand hurt. A constant, thrumming pain that made her want to cry, and was probably the only thing that kept her from actually thinking about the fact that she'd *lost a finger.* Cresy seized control of herself. *Don't think about that. Don't panic, we're not done yet.*

"Hey! Hugghuhkukuh, whatever your name is! Hey, stop!" Cresy slithered down a pile of broken bricks, hastily cleared from the street in the face of the advancing monsoon. "Where are you *going*?"

The sharpsie looked at her. "Ngaechaeg."

"I don't know what that means."

The sharpsie pointed west, then shook his head, and pointed south.

"That's towards the Mireside. No," Cresy told him, as the sharpsie nodded fiercely. "No, you don't want to go to Mireside. You think the men here are bad? They're twice as bad in Mireside, and there's no way to get you out. Just Marsh Boys, and even if they wanted to help you, you'd just be stuck in the jungle."

Faint shouts reached them over the now omnipresent wind. Cresy looked down the avenue to see three men racing towards them, red and blue lanterns in hand, knives and sticks at the ready. The group had, apparently, broken into smaller numbers, the better to canvass the area. Fortunately, most sensible people were inside, their doors and windows barred against the hurricane, so it was unlikely that any angry neighbors would come out to swell the numbers of the mob.

"We have to *go*," Cresy told him. The sharpsie shook his head, and ran south. Cresy rolled her eyes and followed. *I should just leave you*, she thought. *You bit off my finger. I should just leave you to find your own way out.* But she knew she wouldn't; she'd started this, she would finish it.

At least they didn't have to run against the wind, now; the storm gusts came roaring in from the west, tossing bits of debris — broken wood, bamboo, tattered cloth and ashes, and a veritable flock of old broadsheets — in a haphazard migration across the city. The wind was strong enough at times that Cresy felt almost as though she was being lifted from the ground, and it was strong enough to slow the sharpsie down a little, at least.

They tumbled into an alley with a high back wall — too high for even the sharpsie to ascend, as he now demonstrated a remarkable, but ineffective, vertical jump.

"See?" Cresy told him, mercifully no longer needing to yell. The alley sheltered them from the wind. "You don't even know where you're going." The sharpsie just stared at her. "You're *lost*. That's because you just run around like you'll figure it out, and you don't *think*." The sharpsie did not move, then, or speak. The pain in Cresy's hand was almost unbearable, now, and watching this sharpsie just look at her, and not even move, not even...

She walked up to the snaggle-toothed humanoid, and kicked him in the leg. He yelped and blinked, his face cocked into the sharpsie approximation of surprise. "Stupid," she told him, then kicked him again. Then punched his chest with her good hand. "Stupid, stupid, stupid! You don't know what you're doing! You can't just run around! You're going to get us killed!" She kicked him again, as he panicked and backed up against the wall. "You bit off my finger! You dumb, ugly, nasty..." she punched him in the stomach, hard, right below his sternum.

The sharpsie doubled over, coughing, making choking sounds, and Cresy didn't know if he was *actually* choking or if he was just speaking Sharpish.

"Young lady."

Cresy whirled. Egbert Rowan-Vie stood at the mouth of alley, still in the wind. It whipped around him and tore at his coat. The air had grown thick with a fine mist of rain, a prelude to the torrents held in towers of thick black clouds. The long-pin, a study in cruel lines and gunmetal blue simplicity, was pointed at the sharpsie.

"Miss Gyre." Egbert smiled around his brass tooth. "Step away from the animal." He drew up his rifle.

"What..."Cresy asked him, immediately standing between Egbert and the sharpsie. "What are you going to do?"

"My duty, Miss Gyre. Or, my obligation. The Esteemed Families of the Empire have an obligation, we have obligations to protect the common ones. So I'm going to shoot that beastie. You've done an excellent job, quite excellent, Miss Gyre, tracking it down and getting him away from your father. Now step aside, and I shall kill it."

Cresy didn't move. The wind howled around Egbert, as he raised his long-pin rifle and triggered it—the weapon's sharp retort was lost to the churning air, and chips of stone exploded at Cresy's feet. She yelped, and hopped back, only to find herself filled with a pure, abiding fury, burning away every last inch of fear and pain. She set her jaw and lifted her chin, and glared with her predator's eyes right down the barrel of the rifle.

Egbert grimaced. "I won't...I won't ask again." He had to shout to be heard over the monsoon. "I *will* shoot you, girl!"

Cresy had no idea what she would do. The man was too far away for her to reach him, too far away to throw something at him, the alley was too narrow to move in, and there was nowhere for her to hide. Maybe Egbert could be convinced that this was a terrible idea? Even if he could, she had no idea how to do it. All she knew is that she would not be moved, not by him, not by anyone.

"Don't make me do this!" Egbert screamed. He leveled his weapon at the girl, his lips pulled back into a pained rictus. "I will...I will—"

Egbert did not. A small wooden shutter, torn free of its hinges by the growing storm, at that very moment whirled through the air and struck Egbert across his temple. The portly gentleman took two staggered steps, a befuddled expression on his face, then abruptly collapsed in a pile of fat belly and fancy suit, letting his handsome rifle clatter to the ground, unfired and now impotent.

The sharpsie pulled himself to his feet, and he and Cresy shared a moment of muted surprise, looking at the prone heap that was Egbert.

"Well," said Cresy. "Huh."

"Ngaechaeg," said the sharpsie.

"You said that already, I'm telling you, you don't want to go to Mireside."

"Ngaechaeg."

"Fine. Fine, just follow me."

Now even more mindful of the dangers of the storm, Cresy led the sharpsie through a last few twists and turns, into Mireside — a narrow district at the very south end of the city, along the southern fork of the Corasi River. At the sharpsie's urging Cresy took him, crouched low against wind and prying eyes, through the derelict neighborhood to the very edge of the river, here called the Mire. It was ordinarily broad and flat and muddy, but now its brown waters were whipped up into tiny waves. On the far side of the river, barely visible in the dark, was Corsay's dense, malarial jungle.

"See?" Cresy said. "There's nothing h — "

Without a word or growl or anything, the sharpsie leapt from the stone jetty and into the muddy Mire. He disappeared beneath the surface, almost immediately.

"What are you doing?" Cresy screamed at him, but too late. He was gone, and there was no way that, now, bruised, bleeding, and with her crippled hand, she could possibly swim after him. Not with a monsoon brewing that would turn the Mire into a churning deathtrap.

What was he doing?

The threatened rain finally began to fall. The misty, pre-hurricane spray gave way to big, fat drops that began to clatter noisily against stone streets and wooden and tin roofs. Cresy could hear the shimmering noise approaching in a wave from the west. She squinted at the Mire still, eyes sharp for some kind of sign, for something…

There. The sharpsie's head crested the surface for a moment, and he disappeared back beneath the waves — fully twenty yards out into the river. Sharpsies were, apparently, strong swimmers as well as champion sprinters. She saw his head once more, even further out. And then…

In the distance, in the jungle...were those lights? Tiny glimmers of phlogiston-blue light? Were there *people* out there?

As the marching raindrops thundered towards her, she could faintly discern the sound of...something. A voice, crying out — something with the mournful melody of a wolf's howl. The voice that sang was ragged, keening its rough-edged note. After a moment the sound was joined by a second voice, and then a third, making a peculiar harmony in a register just above the wind. Distant, slender shadows were visible across the Mire, and if Cresy squinted hard, she could just see the sharpsie that she'd helped struggle free of the muddy waters and join those shapes, then raise his voice to join the song.

For a moment, Cresy forgot the pain in her hand, forgot the storm, forgot the exhaustion from her run through the city, forgot Egbert and his gun, the mob and their torches...fear and anger, guilt, worry, all of it just melted away, as she listened to a family singing aloud for the brother that had been returned to them.

The rain washed over her then, thundering across her aching body like she'd just plunged into the river herself. The distant river shore and the sharpsie's music was carried away, as the storm insisted on her attention. Cresy squinted against the water in her eyes, and looked down at her hand. The makeshift bandage was soaked through and black with crusted blood. Her skin was an alarming shade of purple.

Hospital, Cresy thought to herself. *I'd probably better get to a hospital.*

Afterwards, though she took a special delight in horrifying both teachers and classmates with her terrifically mutilated hand, Cresy felt a powerful unease at the thought of seeing her father again. By freeing the sharpsie, she had done the right thing — she had no doubt about that. Still...

...*still,* she thought, *maybe I should stay at school for a little while.*

www.ingramcontent.com/pod-product-compliance
Lightning Source LLC
Chambersburg PA
CBHW061144170626
46809CB00003B/982